VALLEY OF PROGRESS

CHIGOU

1

Cory Sheldon

CHIGOU
VALLEY OF PROGRESS
BOOK 1

Published by Ooi Iro

Illustrations by Cory Sheldon
Edited by Linda Cuckovich
Layout by Melissa Olson

Library of Congress Control Number: 2016911106

ISBN 978-0-9975692-0-9

www.valleyofprogress.com
twitter @valleyprogress
www.corysheldoncreative.com

FIRST EDITION

In Memory of Ross M.

Friend
Dreamer
Thinker
Believer

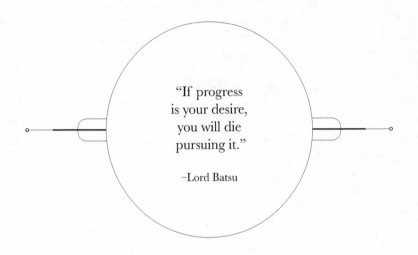

"If progress
is your desire,
you will die
pursuing it."

–Lord Batsu

1
TRUST

The sun set behind the western rim of the Murde Mountains, casting its light across a towering forest of metal and glass. Nature and industry fought to control the profile of the landscape. The city looked small compared to the unprecedented mass of mountains that cradled it, but its glimmering surface commanded attention like a flame in the dark. Although bright enough for the entire world to see, he sensed the light's brilliance about to fade.

He sat there scratching the gray hair of his temple, wondering as to why he still kept that thing on the wall. Opaji Batsu had commissioned the rather large painting to be a gift for his father's eightieth birthday. Gaimen Batsu admired it for a good five minutes before returning it straight back to his son. It carried with it a message, one containing all due respect and gratitude: *A father didn't need an artificial representation of his own empire.* The action verified a truth that nearly all in the valley already assumed, that Father and Son had clearly grown further apart than the distance between their two cities.

Opaji hung the painting next to a massive bay window in his office, looking down on northern Chigou. It reminded him of what he left behind, a once remarkable city that slipped into contentment under the uninspired guidance of his father Gaimen. At a young age, Opaji's zeal carried him out of Primichi on a quest to build a superior city of his own design. When reporters asked the young enterpriser why he wanted to leave his father's city, he would always correct them, saying his father only lived in what his grandfather had created.

Many decades earlier, Jean Batsu had taken a convoy of progressive thinkers and guided them through the highest point of the Murde Mountains. There he discovered a truly unique land, one he described as the only place capable of holding his lofty ambitions: the Naifin Valley. Cradled by soaring peaks, filled with electrical wonders and steam powered might, the city flourished into what many initially dismissed as an exaggerated, futuristic fantasy. When the settlement's first photograph made its way back to the coast, a historic image taken on the world's first airship, all came to agree that the future had arrived.

During its first few decades, Primichi easily retained its crown of progress. That fact confused many when Opaji declared that he planned for a greater creation, something many dismissed as an inflated proclamation. Gaimen disregarded his son's youthful fervor, but the senior Batsu understood his Grandson's far reaching ambitions. Frail and wrinkled, Jean Batsu watched from a wheelchair as his Grandson leaped off of his own creation, creating a new city on the horizon. Jean Batsu passed on as Gaimen watched his son's brazen claims actually rise into existence. Quickly, Opaji's city of Chigou claimed the southern end of the Naifin Valley.

Spending decades developing excuses not to visit, Gaimen eventually sent an assistant down to Chigou to evaluate his son's sprouting metropolis. After spending two weeks with Opaji, the assistant came back with a detailed report and single gift. Gaimen ripped off the golden wrapping paper with a note that read, *My favorite Old City*. He held the well crafted painting of Primichi and stared at it as the assistant began to rattle off the report. Halfway through the exhaustive list of data, Gaimen stopped the young man, asking what his son's city felt like. After a brief reflection, the assistant looked up and simply replied, "it's like Primichi, only better." Gaimen promptly asked the young man to return the painting to Chigou, and stay there.

A shadow then fell upon the portrait of Primichi, snapping Opaji out of a memory, one of his Grandfather's frail body resting in a brass wheelchair. Out of the window, an Unyo-class airship approached, casting its shadow a thousand feet below onto the street. The sun glistened off of the polished trim surrounding its handsome wooden deck. In Opaji's eyes, nothing physically represented his ideals better, and he always enjoyed riding in it. He gathered his hat and exited the office.

Mali Opree got out from behind her desk inside the vestibule, a brilliant room covered in expertly crafted details, all matching Opaji's airship. Then, as she had done countless times over the past sixteen years, Lady Opree handed her chief his cane and overcoat.

"Will you be back by the end of the day?"

"I'll have to see how this meeting goes. You can go ahead and head home early."

"Thank you, Lord Opaji."

After starting his own city, Opaji Batsu decided to go by a single name.

"Actually, Mali, have Bardin make a report on all corporate acquisitions Kasic has made in the past three years."

"Yes, Lord Opaji."

"And I want him to tell me something exciting Kasic plans on doing in the next six months. Tell him there better be a real answer."

"I will do that."

"Then you can leave early."

"Very kind of you."

Opaji clutched his things and walked towards the stairs leading to the airship dock. He walked up between thick, polished layers of metal trim. Po'Kin had long established itself as the primary style in the city of Chigou. Opaji's Telakai tower soared as its preeminent example. Various industrialists occupied most of the building, but the top floors all belonged to Opaji. Practically speaking, it was his home, and few outsiders ever visited.

Light poured in from the top of the stairwell. Opaji pressed down his hat as he walked out onto the windy roof. His feet crossed a large metal relief of the Telakai logo that could only be seen clearly from the sky. As the airship settled into the dock, the roar of its massive engine drowned out the sounds of the busy city below.

Although many large dirigibles hovered over the Naifin Valley, Opaji's Unyo class airship existed as the crowning jewel. The belly of the airship consisted of an exquisite two-level gondola. When in flight, its many windows offered an incredible view of the city and surrounding valley. A dignitary cabin took up the rear of the ship; Daimó sat there waiting for his meeting with Opaji.

The upper level contained common quarters, a cockpit, and engine room, all accessed along a wooden boardwalk wrapping around the ship. Stairs led up to a large deck that sat at the bow of the aircraft. With a wood floor modeled after Chigou's famous Dorsan Ballroom, it would urge one to quite literally dance amongst the clouds. The act, although experienced by few, became an often-used metaphor for freedom or indulgence.

The ship's mooring anchor finally clamped down, and the engineer waved Opaji on to the windy deck. The industrialist felt the subtle vibration of the throttled-down engines. Immediately a crew member greeted him with a quick bow before guiding him down the boardwalk. It got much darker as Opaji finally entered the central lobby. A staircase of white wood and dark brass spiraled down to the lower level. He went straight down before heading back to the rear cabin.

His eyes adjusted to the light, the seated silhouette slowly revealing its identity. He finally made out a face with small eyes set deep into thin features. The man stood up to greet Opaji, who walked straight past him and grabbed a support rail by the window.

"You might want to sit back down," Opaji offered.

Suddenly the engine roared as it thrust the airship off of the mooring anchor, knocking Daimó back into his guest chair. The ship backed out of the dock as Opaji remained still by the window, observing his city below.

"Your name is Daimó, yes?"

"That is my name."

"Come here. Tell me what you see."

Daimó approached the large window. Below, the city of Chigou pumped citizens and vehicles through its industrial vascular system, wrapping around towers of alloy and glass. The city tapered off into smaller and smaller buildings until fading off into the flat, rural land of the valley. Turning towards Opaji's static face, Daimó constructed his answer.

"It is an organism, a growing organism."

"Growing stronger? Growing . . . fatter?"

Daimó continued to look at Opaji, who had yet to return his gaze. He saw an older man musing over his child, a child that had grown up and started to run away. Although an impressive city by any standard, the Batsu family never claimed to covet humble goals. Chigou had grown up along with its creator, but now, Daimó concluded that they were merely growing old.

"There are limits to how big anything can grow, but there is always a choice in how to improve it. Chigou is the crown of the valley, towering above even your father's Primichi to the north."

"It was my grandfather's city. My father merely maintained it," Opaji interjected.

Daimó had nothing to add to the clearly personal sentiment; he continued with his answer. "The city is strong, but even a mountain can fade away with enough time and wear. What I propose to you is refinement and conditioning. Stimulating growth while cutting away the excess. I can be the stone that sharpens the edge. Independent of the tool, yet always working to maintain it."

Opaji's eyes reflected the horizon off in the distance as he finally turned towards Daimó.

"Such words I have spoken to myself many times before. What gives you confidence that you could actually do what you propose?"

"I have power that is not seen. I have no persona to protect, no public opinion to nurture. The relationship between a father and his children can be a complex one and becomes only more so over time. I can act with singularity."

"That is quite a claim. You think you can be influential and invisible?"

"As I know you are aware, I lead organizations that keep just small enough to be ignored, but hard enough to hone what has dulled."

"Across an entire city?"

"Depending on the results of this meeting, yes."

Opaji looked back down on the city, the result of meticulous design. He wondered if there was anything more he could do with his project, or if the vision had reached its threshold.

"As long as you're engineering my vision for this city, I'll give you what you need to do it."

Only that single condition concerned Opaji. Daimó embraced the blessing; however, Opaji's vision was of no deep concern to him. There had long since been a plan for the valley gestating in Daimó's mind, and he finally believed that nothing could keep it from executing. The arcane man forced his excitement from reaching the surface.

Opaji finally sat in a chair and poured himself a glass of Shumé. "Where are you from? Were you born here?"

"Do you mean the city or the valley?" Daimó said, still looking out.

"I mean, are you ever going to get tired of this place and move on?"

"I am of the valley, and I would only leave if I had no more purpose here."

A sea of burning light washed across the sky as the sun sank below the mountains. The cabin turned red as the engines continued to roar over a city too far away to be heard. Small electric lights began to appear below as the Murdes cast their inescapable shadow upon Chigou.

Opaji took a long drink of the distilled green spirit.

"So, what will be your first act in maintaining a path to the future?"

2
PURGE

Opaji anticipated vast growth from the very beginnings of Chigou and meticulously designed his city accordingly. He knew that energy needs would be substantial but wanted to keep the pragmatically named *Industrial Quarter* far away from the bustling life of downtown. It straddled the Long Frost River downstream so that it would not further pollute the water already stained from Primichi many miles north. The area quickly grew into a gray, mechanical muscle that breathed fire and pumped industrial blood day and night.

Initially a mix of proven and experimental construction operations sprang up. Steel had been a coveted building material even during the first days of Primichi, but a costly, temperamental process kept its availability limited. Opaji brought in iron workers to help quickly establish some structures in Chigou but assumed their usefulness would not be long lasting.

Conveniently, at the time Opaji was getting ready to start building up into the clouds, a young engineer by the name of Haroul Kasic developed a steel-forging process that would make almost all other processes obsolete. It involved a firing stage that required only one-tenth the time of conventional methods and produced a far-stronger steel, vastly improving strength-to-weight ratios. For Chigou, it meant rapid expansion outwards and upwards; for legacy industrialists, it meant the end.

As the city grew, the identity of Industrial Quarter grew equally in size and complexity. The men and women who operated the mechanical region were often identified by their oil-and-soot-stained skin and garnered the nickname *black-hands*. The term developed a complicated identity that found itself spoken with pride as often as it was with indignity. It reflected a growing divide between those who bathed before work and those who needed to scrub down after.

The name of Industrial Quarter further exposed its distance from downtown when it popularly became known simply as IQ. It was an efficient way for black-hands to refer to their neighborhood while many uptown used it as an ironic insult, based off of the *Intelligence Quotent* test that had been developed around the same time. Opaji's plan to keep the industrial and intellectual regions separate ended up developing even stronger than he had intended.

In the heart of IQ resided its oldest and least understood residents outside of the district. A close-knit group of hard-working iron workers had formed a network of buildings that mixed residential and industrial structures into a single, complicated city within a city. Nearly half of its tenants shared a single family name that also doubled for the name they gave their maze-like neighborhood: *Roukot*. Opaji wanted to make way for new technology, and Roukot stubbornly occupied what he considered the prime location for new industrial development.

Daimó had long since noticed the Roukots' resistance to leave their self-proclaimed neighborhood and found gracious persuasion inefficient; quick expulsion was a far more practical option. It would be his first major operation since Opaji had brought him in to help refine the city. Daimó carefully considered the type of pressure needed to dislodge such a massive congregation.

The municipal element of force was officially maintained and distributed by a group called Civil Enforcers. The Enforcers in Chigou were known to be very professional, if not a little harsh. They lacked the casual, neighborhood charm of their Primichi counterparts up north, and their uniforms matched accordingly. Dark blue fabric was symmetrically adorned with bold, albino brass fittings. Lord Enforcers, identified most easily by a white neckerchief and shoulder patch, were the only guards to carry firearms. Their presence was never taken lightly.

Carrying a reputation for being perhaps the toughest district in Chigou, Roukot found itself getting the most imposing Lord Enforcer in the city. He had a history in the military before moving to Chigou, where he then received a formal education and graduated with honors. While this helped him to shoot up through the Enforcer ranks quickly, the respect he received in the field almost always came from another reason. Lord Z, as he became known, was always the largest man in any room he would enter; typically people did not get around to asking about his academic credentials.

Daimó had heard of the massive captain and requested a meeting to discuss the removal of resistance in Roukot. They convened at a small office—one of many—that Daimó used when he needed to be discreet. Lord Enforcers rarely entertained a meeting outside of their station building, but the request had been officially vouched for by Opaji himself.

Lord Z walked into the office where Daimó stood, looking at a dingy alley through a window. He turned around to greet the civil servant, then looked up in order to actually make eye contact.

"Thank you for meeting me away from the station."

They shook hands, or rather, Lord Z's hand engulfed Daimó's.

"Please, have a seat."

"I'll stand." Lord Z offered.

Daimó conceded and sat down. "I've been informed of your background, and now that I've seen you in person, I am certain you will be well-suited for the task. We have some citizens whose usefulness has expired, and they need to be removed from the critical land they are occupying."

"Are they illegally occupying this land?"

Daimó had hoped the Lord Enforcer would be quick to obedience and slow to inquiry, but the question suggested otherwise.

"There was no crime when they first occupied the zone, but they are now impeding progress and the greater good of the city. They have become a cancer, and every cancer needs to be purged."

Lord Z shifted his stiff posture. The vagueness presented by this stranger only compounded the suspicious feelings Lord Z had of the meeting.

"Perhaps in order to give you a meaningful response, I should be given the details on who exactly I am to remove and from where."

Daimó spoke slowly and clearly. "Roukots."

There was a brief pause before Lord Z spoke. "You're suggesting to remove all of the Roukots from Roukot?"

"Do you think you can manage that?"

Lord Z cleared his throat, the deep, penetrating sound shifting into a less reverent tone. "Who are you?"

"I am the man you were told to perform a task for, and now that I have tasked you, I inquire if you are capable of managing it."

"I know my chain of command. I was told to come here and meet you, but I am not about to take orders from some nameless man in some nameless building."

Daimó's patience started to strain. He quickly assessed how long he would tolerate the line of questioning before implementing alternate actions.

"I look after the best interests of the city, and right now the city's largest employer needs space, which is currently being occupied by citizens that can't see more than five minutes into the future. As far as my credentials go, we both know who ordered you to meet me, which should be sufficient for a service man such as yourself."

Lord Z quickly replied, "Roukots are not pedestrians to be displaced by mere suggestion from an authoritative voice. They have deep roots in this city, and I imagine the only way they would leave would be through tangible incentive or physical force."

"Yes, we have already tried to negotiate their relocation and offered rather generous incentives. They turned it down, so now your course of action seems to be rather clear."

"They are a proud and resilient people," Lord Z spoke with raising volume. "And you are right, their actions tend to take the immediate future into consideration and not much else, which is why if I walk in there and demand a swift evacuation, it will not end with an ungrudging submission by anyone. As an Enforcer, I am willing to accept the potential of violence, but I am not pledged to provoke it."

Daimó's voice remained steady. "So again I ask if you will manage the task presented to you, or will you accept the outcome of someone else taking responsibility for the job instead?"

Lord Z detested the stranger's cold and objective tone. Although he felt the task to be foolish and dangerous, it was likely to be carried out regardless of his participation. The Lord Enforcer refused to pass on responsibility that would put another in harm's way. He reluctantly responded, "I will see to it."

With an awkward hesitation, Daimó smiled—not out of joy, but more as a courtesy of reciprocation. Lord Z felt there was nothing to reciprocate. He walked promptly out the door.

○ ○ ○

A clear sky cast down over the Naifin Valley, but in the heart of IQ, a cloud of byproduct kept the sun from shining through. The Industrial Quarter had a gray and dull quality unique to that part of the city; one could taste the metal in the air. Because of the constant hum of machinery—from grinding gears to boilers whistling—the sounds of nature were sparse.

The outer region of IQ consisted almost exclusively of factories and furnaces. Between the massive structures a diner would occasionally exist—soot-stained, cramped, and practically invisible to any outsider. The perimeter created a divide between the island of black-hands and the ocean of suits and dresses that surrounded it. Both sides had an acceptance of the separation, feeling moderately comfortable if the need arose to cross over. At the center of IQ, however, Roukot existed as a dense mystery that rarely saw anyone from the outside cross into.

Near the center of Roukot and just off of the Long Frost River, a dormitory existed that only looked habitable relative to the rugged machinery surrounding it. Locals typically identified it by the somewhat facetious name of "Storage." Various tunnels and bridges connected the living spaces with the factories where its inhabitants worked. This walled-up inner city provided for many needs of a typical black-hand. If little desire existed for clear skies and green grass, one could stay in there for months at a time without leaving, and many did.

Just north on Chikance Road, Lord Z lead a small string of Civil Enforcers driving standard-issue vehicles known as Voikatsues, or Voits for short. With streamlined paneling covering most of the wheels, their design emphasized an impressive combination of strength and speed. Their noticeably unique sliding doors made them seem fantastical to children. A single Voit would typically be a comforting sight in more passive neighborhoods, but they had a more complicated reputation in Roukot. Seeing a string of three or four, any black-hand would know that trouble was either well underway or about to start.

Lord Z pulled up to the front of Storage, followed by a line of Civil Enforcers. The unmistakable smooth hiss of a Voikatsu steam engine pulled in the attention of any nearby pedestrian. The shining procession looked like an assertive force ready for any resistant mass. Upon stepping out of his vehicle, Lord Z felt the heat steaming off of the road.

The six Enforcers who came with Lord Z gathered around him, their well-trained eyes scanning the surroundings. There were countless alleys, windows, and corners for something to emerge; so far it was just a swathe of peering eyes. He gave his first instruction.

"Stay out here."

A young and ambitious CE responded, "Who would you like to back you up?"

"A single Enforcer can invoke a number of responses. A group of seven leaves fewer interpretations to be made."

"I can back you up if . . ."

Lord Z looked into the young CE's eyes. "You've been briefed on who's up there, and that we're telling them to leave. Those people carry the name of this neighborhood. If we all go up there and box them in, our severe presentation will quickly evoke an equally severe response. Don't come unless you need to." Before the CE had time to ask his last question, Lord Z cut him off with the answer.

"You'll know when."

With that final briefing, Lord Z turned to face his task. The hallway to the living complex looked as though it was tunneled out from a previously collapsed building. The ceiling hung low and bowed in at points, and the largely metal walls appeared patched together. Random belongings lined the narrow corridor, and Lord Z struggled to get his massive frame through. He identified a few children scattered about with tattered clothing and soot-stained fingernails, feeling as though he may need to step over them. Quickly, hands and eyes appeared around doors. Parents collected their little ones and locked themselves inside their small quarters. Soon all Lord Z could hear were the muffled sounds of steam and machinery pumping from somewhere else.

The Enforcer walked towards a stairwell that ran up through the center of the building. He had a request from Opaji's office to specifically deal with Hugou Roukot, the senior most member carrying the neighborhood name. The tip had him living up on the third floor, probably among a loyal group of visceral black-hands. Lord Z knew any hope of a successful negotiation was razor-thin at best. Regardless, he moved on.

The iron stairs rang an echoing tone with each step, blending with the pervasive symphony of industrial noise. The Lord Enforcer decided to keep his intimidating firearm holstered as to keep tensions low, but his mind's grip stayed on the handle. He spotted dust swimming through a thin ray of sunlight from some crack in the roof or a skylight; he couldn't tell through the ascending cluster of pipes.

As he reached the third floor, Lord Z immediately identified his destination. The hallway contained a single, massive iron door that looked as though it was stolen from an industrial furnace. He slowly began to walk, his eyes locked on the door, certain that those behind it were already aware of his presence.

When he reached the iron barrier, he gently pressed his ear against it before firmly knocking.

"Civil Enforcer, open up," he called out.

Voices could be heard in quick bursts. Lord Z kept his ear to the metal. As the sound of footsteps approached, he took a step back and put his right hand just off of his sidearm. The voices vanished as the door opened up; the room looked empty behind the broad-shouldered man standing in the doorway.

A dark, roughly trimmed beard covered the middle-aged man's thick neck. Well-worn clothes matched the look in his eyes, which quickly scanned the Enforcer's uniform. His gaze paused on the white neckerchief identifying the visitor as a Lord Enforcer. The tension was mutually felt.

"I'm here to speak with Hugou Roukot," said Lord Z.

The bearded man discreetly glanced back. The space looked

like a rec room built out of pieces salvaged from a train wreck. "He ain't here."

"Then I'll wait."

Lord Z closely watched as the man pondered which move to play next.

"Well, it may be awhile. Perhaps you'd like to just come back another day. I'm sure you got other business to deal with."

"He is my only business at the moment. I'll wait."

The man stroked his graying beard and again glanced back over his shoulder. Standing in silence, Lord Z felt sweat beading up on his face. Suddenly, a voice came from a man hidden within the room.

"Let him in, but if he's here to talk about moving, tell him he ain't staying long."

The bearded man slowly sidestepped and let the large Enforcer enter. With the stocky black-hand following, Lord Z walked forward, his eyes thoroughly evaluating the perimeter. His peripheral vision was on high alert. The iron door shut, echoing behind him as he stepped into the room.

Scattered ale bottles sat atop scratched table tops. A small bar to the right appeared to be functioning as a kitchen. Iron beams supported the center of the room, mixed with storage lockers and an assortment of ductwork. Five men then began to appear from behind thick beams and lockers, all with eyes firmly attached to Lord Z. Finally, an older man with a long, gray mustache appeared from around a center column.

"So, tell me, civil servant, are you here to convince me to leave my home?"

The man was clearly Hugou Roukot. Lord Z made sure to keep his movements subtle and deliberate, keeping aware of every set of eyes in the room. "I'm here on behalf of the city. They plan on redeveloping this area and have discussed with you options for your reassignment, so I have been informed."

"That sounds about right, and I told 'em we ain't leaving our home. So I guess you can scuttle back to your boss and repeat what he didn't seem to hear so well the first time."

Lord Z quickly concluded that persuasion through incentive was futile. Having already decided to not leave the matter to another Enforcer, he decided the only thing left to offer was preventing their destruction from the inevitability of progress.

"You deserve to keep your home, Roukot. I'm not here to convince you otherwise. However, the city has decided this area needs to be used for new industry. It is clear to me that neither of you intends to sway your direction, but the simple matter is that you are in their city, and it may be in your best interest to take advantage of whatever they offer you."

As Hugou took a step forward, Lord Z kept his eyes on the men around the perimeter. One man looked as though he held something behind a storage locker, something that made the man anxious.

"What they offer is a reward for having no spine. You tell them their proposal ain't worth the toxic spit in their mouth. We ain't going nowhere." Hugou's voice focused. "But judging by your size, I'm thinking maybe they didn't send you here to just deliver words."

A beat of pressure stepped up in the room as every man subtly shifted his weight. The air felt heavy, carrying the sound of steam leaking from a boiler in the back of the room. Lord Z heard the bearded man inching up behind him.

"The situation is not great for anyone, Roukot, but we don't have to make it worse."

Hugou's eyes subtlety looked past Lord Z. It did not go unnoticed.

"We decide what happens with our home."

With that final declaration, Lord Z refocused on the bearded man, who slowly reached for the Enforcer's sidearm. In a flash, instinct drove his powerful hand onto the bearded man's throat. The Enforcer thrust him against the wall, paralyzing his lungs. With the man securely stunned, Lord Z quickly applied his attention to the rest of the room.

The keyed-up man behind the storage locker finally raised what revealed to be an old hunting rifle.

"Don't!" Lord Z begged in vain.

As the man continued his motion, the Lord Enforcer's training took over. Impossibly fast for a man his size, Lord Z removed the heavy-caliber pistol from his holster and fired a shot right past Hugou's left ear. The rifleman behind the storage locker yelled out as his body slammed to the ground.

It felt like the air had been sucked out of the room, and for an instant, everyone stood in shock. Then, neurons fired in an explosion of panicked realization. Clearing his cover, Lord Z immediately swung his pistol backwards at the bearded man to finish incapacitating him; he collapsed to the floor, unconscious.

With a quick head turn, Lord Z saw each man in the room bracing behind cover with a vintage firearm in hand. He dove down behind the kitchen counter, cracking the wood floor. Deafening shots rang out through the room as bullets buzzed over his head and ricocheted off the back wall.

On the street, the line of anxious Civil Enforcers heard the noise two floors up and jumped to attention. Without hesitation, the Enforcer next in line shouted his commands. "Up now! Enforcer Elou, hold the street."

The men lined up, releasing their batons, and activating the electrically charged rings at the end. They marched quickly into the building, covering each other through the bent hallway.

Above, as another shot skimmed the counter, Lord Z leaned in with his pistol raised. He heard shuffling in the back of the room and then Hugou's voice.

"Those suits uptown think we're some property they can just demolish whenever they feel like it, but we ain't going down, Enforcer."

Lord Z then saw a moving shape reflect off of a tea kettle. A gunman approached, but his weapon wasn't fully raised. The Lord Enforcer braced himself and raised his weapon, ready to fire. In a quick breath, he leaned around the corner, squeezed the trigger, and shot the approaching man in the leg. He went down screaming, his gun discharging into the wall.

As the ringing gunshot phased out, the Enforcer heard the men shifting their positions again. He slid away from the wall towards the edge of the counter. No one was visible. With the man still screaming to his right, Lord Z quickly crawled to cover the flank. Directly below, the rest of the Enforcers approached the stairwell, moving faster on the sound of the last gunshot.

Between the wounded man's screams, Lord Z took a second to listen down the left wall. He readied his sidearm and quickly leaned out past the edge of the shelf. It looked clear, but he heard the sound of shifting feet. A man appeared around a column, raising his cluster rifle. Seeing that the LE had him sighted, the man quickly jumped back behind the column just as Lord Z fired off another shot. The large-caliber bullet whistled by the man's face and smashed into the metal boiler behind him. Everyone turned towards the piercing high-pressure whistle. The men tried to dive around the other side of their cover, but it was too late.

A concussive blast instantly filled the room as the boiler erupted. All sound turned into a numbing ring as a swarm of debris blasted over Lord Z's head. He tightened into a ball until the air came back into the room. With his vision blurry, he fought to see through dust and smoke. His training and instincts quickly cut through the fog, and he began to check his flanks, straining to see through his dust-filled eyes.

He glanced to the left and saw nothing but smoking chaff. To the right he saw a gun. Blinking to clear his vision, he saw the arm of one of the men holding a gun, separated from the body and smoking where there was a shoulder five seconds earlier. It wasn't the first time the experienced Enforcer had seen such a thing. The horror got pushed aside, and he quickly raised up with his firearm aimed.

The room was utterly destroyed. The better half of the walls were missing, and he could see two floors up. Pieces of everything were scattered away from where the boiler once was; nothing was distinguishable from anything else. Wood, metal, and bodies were covered in ash and dust. As his hearing gradually returned, he heard the sound of a woman screaming.

He slowly stepped around what remained of the shelf and looked down through the gaping wound in the floor. A glow came through the smoke, and he could feel a surge of heat. It was fire. He looked up and saw the remains of an apartment collapse down into the hole, smashing onto the ground. The floor continued to collapse; it was time to leave.

Lord Z stumbled to the entrance, bracing himself against the wall. Trying to navigate the thick smoke, he raised his gun when three men appeared directly down the corridor. Their hazy silhouettes then materialized into recognizable forms. The senior Enforcer quickly ran up to him, trying to reinforce his massive physique.

"Lord, are you all right?"

Lord Z gave no answer.

"What happened in here, Sir?"

The Lord Enforcer looked back into the scattered remains with his jaw clenched. "Exactly what he knew would happen."

"Who, Sir?"

Lord Z looked back to the officer. "We need to get out of this building." He nodded as another man arrived and aided the pair towards the stairwell. They fought to maintain balance as the building around them crumbled. Everything was shaking. He could see horrified civilians stumbling around, covered in debris and blood. In one apartment, murky light poured in from a hole where the ceiling used to be. Inside, a little girl sat crying over two adults lying motionless on their stomachs. Her young, terrified face immediately burnt into his memory, where it would never leave.

Making his way back to the outside, Lord Z continued to hear screams as pedestrians crowded around the building. He watched as some zealously ran past others frozen in shock. The accompanying Enforcers leaned him against a parked Voikatsu before going back to manage the chaos.

Minutes later, he heard sirens echoing from the fire brigade and the Med-Vac units. He looked down at the firearm in his right hand, now covered in ash. Gripping it firmly, he threw himself into the Voit and closed his eyes.

The sounds bounced around in his skull like animals trapped in a cage. They were the sounds he had trained himself to run towards, but in that moment he wanted only to block everything out. Eventually his consciousness began to slip, and the sounds of the nightmare slowly carried him away.

Downtown, Daimó looked out of the window from an unmarked office. In the distance, a red glow released a tower of black smoke. It looked as though the entire Industrial District burned. He raised a cup of tepid water, his eyes fixed on the inferno.

"How efficient," he said, taking a sip. He then sat down and looked at the plans he had drawn up. They were titled "Industrial Quarter Purge."

3
RING

Frantic steps could be heard down the long, towering hallway lined with massive columns. Carmin ran across the recently waxed floor with arms full of technical drawings. He dodged coworkers who briskly walked to wherever they needed to be. His Toki chimed, signaling that his meeting had just started. The young engineer hurried up, being careful not to rip his deceptively cheap designer suit again.

As he ran faster, the Po'Kin-style wall sconces began to blur by. His slicked hair flopped about as he rounded a corner, trying hard not to slip on the shiny floor. The blurred field of view then became filled with a huge cluster of children; there wasn't enough time to stop.

His shoulder collided with something that sent all of his drawings floating down like large feathers. Carmin instinctively bit his tongue, trying to keep the adult word in his mouth from launching into the sea of innocent young ears.

"Sorry, sorry, sorry."

Carmin started to frantically pick up his drawings, his blood still pumping like a flooded river. He then saw a rather elegant adult hand appear amongst the scattered drawings.

"I'm so sorry, I'm late to a . . .." Looking up, Carmin's thought dislodged at the sight of a rather striking set of eyes.

"Are you okay?"

"Uhm, yeah. I mean, I'm sorry. Are you okay? That was terribly irresponsible of me," Carmin explained.

"It's okay, I can't fault you for being ambitious."

He managed to grab all of his drawings, and they both stood up. Carmin couldn't help pausing to look at her. The long skirt and scarf had a carefree feel that looked out of place in the rigidly designed headquarters; however, he noticed that it fit her quite nicely.

"You move rather quickly being in such a handsome suit."

"Thank you." Now noticing her face, Carmin stood there fixated.

"I suppose you were in a hurry?" she smirked.

"Yes." Remembering his panicked state, Carmin then sprinted off with his drawings flapping like clipped wings. The woman watched him as he disappeared behind the pool of children snickering over the collision.

The woman stood tall. "So who is ready to see some fire?"

With eyes lighting up, all of the boys and about half the girls let out a politely restrained "yes."

"Next we are going to view the steam-engine room that generates much of the electricity that powers the city. They have to heat up water to make steam, which makes pressure, which forces the engine to move."

A small boy raised his hand, a look of concern on his face.

"Yes, Lakou?"

"Is it going to be smoky? Smoke makes me cough." He asked, thinking of his uncle with the yellow teeth.

"That is an excellent question, and I'm glad you are thinking about that. All of this power and technology can do wonderful things, but we need to make sure that we are responsible with it. With many advancements, there is a cost, and we must always maintain balance with the land and not take more than we can give back."

The dumbfounded boy had not moved. "So, is it going to be smoky?"

The teacher smiled. "I think we will be safe."

о о о

Kiara could see a reflection of clouds moving swiftly in the *Colour, etc.* store front window. The sun had warmed up downtown Doulan, a pleasant and somewhat bohemian neighborhood in northern Chigou. The breeze shifted Kiara's long skirt as she tried to keep her sandy-colored hair from blowing in her eyes. She put her hands up to the window to take a peek in.

A set of colorful oil pencils that she had been planning on purchasing for quite some time sat neatly in a box. The long hours of teaching art at the regional youth academy had taken a little spark out of Kiara's urge to undertake personal projects. She thought if she got some shiny new materials, the motivation would come back again.

Sliding her hands across the window, Kiara then saw some newly arrived sculpting material. The brilliant color came from pigments harvested near the edge of the red valley—hard to harvest and quite expensive. Images then flew around in Kiara's mind, ideas of what she could create if she gave herself the time to sculpt again. A faint sigh slipped out.

As she leaned back, Kiara noticed the reflection of someone standing next to her. Looking through the window himself, a man stood holding a tattered mechanical pencil. She noticed the sharp wardrobe on his fit frame—a bit fancy for her tastes, but nothing that screamed for attention. A spark of recognition then ignited a little grin.

"So did you make it to your meeting on time?"

The man turned towards Kiara. Three blank seconds later, his face lit up. "Yes! Yes, I did. Thank you for asking."

"That's good to hear."

"Sorry again about running into you. That was really careless of me."

"It's fine. I'm tougher than I look," Kiara said, shifting her grin.

Carmin happily took a second to reassess her look. "I figured that you don't work at Kasic. I'm guessing you teach art."

"Is my outfit so obvious?" Kiara didn't like being obvious.

"It's more that you are standing in front of an art store."

Kiara turned her grin into a proper smile. He took the invitation and stuck out his hand.

"My name is Carmin."

Kiara took his hand and spoke with playful directness. "You are much more gentlemanly outside of the office."

"Yeah, I turn into a real monster when I'm going to a finance meeting."

"My name is Kiara." Noticing that their gentle handshake had

Colour, etc

IN DOWNTOWN DOULAN

lasted a rather long time, Carmin went to fiddle with the well-worn pencil. "That's a fitting name."

"Oh, how so?"

"Well, it's very pretty."

Kiara coughed out a laugh. "I never figured a Kasic man could be so downright charming. I wonder what you're like outside of the city limits."

"If I ever find time to leave, I'll let know."

Kiara looked past Carmin towards the northern valley. The sun began to descend as the clouds cleared away.

"You never leave the city?"

"I'm glad I manage to live at least this far from downtown," he mumbled.

"You don't live in this neighborhood, do you?"

Carmin laughed as he looked over his outfit. "Well, I *thought* I did a decent job of not completely looking like a salary man."

Joining in the laugh, Kiara again noticed his pencil, which must have produced a thousand drawings. "I think they close soon."

A breeze blew in, and Carmin noticed Kiara's elegant hand gently move a strand of hair behind her ear. Her face seemed to glow from the sunlight radiating off the store front window. "Actually, I think my pencil can wait if you'd let me buy you dinner tonight."

Kiara's eyes looked away as she tried to hide the red flushing in her cheeks. "Well, I wouldn't want to get in the way of you doing your work."

"Says the girl who knocked me to the floor on the way to my meeting."

"Hey, you ran into me, good Lord," Kiara assertively said.

"I did, and I couldn't live with myself if I wasn't able to make it up to you."

Kiara looked around for a bit before speaking sternly. "Well, I suppose it's the least I could do."

○ ○ ○

Starting as a small bakery, Izzy Kai quickly grew into a full cafe. It specialized in breads made from Blashu Wheat grown exclusively in the Naifin Valley. Its warm quality went well with sweet and spicy baked goods. Over the years, such treats gained a reputation of putting one in a rather friendly mood. Sticky braids became especially popular with young couples.

Carmin tried to keep his destination a surprise, but the aroma flowing down the street from Izzy Kai had long since given his intentions away. The smell even overpowered the fresh Tulú flowers potted all along the front of the cafe. Kiara found the choice a bit forward but hardly disagreeable.

"You aren't wasting any time, are you?"

"I don't know what you are talking about," Carmin defended.

"Mmm hmm. Well, just don't get any sticky braids, because I may end up ignoring everything you say as I slip into a buttery trance."

"Well, as much as I'd love to talk the night away, I suppose looking at you for a few silent hours would not be the worst way to spend an evening."

Carmin opened the door as Kiara walked in, trying to shake the smirk off of her face. They sat by the window and got a box of sweet Blashu drops along with two smoked coffees. Smoking coffee had become popular in Chigou since it gave the invigorating drink a smoother, more complex characteristic. Kiara looked up to Carmin with raised eyebrows.

"No sticky braids?"

"I don't think that would be appropriate for a first date."

Kiara slipped out a laugh.

"I didn't see you as a smoked coffee kind of girl, though."

"I'm not surprised. You couldn't even see me enough to keep from running into me."

Carmin bowed his head. "You make a fair point, Lady Kiara."

"Actually, I am rather fond of smoked coffee. It's good when you're trying to get a project done and the sun is going down," she said, looking out the window.

"I couldn't agree more."

A warm and comforting sensation sat in Kiara's stomach. She felt herself disarming quickly from her date's gentle sincerity; perhaps it was okay to call him a date. She rarely trusted anyone so quickly and felt a bit silly because of it. Carmin had trouble

IZZY KAI
CAFE & BAKERY

IN CENTRAL DOULAN

IRRESISTIBLE
STICKY BRAIDS &
BLASHU ROLLS

THE BEST
SMOKED COFFEE
IN CHIGOU

moving his attention past the captivating grasp of her eyes.

"So did you always want to mentor youthful creative tendencies?"

"I was always an artist. My parents exposed me to drawing and sculpting before I was even talking. I like sharing what I love with anyone interested, but I don't have a kid of my own."

"You just have thirty kids you can send home when you get tired."

They both laughed as they sipped coffee, giving their minds a second to wander.

"So what is it exactly that you do at Kasic? You seem . . . how shall I put this . . . less afraid to smile than most people I've met over there."

"Yeah, it's perhaps not the warmest place to work. I do like the opportunities there, though, designing and creating better ways for people to live here."

Kiara focused in. "So what are you working on now?"

Carmin hesitated to speak, thinking of how dry his explanation would sound given his current company. Kiara broke the silence. "What, are you afraid it might be a bit technical for me?"

"No, it's not that."

"You afraid you'll bore me into the grave?"

Carmin laughed. "Well, it's not that bad. Maybe just a yawning out the door."

"You might be surprised." Kiara took a long sip of coffee.

Carmin sat up a little bit. "Okay. Kasic is thinking of putting up a dam just north of the city so they can install generators."

"And you're designing it?"

"No, I'm trying to convince them that they shouldn't build it."

Kiara leaned in. "You don't think they should try and generate electricity in a way that doesn't involve huge clouds of black smoke?"

"No, no, not at all. Hydropower sourcing is great; it's the dam that's the problem. It sounds tempting, but I think it'll just make the water quality even worse than it already is from all the runoff coming out of Primichi. All of that would end up settling and make a bed of toxic sludge. It'd be nice at first, but I think eventually it'll do more harm than good."

Kiara sat back, contemplating the surprising complexity of the young man.

"So, you'd rather have clean water than all that power?"

Carmin rubbed his stubbled face.

"Well, yes. So, you can probably begin to imagine just how popular I am there. I just think we can come up with better ways to generate power than compromising our biggest source of fresh water. I don't want my children to have to fix my lack of foresight."

Kiara's eyes popped open. "You have children?"

"One day, if I am to be so lucky."

Kiara subtly took a deep breath and began playing with the rim of her coffee cup. Inside, she giggled over how attractive the whole conversation made this engineer seem.

"Hopefully that wasn't too boring."

"No, not at all. Actually, I find that very interesting."

"I wish my boss shared your sentiment."

"Oh?" Kiara playfully responded. "So why do they keep you around?"

"Because I'm the best design engineer they have."

Kiara raised her eyebrows. "And so humble! How lucky for them."

Carmin pulled out a Blashu drop and popped it in his grinning mouth. Kiara then sent her gaze to the table and out of the immediate conversation. After swallowing the sweet dough, Carmin became self-conscious and immediately wondered if she found him to be arrogant. With a less playful tone, Kiara raised her eyes.

"Have you ever heard of the company Etilé?"

Carmin thought for a moment, unsure of where the question came from.

"Yeah, I've maybe heard of them once. I don't know anyone who works for them, though."

Kiara sorted through lingering, unresolved thoughts.

"So you don't know who runs that company?"

"No, why do you ask?"

"I have a friend who lives in Primichi. She ran a simple but really nice vegetable farm in the south west. One day a man from this *Etilé* showed up saying he wanted to test the ground, something about fuel research. He promised she would barely notice him being there and offered her a lot of money."

"Sounds like a decent deal. Did she take it?"

"Yeah. He did his tests, paid her, and then left."

"So she retired early?" Carmin said, trying to lighten the mood. Kiara didn't notice.

"Two months later the ground became toxic, and ninety percent of her crops died. The farm was basically ruined."

Carmin dropped his self-conscious paranoia. "That's awful. Was she able to find him . . . did she tell any Enforcers?"

"No, she couldn't find him, but she heard about someone looking at farms in northern Chigou trying to do the same thing."

"Was it the same guy?"

"I don't know. Probably. I took my bird for a walk up north and asked one of the farmers about it." Kiara thought for a moment. "I'm sorry, I don't know why I'm talking about this."

Carmin's mind quickly shifted, and at the risk of sounding inappropriately merry, let out a small giggle. "You took a bird for a walk? Do you normally travel with a bird?"

"Yeah, sometimes. Is that strange?" she asked.

"Well, it is perhaps a little unusual. But . . . I'm sorry, please continue."

Such a comment would normally agitate her, but instead she felt a pleasing sincerity about it. "When I arrived there was a man who passed me as he was leaving. He didn't say anything, but I'll never forget that face."

"What did he look like?"

"Nothing exceptional. It was more just the look on his face, or lack of a look. He had the most lifeless eyes I'd ever seen."

Carmin took another sip of his cooling smoked coffee. "So what does this have to do with Etilé?"

"A few months ago I took some lucky students for an airship ride from the North Dock. I overheard a man at the front desk saying he was getting picked up on an Unyo airship. Opaji's, actually."

"Wow, he must have been someone important."

"That's what I thought. I wondered if I was going to luck out and see the great Opaji up close and personal."

"That would be lucky. I basically work for the guy, and I've only seen him once, about forty meters away."

Kiara took a breath. "I looked over at him. I heard the man say he had some company called Etilé, and then he turned and looked right at me. It was him, I know it was . . . with those soulless eyes." A shiver ran up Kiara's spine. "I still feel creeped out when I think about it. Anyways, I wondered if he was going to start working with Kasic."

Kiara reached for a blashu drop. "I'm sorry, that was a long story."

Carmin mused on her last statement. "But you're not really sure who this guy is, though. Right?"

"Not except for what I just told you. I mean, I don't always agree with what Kasic does, but I think they're . . . okay. I do. I just worry about the future, and this guy . . . well, you seem like someone who might want to know what he's done in case you ever have to deal with him."

A quietly comforting moment fell between them despite the heavy nature of the story. A waitress then walked up and warmed their coffees.

"Well, if I find anything out, I'll let you know," Carmin offered.

Kiara took a moment to think over his suggestion, and then a glow started to come back to her face.

"Is that a subtle way of saying that you're going to ask me out again?"

"Or tackle you with an arm full of schematics, whichever gets your attention."

The blood vessels in Kiara's cheeks started to dilate again. "Oh, no need to worry about that, Carmin. You have my attention."

They both looked down and took a sip of warm coffee.

○ ○ ○

A gentle breeze floated across the Naifin Valley, pushing the grass in flowing waves. A small crowed carried on with quiet conversations, all of them looking rather dapper considering the location. They sat facing forward, an aisle between them.

Already renowned for its natural beauty, Kora farm had never looked more lovely. Originally a good distance from Chigou, the city had slowly been expanding towards the second-generation farm. Anticipating the urban encroachment, Kojo and his wife Clora purchased much of the neighboring property, successfully preserving the surrounding natural landscape. The healthy older pair sat in the back, holding hands. The scene reminded them of their first day on the farm as a couple.

Kiara stood in a long white and yellow dress, impressively embroidered with Bollo blossoms matching the ones pinned throughout her hair. Carmin started the day with a bit too much coffee but eventually settled down enough to handle everyone staring at him. Once Kiara appeared, however, all attention promptly focused on the fresh-faced bride draped in the dress of her own making.

A rather large gentlemen named Gozen conducted the simple service. He visited the farm a few times a week to mentor the youth who worked there. The brief ceremony charmed everyone in attendance, with vows written by the young couple stirring up a tear or two. One of Kiara's longtime friends provided the rings, having engraved their names on the inside. The rings differed only by an elegant etching of a Whisping Bird on Kiara's band, her favorite animal since childhood.

With their hands shaking and gently grasping one another, the couple kissed to close the ceremony. A promise sealed, looking forward to the days to come, regardless of what circumstances lay before them. Back at the barn, Clora and Gozen had prepared a brilliantly constructed banquet. A spiraling tower of sweet blashu drops rose up at the center of the table, a request of Carmin. He planned on saving the sticky braids for later.

The small guest list comprised a fairly even mix between corporate and bohemian types, but the mood could not have be more harmonious. Between the sunny weather and the sweet image of lovers promising themselves to one another, the day felt perfect and pure.

As a few of Kiara's childhood friends gushed over her, Carmin took the moment to officially thank the gentle giant that ceremonially bonded him to his new bride. He approached Gozen, who fussed over a pyramid of hot-berry grands coated in chocolate. Carmin noticed how charmingly odd it looked—the strong fingers so elegantly attending to the delicate confectionary tower.

"Despite what your size might imply, you have one of the most thoughtful dispositions I've ever had the grace of experiencing. I'd like to thank you for such a warmhearted ceremony."

Gozen carefully adjusted one last berry before conjuring up the will to break his compulsive attentiveness. "It was my pleasure, and it is kind of you to say such a thing."

"And thank you for not crushing my hand."

"Strong handshakes are for men who fear being perceived as weak."

"My delicate fingers are glad you think so," Carmin laughed. "So I heard you work with children here at the farm and at the North Orphanage. I think that's great."

Never comfortable gloating on his own acts of virtue, Gozen simply retreated back into managing the hot-berry grands.

"There are many young ones in this city who unfortunately lack the care and guidance they deserve. I merely do what I can to rectify the situation. Perhaps you and your lady plan on having children soon."

Carmin coughed. "I just got married, Gozen. One day at a time."

As the pair laughed, they saw the new bride approach with the farm caretakers. Gozen gave Carmin a wink and then went off to attend to the structural integrity of other banquet items. Kiara stood next to Clora and as usual, Kojo stayed a step back and let his more charming half lead the felicitations.

"I have to tell you, dear, this old place has never looked so lovely. Oh Carmin, your bride looks like . . . like something out of a dream," Clora said in her warm voice.

Carmin looked over his bride, wondering how he managed to find a woman who looked like she just stepped out of a fairytale. "I couldn't agree more."

"And thank you again for letting us use the farm. I love this place so much. Everything is so pure and good here. I couldn't think of a better place for us to start our lives together."

"We felt the same way when we were just a couple of kids trying to make a life for ourselves outside the city. We had a few friends over, nothing like this, of course, and I certainly didn't look anything like you."

Carmin stepped up and put his arm around his new wife, feeling the soft skin of her shoulder under his hand. He grinned at Kojo, who seemed more comfortable keeping a step back from the sentimental conversation.

"I bet your husband might disagree with who was more beautiful on their wedding day," Carmin offered.

Kojo diverted his eyes. "That sounds like a trap, but I can safely say we are both very lucky men."

Carmin looked into Kiara's eyes and saw his future staring back up at him. He had never felt a warmer sense of hope in all of his life. "Yes, we are."

Kiara turned back to the older couple. "So we haven't met your children yet. Certainly you two don't run this place by yourselves."

"You'd be surprised what we are capable of," Kojo confidently declared.

Clora patted her husband's graying hair. "Yes dear, I'm surprised all these young ladies aren't tumbling over themselves for a chance to dance with such a spry man."

"Well, I certainly hope to get one before the night is up," Kiara confessed.

Kojo's response got stuck in his throat. Carmin graciously bailed him out. "So, your children are here?"

Clora rubbed her hands together as she considered the question, her smile feigning a bit. Kojo stepped up right next to his wife and put his arm around her.

"We are very fortunate to have young ones from the city stay here and help out. They get to learn how to live off of the land, and we get to have more children than most couples could hope for."

Kiara noticed Clora's bittersweet face. "I'm sure they are very lucky to spend any time here that they can."

Clora took a long breath and perked up. "And you two better get to work soon and bring a little troublemaker of your own up here. Nia needs someone to run around with."

Kiara scrunched her brow. "Who is Nia? One of the animals?"

Clora let out an endearing laugh and pointed to a short rock wall. "No, dear, but you're almost right. She is that little girl running across the wall. Nia came to us a few months ago and is finally getting her spirits up. Now she just needs a playmate."

"Well, we vow to bring one of those up here someday," Kiara said.

"That would be lovely, dear. It really would."

The shadows stretched out as the sky had turned into a warm glow. Kojo rubbed the shoulder of his Clora. "Well, it's getting late, and I'm sure these two are eager to do something about giving Nia that playmate."

Carmin cleared his throat. Looking down into his new bride's eyes, he couldn't agree more.

4
CROWD

She sat at the kitchen table with squinted eyes, her tiny fingers grasping a wax pencil. Bright blue lines filled in an oversized engine attached to an imagined airship. The girl's mind focused, blocking out the swarming sounds of grown-ups getting ready for work.

The kitchen had wood floors and a thick counter made of polished plate rock. The counter displayed an assortment of appliances with exposed piping, in line with Chigou's fondness of the industrial chic aesthetic.

Carmin fastened up his tie as he hustled into the kitchen, his forehead developing a light layer of sweat. "Did you move the drawings I had on the counter?"

Kiara arranged her daughter's lunch into a meal box. "Oh no, did you lose your plans to clog up the river?" she spoke with a smirk.

Carmin stopped, closed his eyes, and took a deep breath. "Kiara, I'm running late. Please just tell me . . ."

"I moved them out of the spill zone and into your clean, dry office, Lord frantic."

"Thank you," Carmin said from the hallway.

Kiara tied up the lunch box and set it on the table next to Suzu's airship drawing.

"I put a Molou roll in your lunch today. I hope you're okay with that, Lady Suzu."

Suzu looked up from her drawing and smiled, her black hair falling past her bright green eyes. Kiara playfully rustled her daughter's hair and walked back to the counter.

"Mom!" Suzu exclaimed, attempting to fix her hair.

"Uh oh, look at that mess. I think I better fix it up and put a specky on it."

Mom suggestively raised a small hair clip out of her pocket adorned with small colorful spheres. Suzu pouted her lips and slouched in submission. Kiara then walked straight over. "One day you're going to be begging me to buy pretty things to put in your hair."

Before dolling up her daughter, Kiara placed a small, white dance outfit onto the table. It had white leggings and a small skirt made from stripes of every color. Kiara flattened out the two, blank sleeves.

"So, what do you think of this for the arms? I thought the full-spectrum-look was fun."

Suzu sat up on her feet and looked over the costume. She wiggled about as a toothy grin sprouted. Kiara volleyed back with a suspicious smirk. "You sure it's not getting a little too bright and cheery for you?"

"No, I like it. It will help me to captivate the judges."

Kiara belly laughed. "Where did you learn to say that?"

"This audition is super important, Mom, and Dad said I have to captivate them."

Kiara hollered down the hallway. "Carmin, have you been grooming our daughter's vocabulary for her audition?"

The frantic engineer smiled as he reentered the kitchen. Wanting to catch him before he finally ran off for work, Suzu tugged on his pocket. "Do you think my airship looks fast?"

Carmin quickly leaned in. "The engines are too big given the size of the gas chamber." Suzu gave her creation a pensive stare as Kiara glared at her husband, clearly questioning his word choice.

Carmin reevaluated his blunt critique. "It looks dangerously fast."

Unconvinced, Suzu crossed her arms. "But too big?"

Carmin leaned closer to his daughter, forgetting for a moment that he was already late for work. "They look rather heavy, but remember, just because something is small doesn't mean that it can't be powerful . . . and very fast."

With a small grunt, Suzu grabbed for another sheet of paper and began to draw some petite, deceptively ferocious engines.

Carmin stood up and gave his wife a smirk.

Kiara returned the sentiment. "Oh, Lord clever? Maybe I should leave the complicated task of smoking coffee up to you today."

A wave of panic flowed over Carmin. "You didn't make coffee?"

Kiara rolled her eyes, "Yes, I made coffee."

Carmin kissed Kiara on the head before quickly pouring coffee into his vacuum-sealed Charban coffee flask, along with some milk. He then reached down by the sink and pulled out a wand connected to the building's central steam system. Carmin gave it a quick test before steaming up his coffee flask through its copper valve.

"I thought you were in a hurry" Kiara noted.

"I am, but not in too much of a hurry for this." Carmin pulled off the steam wand, gathered up his drawings, and headed for the door. "Goodbye, my lovely ladies. I shall see you this evening."

"Bye, Dad."

Kiara walked up to Carmin, cutting off his path, and spoke in a quiet voice. "Are you going to stay on the dam project?"

Carmin raised his eyebrows. "You're asking me this right now?"

"I thought you wanted to switch to your Core-thermic project."

"I absolutely do, but I don't decide which projects get passed at Kasic."

"I just really don't like you working on that dam. I mean, you're going to help them clog that river into a toxic backfill."

"Kiara, I'm not doing it because I want to."

"So don't."

"I can't just stop. I do have a family I need to take care of," he said, motioning to their daughter.

"And that dam affects our family as well as every family in the city, not to mention all life in the southern valley."

"They already budgeted it, Kiara. It's a done deal. What do you want me to do about it?"

Hearing her father's volume jump, Suzu took her attention away from the powerful little engines. Her parents noticed, and Carmin abashedly regained composure.

"You're right, I do need to push the Core-thermic project. Right now I'm helping make the dam be as safe as possible and figure out how to do the right thing for everyone."

Kiara kissed her husband's hand. "You're such a good man."

Carmin grabbed his wife and gave her a hard kiss on the lips as her eyes widened up. Suzu winced before getting back to her drawing.

"Have fun in the big city, little ladies." Carmin said, as he ran out the door.

Kiara walked back over to the kitchen to pour herself some coffee. Suzu's head popped up. "Don't I have school?"

"No, silly. It's a maintenance day, remember?"

"Oh yeah. Can we go get cold cream from Michelou's?"

Cold cream—a frozen dairy product adored for its naturally sour highlight in an otherwise sweet and creamy treat—reigned as the favorite confection in Chigou, and Michelou's was easily the most famous cold creamery in town. Known for having more flavors than one could recite, the shop further beckoned children with a ten-meter slide that spiraled down into a pit of colorful pillows.

"Cold cream and a Molou roll in one day?" Mother questioned. "Yeah!"

Kiara suddenly remembered the reason she needed to head downtown. She had kept the reason from her family knowing they would not particularly enjoy it. Slides and sugar seemed to be a reasonable bribe. "I suppose we can make it over to Michelou's."

○ ○ ○

Suzu held her Mother's hand as they waited in line, her favorite red-and-white-striped sling bag hung off her shoulder. Her tiny lungs gulped in air, trying to recover from the thirteen trips she had just taken down the cold creamery's famous slide. The brilliantly designed space danced with smells of sweet things. Sounds of confectionary machines bounced off of the walls. Regardless of age, everyone within felt like a child.

Above the slide, a rather large music box spun around and constantly chimed a playful melody—a sound that Chigouans found themselves spontaneously humming from time to time. Shining mechanics covered the steam-powered device in a

Chigou's Favorite Confectionary
Delicious!

Michelou's

COLD CREAMERY

fancifully designed layout. It rhythmically released small puffs of vapor as if lifting the music to the ceiling.

Behind the central counter of the parlor, the large Michelou's sign glowed in its iconic red script; one could easily see it from across the street. Kiara cherished seeing her's daughter face light up with every visit.

"Going with the usual, or are you feeling adventurous?" asked Mom.

Suzu pursed her lips, taking the vast rainbow of choices under deep consideration. "I feel like I should stick with my regular today."

"Wise choice."

Suzu noded with confidence. "Mom, what are you gonna get?"

Kiara looked down to see her daughter's favorite: hot-berry and chocolate. Hot-berries were small, red berries that had a sweet but somewhat peppery taste to them. Pairing them with either chocolate or cold cream had become a valley favorite. Suzu preferred to pile them all together.

"I'll take your advice and have the same, if you don't mind."

∘ ∘ ∘

Kiara walked down the sidewalk as Suzu polished off her beloved hot-berry and chocolate cold cream. They approached Kasic headquarters, which stood like a mountain, even amongst the towering forest of buildings downtown. A noise could be heard up ahead, an unusually loud hum of human voices.

Suzu looked up, her lips sticky and smiling. She noticed the sound coming from a crowd that had gathered around the front entrance of her father's work. Some people held signs and spoke with their hands up to their mouths. A sense of confusion set in, followed by an uneasy feeling deep in her swollen belly.

"Why are all those people at Daddy's work? Are they mad?"

"Not mad."

"Then why are they so loud?"

"Well, maybe some of them are a bit upset, but they're just trying to get the attention of your dad's company."

"How do you know?"

Kiara looked up at the crowd for longer than what seemed to make sense to Suzu. She did not find comfort in the time it took her mother to respond. "I told them to come here."

Suzu tried to understand what her mother meant, as everyone there looked like a stranger. "If they want to talk to Daddy, why don't they just walk in like we do?"

"They don't want to talk to Daddy. They want to talk with the company."

Suzu looked from her mom and up the towering face of the Kasic building. She felt the crowd was probably going to be there a very long time, as the building did not appear to have any desire to talk back.

She could then feel a tug as her mother walked them up to the edge of the flock. The noise from the crowd felt heavy to Suzu, a tension that multiplied along with the grip from her mother's hand. Kiara looked down at her daughter and smiled, but something felt strange to the young girl. Suzu sensed her mother covering something up, and the unnatural face compounded the tension in her stomach.

The rather petite Kiara walked up on her toes, trying to see over the crowd. She eventually came up to a tall, thin man in a rather bohemian ensemble typical of what many identified as "Soran attire." Suzu looked up through the current of people pushing into her. It reminded her of being underwater at the North Pool as her mother stood above her, visible but unclear.

Kiara tapped the tall man on the shoulder. Being bumped from all directions, the man didn't notice. She then put her hand around her mouth and leaned into his ear.

"Mouba!"

Mouba turned around and looked down to Kiara. Suzu found his long and stringy facial hair slightly frightening.

"Kiara, glad you could finally make it."

"Had to make a stop at Michelou's," Kiara said with a grin as she glanced down to her daughter.

Mouba looked down to Suzu with an expression that did not reciprocate Kiara's playful reaction. Suzu found his joyless face uncomfortable; she did not like it when people seemed incapable of smiling. The sugar high had worn off, and she wanted to go home.

Mouba looked back to Kiara. "No one has come out. The cowards are settled in their fortress."

"Well, a big group of Sorans is a pretty intimidating sight," Kiara spoke facetiously.

"Is that supposed to be a joke?"

Kiara and Mouba looked at each other, a private exchange of tension in a vat of pressure.

"I see some security, but not reps? You'd think they'd want to talk us out of here, or are they just waiting for us to get *nonviolent?*" Kiara wondered aloud.

"They don't have any justification against our protests to the dam. They're just behaving like the greedy cowards that they are. Why don't you go up front and conjure someone out?" Mouba offered.

The crowd continued to push into Suzu, who tugged on her mother's arm. "I want to go home now."

Kiara looked down to her daughter; she could see the uneasiness in her eyes and feel it in her grip. Mouba again interrupted.

"Are you going to participate or not?"

Kiara rubbed her daughter's hand gently with her thumb. She turned back to Mouba and now noticed him holding a bullhorn. "Do you not know how to use that?"

Mouba tucked in his ego and started to make his way towards the front. The crowd pushed in as his lanky frame fought to its edge. Kiara pulled Suzu in front of her, wrapping her arms around the small set of shoulders. Suzu hung on tight. They finally broke through the front of the crowd.

"We're not leaving until they hear us," Kiara projected above the crowd. Mouba nodded and then turned to the security members keeping the group at bay. He raised the bullhorn to his mouth and began the requests.

Up on the twenty-second floor, a power-engineering intern looked down at a spec waiving its arms. Remi had just gotten married and tried hard to balance his plan for a family against an exhausting load of work and school. It felt like a huge break when he managed to squeeze his foot through the front doors of Kasic, but he currently lacked the energy to appreciate it.

Even at a distance, the shouting crowd made Remi's chest tighten. He hated people that yelled their point across, demanding a bend in their direction instead of working quietly and earning the result. Still, a small spark of envy floated around in his mind as he thought of how freely they set their course. Remi suddenly felt that he had been standing by the window longer than he should have.

"Who are they?"

Remi spun around towards the voice by his ear, nearly spilling his coffee on the stranger. Standing right behind him, a tall man wore the coldest expression he had ever seen.

"I'm sorry . . ."

At first, Remi anticipated some reprimand about slacking off. Instead, the man's eyes, which had the tenderness of steel bearings, simply looked down at the street, never blinking. Remi began to feel uneasy about the unfamiliar man.

"What do you make of these people?" the man asked.

"They are protesting the dam, I think." Remi took a sip of his coffee, its warmth a welcome sensation.

"But the dam is already approved. What purpose does this serve?"

Remi found the question oddly pragmatic, or maybe hypothetical? Men at Kasic tended to condescendingly refer to protestors as Sorans, a mildly derogatory term expressing ideological-environmental-sentimentality. To those it applied to, *Soran* would occasionally be used as a term of pride.

"I don't know. Protestors seem to like results as much as they get motivated by being denied them."

The man took a step forward, his face right up to the glass. "Do you believe once it's built, some would still seek to end it?"

"Destroy the dam? I don't think so." He took another sip of his coffee. "However, I wouldn't be so surprised if there were one or two crazies in there who had the idea floating around. I might put the guy spitting into the bullhorn as a candidate."

The stranger then noticed the man with the bullhorn kept

looking back to the same person, a woman protecting a small child while thrusting a fist into the air. She seemed to be giving the loud protestor directions, channeling every command to the guards.

"Do you know the woman with the child?"

Remi walked up to the window and strained his eyes. The small swarm continued to look like a puddle of dots. He wondered how the man could clearly identify anyone down there as a child, let alone make out their face. Remi then reached for the decorative but functioning monocular setting on the side table. He raised it to his eye and spotted a woman in the center of the crowd who had one arm around a dark-haired young girl.

"I can't really tell. I don't think I know her."

The woman then lifted her arm in the air, revealing a red-and-white striped bag hanging over the little girl's shoulder, a rather unique accessory.

"Actually, I think I recognize the little girl. That might be Carmin's daughter."

The man's rigid posture maintained. "And he works here?"

"Yeah, his wife and kid have stopped by and visited him a few times. I'm a little confused as to what they're doing down there, though."

"A company man's wife protesting at the very place he works. That does raise a number of questions."

Remi put down the monocular and saw the man's eyes looking right at him, through him. His body locked up at the void gaze, and suddenly he wished the man would ask him to get back to work. "Well, I've been away from my desk long enough. I'll leave you to the crowd."

Remi walked away from the man in the straightest line he could. He then bumped into another man as he rounded a corner; Remi didn't bother to stop.

"Whoa, kid, what's the rush?"

Anticipating a reprimand, Remi slowly turned about-face. Recognizing Carmin, he relaxed his posture.

"Sorry, I was just . . . did you see that protest crowd outside?"

Carmin lowered his brow. "What protest?"

"There's people protesting the dam. I think I saw your kid down there."

"Suzu? What do you mean? You saw my daughter protesting?"

Realizing he had never officially met Carmin's wife or daughter, Remi quickly attempted to construct a explanation.

"That guy was asking about her. I mean, I think it's your daughter and wife."

Carmin looked towards the man by the lobby window. Remi waited for a response until his curiosity won out. "So, do you know who that guy is? He's kinda creeping me out."

Carmin's mind failed to pull in a concrete memory, but the motionless man still compelled his focus. "Do I know him? What's his name?"

"He didn't say, and I didn't care to ask," Remi said.

"And he was asking about my wife?"

"Yeah."

The two men stood for a moment, preoccupied with different thoughts.

Carmin finally spoke. "I need to go." He walked away with a heavy expression. Remi then walked off to take refuge at his desk, the idea of monotonous work suddenly feeling rather warm and comforting.

Down below, Mouba yelled over to Kiara, who still stood right next to him.

"If they go through with the dam, we are going to have to get serious, Kiara."

Kiara, who had always felt equal portions of admiration and caution towards Mouba's zeal, started to tip the balance in her mind. "We are being serious."

"We can't let it happen, Kiara. If they don't stop, we have to make them stop, no matter what."

Although they had shared some rather passionate conversations about fighting irresponsible industrializing before, Kiara felt conflicted with Mouba's words. A powerful empathy began to flow through the nervous grip of her daughter.

"Mouba, this is about peaceful responsibility. We are not going to do anything dangerous."

He leaned in so close she could smell his beard. "If you can't commit to the cause, maybe you should step away."

Unafraid of the smell, she leaned in even closer. "I've never backed down, and considering why you left Primichi, I suggest you watch what you say to me about running away."

Stunned, Mouba raised his finger into her face. "You don't know why I left Primichi."

"Exactly. And I don't want you doing anything here that's so careless and harmful that you won't be able to talk about it, either. Don't give anyone a reason to call us criminals, Mouba."

Using her mom's sleeve as a security blanket, Suzu sensed herself being shielded from larger, louder bodies. Tiny lungs struggled to breathe while her head pulsed with confusion. Suzu wanted to leave. She wondered why they didn't escape but was too overwhelmed to ask. She closed her eyes and thought of drawing airships at the kitchen table, quietly.

○ ○ ○

Carmin looked through the kitchen window, seeing the endless range of mountains fade off into a jagged horizon. They looked cold as the sun hid behind them. He took a slow sip of black ale—the first drink he had in a month.

His shoulders felt heavy as thoughts of the future ran through his mind. Nothing seemed clear; no choice seemed to shine through. As Carmin heard his girls walking up the stairs, he swallowed the last of his liquid retreat.

The door opened. Mom and Daughter slid their feet in, sharing the same depleted look. Kiara softly smiled at her husband while sitting her daughter down at the kitchen table. Suzu found her drawings to be a suitable pillow for the time being. Kiara could see Carmin trying to smile, but only making it half way.

"Something on your mind?"

"You two look like you've had quite an adventure today."

"Yeah, it actually was a bit of an adventure. I think her Michelou sugar-high has just about crashed down into the cellar."

Kiara ran her hand across Suzu's dark hair. It felt cold, covering the heat trickling up from her skin. Carmin set his bottle onto the counter.

"Found out from some intern that you took our daughter to a protest today, right in front of my building." The energy in the room changed in a single breath. "Made it all the way to the front door and didn't bother to say hi?"

She stroked her daughter's hair one more time before looking her husband in the eye.

"You were presenting today. I know how much that stresses you out. I thought I'd tell you all about it when you got home."

"Thinking of my daughter in that crowd is actually more stressful."

"I was with her the whole time. She never let go of my hand"

"What if that crowd got out of hand? There's only so much you can do against a wall of people pushing into you."

The volume slid up a tick.

"It was a peaceful protest, Carmin. What are you worried that could happen?"

"Your friend Mouba throwing his bullhorn at some security guard, and then the boiler erupts, and you're in the middle of it. That could happen."

Kiara scrunched her brow in disagreement. "Mouba didn't even speak until I got there and told him to."

"Well, I don't disagree that he's not much of a leader, but he does seem to have a temper and some impulse-control problems. And in a pit of yelling people and armed guards, that's all it would take."

Suzu's eyes started to peek open. She felt the house sounded awfully loud for that time of night. Kiara crossed her arms.

"Do you really think I'd do anything that would put her in real danger?"

"I don't know. I'm wondering about that, actually."

Kiara focused on her husband's eyes, not liking the taste he had just put in her mouth. "Do you really mean that?"

Words clogged up in Carmin's throat. He searched for ones that would be carefully honest. "I'm just saying, it's a lot of emotion and a lot of people. It's potential conflict she doesn't need to be in the middle of."

"You know what? I'm glad I took her. She needs to see what it means to stand up for what you believe in."

"Then why didn't you stand across the street? Kiara, you have to see the potential of how that situation could get dangerous."

"Well, sometimes we have to take on a little risk, right? Or should we teach our daughter to fear anyone who stands up against her and just cower away?"

Suzu looked down at the airship drawing she worked on that morning. She imagined herself sitting atop it as it floated through the clouds—unable to see the ground, too far away to hear the people below.

"No . . . I don't." Carmin took a breath. "You can't control a crowd, though, Kiara. It just . . . it just makes me nervous. And why do you have to be there, right in front of my building? People know you were down there. Do you have any idea how awkward that is for me?"

"You were opposed to the dam before we even met. Certainly people know where you stand on that issue by now, dear."

"Yes, but it's different when I'm simply proposing a better solution as a member of the company. When you're out there it looks like I have a . . . wife I can't control."

Kiara folded her arms even tighter. Carmin regretted his wording before his wife even started her reply. "You would like me under your control?"

"No, you know what I mean."

Kiara stood her ground, silent.

Carmin continued. "You know I don't want to control you. It just looks as though . . . it looks like I have a wife that doesn't have any respect for her husband."

Suzu's tired eyes caught a glimpse of her father's smile. In a small frame sat a wedding photo of her parents, the setting sun illuminating their faces. It made Suzu warm just looking at it. Her parents' loud and confusing conversation faded into a hum.

"I do respect you. We respect each other. We care about the same things. We just don't always pursue it the same way." Kiara offered.

"There's just not many people at Kasic that would understand that, and I don't want to lose my job. I want to be able to make change from within the company, and I want to continue to take care of my wife and my daughter."

Kiara slouched her shoulders and relaxed her face. She could see a heavy sincerity in the eyes of her husband. She slowly lowered her arms and stepped over to him. Giving in to his wife's offer, Carmin gently guided her face onto his chest. Suzu tilted her head up to her parents.

"Sorry."

"No, no," her parents said in unison. They walked over to Suzu, and Kiara put her hand on her daughter's head. "You don't have anything to be sorry for."

"But you kept talking about me really loud."

"Sometimes people just get loud when they really care about something."

Suzu paused for a moment, a reaction going off behind her eyes. She then stood up rather sternly and spoke with the voice of a Lord Enforcer.

"I'm hungry."

Her parents stood, stunned at the volume of her proclamation. A few seconds later, they let out a laugh. Carmin rustled her hair until she smiled.

"I'm glad you feel as strongly about food as I do."

Kiara walked towards the counter, thinking of what to feed her little monsters.

5
AMPUTATION

A pyramid of rolled plans precariously balanced in Carmin's arms as he scuttled down a hallway. He could feel his armpits sweating through his shirt. Although he tried to calm his breathing, the thought of his colleagues seeing his drenched shirt just made him sweat more.

Approaching the elevator, he attempted to hit the button as the plans began to slip. Carmin squatted down in an effort to keep them from crashing across the parquet floor. Half bent over into a paper woven squat, he reached out for the button with his elbow.

"Uhm, did you hurt your back?" Remi casually walked up from around the corner.

Carmin glared up and mumbled out a hot breath of air. Remi reached down and hit the elevator button.

"Thank you," Carmin sighed.

"You look like you're ready for the corethermic presentation," Remi remarked as Carmin slowly stood upright, carefully realigning his drawings. "That is what you're presenting today, yeah?"

"Proposing actually," Carmin countered.

"Oh, are they gonna develop it?" Remi enthusiastically asked.

"No. I'm rather certain they will not, but a proposition I'm going to give them all the same."

The doors opened with the bell chime. The two young men walked in and stood quietly. Remi then noticed Carmin, arms full of proposals, glaring between him and the button panel.

"Oh, right. Let me get that."

With a muffled hiss of steam, the elevator headed towards the forty-third floor. Carmin hoped for a quiet, twenty-two-second break, but Remi's voice expunged such hopes.

"So that Core-thermic stuff is pretty wild, huh? You must like working on it."

"It is a bit of a passion project," Carmin said.

"Right. There's no way I could work on something that risky right now. You must really be all-fired about it."

Carmin coughed. "Well, I appreciate you letting me know not to ask you onto the support team, despite the amount of room it currently has for members."

Remi felt his face flush with embarrassment. "No, no, that's not what I meant. It's just that my wife is pregnant and I'm still in school and . . . well, I'm just not feeling very confident about much right now."

The confession gave Carmin a breath of peace, comfort through mutual stress. "That is certainly understandable. Work, family—it's not always the simplest balance to maintain."

Remi relaxed. "Thanks. Honestly, I think the Core-thermic stuff is quite fascinating. A clean, potentially limitless energy source that no one has been able to harness yet. Very exciting, actually."

The thoughts sunk into Carmin's mind, reminding him of his own passion for the project. "It's nice to know at least one other person thinks so."

"Maybe I will get to work on it someday. Hopefully."

Carmin nodded, *hopefully* he thought. The elevator bell chimed again and the door opened. Carmin walked off.

"Take care, Remi." Carmin disappeared into the hallway. Remi stood up straight and grinned, *he actually knows my name.*

They all sat around a solid wood conference table in their ubiquitous business suits. With his sweaty hands flipping through note cards, Carmin stood alone up at the front. Beside him on a box, a large drawing stood as his only companion. They both waited for the firing line to begin.

The room held a moderate hum of chit-chat as everyone awaited the arrival of Bardin, who himself just finished his briefing with Opaji. Internally, company men recognized Bardin as the highest-ranking executive who actually made his physical presence a part of daily operations. His enthusiasm, much like his sense of humor, resembled the warmth of a frozen corpse. Through the years, Opaji's reputation for ideological ambition seemed to grow proportional to the amount of stability Bardin felt a need to maintain. Knowing this, Carmin felt less than optimistic about presenting an unproven technology that completely diverged from everything Kasic currently produced.

He looked up and gave the attendees a quick glance—the usual mix of aspiring company men. Sitting right next to him, Carmin noticed a man that he had never seen before. The word *man*; however, perhaps didn't apply, as the fellow looked to be on the verge of growing his first facial hair. His porcelain face then turned up to Carmin, naive zeal beaming from his wrinkle-free eyes.

"Heard you've got something pretty progressive planned for us today." The pitch of his voice matched the height of his smirking mouth. "Good luck, buddy."

Carmin checked the room to see if anyone else appeared confused by the young man's presence. "It probably will seem really eye-opening for you. It's a good thing your father let you sit in his big chair for the day."

"I'm sitting here because of what I can do, not because of who I'm related to."

"Well then, perhaps at the very least you'll get to see just how conflicted I can make my boss feel before turning me down in under ninety seconds."

The door flew open and the boss walked straight in. Bardin took his empty chair at the opposite end of the table and sat down with a strained exhale. He mechanically pulled out a pen and notepad.

"Okay, Carmin, let's make it a little quick, shall we."

Carmin gave the young man a wink. "Of course, sir."

He moved to the side and directed the attention to his art board. "The valley has proven to be a vast well of resources, and we certainly are not on the edge of drawing that well dry. The fuels we harvest are in ample supply, but the rate at which we gather them already exceeds the rate they are being replenished. Looking into the future, we will need to incorporate energy sources that require less fuel or ones that are, practically speaking, inexhaustible. Hydrogeneration is a good example of moving in that direction; however, the problems with a dam creating toxic sediment are examples of what we really need to try and avoid."

Bardin huffed. The board filled with sounds of shuffling seats.

"We all know your dam opinions, Carmin. Let's move on."

Carmin deflected and pointed to the diagram on his board. A thin red channel grew up to a theoretical generator resting on a ground plane.

"Since wind is rather mild in the valley, the only real viable option I see, hydrogeneration aside, is heat."

Bardin pointed to the board. All of the eyes in the room shifted to his finger. "So I take it that is a diagram of Core-thermic cultivation."

The eyes shifted back to Carmin. "Now, I'm not suggesting that this will become the primary energy source for Chigou any time soon . . ."

"Carmin, this is a conversation our grandchildren might possibly need to have, not us. I want proposals for efficiency, not fantasy."

"I think it's worth developing the technology now so we can jump on it when the time proves prudent."

Then to the surprise of everyone, a youthfully confident voice spoke up, interrupting both Bardin and the struggling proposer.

"The profile of the valley does not suit itself to Core-thermic energy. The proposal seems impractical at best, so why pursue such an inaccessible source?"

Carmin looked down at the young man, who seemed to be incapable of removing his smirk.

"I'm sorry, what is your name, young man?"

"Kits."

Carmin waited for the rest of the name, but none came. "Just Kits . . . how fun. As I was about to say, since the southern end of the valley has reported to have near surface-level hot spots, I believe there are places in the central valley where thermic pockets would be shallow enough to reach."

A choir of coughs quickly sang through the room.

"The southern valley? Carmin, it is not in the interest of this company to follow unverified reports of an area that only a fool would attempt to even survey. Actually, fools have tried to survey that area and their lives lasted about as long as this proposal. Next time, present something I can actually pursue."

Bardin got up and pocketed his notepad.

"I want you moving your attention to the Dark-spark team. Everyone else, we have an hour left in the day, so let's not waste it."

The company men started to get up and empty after Bardin. Carmin slowly collected the notes he didn't get to. Kits stayed back.

"Tough crowd."

"It's not progressive if it's accepted en masse. It's the role I play here."

Carmin slid his drawing off the block, reflecting over the design he almost got to explain.

"You look a little worried." Kits suggested.

"I just feel like I'm forgetting something."

"Well, Bardin didn't exactly give you time to explain everything," Kits said.

"No, not this. Something else I need to do today." Carmin started to get out his small pocket calendar. The green leather cover hid a small pump-pen engraved with his name—a gift from his daughter.

Kits continued. "Do you really think you could efficiently locate enough thermic pockets to make it viable?"

Carmin stopped flipping calendar pages as he noticed a new sense of sincerity coming from the young man. "What department are you with?"

"I'm not with a department."

"Okay, how are you employed here at Kasic Energy Corporation?"

Kits peeked over his shoulder and spoke with a cautious volume. "I'm not. Not directly, at any rate."

"Well, you must work for someone important since Bardin didn't cut you off mid-sentence. So, who would that be?"

"Someone who might be very interested in your theory, if there's something to it."

"I wouldn't propose it if it wasn't possible."

Kits nodded with strong curiosity. "In that case, you may just end up meeting my employer face-to-face."

"Because he'd have the interest and the means to pursue something like this?"

Kits took a second to consider the question. "He has the means, and I'm sure he'll find it very interesting."

With that, Kits winked and headed towards the door. Carmin stood for a moment, considering the possibility that the only person interested in his proposal might not even old enough to vote. He quietly packed up his materials.

"I need a coffee—an adult coffee."

○ ○ ○

Suzu reached into the front pocket of her red coat, a handmade birthday gift from her mother. Her small hands pulled out a single key hanging on a green cord. She worked the key into the lock, its cylindrical teeth pushing the precisely machined tumblers into place. Suzu loved the sound of tiny machines.

Walking in, she expected to be greeted by her parents. But as she hung up her things, she noticed their keys missing from the rack. The lonely feeling in the room was especially uncomfortable that evening, only hours away from her step-dance tryout. Suzu didn't feel like the most feminine of little girls but step dancing was loud, fast, and the outfits didn't seem too silly.

Suzu walked over and hopped up on the kitchen sink, glowing red from the setting sun. She thought of how high she could jump and how that would impress the teachers at Mon'tape, the dance school. In the quiet room she could hear the hum of a Shinyo class airship heading north.

Airships always fascinated her, so massive and yet somehow weightless. As she pondered over her father's explanation of how the metal transports managed to float, a familiar sound entered the room.

"Suzu, what are you doing home early, dear?" Kiara walked up and kissed her daughter on the forehead. "Are you okay?"

Suzu managed a faint smile as Carmin checked his watch. "Actually, she's the one on time."

Kiara pulled up the sleeve on her orange coat to check her wrist Toki. "I'm sorry, Suzu, I've been so distracted today."

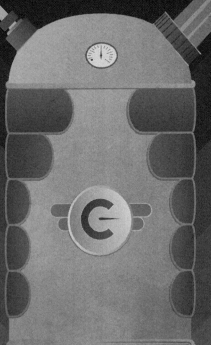

"I should have gotten you a special coffee," Carmin said as he took a sip of his adult beverage.

"I want coffee," Suzu joined in.

Carmin raised an eyebrow. "I don't think you want *this* coffee."

"But I need to be sharp."

Suzu's parents looked at each other a bit shocked. Kiara went over to the kitchen and tussled her daughter's hair. "Maybe you should speak at the meeting tonight."

Suzu's face slipped into confusion as she spoke in a concerned voice. "What meeting?"

"A meeting at the Civil Conclave about opening funds for new energy development. It's a pretty big thing for this family—for everyone really."

Kiara opened the cover to a plate of small, spiced, sweet-cream cakes. She offered one to each of her family. Carmin shoved one in his mouth; Suzu held onto hers.

"We should go; we're gonna be late," Carmin said, shuffling through the mail.

"Is it going to be long?" Suzu asked, looking at her mother.

"No. Well, not too long, and it'll be downtown, so we may have to get a little treat when it's all over," Kiara said, chewing her pastry.

Suzu mustered only the slightest smile. "Okay. I guess I'll go get my stuff." She hopped off of the sink and headed toward her room. Kiara looked down at the kitchen table.

"Suzu, your drawing stuff is over here on the table."

Suzu looked at her mom blankly. "Okay," she said, then continued to her room.

Kiara looked over to Carmin with mild puzzlement. "What stuff? Is she presenting at the Conclave tonight?"

"I'm on the verge of working for a teenager. Maybe the children are taking over."

Kiara walked over to her husband and put her arms around his neck. "So for tonight," she said, dramatically flipping her hair, "I think with my persuasive charm . . ."

"You did somehow get me to marry you," Carmin smugly smiled, which landed him a punch in the arm.

". . . and your smart-mouthed, I mean brilliant project, which already has interest from a new investor, we will pave a path for the future we always dreamed of."

With her sling bag stuffed like a pillow, Suzu entered back into the room. Kiara looked down with a curious grin. "Well, you look like you're ready for something."

Suzu walked past them and into the hall. The curious couple followed their daughter's lead.

The city's streetlights started to hum as the valley went dark. Downtown Chigou had a reputation for being brilliantly illuminated. Sorans often complained of it as wasteful and unnatural, but the allure was undeniable. Downtown perpetually bustled with creatures drawn to the light.

The Civil Conclave appeared in the distance, its curved structure sweeping up to the clouds. A large crowd funneled into the entrance while the building's grand facade reminded them of how small they were. Carmin looked down at his daughter, whose face still harbored some mysterious tension. He then spoke quietly to his wife.

"So when do you think we'll stop doing this kind of thing?"

Kiara briefly glanced over to her husband and then double-snapped back. "What do you mean? Why would we ever stop?"

Carmin took a moment to carefully construct his thought. "I just wonder if some day we're going to come home, exhausted from fighting the good fight, and then realize that our little girl is about to get married to some guy I don't ever remember meeting."

"I'm sure you'll notice the moment our girl starts spending any time alone with a boy."

They both took a peek down to Suzu, as Carmin gently squeezed her hand.

"I just don't want to get so caught up in things that we start to lose focus on the one person who needs us most."

A feeling bubbled up in Kiara's gut, thinking of how quickly she could jump in to defend her ideologies. She felt as responsible for the land almost as much as she did for her daughter. She lived trying to reconcile those feelings and fought to keep her love for either from turning into guilt.

"I don't know, we're a pretty special family. I think we just might have the energy to look after the health of the entire valley and take care of this little one." She kissed her husband on the cheek, who reassuringly smiled back. The family continued to march onward.

Carmin watched he sidewalk drift below his feet before speaking in a reflective tone. "Do you know the Tree House? It's the Northern Orphanage, just on the east side of the river, right up against the water."

"Yeah. They have that big Liazóu tree right where the river bends." Kiara recalled.

"Right, with a cluster of industrial foam pooled up right at the bottom of it. We got a report at Kasic that kids were getting sick there at an unusually high rate. I read it once, but the company never brought it up again."

The image of that beautiful and ancient tree became his personal metaphor for people's existence in the valley: industrial progress on the edge of swallowing the land that supported it. "But there are a lot of kids there, kids who don't have anywhere else to go. They need to have the people in their community standing up for them. Because if we don't, who will?"

Kiara silently smiled at her husband, feeling especially thankful in that moment.

Arriving at the Civil Conclave, the voice of the crowd could finally be heard at full volume. Kiara stepped closer to Carmin who tightened up the grip on both ladies' hands. They approached a painted iron sign that said "Chigou Civil Conclave." Upon making it around the massive nameplate, they stumbled upon the irony of the sign.

A young man fell back on the hard stairs, rolling over once before coming to a stop. A poorly written sign fell next to him, displaying, "Kill the Valley, Kill Us!" The man was clearly a Soran. Carmin pulled in both of his ladies even closer. Up the stairs, they saw a Civil Enforcer wiping his hands of the young man and his protest.

"If you can't act civilized, you have no business being in here." The Civil Enforcer spoke as he looked over the crowd, his hand holding a standard-issue baton. He then slid the alloy weapon into its brass ring holster. As more citizens approached the building, the Enforcer then walked back to the entrance. The young man got up, brushed off his pants, and thrust the sign into the air.

"If you can't be responsible with this city, you don't have any business looking after it."

The Enforcer gave no reaction. Looking around him, the young man then saw a small rock by his feet. He picked it up with his thin arm and cocked it back to throw. Kiara stepped in front of him.

"If you're here to pick a fight, go somewhere else."

The young man paused, startled by the brazen woman. Any desire to retaliate quickly faded upon seeing Carmin stand next to his wife, holding the hand of a nervous little girl. Kiara took a step in and lowered her voice.

"If you want to support responsible change, put that blunt object down and back us up with your voice." Kiara then went straight for the building, the rest of her family following behind in a purposeful march. As they started to hear the volume of the lobby, Carmin leaned into his wife's ear.

"Where in the world did that furnace come from, Lady Kiara?"

"I have no idea, but let's hurry up before it goes away."

The small family approached the front doors being guarded by at least eight Civil Enforcers. People squeezed in past them, staying particularly clear of the two Lord Enforcers near the center.

Framing the entrance, towering iron formations lead to a massive round emblem. The symbol contained an abstract male figure reaching up with one hand, the other behind his back. Protruding just beyond the edge of the circle, the upward hand represented an unending pursuit for progress, all eyes ahead. The other hand reached back—a sincere invitation to anyone willing to board a moving train that never intended on stopping.

Suzu gripped her father's hand tightly as they entered, her eyes fixed on a Lord Enforcer's sidearm. The standard-issue weapon revealed an alluring, masterfully made mix of grace and force. Its nearly spherical, dark iron-alloy cylinder sat in a shaft of polished metal with an white wood handle framed in dark brass. Suzu felt a temptation to touch its shiny surface, an urge so strong she knew it was a bad idea.

Inside, people fanned into the seats set up in the central room. It boasted the second largest capacity of any single space in Chigou, next to the immaculate Rift Theater. The dome-shaped space consisted of a smooth, poured stone surface detailed with brass accents. In the center, tubes of glass formed an elaborate system of lights that looked like the heavens taking root into the ceiling.

Kiara and her family walked up behind the rows of seats, which had nearly filled up. The many rows stepped down towards a circular center stage. Between the black-hands, industrialists, politicians, and Sorans, the room became a crowded bowl of assorted ideals and fashion choices. After a moment of soaking in the grand scale of it all, Suzu looked up to her mother.

"We should stay back here so we can get out faster."

"Okay," Kiara grinned. "If you get tired, your father can put you up on his shoulders."

Carmin looked at his ladies with concern. "What if I get tired?"

"You can get on my shoulders, Daddy. I have strong legs."

He leaned down, close to his daughter. "Thanks for looking out for me."

Facing back at the crowd, a number of big names sat at a long table, including Kasic overseer Bardin and labour captain Martou Latouski. Way out on the end at a little auxiliary table sat Soran-representative Mouba.

Behind them all, a bright face caught Carmin's attention. He finally recognized Kits, once again looking out of place as a handsomely dressed boy among men. Unlike those around him, though, Kits seemed to have no interest in warming up his voice with the crowd. He simply sat patiently, waiting for the event to start up, as if the outcome carried no mystery.

The Chairman then stepped up to the central podium. An electric crackle from the mic reverberated through the expansive space.

"If everyone would please take your seat and subdue your voices, this meeting on the City of Chigou's considerations for energy development will now commence."

Carmin leaned over to Kiara. "You ready?"

After two hours of logistical run-throughs, taking turns and staying on task, the Chairman began to lose his grip on the room's etiquette. Martou Latouski had been standing for at least the last thirty minutes as a devalued voice trying to make a stance between two opposing philosophies.

Latouski didn't want large quantities of resources going into new energy technologies, regardless of how clean they could be. He feared the only jobs created would go to those who didn't need to scrub grime off of their hands at the end of the day. He also demanded better working environments for his group's relatively risky working conditions. Mouba empathized as much as he seemed to be capable of but ultimately found Latouski's vision pitifully short-sighted.

Feeling slighted with his small side table and broken equipment, Mouba finally decided to annex the mic of the city accountant sitting next to him. Down the table, Bardin immediately leaned out of his chair, anticipating his opposition to every suggestion about to come out of the Soran's mouth. Carmin and Kiara both tensed up in the back, feeling their time to speak becoming an inevitability.

"Every day this city decides to push its industrial growth away from a balanced, clean direction, the closer we get to making this entire valley uninhabitable."

Trying to not feed off of Mouba's bait, Bardin took a deep breath and addressed the Chairman. "Being the largest energy provider in the city, we take the impact of our business very serious. We are always trying to make our methods safer for our workers and keep the land healthy. But we have to provide energy in a cost-effective manner because we are an energy company. If we compromise that, we'll cease to exist."

Mouba leaned over the table, the vein in his forehead visible from the back of the room. "What will cease to exist is life in the valley if you don't stop sucking it all up."

"The valley is enormous, and we are far from exhausting its resources . . ."

Sensing the heat pick up, the Chairman started to raise his hand. Mouba cut him off.

"That's your long-term plan? Suck up the valley, die off, and let the next generation figure it out?"

The Chairman cut in. "Gentlemen, please keep it practical."

Bardin followed. "You have the luxury of saying all of this because you're not responsible for implementing any of it."

Mouba's volume continued to rise. "Answer my question: Can you be responsible for the people of today and the people of tomorrow?"

"I'm not defending myself. You have no evidence of your claims . . ."

"Oh no? Well maybe you'd like to hear it. Kiara!"

The young couple clinched up. Carmin leaned over to his wife. "I think it's your turn."

Mouba, buzzing with adrenaline, frantically scanned the crowd for his philosophical comrade. Kiara took a half step forward and spoke loudly.

"A study just completed by Central University concluded that the rate of pollutants being produced is to become unsustainable by the valley on a long trajectory."

Bardin's frustration doubled by the breach in etiquette. "I'm sorry; who is this?"

The Chairman raised his hand again. "Yes, please identify yourself. This is a closed panel, Lady."

"My name is Kiara Komou. I'm a teacher at Northern Primary Youth Academy. I've been observing industrial impact on the valley."

Bardin could feel an ulcer forming. "I'm sorry, did you say a Primary teacher? With all due respect, Lady, you're not an expert and really don't . . ."

"The University Study is completely valid, regardless of my profession. And as a mother and an educator of this city's future, the impact of the study concerns me a great deal."

Carmin silently pumped his fist as Kiara told off his boss.

"Well, we will certainly take a look at the results of the study." The Chairman offered.

"It will only worsen the longer you wait, and you have access to far cleaner technology right now if you would actually pursue it."

Bardin's tone continued to convey his skepticism of this woman who came out of nowhere. "I'm sorry, what is this supposed technology you seem to be privy to?"

Kiara turned to look at her husband, followed by every other set of eyes in the room, then everything went silent. Realizing he was about to repeat a proposal to the same man that turned it down a few hours earlier, Carmin took a moment to rethink his approach. Nothing came to mind. "Uhm . . ."

Kiara poked him in his side, jarring a half-formed thought loose. "I believe there is enough heat below the valley floor that could make Core-thermic cultivation a viable and substantial energy source."

Bardin squinted. "Carmin?"

The Chairman suddenly felt out of the loop. "Are you associated with this man, as well?"

Bardin rubbed his face. "He's one of my employees."

"But I was under the impression Kasic was not developing anything like this."

"We're not."

The Chairman mulled over the moment. Mouba took the two seconds of silence as an invitation.

"You have the opportunity to develop cleaner technology right now and you're not even taking it. The government needs to support people who will responsibly provide for this city."

"Yes, young man, we have all become well-versed on your thoughts regarding the direction of the city."

"So are you finally going to support . . ."

The Chairman raised his hand for the last time. "I think we've covered all we are going to get to today. I will now convene with the Panel and then give my final recommendation as soon as we are finished. Lords, if you may."

Two appointed men then joined the Chairman at the center podium. Kiara leaned into Carmin.

"Looks like we killed this party in a hurry. What do you think?"

"I think I might have just terminated my employment with Kasic."

Kiara grabbed his hand and rubbed his wedding band with her thumb. "Maybe the government will step up and completely fund your new project."

They looked into each other's eyes for a moment and then let out a small laugh. Kiara kept on laughing, a laugh that collapsed into a cry.

"Are you okay?" her husband sincerely asked.

"Yeah," Kiara said as she wiped the tear falling into the corner of her mouth. "I don't know why I'm crying."

"You care a lot about this. You want things to change so bad, but there's only so much you can do."

Kiara smiled and then put her head on her husband's shoulder. Carmin kissed her on the head before looking back to the inner circle, where they continued to convene. The Chairman seemed oddly disengaged from the other two. He then turned his head and looked into the crowd behind him.

Every head in the crowd turned to another, bestowing their certainty of the situation. In the middle, however, one young face was explicitly fixed towards the podium. Rows apart and surrounded by conversation, Kits and the Chairman seemed to share an undeniable exchange in silence.

Their eyes stayed locked until Kits got up, grabbed his scarf, and walked towards the rear door. The Chairman watched him for a moment before cutting off his fellow Panel Lords. The crackle of the mic echoed through the hall.

Kiara lifted up her head and squeezed her husband's hand. Carmin then looked down to his daughter who, despite not understanding most of the evening's discussion, seemed to be even more anxious than he was. Finally, the Chairman spoke.

"Upon review of the evening's deliberations, the panel has decided that at this time there is no eminent need of pursuing any further experimental energy development, and resources shall continue to be put into existing and proven methods. Thank you, we are adjourned."

The blood boiling in Mouba's head kept him from hearing the last few words. "If you won't even react to proof, then what is the point of any of this?"

"We are adjourned, young man."

As Mouba continued to fight past the final bell, Kiara looked up to Carmin. Her smile had vanished. More tears started to well up in her eyes, her body incapable of suppressing months of ambition and frustration fighting their way to the surface. Carmin mourned the hope of his wife.

"I'm sorry."

Kiara started to shake her head, her glistening eyes shooting through the crowd.

"They can't do this. They can't just move on as if we are of no significance."

"We won't quit," Carmin said in an attempt to be supportive. It felt hollow.

"We won't let them get away with this. You saw the Chairman. He didn't say a single word to those useless Lords at the end."

Carmin finished her thought. "He didn't even listen."

"He had no intentions of even considering anything different. This was a show; this whole thing is a mockery of the entire civil process. Damn him."

Suzu saw the people leaving quietly while Kiara continued to look against the current of the crowd. Suzu had never seen her mother so upset, saying such strange things. She pulled on her father's hand.

"What's wrong?"

Carmin saw his daughter's perplexed face. Bending down, he looked her in the eye, wanting nothing more than to comfort the ladies he loved most. "When people don't notice how much we care about something it can be hard and confusing. It'll be okay, though."

Suzu didn't understand that *something* enough to even ask another question. She wanted to be outside. She wanted to be out of that suffocating room.

"Carmin, give me something to write with."

He looked up. "What?"

"I want to write down who those charlatans are before they take their nameplates."

"I don't have anything." Carmin patted down his coat.

Kiara walked behind Suzu.

"They think they can just ignore promises and we'll simply

accept it, but they're wrong, Carmin."

"I believe you," Carmin nodded.

Kiara started to open up her daughter's slingbag, her hands shaking. Suzu's wide and troubled eyes looked up at her father.

"They will be held responsible, Carmin. We're not going to forget . . ."

Suddenly Kiara stopped moving. Carmin's concern then shifted as his silent wife became transfixed with the inside of Suzu's bag. The walking crowd floated past them.

"Kiara, what is it?"

Her eyes started to waiver, taking on a look of hopelessness before they shut, forcing out the suspended tears. Kiara's trembling hands then covered her own face, looking more desperate than even the minute before. She took a deep breath, trying to release the pressure in her chest. Confused and concerned, Carmin leaned down to his family.

"Kiara, what's wrong. What is it?"

Kiara wiped more tears away taking another deep breath. Her mournful face finally turned to Carmin, before reaching into Suzu's bag and pulling out a small dance costume. She held it between her hands, noticing all the work that she and her daughter had put into it over the past two months. She could remember almost every single stitch.

"Her dance audition was tonight."

Carmin's mind rushed to make something positive out of a night that fell apart. "Do we still have time? When was it?"

"No, we completely missed it. We forgot and came here tonight instead."

Kiara turned her daughter around, holding the one-of-a-kind uniform between them. It took Kiara a second to work up the ability to look her daughter in the eye. When she did, she finally understood the anxious concern Suzu had been carrying all evening.

"I forgot about your dance audition," Kiara sincerely spoke.

The words became the first thing Suzu had heard all night that made any sense. Her tired face fought to offer up the smallest and saddest of grins as Kiara stroked her hair. The gracious effort her daughter made to smile felt as painful as it was beautiful.

"But you didn't forget, did you? You came here and didn't complain and waited very patiently like a good girl."

Suzu nodded.

"I'm sorry," Kiara said, offering tears for a broken promise. She pulled her daughter towards her and held her tight. After a confusing and stressful evening, Suzu took her first breath of relief since she got home earlier that day. The moment felt like a small drop of comfort from the sting of a lost audition, a dream her mother had shared with her for quite some time.

Carmin knelt down to meet them. "I think it's time for some cold cream. And lots of it."

o o o

The night grew quiet as the evening rush at Michelou's had long since passed into the street. A few patrons sat around with bellies full of confectionary delights, the purr of neon and steam floating around them.

Carmin ordered chocolate and hot-berry cold cream for the whole family. Trying to smother the evening's negativity, they all got *Murdies*; a mountain of cold cream loaded with sweet condiments. It sounded enticing but looked downright ridiculous when towering in front of one's face. Three at one table looked practically irresponsible.

After thirty minutes, Carmin looked over to his wife, who appeared to be slipping into a saccharin coma. With the eating now ceased, the absurdity of their Murdie spectacle finally became fully apparent. They both snorted out a quick laugh, Kiara nearly choking on a hot-berry.

Suzu had been scraping at the same square inch of chocolate hot-berry for the last twenty minutes. Normally the mere sight of a Murdie would cramp a child's cheeks from excessive smiling. That night, however, Suzu's appetite struggled to appear.

"Not too hungry either, huh?"

Suzu looked over to her mother before silently going back to her scraping spot.

"Suzu, we're going to make sure you get to audition at the school again really soon."

It pained Carmin to see his two precious women in such a state. They looked tired and pale; the cold-cream had done what it could.

"You know where we need to go?"

Kiara looked up, but Suzu hadn't the will or the strength to follow. "To a soft bed?" Kiara wishfully spoke.

"Kora Farm."

It took a few seconds, but Kiara's fatigued mind finally pulled the memory out.

"Yes, that sounds wonderful. And we told them we would come back and visit but we never did. Oh dear, that was so long ago." Kiara pressed her fingers onto her forehead. "I can't believe I forget their names."

"Clora and Kojo."

"That's right. Of course you remember."

"The farm is a combination of both of their names," Carmin said smugly.

"My mind is like porridge right now. It's not my fault." Suzu glanced over to her parents sharing a laugh. She wanted to laugh, too, but she couldn't.

"I think back to that farm, and I swear that it couldn't have been as lovely as I remember. The air was so clean and just smelled like life." Kiara closed her eyes. "Was that real? Does anything like that actually exist?"

Carmin slid his hand across the cool table and sweetly rubbed the top of his wife's hand. "Let's go back."

"Are you serious? Do you even have their wire-type number?"

"No, I do have Gozen's, though."

"Yes!" Kiara leaned forward in anticipation. "Wait, who?"

"Our Cleric."

Kiara furrowed her brow. "We have a Cleric?"

Carmin graciously smiled. "Kiara . . . it's the man who conducted our ceremony. Giant fellow who oddly enough made great, tiny pastries."

"Oh, yes, yes. I'm sorry, I remember, I remember."

Carmin laughed to himself, he always enjoyed it when his wife's excitement would battle her fatigue. It made him feel young.

"Yeah, I think he goes up to Kora all the time, or at least he did."

"So tonight? You should invite him over and we can plan it out."

"I will wire-type him first thing in the morning." Carmin calmly suggested.

Faster than what her tired body would seem capable of, Kiara snapped over towards her daughter.

"Suzu, do you want to go to the farm your father and I were married at?"

Suzu started to answer, but Kiara cut her off.

"It's beautiful, and there are animals you can ride. Oh! And they have a girl, she's probably just a little bit older than you. You two could play and run around. It'll be so lovely and relaxing."

Suzu sat slightly stunned from the sudden eruption in energy across the table. "I've been ready for fun all day."

Mutual smiles cast their vote. "It's settled then."

Kiara took a deep breath. "Okay. Time for bed. Please."

○ ○ ○

The crowd on the street had thinned out to its evening numbers; downtown Chigou was never empty. The eve of Leimikou resulted in the only exception, a holiday celebrating the founding of the Naifin Valley. Parents recounted the story of spirits guiding Batsu and his pilgrims through the mountain fog, providing them with the endless gifts of the valley. Families typically stayed home that eve to play games and eat small treats, a casual representation of mountain exploration and eating rations. In the morning, children attempted to find their pile of presents while blindfolded. A successful discovery set off a bountiful meal, including a toast with Frosted Wine.

During the holiday season, Chigou's already bright downtown converted into an absolute forest of light. Images of the brilliant display bolstered the city's magnificent reputation throughout the country. On the street, local eateries set up hot food stands to reward patrons who braved the cold. Like everyone else in the city, the Koumou family developed a sentimental excitement about the season. Walking home that night, Suzu's thoughts became lost in the lights, and she wondered why they didn't keep them up all year around.

From sixty-six floors up, the family appeared as water bugs

floating along a luminescent river. Daimó often stood at his office window, watching the flow of pedestrians work their way through the provided transit routes. Not once did he ever develop a curiosity of their hopes or dreams; to him they merely functioned as parts of an organism.

Daimó's office sat in a large but otherwise mundane building. He considered it a perfectly suitable location, well hidden in plain sight, and lacking any sort of aesthetic nonessentials. The bare walls framed an iron bookshelf filled mostly with volumes related to industrialization, sociology, and biology. He felt a gust of wind sway the building before hearing a knock at the door.

A sound of gears turning echoed off of the stone walls; the door opened slowly. As Daimó kept his attention on the street below, Kits walked into the cool, dry space. He headed into the kitchen, where he grabbed one of the neatly rolled towels from a steam box. Slowly breathing out, he buried his face into the hot fabric.

"Did everything go predictably?" Daimó's voiced bounced off the glass.

Kits let the steam lift off of his face. "For the most part. Would you like me to go over all of it?"

"Only the unpredictable."

Kits cleared his throat. "Mouba managed to divert the mic I damaged by commandeering someone else's."

"Predictably embarrassing," Daimó said.

"Quite." Kits thought more carefully. "He asked the Koumou woman to contribute."

Daimó finally gave Kits his full attention. "And how did the woman react?"

"Passionately and briefly, then followed up by her husband Carmin. He mentioned his Core-thermic project, which of course was disregarded after some brief drama."

"Is that all?"

"Yes."

Daimó paused at the window; Kits waited patiently. He had become curious about Daimó's intentions regarding the couple ever since the first request to follow Carmin's work. Kits had always found his superior to be a bit of an enigma, resulting in a stockpile of unanswered questions.

Growing up, Kits developed a reputation in his orphanage for engaging in dangerous behavior. One day while he was cleaning the kitchen as punishment for fighting, a businessman arrived with the intention of making the young man an apprentice. No meeting took place to explain why he had been chosen. Years later, the mystery was a normal fact of their relationship, and Kits accepted it in faith; Daimó had given him more respect and responsibility than he ever would have imagined.

"Are you familiar with this plant?" Daimó finally spoke.

Kits looked to where Daimó had silently moved. A small plant sat in a black clay pot. It had bright green leaves that stained red on the edges, an otherwise ordinary looking plant to his untrained eye. Kits had spent little time outside the city.

"I don't know its name, if that's what you mean."

Daimó floated his hand over the plant as if feeling the air around it. "It's the Henka plant, indigenous to the valley, primarily southern. Rather ordinary looking plant, wouldn't you agree?"

"I would."

"Out in the open, the plant will grow wild and expand into an unsustainable mass. It will absorb so much of the ground's nutrients that the soil will no longer be able to sustain the plant that gorged on it. Eventually, it will wither and expire, a suicide of ignorance and greed.

"Deeper into the woods, however, below the mercy and guidance of larger plants dictating its rate of life, the plant thrives. Unable to absorb more light or take up more root than allowed, Henka will not only survive; it will actually benefit the plants around it with a biochemical byproduct. But its survival depends on one greater keeping its growth in check."

Kits bent down to the unimpressive plant, trying to catch some sort of scent. Briefly noticing it once before, it seemed rather frivolous and quaint for such a man. Kits wondered if Daimó kept it as some potted metaphor of the people down below.

"So what if the plant is reduced to a small pot, given just enough to sustain a single stalk?" Kits asked.

"If the plant gets reduced, if it ceases to be a collective, its chemistry will change and it will become defensively toxic. Any animal that consumes it will die within a few hours. A selfish and dismal ending to both predator and prey."

Kits noticed a slight shimmer on the surface of the leaves. He reached in and rubbed a leaf, having always been fascinated with objects capable of lethality.

"Seems like a rather dangerous office plant."

Daimó watched Kits rub the plant, intrigued by the young man's daring curiosity. Suddenly he asked, "What do you think of the Komous?"

Kits took a second to answer, as he always did with Lord Daimó.

"They seem intelligent and determined."

Daimó started to walk over to the iron bookshelf on the side wall; Kits followed.

"Carmin's Core-thermic project, does that seem viable?"

"He certainly thinks so, although I don't think Bardin could be less interested in supporting it. I'm honestly a little surprised he still has a job there."

Daimó pulled a book off of the shelf and opened it up.

"It's because he's extremely talented. Despite Carmin's trying ideologies, Bardin knows it's better to have him under his roof than someone else's."

"Like a valuable plant?"

Daimó flipped through the pages quickly. "If there was a thorn in your side, but it was made of gold, would you pull it out and risk losing it?"

Daimó talked very little about money, a topic most industrialists couldn't shut up about. Wealth never seemed like a personal goal to him; it was simply a transactional tool that society gave an arbitrary value, meaningless outside of its collective acceptance. Be that as it may, Kits knew Daimó had access to a whole lot of money.

"I'd pull it out and trade it for something useful, of course."

"What if, by sticking in your side, that thorn gave you longer life?"

Kits looked at Daimó's hand as it continued to flip through pages.

"Do I want to live longer if I'm constantly irritated and in pain?"

Daimó spoke without skipping a beat. "Carmin's wife, do you think she'll ever stop on the ideological path she marches on?"

The question was easy. "No."

"Do you think there is anything you could do to convince her to abstain her zeal, get between her and her husband?"

Kits felt the query forming into a proposition. "She seems very convicted, and him very loyal. I would imagine nothing short of death would separate those two."

Daimó slapped the book shut. "I want you to go to their home and invite them here for dinner."

He put the book back on the shelf and walked over to his desk. Kits looked up to see the title of the book. It read *Amputation, by Poel Jastoú.*

6
ADOPTION

The proofing box hissed with steam, the mist vanishing as it hit the ceiling. A brass gauge displayed the temperature of the fermenting dough. Kiara prepared what would be a part of the next day's breakfast: peppered cream eggs in biscuits. Two days had passed since forsaking Suzu's dance audition for a worthless energy panel. If the family still insisted on being downtrodden, she hoped to force them into good spirits with hot pastries, and the smell of baking bread always lightened the mood.

In his den, Carmin mulled over his Core-thermic project. Pursuing the technology at Kasic began to feel entirely futile, but with an energy source so potentially clean and limitless, he felt compelled to keep going. He pondered what ambitious investor would be willing to support a trial, but the question concluded with only one answer: No one would ever fund a project in the infamous *red valley*.

Suzu peeked around the door and saw her father tapping some paper. She walked in silently on the balls of her feet. As she approached the edge of the desk, Carmin finally noticed her curious face.

"What are you working on?" Suzu asked.

"My Core-thermic project."

"The one your boss doesn't like?"

Carmin laughed, then sighed. "That is the one. One of many, actually."

He looked back to his drawings, Suzu's gaze followed before returning to her Father. "That's bosses for ya."

Carmin laughed. "I think I talk about work too much at home."

Suzu looked over the drawing, fascinated by all of it's mysterious detail. "So, how do you know where the hot ground is?"

Suzu expected an amazing description, the kind her father almost always gave her.

Carmin cleared his throat. "Well, we think that the world is mostly made up of very hot rock and metal, and only the very outside is cool; rocks, dirt, water and such things. So in spots where the ground is thin enough, you can dig down and get to the hot stuff."

"Like when I tap on the crust of a pie that Mommy made to steal a Bollo?"

"Yes, delicious metaphor, Lady Suzu."

"Can we get a shovel and go look outside?" Suzu proudly suggested.

"Hah, no. I think our shovel might be too small for ground this thick."

Smiling, Carmin pulled over another drawing, one of a harmonic pulse probe he designed. A key component for the development of the project, it had yet to reach even the prototyping phase. The drawing showed a box fitted with a large battery and a number of gauges. Suzu thought it looked very complicated.

"If your father ever gets to build this, we might be able to find some hot spots, if we look where the ground is thin enough."

"So where is that?"

Carmin felt a recurring temptation to tap into his inner frustrated writer and conjure up some fantasy. He loved to enchant his daughter with tales of science, magic and mystery. This story, however, needed no such embellishments.

Lowering his brow and scanning around as if suspicious eyes lurked about, Carmin spoke, cautiously.

"Many, many years ago, a group from the far east climbed through the frozen paths of the Murde Mountains. Then, the Naifin Valley was discovered, at least for those who survived the journey. Once they had settled, their leader Jean Batsu sent out four groups of three men in four directions to see what precious raw assets were hidden in the valley."

"What are raw assets?" Suzu interrupted.

"Uhm, useful natural things. Rocks, wood . . ." Suzu nodded, her father continued.

"So the first three groups left for only a few days and returned with good news, but the group that went south was gone for a very long time. They went beyond where we are now, farther south to where the ground slopes downward and is thick with trees that pierce through the eternal mist."

Suzu was hooked.

"It was many, many days before Batsu saw any sign of the final group. Three men he had sent off; however, only one man managed to make it back, and he was found with a face as white as a ghost."

"What happened to the other two?" asked Suzu.

"Nobody knows. The man could hardly explain what he saw. All he could say was that they ran into something red, something he had never witnessed before, and those men were never seen again. Decades later, Lord Opaji started the city of Chigou and decided to build roads into the woods of the southern valley."

"Opaji?"

"Yes, the very man I work for but have never met. As a younger man he wanted to explore the mysterious valley and see what treasure it hid below. A team of thirty men built only a few miles of road before some of them started to disappear. No one could explain why, but some men refused to go back, saying the forest was haunted. Opaji refused to believe such a thing and decided to double the pay for any man willing to go back. A few decided to take the risk. Their third day back, though, was the last day anyone has ever been down there. Do you want to know why?"

Transfixed, Suzu cautiously nodded up and down.

"People say that, once again, only a single man made it out alive. He seemed ill with shock and could hardly manage a simple thought about what he had seen. All he managed to say was . . ."

Suzu's fingernails dug into her father's wooden desk.

". . . they came from the forest. They were red."

"Daddy, you're not going down there, are you?"

Carmin took in a dramatically large gulp of air, then casually sat up.

"No. I can't, actually. No one can. There is a small guard

station on that unfinished road, the only road that leads down into Goraka."

"Goraka?"

"That's right, the Red Valley. Nobody really knows what, or who, is down there. If we could get down there, though, it could be the key to making the future of Chigou prosperous *and* healthy."

Their contemplative moment got interrupted by the smell of baking bread.

"All right, now go and see what your mother is doing about dinner. Your father's stomach is caving in."

Suzu quickly sprinted out of the room but stopped short of the kitchen, peeking slowly around the corner. You never know who, or what, could be lurking in there.

In the kitchen, Kiara wore a bright red apron. A long, white head scarf held back her hair as it always did when she baked. Beside her, a mist of flour danced in a beam of sunlight, and Suzu stopped to watch. It was an image she would never forget.

"Father wants food."

Kiara turned around, playfully responding with her spookiest voice. "Well, I suppose we better feed him before he turns into a monster."

She expected a smile from her daughter, but Suzu's mind didn't allow it. "Daddy said there might be real monsters in the valley."

Kiara set her fist on her hip. "Oh, did he now?"

Suddenly they heard a knock at the front door. Suzu spun behind the kitchen doorway as her mother gasped. They exchanged looks, neither sure of what to make of it. Another knock echoed out. Carmin walked up through the hallway and joined the confused faces. He then slowly opened the door. Suzu leaned over to catch a glimpse of the mysterious guest.

In front of Carmin, he saw what appeared to be a teenager dressed as an adult. "Hello, Kits."

Kits peeked inside over Carmin's shoulder. "Smells good. These lovely ladies must be hard at work," he said through a grin, too large for Carmin's comfort.

Carmin looked over his shoulder, blocking the entrance with one arm. "Well, the one in the back is married to me, and the little one is never allowed to date. Beyond that, I don't remember inviting you to dinner, or giving you my address."

Kiara started her way to the door after deciphering her husband's tone.

"Carmin, is this the young man you were telling me about?"

Kits smirked. "You've been talking about me. I'm flattered."

"About your boss, actually, whom I still have yet to meet," Carmin lobbed back.

Kiara broke through her husband's arm shield and offered a hand to Kits, who shook it like a gentleman.

"Oh, don't give this young man a hard time. Please, come inside."

"Thank you. I'm actually here to ask you to dinner, but I fear I am too late."

"You want to take me to dinner?" Carmin questioned.

"All of you, actually. I do intend for you to meet my employer, but yes, dinner will most certainly be served."

Carmin slowly looked over to his wife and began to open his mouth. Kiara spoke with better haste, "We would love to. Suzu, lets get our coats."

◦ ◦ ◦

The lights seemed to do little against the darkness of the room. The Komous sat on one side of a stone table, patiently waiting for a dinner they had been craving since back in Doulan.

Kits sat across from them, wearing a grin that seemed permanently stuck on his face. "Are you all right? Is it perhaps too chilly in here?"

Kiara answered. "Just a little, but it'll be nice once all that hot food comes out."

"Very well. I should go check on dinner."

Kits walked back into the kitchen. Behind Daimó, were two plates on a table and another three on a tray; the food appeared ready. Daimó locked his gaze onto Kits, who tried hard to hide how uneasy it made him feel. He stood there waiting for something substantial to become apparent, but his master said nothing.

Kits tentatively walked up to the tray and grabbed it with both hands. He felt something far more significant than serving dinner looming ahead. He could feel Daimó's eyes on his back as the smell of steamed fish filled his nostrils. As he took a step towards the guests, a piercing chill of realization stabbed him in the stomach.

Sitting just behind the food tray, the most unassuming object sat alone. Its plainness kept Kits from noticing it initially, but now the simple black pot consumed his attention. This particular pot, however, contained no plant, no life at all. For only a second he considered its existence, but the placement was unmistakable.

Kits looked over his shoulder, hoping that Daimó would say something contrary to what lay before him. There was no change, no reaction; Daimó's gaze was fastened with steel bolts. The young man looked back down to the empty pot, then to the tray; three plates of food, three guests. Kits lifted it up, and his nerves began to tighten at the sound of the metal plates rattling. He suddenly understood the task set before him. There would be no deliberation: He could either deliver the tray or walk out the front door.

The family sat in anticipation, their eyes fixed on the steaming tray. Kits approached them with a developing feeling of nausea. He had never found it too difficult to bloody another man's face in defense, or even out of provocation. But this felt cold and soulless, and his hands trembled. He set down the tray, met with smiles from those unaware of what they were being served.

Kits first handed Carmin a plate, who sat confused by the sudden lack of smugness on the young man's face; something felt off. Kiara then nudged him, "aren't you hungry?"

A reflex of etiquette took over and Carmin finally grabbed the plate. He watched as the suddenly pensive young man went down the table.

"This looks beautiful." Kiara gleefully moaned, breathing in the aroma as she grabbed the plate.

Kits then got to the end of his line, where two large green eyes gently looked up at him. Suzu's innocent face sat framed in colorfully adorned hair as she sat on her hands. Kits stood shaking as the question entered his mind; could he give what was on that plate to the young, defenseless child?

Suddenly, Kiara grabbed the plate and placed it in front of her daughter. Suzu looked down at the steamed fish with strangely large eyes; it seemed like a long way away from a bowl of cold cream.

"It's okay. She just isn't accustomed to seeing whole fish on a plate," Kiara said before.

Suzu sat there, battling feelings of obligation and appetite. While he held his breath, an impulse suddenly jumped into Kits's throat.

"She doesn't need to eat this. Please let me get her something else." Kits grabbed the plate with haste. Kiara tried to stop him, but her etiquette was no match for his guilt. "We have fruit, maybe something sweet," he quickly suggested, stumbling over words. Suzu smiled at the new suggestion.

It was enough for Kits who turned around quickly, feeling he couldn't get that plate away fast enough. He took one quick step before he nearly collided with Daimó, who stood holding two plates. Kit tried hard to keep his voice from trembling. "The young girl would prefer some fruit."

Daimó simply stood still. Kits lowered his eyes and scurried back to the kitchen. His behavior further perplexed Carmin, finally seeing the mysterious industrialist and apprentice together. Daimó laid down the plates for himself and Kits.

"My apologies about the fish. I don't feed children often, so I forget how different their appetites can be." Daimó sat down. "I should introduce myself. I apologize for not doing it sooner, but the kitchen demanded my attention. My name is Daimó. This is my office, and it is good that you have come tonight."

In the kitchen, Kits immediately threw Suzu's food into the waste bin. The smell of the garbage and steamed fish collided with the tension in his stomach, causing him to nearly vomit. Holding his nose, he desperately looked for the discarded Henka plant, hoping the empty pot to be merely a test of will and obedience. The plant proved to be elsewhere.

Kits then grabbed a large chef's knife and hurried over to a basket of forest fruit. He grabbed a few pieces and began to chop and peel. He tried to steady his breathing, his one hand shaking as the other frantically pulsed the steel blade up and down. Misjudging the distance, Kits then caught the back of the blade on his index finger. He caught a scream before it left his lips, then reached for a towel to stop the stream of blood pouring from his wound.

Kiara began to introduce her daughter as Daimó noticed the noise coming from the kitchen. He kept his attention on his guests.

"And this is my daughter Suzu. She's got the technical comprehension of her father and my hunger for creativity, so we might all be working for her in about ten years." Suzu smiled, never before knowing she had *technical comprehension*. Her stomach growled.

"Then let me hope to leave a good impression by saying my deputy should be out here soon with some more appealing food. Something without a face, perhaps." The couple laughed as Daimó began to cut into his fish, having no reaction to his own sense of humor. "You proposed to Kasic that they should pursue Core-thermic energy, by way of a project of your own design,"

Carmin hesitated, analyzing his host's odd demeanor. "Uhm, yes, actually." Carmin sat upright. "I believe that one day it could possibly be the primary energy source for Chigou. Certainly enough of a possibility that it is worth pursuing."

"For testing, you even suggested going to Goraka."

Carmin became stifled from hearing his own words. The hypothetical suggestion of sending men to the red valley, the valley of death, suddenly sounded wholly irresponsible.

"It was a statement I made based on its geography, surely not a practical suggestion. Certainly not a stipulation."

"The suggestion demonstrates your conviction, hypothetical or not."

The conversation broke its flow. On the Komou side, an awkward ambiguity developed. They welcomed the expressed enthusiasm, but Daimó's statement on potential danger felt uncomfortable. Carmin and Kiara both took a bite of food.

Kits walked up to the table and spotted the two silent eaters before Suzu looked up at him, hopeful for what rested on the plate. He fought an urge to look at Daimó and kept his eyes on the smiling girl.

"I'm sorry," Kits said quietly. He handed Suzu the bowl and sat down. Unintentionally, his eyes caught Carmin staring directly at him. Very slowly, Kits then ate a bite of food as if on a dare.

Daimó spoke again. "This is not the first time Kasic has rejected a proposal of yours; however, you have continued to push for unpopular designs. Will you continue to maintain your efforts at a place that does not fully support you?"

Carmin asked himself the same question almost daily. "I have hope that my influence is at least doing indirect, long trajectory good." He looked over to his wife. "Be that as it may, I'm not against putting my efforts somewhere else."

Kiara wiped the corner of her mouth. "Lord Daimó, my husband and I are very committed to this."

Daimó responded, "I doubted that very little before you came here this evening, and I doubt it even less now."

"We are curious," asked Carmin, "but what is your interest in this project, exactly?"

Kiara leaned in. "Yes. Pardon the bluntness, but I'm trying to figure out who you are or what you do."

As Daimó considered his response, Kits noticed Suzu lift a large piece of green fruit to her mouth; a drop of his blood faintly hung on the back. His mouth opened but nothing came, the piece slipping into her mouth. Finally, Daimó responded.

"I am an overseer. I monitor certain developments in the city and see to it that they advance in the appropriate way. In a city such as Chigou, energy development perhaps deserves the most focus."

Carmin raised his hand to his chin. "Are you with the government? I ask as Kits never mentioned the name of a company."

Kiara offered a large fork full of mountain vegetables to her daughter. Kits clenched his napkin as his heart nearly stopped. Suzu shook her head, so Kiara ate the large mouthful and smiled. The sacred glance shared between mother and daughter seared Kits's conscious. He vainly tried to ignore it along with the fluxing nausea in his stomach.

All attention went back to Daimó as he answered. "I am an industrialist, but more importantly to you, a means to progress. It is for this reason that you sit here tonight, frustrated as a voice with no real authority in a mechanism that is ruled by its own inertia. I sit before you, free to pursue as I wish."

Carmin shared a hopeful glance with Kiara as Kits sat wide-eyed. He had never heard Daimó explain himself to anyone. He felt afraid to speak or even move. Daimó dug out the eye of his fish with a knife and raised it to his lips. His teeth sunk down until hitting the lens and then sucked out the warm liquid within. He placed the remainder of the eye back onto the plate.

"We could continue to discuss decorum all evening, but I believe we have already made our decisions regarding the future."

Suzu squirmed in her seat. The young couple looked at each other, hope radiating off their faces. Kiara then took Carmin's hand. "Yes, I believe we have."

○ ○ ○

Daimó stayed back at the table as Kiara helped Suzu put her coat on in the hallway. Carmin stepped over to Kits, who held the door open. He then shook the young man's hand with a small bow, looking him directly in the eyes.

"Thank you."

The words cut like knives. Kits's throat tightened up, allowing him to muster only a simple nod. Carmin walked out the door and took the hand of his daughter. Kits watched the family walk down the corridor hand in hand, their eyes gazing at visions of the future. He then felt a cold air cross over the back of his neck as he shut the heavy door.

Daimó stood just a few paces away. Kits felt as a child; scared, small, unsure of his surroundings. His dry lips trembled. "I don't know what I've done."

Daimó spoke with what Kits took as some grotesque form of compassion. "You have answered a question about yourself most never manage to acquire. You acted in faith and you acted in fear. The young one's life is now changed forever, set on a path you have forged. Perhaps years from now your paths will cross, and then you shall have the conclusion to your uncertainty. She will undoubtedly make certain of that."

As the family traveled back to their apartment, they glowingly mused over the evening. The wintery parade of holiday lights kept

Suzu awake. Carmin mentally designed his new dream office for the Core-thermic project while Kiara, her mind now settled past the initial excitement of the evening, came to a more complicated conclusion.

"I've met him before."

Carmin glanced over as Suzu faintly listened in. "Yeah, I think Kits may be in the same class as Suzu."

"No." Kiara dismissed her husband's foolery. "Daimó. Don't you remember that name? And how did I not recognize his face, those eyes?"

"You've met Daimó before?"

"Well, no. He's that guy I saw at Kasic who was getting onto Opaji's airship. His company was Elite . . . or no, Etilé, I think."

Suzu had never heard Etilé before and she spent the next minute repeating the odd-sounding word in her head.

"Is he that guy you mentioned on our first date?" Carmin fumbled through his memory banks.

"Yes, I'm almost positive. He's the guy who ruined my friends farm up in Primichi."

The evening's exhilaration now seeped into conflicted limbo.

Carmin questioned the possibility. "Are you sure?"

Kiara struggled with her thoughts. "I think so . . . ugh, I don't know."

"Well, are you concerned about it?"

Kiara hated to spoil the night's excitement from what might be exhausted confusion. "I don't know. It's probably okay . . . maybe?"

"Well, we'll just keep an eye on things. We got time."

Kiara took the comfort of her husband's words and leaned on his shoulder. Suzu watched the density of lights fade out as they got closer to home, repeating the word "Etilé"over and over to a tune she had just made up.

○ ○ ○

Light flowed in as her eyelids opened with surprising ease. Unlike her mother, Suzu had always been a nocturnal creature and found dawn to be a rather unnatural time to wake up. Her room filled with a golden glow that seemed strangely bright, as if she had slept through the morning.

Suzu hung her feet over the bed before jumping down, the floor carrying a sharp chill against the mild air. She followed the warm hallway down to the kitchen as her stomach growled. She imagined her mother working at the counter.

Suzu then stepped into the silent kitchen filled with dust slowly swimming in the sunlight. Still waking up, she squinted at the radiant space. The kitchen smelled like it always did when her mother baked, but she heard no sounds to match. Suzu felt strange, as if standing in a half-formed memory frozen in time.

Her throat started to burn, so she walked over to the sink and pulled up a small step. She got on her toes and filled a clean glass with water. Suzu then got off the stool and went to wake her parents. Trying not to spill her water, she walked up to the open door and peeked in. The room sat still and quiet, her parents still under a sheet sleeping. Thinking with her belly, she walked straight towards the baker of the house.

She placed the glass on the end table, next to her mother's still face. Suzu lightly poked her shoulder, too lightly, it turned out, as her mother didn't move. She then grabbed her mother's arm and shook it gently. Suzu quickly pulled back as the tiny hairs on her arm shot up. Her mother's arm felt colder than any skin she had ever touched. She shook her mother's arm again, frightened and desperate, but there was nothing.

Suzu felt small and alone. She stumbled back, unable to look away from her lifeless mother. Her hand then hit the glass, knocking it into a hundred pieces across the floor. Suzu gasped and leaped away from the piercing noise.

"Daddy!"

Suzu ran over to her father, her feet slipping on the wet floor, tears forming in her eyes. She grabbed his arm tightly and shook it. Her fingers could feel the cold skin through his thin sleeve. His face remained calm, motionless.

An overwhelming fear began to course through her veins. Her parents lay impossibly still, like a painting. The horror became surreal, like something that could only exist in a nightmare. She gasped as a loud ring echoed down the halls.

Suzu clenched her hands up to her chest. She stared out into the hallway, but the apartment had gone silent. Suddenly the rattle of the bell rang out again, bouncing between the walls.

Nearly too afraid to move, Suzu forced herself to run for the door, desperate for help. With her chin quivering, she grabbed the heavy brass handle and turned. As the door swung open, she discovered the largest man she had ever seen.

Upon looking down, the large man's grin rapidly dropped into regard. A thin smear of blood ran from her toes towards the hallway; her state of shock blocking the pain of shattered glass embedded in her feet. A deep and gentle sound then came out of his mouth.

"Is everything okay?"

Suzu's trembling voice spoke. "They won't wake up."

Gozen leaned down as much as his massive frame would allow. He then took the girl's small, colorless hand and gently covered it with his powerful fingers.

"It's okay. I'll help you."

7
MEMORIAL

As Suzu's head rested on her arm, she could feel the hum of the engine. She looked up at the display of scattered clouds, occasionally obscured from her hair blowing in the wind. Buildings rhythmically passed by in a blur, one unclear image getting replaced by another.

Suzu replayed parts of her parents' funeral through her mind again and again. Quiet, sad interactions mixed with unnatural images; the event felt more like some eerie dream. She recognized a few of her parents' friends, most of them cried when they saw her. She heard the word "sorry" over and over and over and began to hate it.

One young man introduced himself as Remi Jounaka. He had worked with her dad and seemed to like him a lot. He cried the hardest when he brought over his wife, who looked like she was going to have a baby soon. He also said something to Gozen about being available and looking out for her. Suzu didn't understand what he meant, but thought he was nice. She remembered how sad everyone looked, all dressed in black. Everything confused her. Suzu couldn't even figure out how to cry despite a hive of tears buzzing inside, fighting to get out. The feeling lingered into a sickness that seemed like a prison.

Gozen looked over to Suzu from the driver's seat. The large, custom-built cabin dwarfed the small girl. Her gaze stayed outside, never looking at the sundry display of levers, switches, and glass gauges. Of all the children he had allowed in his truck, she was the first to ignore its array of shiny mechanization.

He wondered what she would be like under different circumstances . . . normal circumstances. Gozen wished he knew the family well enough to even know what *their* normal looked like. The current situation seemed thin on options as the funeral failed to produce any relatives. Gozen decided to give her a new home at the North Orphanage, a humble hope for a frail child.

Steam whistled out of the truck as it squeezed in through the entrance of the Tree House, the orphanage's more colloquial name. It had an iron gate with black, peeling paint that made it look older than it was. The patchy, small lawn provided at least some natural surface for the children to play. The massive truck finally rested by the front of the house, which Gozen always described as looking beautifully resilient.

Gozen shut off the engine and turned towards Suzu, who continued to look out the window as if scenery still passed by.

"Well, we're here. I'm going to go talk to the mother of the house. She's looking forward to meeting you." The words felt weak as he spoke them. In the time that he had met the frightened girl, nothing he said ever felt significant.

"You can stay here if . . ." Before he could get his next word out, Suzu scooted across the seat, her cold hands gripping on to his forearm.

Gozen leaned down. "You can come with me if you want."

He felt her tiny head nod faintly against his arm.

They walked through the front entrance, Suzu's small arm looking like a string as she held Gozen's hand. Their steps creaked as they entered the hallway. A few pictures hung on the walls, mostly of the Murde Mountains and even a small one of Kora farm, natural beauty not so easily found that deep in the city.

A woman about Gozen's age then came out into the hallway with a perfectly formed bun and elegantly folded hands. A simple blouse tucked into a straight skirt hiding behind a Granai belt. Fastened with thick buttons, the high-waisted band kept her posture up and the cold air out. Suzu peeked around Gozen's arm, seeing the woman as a striking combination of grace and sharpness.

"So this must be her," the Lady postulated.

"Yes, this is Suzu. Suzu, I'd like you to meet the mother of the house, Lady Kyoumére."

Lady Kyoumére looked down, as Suzu timidly disengaged her eyes towards the floor. Lady Kyoumére then spoke with perfect enunciation.

"Lord Gozen told me you had to endure something very difficult recently, something many of the boys and girls here have gone through as well. He also told me that you are a very brave young lady and needed a place to stay for a while. We would be very happy to have you stay here, Suzu."

Suzu pressed her cheek into the back of Gozen's arm. He looked to Lady Kyoumére, who shared his hope and trepidation. The housemother then turned towards an older girl walking down the stairs.

"Lucette dear, Suzu just arrived and needs help moving into the yellow room. Would you take her up there, please?"

Dressed in an eclectic getup, the fair-skinned Lucette bent down to Suzu with an inviting grin, her long and intricately braided hair swinging about her cheery smile. "I know it looks big and old, but the house isn't so scary once you get used to it. Plus, you probably got the best room in it—my old room. Do you want to see it?"

It took a moment, but Suzu slowly revealed her eyes. She offered a quick nod before retreating back to Gozen's arm. Charmed by the girl's bashful demeanor, Lucette gently offered her hand. Suzu looked up at Gozen for permission to not be afraid.

"It's okay, I'll just be down here talking with Lady Kyoumére. It's okay."

Suzu peeled her face off of Gozen's arm and timidly took Lucette's hand. She led Suzu upstairs, who promptly transferred her cheek straight onto Lucette's sleeve.

"She's still pretty stunned." Gozen watched them round the corner.

"Of course she is," replied Lady Kyoumére. "And I anticipate she will be like that for quite some time."

"I haven't told her how they died yet. I wonder if somewhere deep down she senses it, though."

"The report stated it was from some toxin they ingested, probable accident."

Gozen rubbed his neck. "That is how it was stated and that

part she knows, but I'm willing to bet it wasn't an accident."

"That sounds like the Gozen I used to know many years ago."

"A time I wish I could forget."

Lady Kyoumére folded her arms. "We first met back then."

"Well, I suppose there is some small value in what I used to be good at," Gozen smiled. "I don't know, perhaps it's nothing."

"Well, I'll leave all of that concern with you. Right now, I need to make sure this young lady feels safe and has some stable ground to walk on."

"And for that, I thank you."

"I would love to promise you that she'll leave here a healed young woman, but we should know that all I can ultimately offer her is hope."

"Hope from you is better than a promise from most," Gozen smiled thoughtfully. "I'll go get her things."

Lucette led Suzu down the quiet hall. They could hear all the children in the back yard playing near the large Laizóu tree, the one that gave the orphanage its nickname. Its form impressively bent around as though peeling out of itself. Finally, Lucette opened up the door to her old room.

Suzu squinted before quickly figuring out the reasoning behind her new retreat's name. The entire room had been painted with various shades of yellow. A blindingly intense dresser stood against a wall that Suzu imagined to be the color of a warm summer wind.

"What do you think? Is this room bright enough to pull a little smile out of ya?"

Suzu quietly continued her evaluation. Two beds stood against the opposing wall, both aged but otherwise nicely made. Something near the back wall then grabbed her attention. A single chair sat at a faded wooden table covered neatly with used art supplies. Letting her hand slip out of Lucette's grip, Suzu walked to the back of the room.

As she approached, Suzu saw a box full of colors. The set of pencils seemed in good shape but not as nice as what her parents always gave her. She thought of how much her parents liked giving her *the good stuff*, as they would put it. Suzu then reached down and let her fingers slide across the surface of the paper, remembering how much her father loved the feel of it. Standing back, Lucette adored her new housemate's gentle exploration.

Across the table in a tin box sat colorful scraps of fabric next to sewing tools, which always reminded Suzu of her mother. Almost daily, Kiara would try out little fashion experiments on her tiny model. Suzu had thought it to be annoying but now found herself strangely longing for it. She thought of the outfit they had made together for her dance audition, the one she never got to wear.

A nausea then built up as if her heavy heart pressed down on her stomach. Suzu struggled with the memory, too painful to hold but too precious to let go. She felt confused and overwhelmed. Tears started to well up in her eyes; she wanted to hide and ran for the door.

"Suzu," Lucette said as she stepped towards the troubled girl.

With her vision blurring, Suzu ran straight through the door and down the stairs until colliding with a wall. She flailed, trying to get free until realizing the wall was actually Gozen.

"Careful, it's okay."

Gozen knelt down with a thud, cradling her in his large arms. Her breathing slowly started to settle. He then saw Lucette on the stairs, as she shrugged her shoulder.

Shrugging his own pair of heavy shoulders, Gozen looked up to Lady Kyoumére. She greatly admired his concern for children, especially as a man who spent many years dealing with the hardest parts of the city.

She spoke softly. "None of us know what will come past the next sunrise, but be confident you are doing all that you can for now. Her time here will be hard, at least in the beginning; there is no escaping that. Still, she may just grow into a strength none of us can yet foresee."

Gozen took the words to heart, coming from a woman he had long since learned to cherish. He slowly released Suzu, allowing the Lady to offer her hand to the cowering girl. Suzu took her new guardian's advice and accepted Lady K's hand.

° ° °

Chigou prided itself on its image: clean, powerful, and progressive. The downtown perpetually radiated light, swinging between the glimmer of an ancient sun and the world's most impressive display of electric light. Opaji pushed the image from the beginning, and over time it became a cultural norm. He considered anything outside of a brilliantly clean presentation erroneous.

For the citizens, maintaining the city became a common matter of pride, but the spotless veneer hid an ever-growing fracture. An economic divide began to widen over the years, and Gozen knew of both ends better than most. As one who once formally protected the lofty image of Chigou, he now spent most of his time working with those supporting it from below, trading in a white scarf for black hands.

Gozen drove Neko, as he demanded she be called, through the northern end of the Industrial Quarter. A rather massive vehicle, Gozen built the split cabin and trailer truck as a long-running custom project. The design focused on strong lines, giving an impression of speed despite its hefty mass.

Its cabin, furnished as a micro apartment, connected to the trailer via a rotating passageway, allowing interior traversal at any time. Gozen lived in the striking vehicle as much as he used it for work.

Neko pulled into an alley towards the Karoburn loading bay, announcing her arrival with the screech of a steam whistle. Workers took a step back as Gozen pulled into his spot. Before stepping out onto the wet pavement, he hit the small lever opening the rear door of the trailer.

A weathered sign above the bay doors stated "Karoburn heavy loading." One of Chigou's primary fuel producers, Karoburn specialized in the manufacturing of Jinouki, a paste fuel used in steam engines. Jino, its colloquial name, was comprised mainly of the mineral Jinsper and oil from a special breed of Tulú flower called Tulúki. Kora farm had established itself as a foremost supplier of the Tulúki flower.

Like it had many times before, Neko's trailer held a mix of crates containing Kora-grown Tulúki and fruit for Varis Market. Two young men then walked out the rear of the trailer: the tall one, Legou, eating a red Bollo fruit; the short one, Joushi, eating a green one.

"I hope you're enjoying that free lunch," said Gozen.

"Oh, we are," they both smirked with a mouth full of fruit.

"Did you manage to save a crate or two for our actual customers?"

"Hey, us disadvantaged youth need to eat somehow," Joushi followed.

"You could buy food with money like normal working people, but then again you'd have to do actual work for that."

Joushi threw his last Bollo at Gozen's head. He effortlessly caught the fist-sized fruit before devouring it in two bites.

An employee door opened by the loading area. A man walked out, his face looking as though it had lived two full lives as a black-hand. With a cynical glare, Delrico stopped next to Gozen. "Everytime you pull in here, it's right before lunch, and then I gotta stare at these crates of Bollo I'm not allowed to eat."

"The most beautiful fruit in the valley, and I'll give you as much as you want if you take these two freeloading, bottomless pits with you."

"Hire new workers? Yeah, you're as serious as you are small. I'll be lucky to still have my job in a year."

The statement pricked Gozen. Karoburn had grown into Kora's most solid customer, as Chigou perpetually longed for the Jinouki feeding into its countless steam engines. "You were managing the loading bay long before I started delivering. They can't get rid of you."

Delrico pulled a collapsible Spark Pipe out of his pocket. The collapsable smoker had a mouthpiece that could swing out. The action also released a small lever on the side used to spark the fill chamber. Rugged and convenient, they were a favorite of black-hands.

"Well, Gozen, this isn't official news, but I'm pretty sure we aren't going to be a Kasic subsidiary much longer."

"Buyout?"

Delrico nodded as he blew a puff of smoke out of the corner of his mouth. "And seeing as how the boys upstairs aren't making it official news, I'm bettin' it's because it ain't gonna be good news for a lot of us down here."

Gozen looked up from out of the shadow to where the sun struck the upper floors.

"Darou!" Gozen jerked his head as Delrico yelled back to the door. "Come here and help these guys get the crates over to dock four. The loader's backed up." Delrico took another puff off his metal pipe.

Gozen spotted Darou, a rather scrappy but good looking young man. Darou obediently walked over to the crates with a swagger that tried hard to look indifferent.

"That's your boy, right?" Gozen asked.

"Yeah, he's a good worker when he ain't being a little punk."

"Definitely your kid then," Gozen smirked. Delrico smiled the way well-weathered men do to deflect.

"So that's a bit surprising. You'd think Kasic would want to hang on to something as fundamental as making Jino."

Delrico shrugged his shoulders. "Yup. I tell you, Gozen, there's something strange going on. Like there's some company lurking down below, sticking its head up out of little holes all over the city, movin' things around even though ain't nobody seems to be actually working for them."

The suggestion lined up with Gozen, who had been hearing similar news elsewhere. "You think someone is setting up a hostile maneuver?"

Again Delrico shrugged his shoulders.

"You heard of a name?" Gozen inquired.

Delrico shook his head. "Nope. Not that it matters. Whoever they are, they ain't gonna care one scrap about how many years of my life I've given over to Karoburn. I'll be pitched out with the rest of the long-timers to make room for more kids who'll work for nothing. Anyways, good to see ya, Gozen."

With his hands in his pockets, Delrico walked back to the door. Daroú, Lego, and Joushi had already gotten to the last crate of Tulúki, so Gozen walked over and met them by the side of Neko. "You two move pretty quick for carrying all that food in your bellies."

"Well, when you love your job . . .," Legou said smugly.

Gozen pulled some money out of his pocket and started to

count it. "So you two don't need a ride anywhere?"

"No, we'll be fine. Thanks, though, big guy," Joushi said.

Gozen handed them each a roll of money. "You guys are doing great at the farm. I hope to keep seeing you up there."

The young men simply nodded at the brief, genuine compliment.

"Kojo and Clora were telling me about new possibilities for you two."

"Does that mean no more riding in this dungeon on wheels?"

"Hey, you be nice to Neko," Gozen playfully threatened.

Legou patted the back door of Neko and pouted. Gozen then gave the two guys a shove. "All right, get out of here." He took one last look over the industrial yard full of long faces before getting back into Neko and driving off.

o o o

Since it was an unusually chilly evening, Gozen tucked himself into the back of Neko's cab, his girth barely fitting into the padded nook. He chomped on a savory Blashu knot filled with spicy ground meat. He bartered for the filling pasty at Varis Market— only cost him one bollo. His other hand shuffled through a week's worth of letters just picked up from the post.

Only one piece managed to stick out: a letter written with notable elegance. Reading the return address gave him a subtle flutter of guilt; he had not visited the North Orphanage in nearly two weeks. In the months following Suzu's arrival to the Tree House, Gozen had slowly been shifting his time away and more towards Kora. His confidence waned when, after each visit, the unfortunate girl continued to seem no better off. He fully trusted Lady Kyoumére with Suzu's betterment but feared this letter would tell of no such development.

He cut open the envelope with a geared pocket knife, a Civil Enforcer special issue. The perfectly graceful writing undoubtedly came from Lady Kyoumére.

"Dearest Lord Gozen, we have been missing you at the Tree House but I am sure that Kora Farm has been blessed by the time you have been spending up there. They are wonderful people and it is fitting that you have such a good relationship with them.

"What I am writing to you now I know comes as no surprise,

despite that which we have wished for many months. The dear child Suzu has physically grown since you first brought her here, but her spirit seems to be frozen inside of her. I feel that we have done well in making sure that the tragedy she had to endure has not dragged her down into the darkest of depths, but she still floats just below the surface. I now believe that her growth will not be pioneered here, and it will be best if she moves on.

"Perhaps as it is the first place she has lived since the loss of her parents, it has become a graveyard for an impassable memory. Conceivably the city reminds her of a life that she longs for but can no longer have. It is for these reasons that I think taking her north could be the best place for her, out in the open and out of the past. I humbly suggest she try a stay at Kora Farm. Certainly, Clora and Kojo will take her with a gracious heart.

"She is always brightest when you arrive and will certainly follow where your guidance leads her. I have valued our time with her as I value her future, a future which I give back into your capable hands.

"For a faith I reserve for but a few,

"Lady Kyoumére."

Gozen folded the letter and neatly put it back into the envelope. The mattress creaked as he stepped up into the center of the cabin. Steam hissed out as he pulled a small steel lever, rotating a track of shelves. He placed the envelope in an open space before noticing a wooden lock box on a lower shelf. Gozen carefully opened the lid, revealing a small metal badge. At the bottom, a label read "Civil Enforcer Academy;" its albino brass finish had tarnished a bit.

Gozen closed his eyes, clutching the small metal certificate. His mind began to fade in and out of thoughts, moments unresolved for a younger man trying to seek his virtue. The image of a decaying building entered his mind, memories and dreams mixing together. He tried to shove the vision away, but guilt and duty pushed him towards it.

He imagined the inside of a hall and he could see people crouched along the walls. Some held children whimpering in tattered blankets. The air felt thick, a mixture of smoke and steam that he had to force in and out of his lungs.

His daydream marched forward, more eyes began to appear through the thickening smog. They shined like old lights through a dirty lens. Frightened faces watched him make his way down the hall, their bodies still like statues. Suddenly, he heard a young girl screaming from the floors above, but it was not Suzu's voice.

Gozen ran to the stairwell, stepping around transfixed bodies.

Suddenly he stood in front of a heavy door. The strained cries were inside, like a voice exhausted from its own lament. He reached for the twisted handle of the door; it felt hot and he could hear the other side hissing at him. Fear tried to pull him away, but the cry refused to let him go. He finally opened the door.

Muggy air rushed into the room like the deep breath of a dragon. Debris and smoke filled the space; it hurt his eyes to even look. All sounds then muffled out, leaving only the quiet voice of the girl sitting on the fractured floor.

Gozen started to walk forward, wanting to bend down and help the tormented child. As he approached, he could see two bodies lying in front of her. As the smoke dissipated, he saw their heads tilted back, their mouths gaping open with those placid glowing eyes.

Sounds began to rumble in, the smoke shifted more, and he could see that their heads were hanging on the edge of a broken floor. The swarm of noise grew louder, twisting metal and desperate screams. The cloud quickly flushed back to reveal the room blown apart, destroyed along with the rest of the building.

The broken floor shook below his feet. His ears began to hurt with a swell of chaos, the screams of the girl rising above it all. Looking down he saw her head begin to turn. Her mouth stretched open and her sad eyes burned. Through the hell-storm her screech tore through his ears, feeling like it would rip through the back of his skull.

A horn blared from outside Neko and suddenly everything vanished. Gozen again opened his eyes and saw the metal still sitting in his hand. Gozen could feel his heart racing and grabbed a flask, quickly forcing down a gulp of spirits. A faint ringing still bounced around between his ears. Gozen set the Enforcer badge back into its box and onto the shelf. Hitting the lever, the shelf rotated to hide the heavy emblem into the darkness, carrying the memories with it.

o o o

Suzu subtlety looked back to a perfectly composed Lady Kyoumére, whose warm face suppressed a sadness. Behind her stood a far less rigid Lucette, her eyes glossy from a recent bout of tears. As Neko began to pull away from the orphanage, the two women faded in the rearview mirror. Suzu looked at them with her head on the window, quietly fighting back tears of her own.

Gozen tried to count how many months it had been since he first saw Suzu. She looked noticeably older but in a way that didn't seem to match up with time. As a silent drive finally got them to the edge of the city, Gozen conceded that Lady Kyoumére was correct.

"I'm sorry about pulling you away from your friends. Lady Kyoumére thought it might be good for you to get out of the city and into the open."

Suzu kept her head down until they passed by a small crowd outside of the Northern Ice House. Picket signs bobbed amongst heads chanting frustrated protests. Gozen heard that the Ice House had recently modernized its business. No more antiquated plucking ice from the mountains as everything began turning to new Cold Charge technology, which took half as many employees and cost no more. In line with other glowing acts of industrial growth, the maneuver seemed a lot less inspiring from down on the docks.

With tall buildings disappearing behind them, along with the sounds of protest, the gray landscape transitioned into a vibrant green.

"Have you ever been out of the city before? The farm we're going to is really nice. I think you'll like it." Gozen's words floated in a cloud of awkward stillness.

A few more minutes went by. Gozen resorted to watching the occasional fruit tree pass by. The sun shined clearly through a few clouds, typically lovely weather in the rural north. Recently, however, the landscape had developed a rather noticeable alteration. They both raised their heads to see the massive spectacle approach.

Along the river the pair saw one of the largest construction projects Chigou had ever undertaken. Suzu already knew quite a lot about the project, especially for someone her age, and the sight of it felt bitter. Many of her parents' final conversations revolved around their opposition to the project, which now seemed to be laughing at them with a mangled grin. A massive portion of land around the river had been torn up, making way for an army of giant machines loaded with concrete and steel. The Long Frost Dam appeared well underway.

Kasic executed the construction through a collaboration with the city, allowing ultimate responsibility to stay ambiguous. The dam site sat closer to the city than the planners had hoped, the result of Clora intuitively buying up a buffer of land south of Kora. Some thought of the dam as a progressive power source, providing the added bonus of a new lake. To anyone with more of a Soran persuasion, the project promised an arrogant mutation of the natural landscape. Suzu's feelings leaned towards the later as she sat holding her knees up to her chest, awaiting yet another unfamiliar destination.

"Why are you taking me up here? Do you like leaving me at places?"

Gozen rarely acted impulsively, even in his Civil Enforcer days. Strong and steady always felt the better fit. The troubled enigma sitting next to him, however, managed to pull out something rather rash.

He hit the brakes and Neko came screeching to a stop. Shocked, Suzu slowly turned and pulled back her messy locks, revealing two very large green eyes. Gozen squared up his face right at her.

"Nothing has broken my heart more than the day I first met you, and ever since I have been trying to think of what I could possibly do to help you deal with such a horrible thing. The answer I have is that I don't know what to do for you. So today, we're driving up to a lovely little farm where you're going to live. What's going to happen there, I don't know, but it's beautiful there and the people are nice and I hope you like it. And no, I do not like leaving you places."

Gozen faced back down Long Frost Road, hearing only the sound of his breathing.

"Okay." Suzu had been sitting like a statue the entire time. Slowly, she rested her head back on the window. "Thanks."

8
KORA

Driving parallel with the Long Frost River, they finally reached the lengthy entrance to Kora farm. They crossed a drawbridge that usually stayed down, reflective of the inviting spirit Clora and Kojo always extended. On the farm side of the river, two decoratively constructed iron wheels could lift the bridge to one side. Along with colorfully stained wooden beams, it looked as if something a child would dream up.

After Gozen expertly squeezed the large truck through, the suddenly curious Suzu watched the bridge shrink in the distance. The air had an unfamiliar quality to the girl, an organic scent of life void of metal and smoke.

A simple farm house began to appear over an approaching hill. Wide, cylindrical silos sat scattered around the property. With their rounded roofs, Suzu thought they looked like giant blashu rolls baked in a tin. Further beyond, endless fields and groves covered the land in massive, colorful squares until disappearing into the horizon.

Although she had never been there before, an odd familiarity began to grow in Suzu. She searched her mind, but the feeling stayed frustratingly vague. As they approached the house, the familiarity started to slip into the surreal, as though she was peering deep into a photograph.

Gozen drove Neko to a stop, very slowly.

"Sorry about that scare earlier," he said with a grin.

By pulling a small lever, a step extended out from the thick, round guard, and the two stepped down. On opposite sides of the truck, they both stretched their arms with a long moan. Suzu's nose scrambled to make sense of the botanical swarm all around her. The usual buzz of Chigou had been replaced with equally confusing sounds, all soft and random; it didn't feel real.

Gozen walked around to her. "So this is Kora farm, a special place to many people dear to you."

Suzu looked up to her driver. "You think that includes you?"

Gozen squinted one eye. "I see that you've picked up some of that orphanage spunk. I guess you weren't sleepwalking over there after all."

Typically, Gozen responded to juvenile sass with twice the wit at a fraction of the words, but never reciprocating disrespect. He knew it typically came from fear or insecurity and a certain lack of structure. Rarely did he enjoy hearing it, but Suzu had never sounded so lively. Not wanting to encourage a sparky mouth, he kept his jovial reply in his throat.

Suzu turned to the beautifully kept house, which looked surprisingly old for the relatively young valley. The two-story home anchored to a tall tower on the north end, all made from white brick and wood trim. Suzu immediately got an urge to climb up the tower and gaze out from its circular walkway.

Gozen saw Clora walk out of the front door, her silver hair shining in the sunlight. He then bent down to Suzu, whose stare still swirled across the farm like a curious wind.

"There's a lot of room out here. Why don't you go make use of it?"

Suzu looked up to him, unsure of how to respond; she had never had access to an area so open.

"It's okay," Gozen said with assurance. "Go run around, kid."

Suzu then ran off through the shin-high grass, gulping in the vibrant air. After months and months in a little room, locking her mind in an even smaller space, the sight of the tortured young girl running free brought a powerful rush of joy.

Clora approached the musing chaplain, negating her need to ask about what she could clearly see in his eyes.

"It's amazing what freedom can be achieved when we allow ourselves to look away from the familiar," said Clora with her typical honesty.

"I just hope freedom is the right choice for her. Lady Kyoumére seemed very sure of it. I think I believe as much, I can't imagine her being better anywhere else." Gozen responded, sitting down on Neko's bumper as to be a bit closer to Clora's eye level.

As Suzu disappeared behind a large silo, Gozen gently touched his small host's shoulder. "Thank you for letting her stay here indefinitely. Your graciousness provides hope."

"You speak awfully sweet for such a big fella."

"As long as you think so."

Clora smiled. "I remember so clearly the day you first came here. You probably were just about as lost as this little girl seems to you: dislodged from your past, desperately seeking a reason and a meaning."

Gozen imagined what adventure or trouble Suzu might currently be considering. "Working with the kids here has probably helped me more than I've helped them. With this lady, though, I don't know. I've never had one all to myself. The only plan I have for her is hope, really. Not sure if that's faith or foolishness."

Clora looked off to the silo. "It's an answer we get to seek all of our lives."

"You sound not unlike another wise woman I know."

"Yes, and you should feel lucky to have so many astute ladies at your disposal," Clora suggested with a grin. Suddenly, her stomach growled loud enough to derail their collective train of thought.

"Mentoring you is making me hungry, young man. Come help me make some lunch."

○ ○ ○

Grass grew tall up against the smooth brick walls, flowing in a long curve. Suzu ran her hand against its sun-warmed surface. She came upon a dark wooden door with a small, circular window too high up for her to see in without jumping. She grabbed the door's thick handle and slowly pushed it open, wondering why farm doors needed to be so heavy.

Contrasted against the radiant sun, the interior appeared black. Suzu felt a cool flow of air drift over her face, foreign smells of the farm traveling along with it. After a quick hesitation, her curiosity pushed her inside.

Her eyes started to adjust as she began to notice circular skylights tucked behind a web of support beams. Stalks of harvested crops tagged with colored labels piled up in round crates along one wall. She had never seen food stacked up in such large amounts.

Farther along the wall, strange machines stood as a sleeping army, their purpose a complete mystery. They ranged in size with all sorts of wheels and hinges amongst a rather intimidating assortment of blades. One machine in the back had a glassed-in-cabin just large enough for one person, perched high on its complex pile of metal parts. The vehicle looked large enough to devour a garden in one gulp. She walked straight towards it.

As she approached it, Suzu could make out large metal teeth set near the floor. They stretched back into something that looked like a giant, horrific comb. Her parents had shown her massive machines before, but nothing that could drive around. It looked as though it could give birth to a normal car. Behind it, small rungs led up to the cabin, leaving just enough space to climb up.

Suzu wedged her body between two machines, hitting her shin on some sharp metal edge hiding in a shadow. She yelped out in pain, but the awkward space prevented her from bending down to check the injury. Instead, she reached up to grab the first rung. As she stepped down, a sharp sting ran up her leg, nearly causing the other leg to buckle. Determined, she pulled up even harder with both hands. Fighting through the intense ache, she managed to get her foot up.

With the hardest part over, she climbed up the rest of the way. She twisted an oddly small latch and the cabin door swung open. Levers, dials, and buttons filled the mysterious buffet of colorful things that did stuff. Suzu felt her heart beating a bit faster.

Carefully, she slid onto the seat surrounded by sharp, metal edges, finding it surprisingly cozy. Unable to restrain herself, she let her fingers gently glide across the knobs and switches. One button near the bottom had a beautiful emerald color, glistening like some of her mother's fancy rings. She pressed harder to get a better read on its texture, and then Suzu's heart nearly leapt from her throat.

A horribly loud electrical whine sounded from below, followed by a pulsing mechanical roar. She felt the entire cabin shake with that blaring cacophony, louder than anything she had ever heard. Her chest tightened, and she frantically looked across the instrument panel for something to turn it all off; nothing made any sense.

The shaking cabin felt like it could collapse at any second. Suzu opened the door and looked below to see any way to leap down and escape. She stood up and grabbed onto the door frame, leaning out to see what kind of mechanical madness existed below. She saw a small patch of safe ground, right behind a storm of ferocious metal shifting back and forth.

While the machine convulsed violently, Suzu felt her body go numb. The moment became overwhelming. She then gained just enough sensation to feel her foot tipping on the edge, and her fingers desperately clenched the metal handle. But her shoe slipped off, and momentum ripped her tingling fingers from their anchor. Suddenly, she was falling.

Time slowed to a terror-filled stop as she floated above a swarm of slicing death. Her shock then began to recede as she realized her fall stopped just short of demise. The flood of mechanical sounds then suddenly collapsed into silence.

"I admire curiosity, but you're just being stupid."

Suzu felt her body shift around, She could then see what, or who, held her up. A young woman impressively braced herself off the top of the cabin, hitting the kill switch with her foot while holding Suzu by the ankle. She looked like a spider, but a lot less scary as she set the little visitor back onto the seat. Feeling as though the world had flipped around, Suzu then found her athletic savior staring at her, hanging upside down.

"So who are you and what are you doing up here?" the inverted face demanded.

Suzu felt too small to speak.

"Okay. Well, I'm going to bet that your silence is from a recent near-death experience. Also, that you have learned never to get up on the harverster again."

Suzu managed a nod in agreement. The young lady then offered her hand.

"My name is Nia. And what do I call you, if you've gathered

enough breath to speak yet?"

Suzu raised her right hand and then switched to the left, confused by her first ever upside-down handshake.

"Suzu. My name is Suzu."

Nia took her hand. "Well, Suzu, now that we're acquainted, what do you say we find a more comfortable place to chat?" Suzu nodded her head very seriously.

Like a bird floating to the ground, Nia perfectly flipped down between the closely parked harvesting machines. Suzu gasped. She had never seen anyone move like that before. Nia dusted off her hands.

"Now, I know you can get down if you managed to get up there all by yourself."

Suzu felt funny, unsure if the acrobatic marvel had just complimented or mocked her. She grabbed the door handle that failed her a minute ago. Nia stood below, playfully impatient, until she noticed the young girl avoid putting weight on one foot.

"Hurt your leg?"

"Yeah, I kicked that thingy climbing up," Suzu said, gesturing to the front of the machine.

"Well, if that's the situation, I suppose I can help you down then."

Nia reached up and gently spun Suzu down into her arms. It reminded Suzu of the slide back at Michelou's. The athlete then hopped up on to a narrow piece of frame and carried Suzu off the machine in perfect balance.

Back on solid ground with everyone upright, Suzu finally got a good look at Nia. Bright, golden-red hair flowed out of a scarf and down her back. She wore a rugged, bluish-green jacket with brass buttons that showed off her athletic frame. A short gray skirt then covered striped leggings underneath. Suzu liked the outfit, wondering if it matched normal farm fashion. She then thought of what her mother must have looked like as a young lady.

Nia cleared her throat. "So as I was saying, I don't ever remember seeing you here before."

Suzu finally felt able to speak normally. "I came here with Lord Gozen. Lady Kyoumére thought it would be good for me to stay at the farm."

"Oh, were you staying at the Tree House?"

"Yeah. My parents died."

Nia took strong notice of the quick statement. She then knelt down and spoke softly. "Yeah . . . I lived at the Tree House when I was younger. My parents died a long time ago. It can be pretty hard sometimes, huh?"

After months in the orphanage, Suzu felt odd over how normal the conversation sounded.

"But I think the Lady was right. It's pretty good here. I think you'll like it."

"Yeah?" Suzu spoke with soft sincerity.

"Absolutely. Now let's get you back to the house to see how bad your leg is."

Suzu nodded, thinking that her leg already felt a bit better.

o o o

After a few days, Suzu's leg looked pretty good, and Nia had helped her avoid any further injury. Suzu's rapid spark of curiosity made Gozen a bit nervous, but he knew Nia to be trustworthy. With things going so well, Gozen decided to get back to work.

Kojo went over to the Tulúki seed silo just as Gozen backed Neko up to the loading bay. Legou and Joushi sat up on towers of stacked seed crates, sporting their usual mischievous grins.

"For a mere twenty Fins, I'll be more than happy to load one of these crates for you, big guy," Legou graciously offered.

"How about I pay Joushi ten to pull out the bottom one while you're still sitting up there?" Gozen counter-offered.

"All right, boys, get off so I can weigh 'em," Kojo commanded. Legou and Joushi jumped off their respective towers, laughing about something the older men easily ignored. Gozen approached Kojo as he worked on an invoice with a Chipi, a portable type printer that could interface with multiple devices. Aya Precision manufactured the impressive device, typical of most products created by the Primichi-based company.

"Let me know if you need help with that simple math, Kojo," Joushi offered.

"You keep up with the smart talk, and you'll need help spelling your name," Kojo replied, raising the metal Chipi.

Legou laughed. "Haha, Kojo is going to beat you with a Chipi." After a few punches to the arm, the fellas got to work.

Gozen leaned into Kojo and spoke discretely. "I talked with Delrico last time I made a drop at Karoburn. He seems to think the company is going to be bought out."

Kojo scratched his jaw. "Hmm, what's making him think that?"

"He really didn't say much beyond just that."

Kojo scrunched his brow. "Are you concerned?"

"I'm getting there."

Kojo continued printing an invoice. "Should I be?"

"Eh, I'll let you know."

As Kojo finished printing, he looked over to Gozen, who appeared lost in some lingering thought. "Concerned about your little lady? I'm sure she can handle a day without you."

Gozen mumbled something before changing the subject. "Did I ever tell you how her parents died?"

"Just that they died at home."

Gozen nodded his head, a sentimental pause before his inquisitive instincts took over. "I talked to an Enforcer friend of mine, said cause of death was inconclusive; probably accidental or suicide. Neither of those add up to me."

"That sounds like a younger Gozen talking."

The older Gozen moaned again; he did not think of his youth as positively as most others did.

Kojo noticed. "Either way, little Suzu is lucky to have a guy like you looking after her."

Legou and Joushi finished loading the last crate. Gozen turned towards them, ready to finalize logistics. "You two got somewhere to be after the drop-off?"

"Sure, boss, we'll give you some alone time with Delrico," Legou kindly offered.

"Get in." Gozen headed to the cab.

o o o

The Naifin Valley produced stunning sunsets, and the citizens of Chigou regularly made a point to watch them, if only for a minute. The sun caught particularly well in the northern neighborhood of Doulan, and Gozen made an effort to drive through the tranquil scene every time he entered the city. His feelings of the neighborhood had grown complex, however, since discovering Suzu's childhood vaporize in a single sunrise.

Gozen squeezed through downtown and entered the loading dock. Upon backing in, Gozen looked around until he found Darou and his father. After the younger men finished unloading, Gozen approached Delrico, eager for any news about the state of Karoburn.

"Well, no more Karoburn," Delrico gruffly stated, his mouth full of seeds.

"What? It got bought out already?" Gozen asked.

"Welcome to Etecid, Jinouki fuel manufacturer of the future," Delrico said with a cynical prick.

"Etecid?" Gozen asked. "That even sounds scheming."

Delrico just shrugged.

Increasing suspicion nudged Gozen to look around. "So, what have they told you? Any changes, or are they basically keeping things as is?"

"Oh no, they haven't said a damn thing other than there's nothing to worry about. But I tell you what, big guy—nothing makes me worry more than a stranger walking up to me and telling me I have nothing to worry about."

"So that's it?" Gozen again asked.

"Oh, I'm sure someone upstairs knows, but they don't generally seem too concerned with our feelings down here on the dock," Delrico grumbled. "Next time you come here, I bet you twenty Fins my boy is gonna have my job, and I'll be out on Gris Ave begging like a bum."

Gozen looked up towards the executives convening behind closed doors, possibly on the verge of discarding these hard-working people out of convenience. If so, he swore to himself not to remain idle.

Delrico's tired eyes looked over to the Karoburn sign, which he had worked under for what seemed like a lifetime. Signers were already tearing it down, replacing it with something younger. He spat some seed husks onto the ground and then walked back from where he came.

Darou quietly watched his father give a conflicting glare before slamming the door shut. Gozen wanted to tell the young man something positive on his way out, but nothing in his mind seemed to qualify.

He then thought of another father, whose tragically short life was probably being boxed up at that very moment. He left to go collect.

○ ○ ○

Carmin's old office had barely been entered since his untimely death. Remi had thought it strange the company never issued a request to collect Carmin's things. When he heard that someone finally planned to get them for Carmin's daughter, he quickly volunteered to take care of it.

Remi had hoped to work one day on a project of Carmin's, work that now sat motionless underneath a thin layer of dust—a mutual death, as it turned out. He missed hearing about Carmin's projects, always something new and a bit daring. Remi found his current assignment interesting enough, but it lacked any real inspiration. He had slowly come to realize that the best projects birthed out of a personal passion, something Kasic rarely seemed to value in action.

While Remi packed up the remnants of Carmin's suspended career, Neko pulled in down below. Despite conducting the man's wedding, Gozen had only seen Carmin that one day. He wondered what things Suzu would particularly cherish; perhaps as long as they were her father's, it wouldn't matter. A memorable three-note chime sounded when Gozen reached the thirty-seventh floor on the steam lift.

The big man made it over to Carmin's quiet office and noticed the door left slightly open. He slowly stepped inside and saw Remi leaning over a box, a set of schematics in his hand. Gozen waited for the young engineer to notice him. It took a few seconds.

Remi popped up. "I'm supposed to be in here."

"I hope I am, too."

Remi lowered the drawing below his tense shoulders. He couldn't help feeling nervous sorting through a deceased man's things. "Oh, you must be the guy picking up the belongings."

Gozen looked over the room. "I believe that's the plan."

Remi stepped around the desk, and the two men shook hands, giving a slight bow to one another. While still common up in Primichi, the etiquette of bowing had largely faded down in Chigou.

"I was just looking over some of his old work. Rather interesting. I really wanted to work with him some day, but as it were . . ." Remi held out the drawing. Gozen watched him thoughtfully admire the schematic.

"So you are taking care of . . . what is her name?" Remi continued.

"Suzu."

"Yes," Remi quickly replied at an awkwardly loud volume. "His only child, if I remember."

"Correct." Always conscious of what information he gave and to whom, Gozen decided this guy seemed harmless enough.

"Well, anyways, thank you for coming all the way down here." Remi shifted through the box. "I'm not sure how much of this the young girl will want. I archived some of his work, but since a lot of it was in such an early state of development . . . well, here ya go."

"I'm sure sooner or later she'll come to appreciate all of this," Gozen suggested.

He appreciated the admiration Remi clearly had for Suzu's father. "Maybe you could help explain all this when that time comes."

Although taken back by the statement, Remi quietly agreed. Then, as it often did, Gozen's former profession took over. An impulse arose to collect info on a pertinent cold case.

"Exactly how well did you know Carmin?"

"Well, we actually were not that close. I was fairly new here, just kind of a wide-eyed kid looking up to one of the more progressive minds at the company. He seemed like a really decent guy, too," Remi reminisced. "Did you know him well?"

Gozen thought of the last time he saw Suzu's father, not something he wanted to discuss. His mind instead shifted to the beautiful wedding between two bright-eyed dreamers. "Briefly, before he . . . they had Suzu. They had a lot of optimism, more than perhaps most couples making a promise for a future together. I wish I could have seen them again."

Remi reached into the box. "Actually, there is one item in here that I know was for his kid. I saw him working on it a few times. Plus, I'm nosey, and he was kind enough to tell me about it."

Remi lifted his arm out of the box and held a small cylindrical case made out of Bokai and White Wood. Masterfully crafted, small strips laid out in alternating rings. He carefully opened up the box, tilting it forward for Gozen to see.

Inside the box sat a round Toki made out of albino brass and dark alloy. A portable time piece, Tokis had a specific popularity for always having an alternate, hidden function, known as a Special. The most common was a compass, but often the secondary function remained a secret to everyone but the owner. Generally cherished items and often crafted for a specific person, this one appeared quite precious.

Inside, smooth metal rings framed a brilliant white face of polished minerals. The brass clock hands floated in panes of glass—impressive by any standard. Gozen could see why Remi had so much respect for the work of its maker.

"I'm not sure what its Special does," Remi confessed, spinning a dial around the outside of the Toki. "I thought it might point north, since that's the common one, but I suppose that was a foolish assumption since Carmin made it."

He placed the wooden case into Gozen's hand, the final gift of a father who would never see his daughter's face as she opened it. The thought of it made his heart ache.

"Thank you. I'm sure this will mean a great deal to her."

As Gozen headed back to Kora, memories in hand, Remi went down a few floors with an old schematic. The plan displayed sketches of the Core-thermic project, Carmin's last. The two had once discussed the concept with much zeal, but now that the creator ceased to be, he decided to keep such fascinations to himself.

Remi entered the office of his current assignment, the words *Pirou Naizen - New Engine R&D* labeling the door plaque. As it was one of the smaller research and development labs in the building, only he and his superior worked inside. Small lab equipment lined the walls: combustion chambers, exhaust systems, fuel mixers, and other scaled components for engine testing. It all surrounded a main desk with Remi's flat plank of wood, or what he called his desk, off to the side.

Upon getting the assignment, Remi felt optimistic for what seemed a suitable alternate to working directly with Carmin. Recently, however, he had become suspicious of the project and its lead engineer, Lord Pirou. Remi tried to dismiss the feelings at first but found it hard not to be skeptical of Pirou Naizen's credentials, for Bardin Naizen—Pirou's uncle—had hired him.

The current project focused on Dark-spark engines, a direct-fuel technology that competed with steam power. The theory had been put through initial testing and revealed a number of promising aspects, some even calling it a revolution in industrial power. Still, the technology remained young and its long-term impact largely unproven.

Pirou Naizen worked at the main desk, carefully guarding his research. The assistant walked in to see his boss hunched over his desk with a cup of coffee likely to be at least a day old. Pirou turned around like a sick cat in a corner. Upon noticing it to be Remi, he decided not to bother with eye contact.

"Where were you?"

"Collecting Carmin's things. I told you." Remi sat at his wood plank.

"What do you mean? Didn't he die, like, a year ago?" Pirou's voice was devoid of any sympathy.

"Yeah, but nobody came to pick it up until today."

"So why did you pack it up?" Pirou sounded agitated. "Can't some lady from HR do that?"

"I don't know. I mean, I knew him. I felt bad for his daughter, so I just volunteered."

For a fraction of a second, Pirou glanced over to the black-and-white photo of his wife, daughter, and son before quickly getting back to his papers. "Well, we're behind. I need you to read me the report on Batch 37's performance. Quickly."

"Okay." Remi rolled his eyes, feeling safely ignored. He reached to the back of his desk and pulled up a folder. He thumbed through some pages before turning to Pirou.

"Where did we get all the Kurokinojinsper for this?" Remi plainly asked.

Pirou half turned. "The what?"

"Kurokinojinsper, the Dark-jinsper we used in this fuel batch. I didn't even know this much was being mined."

Pirou became perturbed enough to give his subordinate nearly all of his attention. "Remi, what do you care? It's not your job to manage material acquisition. Just go over the report." Pirou went back to his papers.

Remi looked over to the scrap of paper with Carmin's Core-thermic notes, put it in his pocket, and mumbled to himself.

"What?" Pirou hastily demanded.

"Nothing," Remi dismissed. "Here is the report; I think you'll be happy. Power was decent at about 38.5, efficiency, though, was the best batch yet at 62."

Pirou finally sat up straight. "38.5 and 62?"

"Happy day," Remi flatly stated.

Pirou covered his mouth with ink-stained fingers. He looked blankly around the room as his mind raced. Remi continued thumbing through the report. "If you project these numbers out, it looks like this trajectory could certainly shoot past steam engines in a few years."

"This is it. This Batch is going to be the launching platform for the entire engine redesign." Pirou spun around, nearly in a stunned state of euphoria. He looked back down at some papers on his desk, his brain too active to settle on anything. His eyes gleamed with a ravenous hunger for what he saw in his mind, finally in reach.

"Too bad it still produces a black cloud of death," Remi casually declared.

His assistant's words took a few seconds to process through the storm of glee running through his head. Pirou finally stopped and glared at Remi. "What did you say?"

"Well, between the refining process and the combustion process, this stuff produces incredibly high levels of byproduct into the air and water. Toxic byproduct. Too bad. It's got a few things really going for it."

Pirou took a step towards him. "A few things going for it? With these P & E numbers, what else does it need to do?"

Although still a few steps away, Remi could feel Pirou pushing into him. "Yes, those are good numbers, and important numbers, but aside from the fact that it would essentially poison the city, we don't even know how much Dark-jinsper there is in the valley."

Pirou stepped forward again, the closest he had intentionally gotten to Remi during the entirety of their shared time in the office. "Look, you're not here to dream about worst-case scenarios happening long after we're dead. This isn't some Soran social club. You're here to study results and make reports on how powerful and efficient these fuel batches are in my engine. That's it."

"Okay." Remi backed into his chair, as he found the warm breath of Pirou to be rather stale. "I just remember when Carmin presented his Core-thermic idea, it seemed like such a win-win-win . . . if he ever got a chance to develop it . . ." Remi began to grasp what he said, and who he said it to. He lowered his voice. "I just don't think this has the same kind of . . . perfect-solution potential that Carmin's did."

Remi clenched up as if about to be hit by a balloon full of piss.

"Carmin is dead, his idea is dead, and every second you spend on that idea is time and money wasted by this company." Pirou's spit flung onto Remi's face. "Do you like having a job here?"

Remi typically did not take lightly to patronizing remarks, but he wanted the current stream of rancid humidity out of his breathing space. "Yes."

"Then start acting like an assistant whose desk is just a sad little scrap of wood. Respectful, compliant, and quiet." Pirou went back to his desk.

Remi turned around and rubbed the plank of wood. "I like my scrappy little desk."

○ ○ ○

When Gozen arrived from Kasic with Carmin's things, Suzu seemed almost indifferent to seeing them. She slowly went through each item in the box, professional pencils and notes, her reaction nearly void of emotion. Not until she got to the wood Toki case did she even bother to take anything completely out. When she opened the fine container, her eyes dove through the shining face of the Toki. For quite some time, her focus remained on its brilliant surface as if an infinite amount of detail needed to be observed.

Gozen shared what Remi had told him, hoping a bit of back story would help give the object some connection. He explained how the Special for that particular Toki remained a mystery, suggesting that it might be fun to figure it out. Instead, he found his words drift around the room unnoticed. Suzu just stared blankly at the final gift.

Gozen imagined Carmin giving his daughter the precious expression of countless hours of work. He imagined the father's face, beaming as he explained all that made it unique. He wondered how many times Carmin daydreamed about that precious exchange, but the moment would never happen. With nothing left to say, he gently patted her on the back and retreated downstairs.

Gozen's heavy footsteps quickly faded out of Suzu's consciousness as her eyes continued to pry into the mysterious device. Its albino brass surface brilliantly reflected the light over her bed, its hands slowing turning, trapped behind the glass face. She began to run her fingers along its edge, feeling for some sort of switch to bring its Special alive. She felt the perfection of its construction, a perfection that matched only the memory of her father. She wanted so badly to ask him questions like she always did, but the secrets of his gift remained quietly locked away.

A storm of emotions then seeped out from her core. Suzu's fingernails began to dig into the Toki's seams, too perfectly machined to let anything in. A pain began to fire through her fingers as it denied her an answer. She demanded to know why it sat there looking so perfect and lifeless. Frustration pushed out tears. She dug harder, and blood began to seep out from under her nails. She clawed to tear out the answer buried beyond her reach.

Finally, she cried out to her father as she slammed the Toki onto the dresser. The hardwood top dented in but the Toki remained

KA$IC

LEADERS IN ENERGY

LEADING TOWARDS
THE FUTURE

unaffected, still pristine and paralyzed. She clenched her jaw and slammed it down again. It did not answer. She slammed it down again and again and again. Wood splintered into her face as a scream gnarled out between her teeth. Her blood began to smear across the otherwise immaculate surface.

She then collapsed on the floor, giving up on hearing a voice trapped under six feet of dirt. She laid there as her rage slowly evaporated.

Down below, Gozen silently listened as the violent sounds finally came to a halt. His instincts told him to go back up, but something kept him from moving. So badly he wanted Suzu to escape her tragedy, to resemble the kind of girl he imagined Kiara and Carmin would have raised. Instead, the world showed just how cruel it could be and she lived with it. Eventually the house fell quiet, and all decided to retreat to sleep.

○ ○ ○

The next morning, Gozen sat with Clora over some smoked coffee before breakfast. He expressed his frustration with Suzu before apologizing for rambling. Clora tried to comfort her friend, reminding him of his good heart and the danger of expectation. He had been contemplating going back into the city when they both heard light footsteps coming down the stairs.

Suzu walked past the breakfast room in nightclothes, dragging her long socks down the hallway. The adults watched the girl then quickly return into the room with a rather odd expression. "So is someone cooking breakfast around here?"

Gozen smiled, suddenly feeling hungry.

9
GRAVITY

The country breeze always blew gently at Kora, unlike the swirling bursts she felt in the city. Suzu loved how it softly pushed the grain fields around like oceans of gold dust. Farmworkers bobbed around in the waves, wearing bright, fruit-colored jackets. She quickly discovered about half the workers at the farm were orphans or, what she overheard someone once call them, "troubled youth." Suzu felt exempt, as she had yet to get in trouble since turning on the harvester.

For a first job, Suzu harvested Bollo fruit in the west orchard. Bollo trees grew to a height of three meters and blossomed fist-sized fruit, starting white and quickly turning bright red. Sweet and filled with juice, she found the fruit extremely tempting to snack on while working in the sun. Nia gave her permission to nosh one or two if she got hungry, giving Suzu less guilt about the ones she already ate.

Gozen often worked with Suzu, mostly enjoying her developing conversation skills, occasionally spotted with adolescent sass. Quickly, the odd pair developed their own system for harvesting: Gozen holding a big basket while Suzu threw in the fruit as she sat on his shoulders. Although small for her age, it had been years since she sat on anyone's shoulders. Luckily, Gozen happened to be the largest man she'd ever met.

"Are there always so many Bollos? I don't think we can pick all of them."

"No, their season is longer than a lot of crops, but in half a year the trees will all be empty," Gozen maneuvered the basket.

"What's wrong with them? Why don't they grow all the time?"

"There's nothing wrong with them. They just have to go through different seasons. Sometimes they are recovering, preparing for a time when they sprout again."

"Hmm," Suzu pondered. It felt strange to see Bollos on trees instead of in grocery baskets. Growing up in a world full of machines, all of the organic business of seasons and blossoming seemed nothing short of magic. "So Clora and Kojo just put them here? And they just grow?"

"Yes. You can help them in ways, but you can't make them. Ultimately, I suppose it's up to the trees."

Suzu rested her chin on his head, scrunching her face at the idea of trees deciding on anything. She remembered some of her mother's friends mentioning some sort of botanical consciousness. A strange idea, but it seemed to fit at Kora.

Gozen gave a shake. "You better get back to picking fruit. Nia isn't going to be happy if this is all we have."

"I'll just tell her it's because you walk too slow," Suzu threatened.

"Well, I'm carrying the fruit and an entire girl."

"Nia isn't interested in excuses, she told me herself," Suzu spoke with a glint in her eye.

With that, they both looked towards the sound of an engine coming from the farm house. Nia drove towards them in a Quick Wagon—an open, compact utility vehicle great for hauling. One could also fit a small pile of kids in the back, or in the case of Gozen, just himself. He looked down to Suzu. "I'm telling her it's your fault."

Quickly, Suzu jumped off of Gozen's shoulders, "not if I get to her first!" She promptly landed on the front seat next to Nia, a strained look of innocence on her face.

Nia raised an eyebrow, "Uhm, dinner is ready."

"That's good. You get really hungry working so hard." Suzu said, looking straight ahead.

Nia looked at the half empty basket in Gozen's hands and shook her head with a smirk. "Shameful."

Around the farm, most of the young day workers returned to the city, but a few gathered in the dining room for a weekend stay. Clora spent the day preparing a large meal. It included her cherished baked Blashu spiral, a soup made from roasted vegetables, and a spicy paste of pepper pods and Tulú oil.

Parking by the house, Gozen unloaded the fruit while Nia and Suzu washed their hands. The smell of Clora's food urged them to hurry.

"So where are we going to eat today?" Suzu enthusiastically asked as she scrubbed quickly.

She had been eating alone or with Nia around the grounds for every meal since arriving at the farm. She expressed no enthusiasm when asked to eat at a group table, which Clora seemed fine with for the time. That day, Nia felt good about making a little change.

"I thought we could eat at the big table today," Nia casually suggested.

Suzu stood there, her smile tapering off into a straight line. Hoping for some sudden sound to distract the proposition, Suzu gave in with a gentle nod. Nia smiled, then shouted towards Gozen, who was stocking fruit in the pantry. "Hurry up in there, old man. We're hungry out here."

Putting up the final basket, Gozen let out an exhausted laugh. "For such a peaceful farm, this place has a rather high concentration of brash-tongued women."

⚬ ⚬ ⚬

Kojo sat at one end of the long table, filled in by young workers. Suzu hid as best she could at the other end, sitting next to Nia.

Clora walked in with the final platter of food—roasted Chitori—and placed it down between the soup and pepper paste. Nearly everyone sat up to catch a better whiff of the steaming field bird. The mother of the house finally took her seat.

"Gozen, would you please express our gratitude for the moment?"

"Certainly. Today we have food, prepared by a mother, gathered by children, and shared by a community I am thankful to be a part of. We come from many different places, but we have united here, and though we do not know what will come with the rising sun, I am thankful for what we have today and faithful that good will come of our union."

"Goúbon," all said collectively, all except for Suzu. Immediately hands began passing plates around. Now able to finally eat the crops they had been harvesting all day, everyone relaxed their shoulders with gentle smiles.

Eventually conversations sprouted up as people got their energy back. Nia got caught up exchanging sharp remarks with Gozen despite Clora's many glaring looks; Gozen blamed the pepper paste. Clora agreed that she made a fairly mean pepper paste.

As the energy of the room amped up, Suzu cowered into a shadow at the end of the table. The Tree House had been especially difficult for her with its populated meal times, drastically different from what she had growing up. Lady Kyoumére noticed and generally sat Suzu right next to herself. Suzu's current situation proved much louder than anything at the Tree House, and the whole thing began to feel unbearable. Conversations crisscrossed with laughter, and the strong aroma of food became too much against a growing nausea.

Struggling to breathe, Suzu desperately looked up through the noise to catch the attention of Nia. With a mouth full of delicious food, Nia eventually noticed her little friend's state of distress. The acknowledgement was all that Suzu needed, and she ran straight out of the dining room.

Moving quickly, she stumbled through the hallway and towards the nearest exit. Her sweaty hands fumbled with the front door latch as her body ached for a full breath. The metal knob finally cranked, and the door flew open.

The dry, cool air washed over her, and she filled her lungs with it. Suzu ran up to a tree and collapsed. An emotional valve opened and she started to cry, allowing her tense body to normalize. She fought to think of her parents sitting at their cozy little table, their familiar voices wrapping around her.

Nia immediately followed through the front door, quickly hearing muffled sobs by the tree. Nia simply sat next to her, waiting until Suzu was ready.

After the girl finally managed to calm her breaths, Nia gently spoke. "There are a lot of people in that room, huh?"

Suzu nodded, comforted by simple, clear words.

Nia continued. "When I first came here, it felt so strange to me. I was a child of a city that never slept, but here at the farm it was always so quiet and calm. Sometimes it was relaxing, but mostly it made me feel really lost. It took me a long time to get used to it."

She leaned onto Suzu's shoulder as both of them sorted through images of the past. "I remember my dad told jokes, or at least he laughed a lot. My mother always played with my hair, even at our little dinner table. I loved just sitting in a room with her, looking up occasionally and seeing her smile.

"They worked in the southern part of the city, this place called Roukot. Tough neighborhood to grow up in, I guess; it seemed normal to me. Then one day the building they lived in burnt down. A lot of people died. Families. My family."

Nia tucked her arms towards her chest, fighting off the chill. "Anyways, Gozen got me out of there and now I have a new family, and they're pretty great. Different, but still great."

Suzu took her sleeve and wiped off the last little tear. "My parents talked a lot during dinner, but it was just three of us. I didn't always understand what they talked about, but I still liked it. If they got too tired to talk, we'd go to Michelou's."

"You mean the cold creamery?" Nia nudged the conversation up.

"Yeah, it's the best," Suzu said, managing a grin.

"What's your favorite thing to get?"

Suzu's smile slowly dimmed as she thought of that old, familiar conversation. Her mother, always adventurous and suggesting new things, and Suzu always getting her usual hot-berries and chocolate. Such comforts seemed to no longer exist. "I don't remember."

Nia remembered a time when all she wanted was to stop feeling sad and hopeless. Thinking back, she felt that Clora and Kojo didn't just make her life better, they saved it.

"Suzu, I have something special I'm going to show you tomorrow. It is something new, and it will take some work, but I think you'll take to it very well."

Suzu tried to sniff in her runny nose. "Okay."

○ ○ ○

The following morning, Suzu anxiously went to the grain silo, as her new hero Nia had asked. After an exhausting night of crying, she felt reborn in the warm early sun. She put her ear up to the heavy door, listening for a clue to the *special thing*. Nothing revealed itself, so she crept in.

Dusty air filled the spacious room, its curved walls lined with bales of dry grain. The towering stacks absorbed the sound, leaving the room eerily quiet. A dark shape then fell behind Suzu with lithe silence. Hearing the slightest shuffle, Suzu spun around, but there was nothing. Frantically searching, she spun back around before nearly jumping out of her shoes.

"Hey there, sneaky," Nia grinned.

"Nia! YOU are the sneak. How did you get there?"

"I'm sneaky." Nia suggested.

"You're creepy."

Nia glanced up to the rafters with curled fingers. "No, creepy was when I was watching you from up in the darkness."

"What? There is no way you got down here that fast."

"I was," Nia said, leaning in, "and I'm going to teach you how to do it, too."

Always feeling a repressed acrobat lived within her, Suzu anxiously stood at full attention.

"So I take it you're interested."

Suzu's nod slipped into a crooked frown. "But I'm not very good at that kind of thing. My dad used to say I was kinda clumsy like him, but it's okay because smart people can be a little clumsy."

"What would you say if I told you I used to be clumsy?"

"I'd say you're a good athlete and a bad liar."

Nia laughed. "Did your dad teach you that too?"

Suzu stayed with her suspicious gaze. Nia cleared her throat. "Kojo used to say I was so clumsy it made him nervous; said I needed to get my bearings together if I was gonna work here, so he sent me to a circus school down in west Chigou. It was run by descendants of Chomi and Misko, the famous Soultai artists from Primichi."

"I used to have a book about them. It had some really great pictures of them flipping and doing crazy things," Suzu enthusiastically spouted.

"So you must know about how Soultai explores the strength of the ground and the freedom of the air? Allowing one to master their power and balance with their surroundings?" Nia inquired.

Suzu tensely nodded.

"Well then, let us begin."

Suzu could only manage out a little squeak.

"Now, first thing. I want you to stand up on your hands."

Suzu looked down at her hands, farther down to the ground, and then thought of her feet somehow pointing up to the sky. "I think I'm gonna fall over."

Nia folded her arms. "Okay."

"Okay?" The open-endedness baffled Suzu.

"The ground isn't that hard. Go for it."

Suzu envisioned Nia effortlessly walking on her hands, a sight she had seen more than once. She took an exceptionally deep breath and flipped over, imagining the grace of her mentor. Her feet quickly followed along with a burst of ambition, a burst that carried them past their goal and straight down onto the ground. Suddenly in a small cloud of dust, Suzu sat up coughing between moans.

"Well, that was awful, but there are two good things about what you just did," explained Nia.

Suzu sat confused.

"You certainly aren't scared to show some effort, and now you don't have to wonder what it feels like when your butt hits the floor."

"I guess that's good," Suzu spoke, rubbing her sore bottom.

"You okay?"

"I think so. I just hit kind of . . ."

"Good, let's try it again." Nia jumped back to give her student some room.

"Right now?"

A silent standoff quickly formed. Nia put her hands in her pockets as Suzu dropped her shoulders. With a whimper, she lined back up in front of the body print she just made. After a quick nod from Nia, Suzu flipped around, but her feet only managed to elevate about eighteen inches. She landed with a pathetic grunt.

"Just split the difference and you'll be well tuned," Nia brightly encouraged.

"It feels weird."

Nia lined up perfectly beside Suzu and straightened up the slouching girl's posture. "Now I want you to do it again, but this time I'll grab your feet."

"You mean it?"

Nia spoke gently. "Suzu, have I ever given you a reason to not trust me?"

Suzu suddenly realized that since her parents died, she held very little trust for anyone. Everything she had counted on outside of her own skin had vanished. She fought to get the words out. "I trust you."

Nia lightly braced the small of Suzu's back. "Go for it."

Sensing Nia's support, Suzu quickly spun her feet around. In a second, she stood perfectly inverted.

"Do you feel that?" Nia asked.

It was a completely new sensation for the girl. The weight sat heavy on her unconditioned wrists, but something about it felt strangely natural.

"Now you know."

"Know what?" Suzu strained out.

"What it's supposed to feel like."

Suzu's confidence increased along with the strain in her arms. She tried to imprint the feeling onto her mind, thinking of what it would be like stand on her own. She then heard Nia's voice, softer and much closer.

"You learn faster when you believe you can."

She turned her flushed face to see Nia's five inches away; she was standing on her own. The excitement distracted Suzu enough to collapse her back down in another cloud of dust. She let out a bizarre laugh as the shock tingled through her bones.

"Now, I think I should teach you how to fall."

"There's a good way to fall?" Suzu groaned, brushing off the dust.

"Yes, and you certainly do not know what that is."

○ ○ ○

With a bottom carrying a few new bruises, Suzu decided to sleep on her stomach. She lay there with a feeling that she had all but forgotten: the reviving sensation of purpose. She couldn't even remember that last time she went to bed anticipating the next day. Her overwhelmed heart felt raw, as the simple joy seeped out from where it had long been buried. A slurry of laughs and tears spilled into her pillow, and Suzu felt as though she experienced joy for the first time. Eventually, as the built up pressure finished releasing from her spirit, the exhausted girl managed to fall asleep.

In an adjacent room, Nia remembered her time at the Chomi and Misko school. She thought of what she must have looked like back then, smiling at the comparison with Suzu and her dusty pants. Nia's drifting mind then landed on a conversation she walked in on earlier between Clora and Kojo. They mentioned some young man coming to the farm, the heir to some wealthy industrialist. Apparently the plan included him learning the art of living like simple folk while gracing them with the luster of his family's empire. Preparing herself to be unimpressed, Nia eventually fell asleep.

o o o

The following morning, Suzu stumbled into the silo looking as if a block of ice hung from her neck. Nia privately enjoyed the sight of such a youthful face being cradled by the posture of a grandmother.

"It looks as though we might need to loosen that shipman's knot between your shoulders before we begin," Nia observed.

"I hope you don't want me to stand on my hands today. I can't even raise them past my ears," Suzu groaned.

"No, I'm planning on wearing your legs out today."

"Great, then you can just roll me back to the house when we're done."

Nia walked behind Suzu, "All right, you're going to have to sit down for this." Suzu sat down, trying hard not to bend her back; it took awhile. Nia politely attempted to contain her laughter. "Okay, now cross your arms over your chest."

Suzu let out a whimper as she managed to obey. Nia sat down right behind her, wrapping her arms around Suzu. She then pulled her arms out in opposite directions while slowly bending her forward. Suzu giggled in pain, feeling a simultaneous burst of searing heat and relief. After fifteen seconds, Nia pushed and pulled even more, releasing three quick cracks that echoed through the silo.

"Good enough?"

Suzu squeaked, "Yes, please."

Nia slowly got onto her feet; Suzu plopped her back onto the ground.

"Feel better?" Nia said from above.

"Who was the first person to think to try that?"

"Someone smart and very friendly." Nia reached down and pulled Suzu up so fast her head felt fuzzy. As she regained focus, Suzu finally began to notice the explicit arrangement of stacked bales asymmetrically lining the walls of the silo. They looked like grassy stairs.

"I want you to hop up on that low bale and run around the entire silo without ever touching the ground," Nia requested.

Suzu rubbed her eyes, then sized up the bales from beginning to end. A bit of confidence emerged, noting how much softer dried grass felt compared to the ground. With a small grunt, she was off.

Suzu sprinted up to the first bale and managed to get onto it with relative ease. The next bale stood one step up. Not a problem. Running a few more meters she came to a gap; she slowed down a bit before successfully making the leap. Nia raised her eyebrows, critiquing each and every move.

Confidence fortified in Suzu's mind as she approached her first real challenge: a three-stack tower. Suzu slowed down, trying to finesse her timing, finally jumping as high as she could. She grabbed the top and planted her feet on the second bale. Quickly, however, the top bale proved to be an unreliable anchor. She fell straight down and landed with a moan that immediately got muffled from the bale landing on top of her.

Nia walked up to the large wad of grass that appeared to be sprouting arms and legs. She flung the bale back up top. "So, don't climb unstable things like they were stable things. Lesson learned."

Suzu sat up and spat dried grass out of her mouth. "Well . . . it's way too high to jump on."

Nia stood there, silently allowing a response.

Suzu grunted again. "It's not like I can just run up the wall!"

"Hmm." Nia turned around and trotted back to the center of the silo. Suzu brushed the remaining grass out of her hair and dragged herself over to Nia. Once they reached the center, Nia stopped, focused her eyes, and straightened her posture. Suzu gladly took a moment to rest.

Suzu then felt the air swirl as Nia ran past her. She watched her master instructor curve in to match the arc of the wall and hop up to the first bale effortlessly.

Dealing with the first gap, Nia timed her footing so perfectly her stride never broke. Suzu held her breath as Nia approached the impending tower and shifted her momentum onto the wall. As if gravity had turned off, she ran two full strides up the wall, her feet digging into the brick. Finally, Nia vaulted off and landed cleanly onto the top bale; Suzu's jaw dropped.

For a finale, Nia then grabbed onto a support beam and back-flipped down onto the floor.

"How?" Suzu asked in disbelief.

"You'll understand will once you do it." Nia walked back, not even sweating.

Suzu dropped her shoulders and looked back to the tower of stacked grass for an answer; it wasn't talking. Comparing Nia's grace against what she imagined looking like herself, Suzu expelled a defeated breath. "But I can't do things like you . . . and I'm too small."

Nia leaned down. "I can tell you this for certain, Suzu: If you don't believe you can do it, then you most certainly will not. However, if you believe you have a chance, then a chance you most certainly have."

Suzu folded her arms and scrunched one side of her face. "Easy for you to say."

"Yeah, it is," Nia volleyed back.

Suzu waited for the ending of that enlightening statement but soon realized it had already arrived. Suzu reconsidered, but her bank of self-confidence never felt particularly full. "Do you believe I can do it?"

"It'd be a bit silly of me to teach you if I didn't."

Suzu turned back to the gauntlet and envisioned her mentor's adeptness. It could be done, she thought. Suzu dug her toes in and ran for the first low bale. She imagined Nia matching her step for step. Suzu took the gap without hesitation and managed to glide right over it.

She kept her speed up and felt more power than before heading towards the tall bales. She pictured a path up the wall like a flight of stairs; she planted her left foot and jumped up. With a hard scrape, her right foot hit the wall and she could feel herself ascend. The momentum, however, failed, and the foot started to slip. As the ascension leveled off, Suzu's face planted firmly into the hay with a muffled grunt before falling into the familiar spot down below.

Nia jogged over as Suzu sat up moaning and spat out more grass. Nia helped her up just as Gozen appeared. All three convened in the middle as Gozen's face went crooked. He seemed to be the only one noticing Suzu's tussled hair full of harvest grass, some of which stuck to the corner of her mouth.

"You know, it tastes a lot better if you wait until after it's turned into bread," Gozen suggested.

"I'm not baking here, Gozen. I'm learning to run like Nia," Suzu said sternly.

Gozen and Nia both smiled at Suzu's draconian delivery.

"Does Nia run on her face?"

Suzu grunted and made two fists. "I believe in myself!" The girl then ran off and attempted the gauntlet once again. Nia turned to Gozen. "So, what has been keeping you away?"

At least ten things came to Gozen's mind but he carefully minded what business he discussed with her. "There have been some companies shutting down lately. I've just been looking into it."

"That happens sometimes, though. Right?" Nia had developed a strong curiosity over civil matters as of late, and Gozen had noticed.

"Maybe, maybe not. That's what I'm trying to find out."

"But people lost their jobs?" Nia asked.

"Well, this stamping plant just shut down. Nobody expected it, at least nobody on the floor. They got escorted out of the building by sentinels who wouldn't even let them collect their stuff. Things got pretty rough. One guy got hit so hard he may have lost vision in one eye."

"Oh no, that's horrible," Nia gasped. "Why didn't anyone know it was gonna close?"

"That is an important question. Opaji often blesses the closing of companies to make room for progress—his words, but generally out in the open. Lately, though, something feels subversive. It's not the same." Gozen watched as Nia's mind cranked every gear. He felt hesitant to involve her into such matters, ones that he knew could be dangerous, but her virtuous ambition struck him just as hard.

"Hmm. You know, I'm going to start taking some classes in the city soon, business development. I could look into things for you, ya know. Any way I could help," Nia earnestly offered. She then saw Gozen pause, stunned as if a thought had emerged but he feared letting it out too quickly.

Finally, with heavy eyes, Gozen replied, "People's lives are going to change because of you."

The statement nearly floored Nia, and the pair stood there quietly managing an emotional swell. The moment then quickly deviated towards a loud grunt from Suzu. They looked over to see her launch into the wall. She took two vertical steps and felt herself elevate more than before, her chest hitting the top edge. She stretched across and thrust her fingers into the bale. With feet digging in below, Suzu felt hot blood pump into her arms, then heaved herself on top. "I did it!"

"I'm not surprised. Now keep going," Nia directed.

Suzu's dusty face gulped in some air and continued to finish the course. Nia and Gozen both relished in watching the quiet victim suddenly running on a path to conquer life.

Suzu swung around the last pole and sprinted towards Gozen. Noticing her failure to slow down, he started to brace himself. She then ran up his leg, grabbed onto his jacket and pulled herself up onto his shoulders. Proving to be overly enthusiastic; however, she then flipped right off. Nia reacted in an instant and caught the explosion of energy before she hit the ground. "What, are you an Ice Cat now?"

"Feels like one," Gozen said, rubbing his sore hip.

With what seemed to be a developing habit, Suzu gave another very serious grunt and ran off to improve her lap time.

Gozen dusted off his pants. "You're really great with her, Nia. I don't think I could overstate that."

Nia's grin turned awkward as her cheeks started to blush. Unsure of how to handle the compliment, she simply deflected, "Just finishing what you started."

o o o

Eventually they made it back home, and Nia strongly encouraged Suzu to take a shower. Once in bed, Nia combed the girl's wet hair as they talked about the day's progress. Eventually fatigue flushed out the adrenaline, and Suzu managed to lay down.

Suzu dreamt of what other challenges Nia would have for her. Her head filled with images of climbing up walls and jumping over tractors while wearing some stylish outfit, but nothing floppy like a dress. Suzu then fantasized about her mother and Nia discussing how to make the most polished outfit a spunky little girl could hope for.

As she imagined them all laughing together at the dinning table, her heart then began to ache. The perfectly normal laughter that used to fill her old kitchen suddenly seemed so special, and so painfully absent. Suzu then realized the laughter actually came from downstairs. She perked up at the recognition of Nia's spirited voice bouncing up the stairwell. She put her bare feet on the cold floor. Then, wrapping her arms close around her torso, she scooted out into the hallway.

Suzu got to the edge of the stairs and sat down, barely making out Nia, Clora, and Kojo sitting at the kitchen table. They picked at a plate of Blashu drops and sipped on what smelled like smoked coffee.

Suzu began to listen in. They shared a story of Nia as a child, something about running around naked and covered in flour. Each of them contributed to the story as if they would never tire of sharing it, taking turns finishing each other's sentences, handicapped from all the laughing. Suzu pulled her knees into her chest and leaned against the railing. She imagined her parents

SILO : MEDIUM | S05
KORA : N. CHIGOU
SMALL VEHICLE STORAGE

down there with them, sitting across the table, just out of sight.

o o o

In the morning Suzu found the house completely still, the only movement coming from dust dancing in a sunbeam. As quickly as she could, Suzu got dressed and ran outside. She burst through the silo door looking for Nia but found only more silence. The entire farm suddenly felt abandoned and she hated it.

"Look out," a voice echoed from the rafters. Suzu then saw Nia's inverted, hanging body elegantly flip down to the ground. Suzu stood in amazement as Nia stood up, holding a coffee flask.

"You were drinking coffee upside down? That's amazing," Suzu exclaimed.

Nia stepped forward, wiping a little spilled coffee off her chin. "I was thinking that too, but now I'm feeling it's actually kind of a dumb idea."

The two then simultaneously let out a yawn that ended with Nia laughing. "It looks like you didn't get much sleep, either."

Suzu shook her head to which Nia began tapping her flask. "Hmm, maybe we should hold off on what I had planned for today."

"No, it's okay," Suzu brightened up. "What is it?"

Nia took a sip and cleared her throat. "Alright, today you're going to choose how much you trust and how much you fear."

Suzu responded with the voice of a field mouse. "Okay."

"I want you to climb up the bales, all the way up to the rafter . . ." Nia pointed up rather high and swept her finger across the beam, ". . . and walk across."

Suzu seemed to shrink down, the idea leaving her speechless.

Nia bent down, offering Suzu her warm hands. "Suzu, I want to ask you something and I want you to think about the answer before you give it to me."

Suzu again nodded, preparing herself for the crucial inquiry.

"Do you trust me?"

Suzu began to nod. Nia gently put her hand on the girl's face to stop her. "Do you think I would ever do something to harm you or let you really get hurt if I could stop it from happening?"

Suzu found Nia's strength intimidating. The task seemed dangerous, but Suzu concluded that Nia's faith had proven itself stronger than her own fear. "I trust you."

"And you've walked on wood before, right?"

"Uhm, Of course."

"Well," Nia replied, "then you should be fine."

Suzu turned and sized up the path before her. She walked up to the bales and carefully began to climb the steep, grassy stairs. Upon reaching the top, her confidence immediately shrunk to the size of a Tulú seed.

"Why is this so much higher up here?" Suzu asked, lowering to her hands and knees.

"It's not. It's just fear pushing into your senses."

"But what if I fall?" Suzu said, digging the tips of her fingers into the wood.

"I'll catch you."

"But it's so high!" Suzu felt sick.

"If you don't trust me, then you shouldn't go. If you do really trust me, then you have nothing to fear."

Suzu grunted, feeling like Nia should be sharing in some of the panic. A few seconds went by and Suzu finally accepted her two simple choices: go back or move forward.

With shaking arms, she shifted her weight back, slowly managing to stand halfway up. Feeling the beam solidly at the bottom of her feet, she started to let her hands go. Gravity seemed to double, and she could feel it pulling her down to that dusty, hard floor.

She slid one foot forward, tossing dust down onto Nia, whose eyes looked like two tiny green pinheads. Suzu checked her balance, then slid her back foot up. The beam started to feel familiar below her feet; two more small steps and she felt a rhythm develop. Nia took another step forward, matching Suzu's speed. "See, it's just like walking on the ground in a straight line."

A very narrow line, Suzu thought to herself while looking across the beam. Feeling an urge for the entire thing to be over, she picked up the pace. One step, good. Next, still going. On the next step, her foot then caught a splinter. She quickly put it down to balance, but nothing was there.

Suzu screamed as she fell, reaching out and hitting the beam with her elbows. She clawed into the old wood as her feet dangled in the floating dust.

"Nia!"

Out of Suzu's sight, Nia quickly but calmly stepped back. "It's okay, Suzu. You can let go."

"Letting go is not okay!" Suzu exclaimed, confused why anyone would suggest otherwise. Her breathing pulsed, and she could feel the pressure on her fingernails, gravity unrelentingly pulling her down. "Help me, Nia!"

"I will, Suzu, but I can't catch you unless you let go," Nia said firmly.

"No, you have to come up here and pull me up." Suzu's desperate voice shot out from her knotted stomach.

"If I climb up, you could fall without me here to catch you."

Suzu hated everything. "I don't want to fall!"

"Suzu, you decided to trust me when you climbed up to the beam. Don't let your fear overtake your faith."

Despite the panic, Nia's voice somehow comforted Suzu through sore muscles and fright. As fatigue began to take over, the girl decided to simply release. A terrifying instant then turned into a tranquil freefall. Her burning muscles eased as cool air rushed over her warm skin. Finally, she felt the soft impact of Nia's cradling arms.

Suzu kept still as Nia looked down at the girl now tucked into her embrace. "How cute we must look right now."

Suzu started to cry. Nia compassionately smiled, watching the tension empty out and stream down the girl's face.

"I really hope Gozen doesn't walk in right now. We'd never hear the end of it," Nia said before letting Suzu down. The student then wiped her face off with her sleeve. "Sorry."

"It's nothing to be sorry for. You fought your fear. You were brave."

Suzu let out a pathetic laugh. "So I guess these are tears of bravery?"

Nia leaned in. "If you don't feel any fear, if it's just easy, then you're not really being brave."

An odd hum then came in from the outside. It seemed to be

approaching from a distance, a mechanical but strangely elegant noise, unlike that of any of the machines they had on the farm. As Nia started to walk towards the door, Suzu tugged on her sleeve.

"Is that Gozen?"

Nia focused in. "No, I don't think so."

She continued towards the door as Suzu cautiously followed a few paces back. Nia opened the door and the sound shot past them. Coming up the road, they saw a spray of dirt being kicked up behind a small vehicle. It moved faster than anything she had seen before, and within seconds it quickly slid to a stop by the house.

A glare of sunlight came off of its polished surface and cut through the cloud of dust. As it settled, a sleek little car began to appear that looked as expensive as it was fast. The engine shut off and a young man got out of the car, his light hair nearly glowing in the sun. He stood with posture that only a privileged education and perfectly tailored clothes could generate.

"Who is it?" Suzu asked.

"I think it's our rich boy arriving for his simple living vacation."

"Oh, okay," Suzu nodded. "Wait, what?"

"I think it's just this guy from Primichi whose father owns some huge company." Nia explained.

"Should we go meet him?" Suzu asked simply.

"Let's not. Maybe he'll just go away."

Confused with the unusually cold reaction Nia had to this stranger, Suzu looked out at the young man examining his shiny vehicle. "His car is pretty fast though, huh?"

Nia folded her arms. "Well, I suppose we all compensate in our own way."

"Right," Suzu agreed. "Wait, what?"

∘ ∘ ∘

Upstairs in the house, a focused Suzu held her ear to the wall. The new arrival spoke with Kojo in the hallway, something about farm machinery. Only the second day after the young man's arrival, her eavesdropping had already turned into a hobby.

While continuing to eavesdrop, Suzu looked out the window to admire the young man's fascinating car. It had a meticulously streamlined design, an impressive blend of speed and strength. A thin roof hung over the seats that seamlessly flowed with the body; strange, as she remembered no roof when he first drove in. The car looked like something her father would have stopped to gawk at on the street.

Suzu then heard the car owner's voice drift outside. She watched him walk out to the car and open the trunk, just as Nia stepped into her room carrying coffee and two blashu butter rolls. Suzu fixated on the sugary surprise.

"Gimmie!"

Nia quickly offered her the one not in her mouth. "You're already up? What is this all about?"

"I'm spying," Suzu announced, feeling rather impressive.

"Spying? On Mr. Fancy Slacks?"

"Yeah, he's getting something out of his fancy car."

Nia reached out to Suzu. "Well, let's hurry up so we can miss him while he's busy playing with his fancy graduation present."

"How do you know he got it for his graduation?" Suzu looked back out the window.

"Just get your shoes on. Snap snap, little lady."

Suzu quickly slipped on her athletic shoes, tightened them with the tensioner dial, and followed Nia downstairs. As they got to the bottom of the steps, the young visitor walked in with a wire-type machine in his arms. They all stopped where they were, quickly and mutually looking each other up and down.

"Greetings. I am Jin Aya, I originate form the city of Primichi. You must be the daughter I've been briefed on," Jin assumed, standing tall in his tailored vest and white scarf.

"I don't know. I suppose that's possible," Nia responded with forced indifference.

"Do you have any siblings?"

Nia diverted her eyes to the floor. "No, I don't."

"Well, it must be you then that your mother was so eager for me to meet. Lady Nia, correct?"

"Yes. Now I hate to cut this short, but we have work to do."

Nia took a step forward but Jin didn't budge, instead turning his attention towards the shorter half of the pair. "And what would your name be, if I may have the privilege of asking?"

Jin shifted the heavy wire-type to his left hand then offered his right. Suzu lifted her chin. "My name is Suzu." She shook his hand, noticing how unusually strong he seemed for a guy wearing a decorative scarf.

"Suzu, it is an absolute pleasure to make your acquaintance," Jin followed up.

"Well then, we have some important business to get to, so if you don't mind . . ." Nia interjected.

"Why are you here?" Suzu asked. Nia began to tap her foot.

"Well, since you asked, I'll be here for a brief period in order to help evaluate some of Lord Kojo's farm equipment and observe its execution in a practical field environment."

Nia broke her intense nonchalance as she finally processed Jin's introduction. "Aya, as in the Aya Corporation?"

Jin stood erect and cleared his voice. "Yes, that Aya. I am an heir and currently our newest representative in Chigou, as it turns out."

"How fortunate for us. Come, on Suzu; time to be productive." As Nia pulled Suzu towards the door, Jin offered a handsome smile as he gracefully allowed them to pass. Suzu kept her gaze on the intriguing young man as Nia kept her eyes in the opposite direction.

"He stands really straight," Suzu observed.

"Mm-hm," Nia quickly added, leading them a few more snappy steps towards a Quick Wagon.

"He's pretty handsome, too, don't you . . ."

"Didn't notice," Nia responded briskly.

"Hmm. His hair is really light, and so are his eyes. Blue, but like snow or something. And why does he wear such nice clothes on the farm?"

"It's not the least bit important. But what is important is that we get a good haul today. We've been slacking a bit this week. Now get your curious britches into the wagon," Nia commanded as they both got into the utility vehicle. "And don't talk to that boy."

10
UNDERTOW

Despite her warnings, Nia noticed Suzu developing an ever-increasing curiosity about the visiting northerner. She attempted to stay away from Jin, a task that proved rather simple as he generally remained busy with Kojo and the farm equipment. Regardless, Nia kept an eye on the stranger whose presence felt more suspicious with each passing day.

She continued mentoring Suzu, going between Soultai training and harvesting crops. Nia quickly became impressed with the young girl's commitment and ability. She imagined that it wouldn't be much longer before Suzu absorbed most of any instruction she had to give. Suzu already appeared almost unrelated to the fragile creature that first came to the farm under Gozen's wing.

Her large friend had continued to investigate suspicious closings in the city but kept most details to himself. Occasionally, Gozen indulged Nia's curiosity into such matters and took her into the city, but keeping the slightest potential of danger at arm's length. The number of trips increased with Suzu's growing independence, but each time Nia reminded the curious girl to keep away from the rich boy with the suspiciously white teeth.

To Clora and Kojo, Nia's urban excursions became a point of worry. Besides appreciating their only daughter's place at Kora farm, Kojo feared losing the best worker to some civil ambition. Clora's concerns focused on the city she never quite trusted. Only the guardianship of Gozen convinced them to allow such trips to take place at all.

o o o

Early one morning, Gozen received a wire from an Enforcer buddy describing the sudden death of an industrial worker. Such exchanges of information remained the only ties Gozen kept with his former profession. The deceased remained unidentified, but the company name led Gozen to a sickening conclusion.

While he walked out of the house towards Neko, Nia spotted Gozen wearing the jacket he always wore into the city; she immediately ran towards him. Inside the cabin, Gozen sat meditating over the dark complexity of the situation. Finally reaching down to start Neko, he saw a flushed Nia open the door, vainly attempting to mask her excitement.

"Hey, you going into the city?"

"Uhm . . ."

"You . . . doing any investigating?" Nia playfully smirked.

"Well . . ."

"I'll come along and keep you company. You want some company?"

"Nia, you keep asking me questions, but I haven't answered the first one yet."

"Right." Nia dropped her shoulders, attempting patience. "So, you mind if I go?"

Gozen pointed into the cab. "What if I was cleaning my gun? You should be more careful about sneaking up on me."

Nia's eyes widened. "Gun? Ooh, this sounds really interesting now."

No matter the circumstances, Gozen could never smile at the combined thought of Nia and a gun. "You wouldn't say that if you ever had to actually shoot someone."

Nia's energy instantly dropped. Although a spunky girl, she had enough tact to know when to not push Gozen. "Sorry. I really would like to go, though. I won't be pushy, I promise."

Gozen squinted one eye. "You, not be pushy?"

"Oh, stop it. I'm not that bad."

He looked back to the house. "You know, your parents aren't exactly thrilled at the idea of you going into the industrial district with me."

"Gozen, they can either ease into acceptance of me growing up or they can let it smack them in the face. Personally, I think I'm doing them a favor by going into the city with an experienced bodyguard like you."

Nia saw Gozen slip into another one of his melancholy withdrawals, staring blankly out the window.

"Are you okay?" she quietly asked.

Exhaling out heavy thoughts, Gozen managed a smile, accepting the sincere offer of companionship. "Get in, pushy."

o o o

By the time they got to Doulan, Nia had effectively worn down Gozen's resistance to speak of Etecid's suspicious buyout. He thought about the matter far more than he discussed it, so when he finally opened up, the conversation became a flood of theories and corroborating factors.

"I just don't understand why it's so suspicious that this company got bought out," Nia explained.

"It takes no small effort to hide information about buying companies this large."

"Well, maybe this new company just likes to keep things quiet . . . like, out of humility."

Gozen laughed. "That would be a first. Typically when a company doesn't want people to know their business, it's not out of modesty. Actually, it's never out of modesty." Gozen leaned over to Nia. "Which is why I'm so concerned to find out what that reason is."

Neko pulled into the back loading area of Etecid, formally Karoburn. Nia looked out the window. "So, what are you doing here exactly?"

"Actually, this particular trip has to do with a more personal matter," Gozen sighed, shutting off the engine as it started to rain. "But I don't want you to get out of Neko."

"I promised you wouldn't regret bringing me. I'll stay put," Nia said with a smile.

Gozen then saw a young man standing like a ghost with a clipboard. Static amongst the bustling dock workers, Darou looked as if the rain had washed the life right off his face. Gozen groaned, fearing what the image meant.

"Stay here," Gozen instructed before shutting the door behind him.

"You already said that," Nia quietly said to the empty cabin.

Gozen quickly mulled over what to say to the only man not noticing his large body march across the dock. When he finally reached him, the young man still kept his head down.

"Hey Darou, get a promotion?" Gozen casually spoke.

Darou finally looked up from the supervisor clipboard Gozen had never seen him carry before. The rain ran down around his lifeless eyes.

Preparing himself, Gozen leaned in with a softer voice. "Hey, Darou, where is your father?"

Darou looked around and then back up to Gozen. He spoke with an eerie calmness matching his placid look. "He got fired with a bunch of other guys. He got fired and they gave me his job."

Gozen continued to gently push into the conversation. "When was that? Just the other day?"

As if on a delay, Darou eventually continued. "Yeah, he went home and drank a lot." Darou gazed around the bay again. He hated the buildup to what Gozen wanted to know.

"Is he there now? Is your father back at the apartment?"

Darou looked down, clutching his clipboard. "No, he's dead. He fell off the balcony while he was drunk. Maybe he jumped, whatever difference that would make."

Gozen's heart sank as his mournful assumptions were validated. Every sentiment he thought to offer seemed as desperate and frail as the young man before him. Still, he felt a need to offer something. "I'm really sorry, Darou."

Darou pushed his emotions back. "I'm fine."

Gozen knew the young man needed something more than pleasantries. He wanted to offer some kind of hope and stood there quietly, desperately praying for such a thing to reveal itself. Darou began to shift about, awkward in his own skin. "What? I'm fine."

At the last proclamation, Gozen could see Darou unknowingly tuck in his trembling lower lip. Gozen leaned in and put his hand on the young man's shoulder. "Either way."

Gozen looked up into the rain towards the offices of Etecid. The tragic reality of Delrico's premonition settled in. He thought of how a place that used to seem so reliable suddenly felt like a trap ready to drop on its inhabitants. In a flash, Gozen concluded that leaving the boy there was unacceptable.

"Hey, Darou, how'd you like to take a break? Work out in the open air for a little bit?" Gozen asked with light enthusiasm.

"What do you mean?" Darou's face became blank.

"Well, if you wanted to take a little break from the city, we can always use a capable guy like you up at Kora. I mean, if you need to take care of things at home, I don't want to pressure you into anything, but . . ." Gozen left the question open.

Darou thought for a brief moment. "My dad stopped paying rent. I can't live there anymore."

"Yeah," Gozen nodded. "Well, it's really nice up at the farm." Seeing the proposal start to sink into Darou's mind, he continued. "Plus the food is great. I can take you today. Find out for yourself."

Quietly, the young man mustered up, "Yeah, sure. Whatever."

Gozen tried to temper his relief. "Okay, okay. Well, I'll go up and take care of the employment transfer. You can just . . . hang out here."

In the cab, Nia sat with her knees tucked into her chest wondering why Gozen scampered away so quickly. Her attention then landed back on the young man standing alone. She had never seen him before, but he possessed a familiar kind of lost look. She saw it a lot from guys who worked at the farm, guys who needed a break from the city.

She noticed Darou lacked the kind of bulk of most guys in the industrial district. His face had a particularly rugged charm to it, one surprisingly well kept for a dock boy. She wondered what Gozen thought of him.

Upstairs, after sitting for twenty minutes in a small waiting room, Gozen finally got called to the Employee Transitioning desk. A small, older woman sat behind it, wearing a rather petite pair of thick glasses. "And how may I help you?"

"I'm going to have Darou Batet come work for me up at Kora Farm, under the Corporate Partnership Exchange plan," Gozen plainly stated.

"Do you have your Employer ID?" the sweet voice asked.

"Gozen reached into a coat pocket.

"Looking at you, this farm must require some rather heavy lifting." Her left eye winked behind the thick glass.

Gozen coughed. "Uhm, occasionally." He handed her the ID card as she received it with a grin. "I'll be right back."

As she left to another room, Gozen scanned the entire perimeter. He processed what kind of information he might be able to get on the Etecid buyout. Across the hall, Gozen's wandering eyes then paused on a sign reading *Accounting Records*.

With the office quiet, Gozen casually proceeded across the floor, pretending to admire the undecorated walls. He then leaned his ear near the Accounting Records door; nothing. Without hesitation, he swung open the door, ready with the answer of a lost visitor looking for a restroom.

Discovering no personnel, Gozen shut the door. The windowless room held stacks of cabinets containing more files than he cared to estimate. He walked up to the first one on the left, displaying a date from five years back. The next one moved forward chronologically.

Voices then appeared outside the door along with the sound of narrow-heeled shoes, quickly getting louder. He searched for a place to hide his massive size, but none came close. The sound of the crowd made it to right outside the door. Gozen held his breath. The tapping of heels then faded down the hall.

Quickly, he walked to the last cabinet and pulled the drawer. Locked. Gozen reached into his jacket and pulled out an electric Lock Gun he kept around from previous employment. From the handle of the Lock Gun, he pulled out a Tension Wrench, inserted the tip carefully into the keyhole, and turned it slightly. He then inserted the Lock Gun blade above the wrench.

Anticipating the gadget's loud action, he stood perfectly still and listened again for personnel. Nothing. He then triggered the Lock Gun, and a high-pitched buzz rang through the office. The pins pushed up, and the wrench spun the cylinder. Smoothly, he slipped out the lock tools and pocketed them.

Gozen started flipping through files, working towards the buyout date. Knowing the older lady could be back any second, he worked quickly. Labels flashed through his fingers as he looked for something to stand out. The sound of more footsteps emerged from down the hall. His fingers moved faster and then suddenly stopped.

Between his fingers, a label read "Full Corporate Acquisition." Outside the door, the approaching footsteps stopped. Driven completely by instinct, Gozen pulled the file and shut the drawer, the sound matching up perfectly with the opening click of the door.

A middle-aged woman walked in, her eyes immediately locking onto Gozen. He lifted his right arm as if overcome with surprise, his left arm hidden behind his back. The woman examined the room with inquisitive eyes, her posture tense and upright underneath a perfectly tailored jacket and pencil skirt.

"What are you doing?" the woman's voice directly requested.

Gozen always wished his mind to be as fast as his hands. "Uhm . . . being put on the spot."

"Who are you? The data in this room is privileged information." The woman took a step further into the room.

Gozen charmingly rubbed his head to distract from the movement of his other hand. "I'm acquiring a current employee of yours. I wasn't sure if there was anything in here I needed to do."

The woman's eyes went directly towards the file cabinet next to Gozen, the door of which did not manage to shut all the way. "Anything you need to know in regards to that would be explained to you across the way."

Gozen humbly responded, "I figured . . . I was just being cautious . . ."

Her eyes then focused along with her voice. "Why were you looking in that cabinet?"

"I wasn't, really. It was open."

"Those are always locked."

"Yes, I was surprised myself," Gozen coughed softly. "What's in these, anyways?"

Gozen's fingers fidgeted. The woman furrowed her brow. "Reading the information in those files is a criminal offense. I could call security."

Although Gozen had developed a keen ability to control his emotions, threats tended to trigger a particular impulse. He calmed his posture and began to walk towards the woman. His eyes drilled straight into her gaze, which started to shift nervously. Gozen stopped directly in front of her. Her tall-heeled shoes did little against his towering proportions.

He spoke directly. "And exactly what is it that you think security would be able to do?"

The stunned woman searched for an answer, having no set reaction for such a statement. Gozen proceeded. "Because if they decided to lock me away down in the dungeon, how would I be able to take you out to dinner?"

Her eyes widened a little more. "What do you mean?"

"When I make my scheduled trip next week, I'm going to wait around until you get off work and then take you out to dinner. That is, assuming I'm not locked up downstairs, with you up here alone, both of us dying of hunger."

The woman evaded his gaze while rubbing her suddenly warm neck. "Uhm, I'm not sure. I don't even know when you're scheduled to be here next week."

"I'll return the favor and sneak up on you," Gozen said as he gently embraced her left hand and subtly bowed. He then slipped into the hallway, brushing up against her arm just as the older woman appeared across the way. He casually walked towards her as directly as he could. "Ah, yes. Thank you very much, Lady."

The older woman held the folder close to her chest. "Now, before I send him off with you, I think there are a few things you should know."

"Okay," Gozen grinned as he glanced behind him. The startled woman, clearly staring, looked down and disappeared into the office.

"Now, I would like to consider myself to be someone that gives anyone a fair chance, especially a young person who has gone through . . . difficulties."

"Of course," Gozen politely responded.

"Well, Darou, you see, had some trouble with the law before he started working here . . . and while he was working here."

Although the information did not surprise Gozen, it certainly seemed pertinent considering where he planned on taking the young man very soon. "Nothing serious, I hope."

"No, no. Well, I think every law should be respected. They are all rather serious, if you know what I mean?"

"Yes, of course." Gozen started to reach for Darou's file.

"I'm sure with the proper guidance and attention he could develop into a decent man who didn't feel the need to steal or take part in any nasty business like that."

"You make a very good point." Gozen thought of the other woman looking in the drawer he left open, noticing the missing file, which hid down the back of his pants. It was time to hurry.

"I just thought it was the right thing for me to tell you that," the woman said. "Now, you have everything you need in this file . . ."

Gozen grabbed the file. "And I thank you for aiding me so quickly, as I am late to my next engagement."

"Well . . ."

"Good day to you, my Lady. You are a gift," Gozen said, his feet already carrying him away.

Down below, Nia sat snugly in the cabin of Neko, discretely watching Darou. In the distance she saw Gozen walk out of an employee door with an awkwardly quick pace. He headed straight for Darou, looking back over his shoulder three times along the way.

"Got your paperwork. You're all set."

Darou looked up, still in a bit of a haze. "Yeah?"

Gozen continued to glance around the bay. "So look, I don't know if you need to take care of anything, but you are free to join us back to the farm right now, if you'd like."

Darou followed Gozen's finger towards the cab of Neko. He spotted Nia, who quickly diverted her eyes to the floor of the truck, very casually.

"Well?" Gozen asked, tapping his foot with the energy of four smoked coffees.

"Yeah, let's go," Darou answered, looking at Nia.

Gozen gave the young man a thoughtful shove towards the

passenger door. Darou opened it up as Nia stayed put. Gozen coughed. "You gonna make him sit in the trailer?"

"Oh, sorry." She quickly scooted over, and Darou climbed up into the cab, their shoulders pressing up against one another. She tried hard to not look directly at the new passenger, whose wet hair dripped on her shoulder, and smelled like a fuel plant. The young man reached for the door, but Gozen hit the accelerator, shutting the door for him.

After a minute of hearing Gozen's heavy breathing, Nia finally spoke up. "Paperwork tends to put you to sleep. What happened up there?"

Gozen looked like a mischievous child as he drove. "I may or may not have threatened a female accountant on the thirty-second floor."

"Gozen!" Nia accosted with a grin. "What do you mean 'may not'?"

"It may or may not have ended with me asking her out to dinner."

"What?" Nia was shocked.

"Nice." Darou added, nodding his head by the window.

"Regardless, the employment transfer went through, and I may have discovered some other information as well." Gozen raised his eyebrow towards Nia, who reciprocated with a nod. A confused Darou looked out the window.

They continued north towards the farm as the sun went down. Nia tilted her head halfway around, noticing Darou tap his fingers as if to some imagined music in his head.

"My name is Nia, by the way," she said, looking out of the corner of her eye.

"Darou," the young man calmly responded, leaning his head toward Nia. They both settled into their seats as Darou's rain-chilled body finally began to warm up. Doulan began to appear in the distance, and Gozen's mind drifted to its usual thought.

When they arrived at Kora, Clora and Kojo came out with Suzu, who had anxiously awaited their return. Gozen briefly introduced Darou to the farm owners, who warmly welcomed him. Nia then took Darou aside and ensured him that he would love his time there.

It had become rather apparent to her elders that Nia's heart felt for burdened souls. They considered it a wonderful trait full of hope and selfless ambition. As soon as they noticed that ambition attach itself to a troubled young man from the streets with well-defined cheekbones, however, they questioned if it was an absolute virtue. Darou would not sleep in the same house as Nia.

An hour later, Darou settled into his new quarters. Suzu lay in her bed as Nia eagerly awaited Gozen's detailed debriefing back in her room.

"So, did you find out the name of that company?" Nia asked.

"I'm not so sure I should really be bringing you into all of this." Gozen pondered, now with time to clearly think.

Nia crossed her arms. "Gozen, you wouldn't be sitting in my room if you didn't want to talk about it."

Gozen groaned. "Alright, the company's new name is Etecid, but it seems to have come out of nowhere. Oddly, there is no official buyer listed."

"But someone has to own it, right?" Nia curiously asked.

"There was one mention of an underwriter. It's not a registered industrial entity . . . I suppose that could have been the outright buyer, but that's strange. It's like some rich old lady just decided to buy a fuel-processing plant for an after-tea activity."

Nia asked, "So what was the name?"

"Etilé . . . ever heard it before?"

They both shrugged their shoulders, wading in a dead end. Nia then conjured up more curiosity. "So if you've never heard of them, why are you so concerned about them?"

"It's because I've never heard of them," Gozen replied. "You can't buy a company like Karoburn, well, Etecid now, unless you have some seriously deep pockets. And you can't buy it in one day with almost no one noticing unless you have some seriously powerful influence. They are most definitely hiding something."

Nia churned the cogs in her head. "Maybe they wanted to stay quiet, knowing they were going to fire all of those people, like Darou's father."

"That is possible."

Nia sat up tall. "Because if a man killed himself and stranded his son because of them, I think they need to be exposed. We could expose them."

Gozen finally pulled out of the sleuthing mindset. "Whoa there, Lady wild cat. Let's not rush into a war with some mega-corporation."

"Yeah, I know. It's just that we bring in guys like Darou to the farm, which is great, but how much better would it be if they never ended up with those problems that needed fixed to begin with?" Nia said with her hands as much as her mouth.

Gozen replied, "No, I agree, but it's a complex set of issues that typically don't have a simple answer."

"But that doesn't mean we just say it's too hard and don't bother even trying to do something about it."

Gozen softly glared at her, both of them well aware he most certainly had been doing something.

"I know, I know." Nia's anxious tone became nearly apologetic. "Maybe it's just that I feel like I'm not doing as much as I could, you know?" She fidgeted with her fingernails. "Maybe you can take me to a meeting at the Civil Conclave sometime."

Gozen stretched out his back. "I don't even go to those things. The talk to action ratio there is a bit much for me."

"Perfect, you can just drop me off."

"Alone?" Gozen laughed. "Kojo would love that."

"Hey, I can handle a meeting in a Civil building. Give me some credit, old man."

The pair shared a laugh as Nia noticed a small green eye poking around the corner. "Suzu?"

"Yeah?" Suzu spoke, her voice muffled through the wall.

"Do you want to come in?" Nia suggested.

"Okay." Suzu slid around the corner and sat on her allocated spot on the bed. Silence then developed as the older two sat unsure of how to transition the younger one into the conversation. Suzu helped them out.

"You can keep talking about that stuff. I know about it," Suzu confidently informed them.

"Oh, do you?" Nia spoke through a smile. "Well, like you might have heard, it's complicated stuff. I'm not sure we even know what we are talking about. Sorry if we were too loud."

Suzu felt an impulse to speak on things she had rarely spoken on before but constantly sat between at the kitchen table back home in Doulan. "I've been to a meeting in the Civil Conclave."

Nia's eyes widened and found Gozen's doing likewise. Her voice then slipped into a subtly condescending tone. "Really? Did your parents drag you there as punishment? I bet that must have been a bit dull."

"My mother got really upset. She and my dad wanted my dad's company to start using this ground-energy stuff that he was working on. Nobody listened to them, except this one young guy and his boss."

"Oh," Nia spoke with a surprised envy towards the girl. "Well, that's good someone liked his idea."

Suzu spoke again, her voice starting to develop a chill. "We had dinner with them. That's where I heard the word."

Nia asked. "What word?"

"Etilé. You were asking about it." Suzu informed them.

The older two looked at each other stupefied. Gozen then felt an urge to halt the conversation, but Nia jumped forward. "How do you know about them?"

Suzu quietly continued. "It was the last thing my parents ever talked about, with the man who made them eat the poisoned food."

Gozen dropped his shoulders, wishing the sudden rush of clarity had come a few seconds earlier. The room again went silent as the adults fumbled in their heads for something to say. Again, Suzu beat them to it.

"Maybe I could go to another meeting at the Civil building. Maybe we can find that guy. He walks and talks kinda normal, but his eyes make him look like he's dead."

The two sat at a loss, wincing at the sound of Suzu's sweet voice speaking such words. A shared urge developed to console the girl, but nothing came out. Gozen always had his suspicions of how Suzu's parents died and wondered what Suzu thought of it. He realized then that the girl had long since found the answer.

"All right, I think that's enough for tonight. My brain needs some rest," Gozen declared.

○ ○ ○

After a few unsure weeks, Darou had slowly begun to adapt to life on the farm. Nia found multiple excuses daily to cross paths with the newcomer, enticing a curious eye from her parents and student alike. Suzu enjoyed showing off her new Soultai skills to the cryptic young man, and since Jin remained on Nia's blacklist, Darou became the young girl's most consistent audience.

Harvesting began ahead of schedule, so Clora decided to finally have every person on the farm join in one large meal. Knowing newcomers didn't always get along, Clora hoped the comforting food would subdue any hostility. Kojo and Clora declared seats at the ends of the long dining table, putting themselves in a position to flank any friction that might develop. Nia made a point to distance herself and Darou away from Jin. Simply seeing the silver-eyed rich boy sit as if a gold rod ran up his back made her appetite wither a bit.

Gozen finished placing large dishes on the table as eyes and nostrils widened at the fragrant spread. Sitting down, he promptly gave honors. "We are thankful for this food, pulled by effort from the dirt, and thoughtfully prepared at the table. We are thankful for this time that we are united, coming from different places but joining together for this moment."

Nia looked over to Darou, his face filled with unease, his eyes scanning the table as if under interrogation. He looked more uncomfortable in that moment than he did even upon his first arrival to the farm. Nia's heart ached for any soul that felt family interaction to be difficult. She hoped, over time, she could help that to change.

Gozen watched the young pair as he continued. "And we are thankful for hope. A hope which takes what is behind us, no matter how dark, and turns it into a light that illuminates the path ahead. Goúbon." The rest of the table guests repeated the traditional blessing and grabbed their brass.

"Okay, don't be shy. I want this gone before it gets cold," Clora joyfully commanded to no objection.

Suzu had managed to grow far more comfortable since her first meal at the table—so much so that she instigated conversations about the Soultai maneuvers she swore to be on the verge of mastering. Nia kept glancing at Darou, who immediately got lost in his food, rarely looking up. Suzu noticed and decided to help the shy soul out.

She leaned over to him and whispered, "I didn't like eating with everyone at first either, but it's okay. You don't have to talk."

Surprised, Darou looked down to his side. "Thanks for the tip." He then offered the sincerest grin Suzu had yet to see on his face.

Since the beginning of the meal, Jin had taken a strong notice of Darou looking at the small, gold-lined bowl in the center of the table. One could assume the immaculately made centerpiece to be the most valuable thing in the house. The two of them most certainly did.

"Pardon Darou, you grew up in an urban neighborhood, right? What do you think that bowl would go for, street value?"

Darou and Nia both looked up to Jin, confused by the out-of-context question. Unaffected, Jin proceeded. "We have a pair up in Primichi, I remember what we paid for it, but I'm curious what something like that could go for in a street market. It's not something I feel I have a very good grasp on."

The moment felt bitterly awkward to Nia, who anxiously tried to come up with a clever transition. Darou attempted to divert the conversation by shrugging his shoulders and giving his attention back to his plate. Gozen then tactfully began talking about the crop cycle and pondering what fruit would become popular in Chigou over the next few months.

Nia scoffed at herself for being so hesitant in talking to Darou, especially after Suzu managed to do it with such ease. She took a quick drink of water.

"So, Darou, how do you like being on the farm so far? Do you find that you've gotten more sore or bored over time?" Other conversations hovered around, but all eyes slowly started to drift towards Nia and Darou.

"Well, I am a bit sore, but I think I'll manage. Can't very well complain about hard labor next to a young lady as tough as yourself. At least, not out loud," Darou said with his usual downplayed emphasis.

"I am pretty tough, but I think that's the one you need to worry about," Nia said, pointing to Suzu.

"I'll try to not make you look too bad, but I can't promise anything, "replied Suzu, her large grin full of food.

"Suzu, that's an awfully full mouth to be speaking with," Clora smiled.

Nia continued. "Since we've been having you do all this back-breaking busy work, is there anything you think you might like to try out? Any skill you have that we haven't taken advantage of yet?"

Darou's protective smugness heightened along with his insecurity. He shuffled in his seat. "Uhm, I'll just do whatever. I'm not too picky."

"Okay." Nia smiled before taking another bite.

As other conversations started back up, Jin decided his previous inquiry still warranted resolution. "Yes, Darou. I'm curious about your skill set. Being formally educated in noble elect institutions, I find coming here to be a valuable indoctrination to things hands-on and practical. Quite invigorating, actually."

Nia's eyes shifted to Jin, cold and ready to strike. Darou slowly turned. "What?" He tried to maintain composure, but Jin appeared to be taking him to a place that felt defenseless.

"Well, since you had more of a street education growing up— please correct me if I'm wrong—I'm curious if coming here helps by exposing you to long-term structural goals." Jin spoke with such controlled eloquence that the statement almost didn't feel patronizing.

"Jin." Nia's glare drilled into the back of Jin's skull, while trying to keep her protective intentions subtle.

"Yes, Lady Nia?"

Uninterested in a debate, Nia went back to eating. Jin continued his inquiry. "We all gain wisdom and skills that are channeled by the context of our own provenance. I'm simply trying to gain a comprehensive perspective from Darou's tutelage."

By now, the conversations around the table had stopped at Jin's fancy word circus. He channeled everyone's eyes toward Darou, who shifted through a backlog of vocabulary, unsuccessfully trying to decipher them. A painfully transparent smile covered a deep humiliation. Nia wanted to take her Blashu roll and shove it between Jin's shiny teeth.

"I . . . I don't know." It was all Darou could muster. The room went taut with silence.

"I can do a back flip now, real good," Suzu interjected with unintentional reprieve.

Nia managed a small and awkward laugh that squeaked past the knot in her stomach. Darou lowered his head and began to scoot food around on his plate, trying not to be rude, trying not to be anything.

○ ○ ○

In the morning, Nia took Suzu out to the edge of the Bollo orchard. Initially, they sat quietly as Nia slowly sipped her smoked coffee, the steam floating over her pinkish eyes.

"So, are we gonna use the Lansu today?" Suzu spoke with anxious enthusiasm.

Nia took in a deep breath of cool morning air before jumping up with a grunt. "Yes, but you need to learn a little about it before I let you touch it."

"I can't even touch it?"

"This is actually a very special Lansu called a DaiLansu," Nia sternly decreed. "If you don't use it correctly, then you have no business using it at all."

Suzu nodded with a hyperbolic seriousness that Nia forever found amusing. The teacher then pulled the Lansu behind her back with dramatic grace. The handle was of an especially dark alloy. Morning light revealed intricate detailing that rose up just enough to create a firm grip.

"You see that switch in the middle?" Nia asked.

Suzu nodded at the inlaid switch; Nia pressed it down. A bizarre and enchanting sound echoed out, quickly fading its high frequency tone into silence again.

"What does that do?"

"It calls Kola," Nia explained.

"What's a Kola?"

"You'll find out soon," Nia mysteriously suggested.

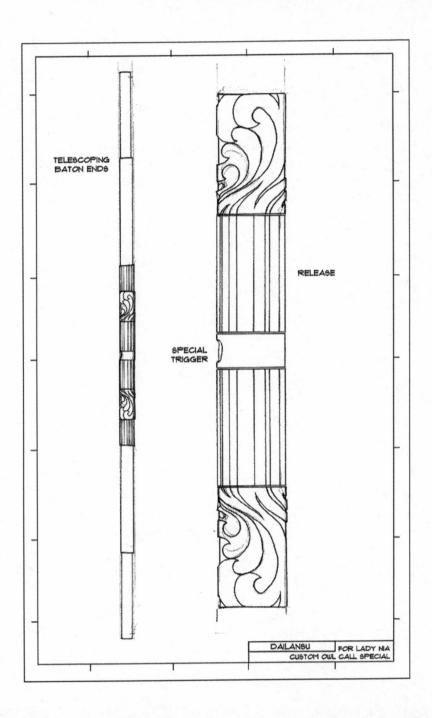

TELESCOPING
BATON ENDS

SPECIAL
TRIGGER

RELEASE

DAILANSU | FOR LADY NIA
CUSTOM OWL CALL SPECIAL

"Why is it so short?"

Nia smirked and took a step back, holding the DaiLansu out. "The staff has static sections that separate two tensioner handles. Twisting them allows the length of the staff to change. Twisting again locks them into place."

Suzu's attention began to sharpen. "How does that work?"

Nia slowly twisted the two handles in opposing directions. She held the staff out, letting Suzu absorb the dramatic pause. Then, with incredible speed, Nia twirled the staff in a blur just half a rotation. The weapon then rested again in her hands, but tripled in length.

"Whaaat?" Suzu's jaw plummeted.

"Spinning the staff allows the inertia of the inner rods to pull out, tightening the handles, and locking them into place. The idea is simple, but mastery is a far more complicated matter."

Suzu's eyes swelled. "Nia, are you a master?" She had never been more serious in her life.

Nia's smirk widened as she took an extra step back. She twisted the tensioners and gave the handle a fast shake back and forth. In a flash, the staff was again at its original length. The show then entered its main act.

Perfecting her posture, Nia swung the Lansu around as one end shot out and then stopped like a bullet tied to a chain. She spun around and began a routine of twirling, planting, and balancing that made the Lansu come alive.

Suzu was in a trance of acrobatics. Nia morphed and spun the DaiLansu around in ways that seemed impossible. Her perfect control made it hard for Suzu to imagine doing the same; it looked fantastical. Nia at one point lengthened the Lansu and actually vaulted on top of it. Standing on her hands, her feet seemed to be four meters in the air.

Nia then finished the routine by twirling the staff at half length above her head with incredible speed. She released one end, threw up a Bollo fruit, and hit it almost as far as the vehicle silo.

Suddenly, like a white harpoon, an owl came soaring out of the sky. As if magically orchestrated, it grabbed the fruit just before it hit the ground.

Suzu was in full disbelief. "What in the brass is that?"

"That's Kola," Nia explained. "It's my owl friend."

Mesmerized, Suzu watched as the white bird swooped around in a massive arch before flying towards them. It quickly seemed to grow in size to Suzu, who ducked as the bird landed on Nia's padded shoulder with one claw, immediately eating the fruit with the other. It had a large white body with black patches over each of its eyes. Its long talons looking properly dangerous.

"So that's why your jacket has one shoulder pad."

Nia winked.

"And where did you get a Kola?" Suzu demanded.

Nia laughed. "I didn't get him; he came here hurt awhile ago and I helped him get better. I think he's from the mountains, but now I can use the Lansu to call him, if he feels up to it. Kojo helped me put the Special in the handle, and another in a Toki. Somehow he knew what an owl call sounded like."

The bird then flew off as the ladies' hair blew back from the force of its wings. Suzu watched the owl fly away past the silo, then noticed something peculiar on top of it. Someone walked on their hands towards the middle of the roof, with posture better than most managed on their feet.

"Whoa, is that Jin? How did he get up there?" Suzu asked with wonder.

Nia folded her arms and dismissively shook her head. "Show off."

Jin continued his controlled ascent up the silo as the girls watched. Then off in the distance, they heard a slamming door. They redirected their attention and saw something going away from the house in a hurry; it was Darou.

Clora then appeared at the door and yelled, "Darou, stop!"

Darou continued to run, holding something in his arms. Nia and Suzu stood for a moment, trying to make sense of the scene unfolding in front of them. Suzu then tugged on Nia's sleeve. "Hey, look."

Pointing towards the silo, the girls saw Jin come out of his handstand and run to the edge of the roof. Smoothly, he slid off, tumbled into a perfect landing, then ran straight towards Darou without breaking momentum. Sensing the urgency, Nia put her hand on Suzu's back and started to jog towards them. "Come on."

"Darou, please stop!" Clora again pleaded, but Darou's attention focused ahead. Jin saw him head for the vehicles on the secondary drive loop, lined up against a freestanding wall. Darou bolted straight towards the cabin of the front truck.

Reacting, Jin cut a corner and headed for the back of the single wall. He launched, taking three full steps straight up the brick face before pulling himself to the top. Suzu gasped. Jin immediately ran along the top of the wall with perfect balance, matching Darou's direction.

Just as Darou arrived at the truck, Jin leaped over it like a predatory bird in a dive. As he landed, he grabbed Darou by the shoulders and spun him to the ground in one motion and Darou rolled. Initially struggling to get up, he managed to stand as he saw Jin walking right at him.

Darou's instincts flung a fist at Jin, who raised his arm, cushioning the blow as it landed on his cheek. Darou lunged with another strike, but Jin, with complete control, grabbed his wrist and flung him straight back to the ground. Darou screamed as Jin held him face down, his wrist high behind his back, locked in a painful submission hold.

All three ladies made it up to the dusty boys at the same time. Hearing Darou's painful cry, Nia jumped in. "Let him go, Jin!"

"Are you going to compose yourself, Darou?" Jin spoke with unnatural confidence. Darou simply moaned out again as agony shot through his arm.

"Jin, stop it!" Nia grabbed his arm.

Jin finally looked to Nia and saw her convincing determination. He gently let go of Darou's hand, which flopped to the ground. Rolling over, Darou continued to groan in pain as he braced his wrist. Nia bent down to him. "What is a matter with you, Jin?"

"Lady Clora was yelling for him to stop. He wasn't stopping," Jin suggested.

"So you tackle him and try to break his arm?" Nia could feel her face getting hot as she tried to examine Darou's arm; he pulled away.

168 o————————————————————————————VALLEY OF PROGRESS: CHIGOU

"I wasn't going to break his arm. I thought he might have stolen something."

Nia looked up to Jin with disdain. "You would think that."

Jin, confused by what he perceived as an attack, defended himself. "But Lady Clora was yelling, and Darou has a history of . . ."

"Just shut up. Just shut your shiny little, rich-boy speech hole."

"Nia!" Clora had grown to appreciate Nia's spark, but she did not approve of speaking to any houseguest in such a manner, even if they did have misguided virtues.

Nia kept her eyes drilled into Jin. "You coming down here for your simple-people research vacation is a complete insult, to me and everyone here. You don't understand us and you never will. Just . . . leave."

As Darou moaned again, Clora bent down to examine his arm. Jin stood silent. He understood the words Nia spoke but did not understand the fury behind them. Nia continued to burn a hole through his stoic veneer, while Suzu walked up to the small crowd. Suddenly, everyone saw her holding a gold-lined bowl, the awkward topic of dinner the evening before. The handle had broken off.

Cutting between Jin and Nia's silent standoff, Clora discretely acknowledged the evidence with her eyes. She then let out a compassionate sigh and continued to carefully tend to Darou's arm.

o o o

After a day of icing Darou's wrist, Nia watched from her window as Gozen drove him off of Kora property. Halfway to Chigou, the silence in the cabin eventually broke. Gozen did all the talking at first, explaining to Darou that he didn't seem quite ready to be in a place like Kora Farm. He then shared a one-way conversation about the challenging balance between forgiveness and pragmatic wisdom.

Once Darou managed to purge a revenge fantasy of Jin out of his mind, he finally shared a simple "I understand." The young man spent the rest of the drive doubting his purpose, or even existence. He felt like a burden being carted around, trying to find the place where he would cause the least trouble.

Their trip ended as Darou saw a sign slowly pass by his window, "The North Orphanage." Gozen turned off the engine and looked over to his young passenger, whose face appeared to drain of its final ounce of resolve. Tears began to well up in hopeless eyes and Darou appeared as though he could get sick at any second.

"What's wrong?" Gozen asked.

Darou half-turned his face towards the only man he still looked up to, now letting him go. "I'm supposed to become a man that can take care of himself. Maybe my dad thought I was, which is why . . ." Darou's voice trailed off into strained breaths. "But he was wrong, and now I have to go to an orphanage and be looked after like some damaged little kid."

Gozen quietly spoke. "That's not why I brought you here, Darou."

"I'm sorry I've wasted so much of your time. I know you have important things to deal with."

Gozen leaned over to the young man trying to disappear. "There are a lot of damaged kids here, Darou, and it's not easy for Lady Kyoumére to take care of them all. I help how I can, maybe not enough, I don't know. But I do know a lot of them in there are looking for someone, not another kid like them and not an old man like me. They could really use a big brother."

Darou looked up, confused over the suggestion, unsure of how such confidence could be put into someone like himself.

Gozen reinforced his suggestion. "I didn't bring you here to be looked after. I brought you here to be looked up to. If you allow it to happen, you might just surprise yourself."

o o o

With Darou no longer around to show off to, Suzu had begun to quietly train on her own. Nia took notice, something that initially stung her pride as the mentor. That insecurity grew as she caught Suzu occasionally asking Jin about his training, which clearly differed from the lady's practice of Soultai. Nia kept her distance, longing for the day Mr. Scarf would pack up his fancy little car and leave. But after days of brooding, Nia eventually decided to stop being so foolish and allow the girl to grow up.

Unknown to Nia, however, Suzu had developed a rather impressive ability to sneak about completely undetected. Her small size, mixed with a newly developed acrobatic strength, allowed the young lady to stick into corners like an invisible insect. This led to a habit of resting up in the rafters occasionally when Jin would go into a silo to train. If aware himself, Jin never let on.

One warm day while engaging in her spying routine, Suzu spotted an expensive-looking black car drive up; everyone assumed it to be a friend of Jin's. Through the skylight, she spotted the driver walk out and talk briefly with Clora, who pointed him over to her silo. Suzu struggled to make out the face of the approaching man through the dusty port window. Then, she heard him enter below.

From behind, the mystery guest appeared to be roughly Jin's age and almost as well dressed. They began to speak, but the words sounded muffled up in the rafters. Suzu walked along a beam towards the center when she kicked off a thick mass of dust. She froze as it fell towards the ground. Seeing it drift past them unnoticed, she carefully sat down and listened in.

"So you have some examples of these flash boilers that I can actually see?" the stranger asked.

"I fit one into that compact utility vehicle. The flash boiler's compact size and rapid energy response suits such a vehicle perfectly," Jin confidently responded.

"Is that the only one?"

"Well, my personal vehicle has one installed, but that's a special project."

"Special as in, I don't get to look inside?"

"No, you don't," Jin responded without hesitation.

The stranger looked around the silo. "Do I get to take a demonstration model back to the city?"

"Lord Kojo owns these vehicles, but I will demonstrate this model." Jin led the way to the Quick Wagon against the wall in the silo. "Pay attention to how fast it fires. You might miss it."

Suzu rose to her feet and silently followed across the beam. As the pair made it over to the vehicle, Jin reached to the starter and ignited the engine. A high-pitched hum rang out immediately.

Wanting a better look, the sly girl waited for an opening. As the two popped open the engine cover, Suzu slithered down a beam and behind a tractor.

She watched them as their voices got drowned out from the roaring engine. Looking through the dusty cabin glass, Suzu squinted, trying to make out the stranger's obscured face. Jin revved the engine; Suzu could feel the heating vibration on her skin.

She kept her attention focused towards the stranger as the hood finally came down, revealing his identity. Immediately her stomach tightened up and she couldn't breathe. The face pierced her mind with bitter familiarity, an image she had seen only once before. The black heat of fear engulfed her as her vision filled with a red haze. She thought of a dark room, coldly unfamiliar, with the last sounds of her parents' voices echoing between the walls.

° ° °

The girls sat alone, eating Bollo Tarts that Clora had just baked. Suzu kept quiet, her mind churning through a heavy fog. Nia, who would normally be quick to notice such a thing, mulled over her own concerns of the day's guest.

"So, did you see that guy who showed up today?"

Suzu's preoccupied mind took a moment to respond, despite being well ahead of the question. "That guy who met with Jin?"

"Yeah, so you saw him?"

Suzu thought of many ways to answer the question, but none of them made it out.

Nia continued, "I wonder if he's friends with Jin. They were in that silo a pretty long time . . . interesting."

The young lady started to notice a twinkle developing in Nia's eye. Her mouth curled up, playfully curious; Suzu started to feel ill.

"He dressed pretty smart, but not so desperate like Jin. Maybe it was a business thing." Nia pondered her own inquiry. "You didn't talk to him?"

Suzu looked down at her tart. It was beautifully prepared, but the idea of eating it made her stomach cringe. "No."

"Oh well." Nia whimsically drew circles on the table with her knife. "Wonder if he'll come back."

"I think I'm gonna go to bed," Suzu declared as a taste of bile built up in her mouth.

After a few seconds, Nia snapped out of her daydream. "Oh, okay. Uhm, well I'll see you in morning, huh?"

Suzu lowered her head and walked straight up the stairs. She then noticed a pain in her thumbs. Looking down, she saw dry blood on her fingernails from scratching her cuticles for the past hour. She didn't bother bandaging them.

○ ○ ○

The morning sun skimmed over the roof and shot a thin bright beam into Suzu's dark room. The chilly air felt aggressive, so she gripped the edge of her blanket and pulled it in tight against her cheeks. Her thoughts floated in a dark gray pool with nothing on the horizon.

A dark red glow rose from below the infinite gray, filling the room. The thick scarlet light began to suck up the air around her. She felt it pull her from something far away. It wanted to be known, daring her to dive in and pursue it. She saw a face deep down, motionless as if it had been there for a long time, waiting for her.

Behind closed eyes, Suzu sensed the light in the room shift. When she opened them, they watered from the small rush of cold air. A shadowy figure stood in her doorway. She tightly closed her eyes again, squeezing the tears out, hoping the image would wash away with them. Suzu slowly opened her eyes again. At the end of her room, Jin stood alone, quiet.

The blanket compressed under the grip of her small fingers. Suzu waited for Jin to do something; he stood there watching, not moving. Feeling the warm blanket get damp from her breath, she slid it down below her chin. Jin held something in his hand: a black rod, half-hidden away.

He then unfolded his arms and held the dark cylinder out just in front of him. A quick mechanical click echoed, and in an instant a long blade shot out from the object. Jin slowly walked towards the girl. Her body lay motionless as her eyes snared onto the sword. His steps quietly tapped and then he stopped, looking down with his silver eyes.

"What do you think?" Jin curiously spoke. "I just finished it. It's a prototype."

Suzu raised the blanket back up over her mouth. Her voice muffled through the quilt, "What?"

"It's a Masu, the traditional Maiashi sword I hinted at one day. I admire their design, their balance, but they are a bit large to be carrying around. I decided to design a retractable one. Quite successful, I think."

Suzu's shoulders relaxed and her eyes began to examine the sword. The round handle flattened slightly on two sides. Small black squares tiled the surface, set into dark matte steel. Albino brass anchored the segmented steel blade, its fittings so perfectly crafted they nearly disappeared. With another small click, the blade disappeared back into the handle. Suzu didn't move.

"Howdoesitdothat?" The muted sound leaked out, almost discernible.

"Pardon?" Jin asked.

Suzu lowered the blanket below her mouth and spoke more clearly. "How does it do that?"

"I anticipated such curiosity," Jin grinned. "It uses a double-spring vacuum mechanism with an inertia switch. The vacuum reengages the blade halves once they fully extract."

Suzu's haunted mind became distracted by the complex mechanical beauty before her.

"Do you think you could manage this without hurting yourself?" Jin asked.

Suzu traded looks between the razor-sharp weapon and Jin's steely eyes. "Or perhaps injuring another?" He followed up.

Suzu felt her pulse raise and wedged her toes into the bed. Jin allowed her to look at it, holding the blade out freely with an open hand. She slowly felt a pull towards the weapon, but the moment passed.

"Perhaps not yet." Jin gripped the Masu, lowered it, and started to walk away.

"Jin." Suzu's voice choked as it tried to speak loud and clear.

Jin stopped and turned around. "How may I assist?"

She took a long breath. "Who did you met with yesterday?"

Jin considered the inquiry before putting his hands behind his back. "An unannounced potential client."

Suzu wrestled with her thoughts. Questions buzzed in her skull, but she wondered if she should say anything more. Jin preemptively answered, "He wishes to do business with me. I was seeing if I wished to do business with him."

The blanket went down to Suzu's waist as she sat up. Jin saw the gears of her mind grinding hard. "Is he your friend?"

Jin simply shook his head.

Suzu spoke again. "Is he coming back?"

Squinting his eyes, Jin altered the tone of his voice. "You have seen him before, haven't you?"

Her eyes again went towards the Masu in his hand. She thought of how sharp its edge looked. She thought of Kits's face through the dusty silo air. "Do you know where he lives?"

Jin let out an amused breath. He again shot the blade out of the handle, reflecting a ray of amber light. "Aren't you something curious." He leaned on the sword like a cane. "I possess an address."

As he spun the point of the Masu on the floor, he noticed Suzu intently watching the twirling, razor-sharp edge. "What exactly do you intend to do with Kits Bodú's address if I were to supply it?"

Suzu retreated back to her bed, suddenly feeling an urge to shut up. Jin then raised the blade slowly towards her. He held it still until the lure became too much. Suzu finally looked back up to him.

Jin spoke with a chillingly calm voice. "Be careful little one." Suzu flinched as the blade retracted back into its handle. Jin walked out of the girl's room, his form disappearing into the shadow of the hallway.

Suzu felt her heart beat as if it was trying to escape. Her thoughts converged onto an idea, an idea that clenched her soul so hard it became a singular thought.

She got out of bed, walked over to her closet, and opened the heavy wooden door. Nearly all that she owned hung inside. Uniquely handmade by her mother, the lifeless memories suspended in the dark, some of which still fit. She reached in and pulled them all to the floor.

∘ ∘ ∘

Gozen worked in the secondary drive under the hood of Neko. Most of the farm prepped for the second Blashu harvest while Nia handed Gozen tools like a surgical nurse. With her other hand she fed Kola hot-berries out of a basket the bird held with its free talon.

"Did they schedule a date yet for the meeting about the Corporate Liability Edict?"

Gozen kept his head in the engine compartment. "At the Conclave? Yeah, finally. I take it you want to go."

Nia cracked a grin. "Absolutely."

"Well, you get to ask your parents."

"I'm not so sure they need to know," Nia smirked.

"I thought you wanted to grow up, Nia." Gozen continued to work.

Nia scrunched her face, popping a berry into Kola's mouth. "What's that supposed to mean?"

"I thought you didn't want to hide what you were growing up to be."

Nia stood for a moment, giving his suggestion a rather serious dose of consideration. "You know, you are absolutely right. I keep talking about it, but maybe I just need to grab Ma and Pa and have a good ol' fashion sit-down."

"Whatever gets you to stop yapping about it every other day." Gozen said, receiving a punch in the arm for his remark. A moment passed, and Nia admired Kola's elegant form against the afternoon sky.

"So, Gozen, you used to be an Enforcer, right?" Nia had easily pieced together as much over the years despite it being something that never got formally discussed.

After a minute, Gozen finally came out from the maze of wires and pipe. "Yeah, a long time ago." Gozen clearly had much more he didn't say. He went back into the maze. "Why do you ask?"

"I don't know." Nia's gaze floated around, sorting through her own sizable mound of thoughts and memories. "I've just been thinking about my parents a lot lately for some reason, my birth parents."

Hidden under the engine, Gozen paused with his corner

wrench. His stomach tightened, the precursor of a conversation he had held off for more years than he could recount.

Nia looked over to Kola, who traded glances between her and the last hot-berry in her hand. She threw it up in the air, and Kola gracefully soared up after it. "I know they died in that big fire in Roukot . . . a big industrial accident or something. I mean, I don't even know what I hope to find, or how I would even go about it. I was just wondering if maybe, since you used to do some kind of investigation stuff, or maybe you had some friends that were still Enforcers, maybe they could help me find out some information on them, something about who they were . . . I don't know. Maybe I'm just being silly."

Gozen's chest hurt keeping it all in; not stories of love and life, only of death and a man tragically devoted to his duty. He fought back tears, hidden and afraid.

"Gozen," Nia continued to softly muse, "you can tell me if I'm just being silly and sentimental. I don't want to ask too much."

Gozen slowly lifted up out of the suffocating engine compartment, calming his voice with a heavy breath. "You deserve to know anything you wish about your family. There's nothing silly about that." He struggled to take another calm breath, hiding from Nia's smiling face.

Her grin quickly vanished, however, as she saw Jin walking towards them. Nia's squinting eyes noticed the unassuming Masu in his hand. Jin immediately gave his focus to the engine block.

"Is it broken? I have a minute if you need some guidance."

Noticing Nia busy biting her tongue, Gozen decided to speak. "Nothing is broken, so unfortunately we have no need of this gracious minute you offer."

Nia covered her mouth as she coughed; Jin felt it sounded strangely like a laugh. "Modifications then? You can reroute the steam exhaust to recoup lost energy in most of these model B engines. I could show you how," Jin confidently offered.

Gozen replied, "Oh, I'm sure you could, Lord Jin, but actually I installed a flywheel for that very purpose. Just finishing it up."

Jin processed the idea and immediately started visualizing the details of what Gozen must have done and how he would have more efficiently put it together himself. "That's an interesting idea. Does it transfer mechanical or electrical energy?"

"Both." Gozen and Nia shared another mischievous cough. They then turned to the sound of the farmhouse door shutting. Suzu awkwardly walked towards them, holding something in her hands. Jin spoke to the pair. "I think the young lady may have something on her mind. Good day." Jin assumed his usually refined posture and walked away.

Looking back to Suzu, Gozen and Nia could now make out what the young lady carried. She had a travel trunk in each hand, both bursting with clothing. Suzu's white knuckles lowered them with a thud. Gozen and Nia looked at one another with mutual confusion.

"Taking a little holiday up to Primichi?" Nia playfully asked.

When Suzu didn't respond, Gozen quickly cut in. "Am I supposed to be taking you somewhere? For a very long time?"

Their shared amusement quickly faded upon realizing Suzu had no interest joining in. The young lady's face conveyed a heavy urgency. Her jaw trembled as if words tried to fight their way out of her closed mouth.

"What is it, Suzu? Why do you have your travelers packed?" Nia questioned.

Two quick breaths finally pried Suzu's mouth open. "I want to go back to the city."

The simple statement quickly germinated into a pile of questions. Searching for some insight, Nia looked to Gozen, who thought of the first time he saw the girl. "Suzu, do you mean you want to go home? Where you grew up?"

Suzu's eyes fluttered around, searching for something undeniable but nearly unmentionable. She continued to force the air through her clenched teeth. Nia walked up to her young student, but Suzu reached for her bags as if Nia was trying to take them from her.

"Hey, it's okay." Suzu avoided Nia's gaze. Gently, Nia put her hands onto the girl's travelers and slowly slid them to the side. Suzu reluctantly let the handles slip from her fingers.

"Why do you want to go into Chigou?" Nia's soft voice started to pull the girl's attention away from whatever held it captive. "Is it an emergency, or can we talk about it for a minute?"

Tears started to well up in the girl's eyes as she finally allowed them to look directly at her mentor. "I need to go back home."

Nia reached out and grabbed her hand gently. She looked over to Gozen, whose compassionate face had no clear answer. Nia spoke lightly, "Suzu, you can't really stay at your old house anymore."

The girl's voice started to settle. "I know."

"You've done really great here, Suzu. We all love having you here." An image flashed into Nia's mind, a scared and lost girl coming to the farm for the first time long ago. "You know you're part of the family here, right?"

A passing airship cast a shadow over the farm, followed by a quick chill. Suzu's vision filled with swirling images of the past and present, passing through an endless red fog. "This isn't my home. I need to go back to the city."

11
SHADOW

Light flickered in and out as Nia sat quietly on the ground, the white owl flying in circles overhead. She watched as the shadow passed over again and again. Jin saw her sitting there, gentle waves of grass flowing around her, as he walked from the tractor silo. It had been weeks since Suzu left Kora, and she had yet to come back for a visit.

In all the time he spent on the farm, Jin had never seen Nia so still. Even after a full day of Soultai training and harvesting, she would manage to joke of her fatigue. He theorized that her mood heavily derived from the absence of her student Suzu. Jin sensed a similar energy change with a number of members at the farm, but none as strong as from the young lady floating in the grass.

Passing under the ever-circling bird that strangely refused to leave the human girl, Jin entered the house. He found Clora quietly sitting in the reading room. An occasional occurrence, the activity seemed to be occupying more of her time as of late. She continued to rock in her chair, emitting long sighs. Jin quietly walked up to his room.

○ ○ ○

Nia eventually got up and made it over to the grain silo. The absence of Suzu left a vacuum, making the space dolefully quiet. She found herself missing the endless questions and youthful energy bouncing off the walls, and occasionally, the ground. It all felt bizarre to Nia, and she couldn't reconcile the girl who grew to love the farm with the one that suddenly wanted to run away.

Kola's voice then pierced through the silo's roof, which Nia took as a suggestion to quit moping. She jogged over to the locker where she kept her training batons. Quickly reaching for an old

Lansu, her attention abruptly diverted.

The spot where her DaiLansu typically hung presented nothing but dusty air. Nia looked around, thinking of where she possibly would have left something so precious to her. It then dawned on her; she would never leave it anywhere other than the one spot where the DaiLansu clearly didn't exist.

○ ○ ○

Feeling an unusual sense of hesitancy, Jin stood in the center of his room, one that had been organized with incredible purpose. A table strategically held paper, pens, and a mechanically floated right angle—a device of his own invention. A working drawing labeled C22 neatly sat in the middle of the desk, revealing ideas for a four-wheel-drive modification to his car. He remembered presenting the idea to his father, who seemed rather uninterested over the project. Jin then thought of sending his family a wire-type and wondered if they ever thought of doing the same.

At the back of his desk, Jin then noticed the smallest of details, but one that clearly stood out to his meticulous eye. His leather address book sat roughly ten degrees off square with the latch not completely fastened. Next to it, a small note pad neatly held a 0.5mm pencil, one that should have been in its holder.

Jin slid the notepad into the sunlight and noticed depressions from writing on the page above, already torn off. From what letter forms he could make out, a hypothesis over the irregularities quickly formed.

Jin flipped pages in the address book, stopping at the one marked with a large K. His finger slid down to the last entry titled *Kits - Etilé*. He then held the notepad next to the entry. His eyes focused in order to make out the forms indented into the paper: *2S11 Oraguine Ave, Apt 4269*. Someone had copied Kits's address.

Jin set down the book and reached for a wire-type machine. His index finger slid over to a seven-digit ID number next to Kits's name before sitting down. With rhythmic clicks, he began typing a message titled *Little Lady Visitor*.

○ ○ ○

As Gozen drove up in the cab, outside Neko's port window, Suzu saw the opening ceremony of Chigou's gleaming new point of pride. A crowd gathered on the giant wall holding back the mighty river. A few proud citizens held a garish sign reading, *Long Frost Dam Inauguration.* She imagined what her parents would have felt, seeing the celebration of what they had tried so earnestly to stop. She wondered how many of the screaming heads were happy that her parents had died. Suzu then imagined the shiny new dam crumbling apart.

Closer to the street, Suzu then noticed a man whose image felt undeniably familiar. He held a bullhorn and scowled at the celebrating crowd. She immediately thought of the name *Mouba.* Although she didn't recall ever speaking it, she clearly remembered it being yelled out between her parents.

The entire sight then vanished in the distance, and she leaned against the railing, her feet dangling off of the high shelf. They swayed back and forth along with the trailer as the passing road hummed from underneath. She looked down at a piece of paper that she had clenched for the past hour, containing but a single address. Her body then swayed as Neko came to a stop.

Effortlessly, Suzu dropped to the floor of the tall trailer, folding up the note and hiding it into her back pocket. She wore Hipans that had been handed down from Nia, knee-length pants that created a rather athletic profile. She then grabbed a matching jacket and leapt out of the makeshift apartment she had transmuted out of Gozen's mobile office. Up in Neko's cabin, she could see the bustling Varis Market, Chigou's second-largest food bazaar and a favorite of Sorans.

"I'll get the fruit ready," Suzu energetically offered.

"Keep a crate of the Mimi in the trailer. We're going to take that to the Tree House," Gozen commanded.

"Oh, lovely," Suzu smiled, looking over her favorite fruit. "Is this a bribe to help convince me to stay there?"

"If it works, then yes."

Suzu hopped to the back as Gozen triggered the motorized rear door. Light poured in and Suzu reached down, grabbing a handful of the small orange fruit. She shoved the tangy cluster into her mouth as Legou and Joushi approached the back of the trailer.

"All right, fellas, all but two of the Bollos like usual, and leave one of the Mimi crates too."

The two young men smirked. "At once, Lady Suzu."

Suzu replied, the sound of popping Mimi coming from her mouth. "And let's not take forever like last time."

Legou elbowed Joushi. "A few weeks with Gozen and she's already talking like a grumpy old man."

Suzu flung a Mimi at Legou's face. The young fellow quickly intercepted it out of the air with his mouth. Suzu playfully growled as Legou carried some produce towards the building, chewing extra loud.

Gozen came around to the back with a bill for the fruit order. Seeing Suzu march around like a dock boss added to the endless stream of confusion the young lady caused him. She had given no further insight about her demand to leave Kora, but Gozen grew in his suspicion that something dark pushed her forward.

His thoughts then swung over to Odetta, a full-bodied manager known as the jovial backbone to Varis Market. Holding a clipboard, she took a quick glance into the trailer. "Beautiful as always. How many?"

"The usual," Gozen replied, filling out the rest of the bill.

"One Mimi crate is for the Tree House, though, so don't take them all," Suzu said, heading back into the trailer.

"Yes, my Lady," Odetta replied, sharing a smile with Gozen. "You working for her now?"

○ ○ ○

Making good time at Varis Market, Gozen and Suzu managed to make it over to the Tree House with plenty of light out. Neko pulled up as Lucette came running towards them, her intricately braided hair bouncing around as she got to the door.

"Suzu!"

The door swung open, nearly hitting Lucette in the nose. Suzu made a charmingly apologetic face and then jumped down. Lucette noticed the suddenly not-so-young girl's dark hair pulled back with slightly angled bangs that looked properly sharp. The eyes, however, felt unfamiliar.

"Look at you, standing tall," Lucette said, before projecting louder. "So Gozen, are you working for her . . ."

"Save it," Gozen interjected. "Already heard that one today."

Lucette lowered her voice and leaned towards Suzu. "Well, it must be true, then."

Suzu looked over Lucette, who wore gray striped pants under a yellow skirt. A handmade scarf hung over her bright purple jacket. "You look sparkly as always."

Lucette bowed before leading her old friend by the hand away from the truck, their faces illuminated.

"Don't worry, ladies. I'll grab the crates," Gozen called out.

"We can always count on you, Lord Gozen," Lucette yelled back as the girls disappeared towards the river.

Lady Kyoumére then came out of the house with her usual grace and perfect Granai belt posture. She warmly watched the reunited young ladies gallop past the house. At the rear or the truck, Gozen met her with a glowing face of his own.

"Reunited friendship between two young ladies. Is there anything more charming?" Kyomére offered.

Gozen effortlessly held a large fruit crate. "I don't remember them having quite that much energy together. I suppose distance builds anticipation."

They watched the girls run to the large Laizóu Tree by the bank of the Long Frost River. Lady Kyoumére tucked a windblown lock of hair behind her ear. "Suzu seems to have come quite a ways, Lord Gozen. I didn't imagine her seeming so old so soon. I would say you're time up at Kora was rather well spent."

"And we certainly have you and your intuition to thank for that," Gozen spoke respectfully. "Nia really took to Suzu. It was like watching sisters almost right from the beginning."

The Lady let out a complex sigh. "And then, suddenly, Suzu wanted to leave."

"I keep telling Nia it's nothing to worry about, but I feel like I'm lying when I say it; why, I don't even know." They watched Suzu swinging upside down from a branch of the Laizóu Tree, slapping hands with Lucette. "I felt like all I wanted for that girl was for her to be able to stand up with a little hope and confidence, and then one day she just materialized."

"And now you don't feel about it the way you thought you would?" the Lady compassionately asked.

"She wants to stay with me in the truck now, cramped in that little space I barely fit in. It makes no sense."

"I don't know. Doesn't sound so awful," The Lady offered through a grin.

Trying not to blush, Gozen got back to the matter. "Or perhaps it's just an old man being foolish and missing the less mouthy version."

"Foolish, maybe, but lovely in a way. In all the time I've spent with the children of this home, I have come to understand this: that they are as beautiful as they are difficult, wanting nothing more than genuine love in their lives."

Gozen took a long breath. "And once again, your voice soothes the unease of my spirit,"

"You flatter me too much," she graciously returned. "Now, since I imagine we won't have this girl's life fully comprehended by sundown, I suggest we get inside and ready ourselves for dinner. May I help you with those crates, Lord Gozen?" Lady Kyoumére took a step forward.

"Oh, that won't be necessary, but you should perhaps have a Mimi or two before the children cause their extinction," Gozen winked.

Lady Kyoumére smiled and elegantly slid her hand into the crate, her wrist rubbing up against the side of Gozen's hand. Picking out the best looking one of the bunch, she popped the cluster fruit into her mouth and gave a quick hum of delight. She precisely turned on her toe and began her walk back to the house. Gozen stood for a moment, smiling rather wide as he watched her elegant frame sail away.

Behind the house, Suzu hung inverted over the patchy yard Lady Kyoumére tried diligently to keep healthy. Lucette leaned against the trunk of the tree, braiding a lock of Suzu's hair. "So you learned all of this circus stuff up at Kora?"

"Yeah, it's called Soultai. I got to practice it a lot up there."

"Pretty nifty, young lady."

"Oh yeah, it's all-fired for sure. I felt like a real bent-wheel when

I first got there, but I can do all sorts of stuff now," Suzu said with a grin.

"So, is that something everyone learns up there? Seems like a pretty amazing place to live," Lucette spoke, thinking of how badly she wanted to visit somewhere farther away than Ella's flower shop in northern Doulan.

"No, Nia just taught me but I don't think anyone else. There was this other guy, Jin, that showed up a while after I got there. Rich kid from Primichi who could do some fancy stuff. Showed me a few things, but Nia didn't like him."

"But you like him, huh?" Lucette suggestively asked.

"Eh, interesting boy, but oddly fancy. This Darou guy lived up there for a little bit, and one day he tried to steal this fancy bowl, but Jin ran him down like some kind of cat and gave him the business."

Lucette's eyes widened. "Darou? Darou Batet?"

Suzu scrunched her nose, "Uhm, yeah, I think so. Why, do you know him?"

"He lives here," Lucette smiled.

"Here? Isn't he, ya know, too old?"

"I think he's the same age as me, but he lives in the annex across the street. I'm sure he appreciates you telling me about him getting worked over by some rich kid, though."

The two laughed just as the dinner whistle blew. Lucette let loose of Suzu's braid as Suzu flipped onto the ground. Immediately, the girls raced to the door, poking each other in the side.

Gozen prepped dinner with Lady Kyoumére in the kitchen, including a blashu grain salad with dried Mimi and root vegetables. Fried fish from the Chioi river topped it off. The Lady and her guest chef enjoyed the relatively quiet kitchen while loud, youthful voices bounced through the hallways. The pair then shared a glass of leftover cooking wine, with the Lady letting out an unusually loud giggle.

Inside the rather long dining room, symmetrically lined with tall windows and large wooden tiles, the kids of the house began to file in and take seats. On the wall hung a pair of wooden Masu swords used for Maishi training; the former owner added the space after visiting a traditional Maki up north in Primichi. The boys in the house all dreamed of taking down the swords for a proper sparing match, but fear of Lady Kyoumére's wrath kept such a fantasy from ever materializing.

Near the far end of the table, Suzu and Lucette sat down, their cheeks flushed. As discretely as she could, Suzu gave her friend one last poke. Lucette flinched back, raising her finger. "You better stop. Kyoumére will sting our little cheeks."

Minding his own business, Darou walked past Suzu and sat down next to Lucette. He gave her his typically minimalistic nod before staring at the table.

Lucette leaned back. "Recognize this portrait, Darou?"

He looked over to Suzu with only the slightest reaction. "I know you, right?"

Lucette looked over and shared a between-girls laugh with Suzu. "Are you sure? I mean you only lived with her."

Reluctantly thinking harder for such a late hour, Darou finally managed recognition of the face away from its usual context. "Yeah, I remember. You look about five years older, though."

"A little time in the city goes a long way, Darou," Suzu replied.

Lucette turned and gave her old friend an off look. "What? Did you steal that from your grandpa?"

"Hey, I never knew my grandparents," Suzu replied, nearly offended.

"Oh, save it for the neighbors. We're all orphans here," Lucette reasoned.

"So, Suzu, right? How is Nia doing? Did she come here with you?" Darou asked.

"Oh, I bet you're interested in knowing the answer to that one," Lucette teased.

"Yeah, I asked the question, didn't I?" Darou countered.

"Yeah, she's good, but I came here alone," Suzu replied.

"A little bit of that place goes a long way, huh?" Darou pried.

Complex feelings prevented Suzu from volleying back a quick reply. Luckily for her, Gozen entered, carrying a steaming mountain of food.

"Hope you're hungry," Gozen announced with a grin. "Really

hungry. I may have made too much."

Lady Kyoumére walked past, brushing against his arm. "Not possible in this house."

She waited for him, which he reciprocated by pulling out her chair; she graciously sat with a bow. Gozen gave a heartfelt thanks as he always did when he visited. The kids sat quiet as the fragrant stream of spices hit their senses. A minute later, the meal was underway. Conversations slowly built up as plates continued to get passed around. For a moment, the two adults held hands under the table.

Moaning from the appeasement of her taste buds, Lucette laid her head on her newly reunited friend's shoulder. Suzu felt Lucette's cool hair against her cheek. Silently, they both said thanks for the reunion. Suzu then caught Darou glimpse at her. Together, their minds both recalled the last meal they had together, awkward and trying. They then shared a smile, feeling as though they had survived into some new, uncertain stage in life.

The orphans eventually slowed down, some rubbing their swollen bellies. They lacked any sense of misfortune, feeling rather privileged in that brief moment. Then, after a minute of satisfied meditation, Lady Kyoumére ordered the table to be cleared before she strode towards the coffee press.

As Gozen set down the platter, Darou walked by with his head low. "Hey, how are you doing?"

Darou stopped and subtly looked around, seeing if any eyes took notice of their forming conversation. "Good."

Gozen took a step closer, lowering his powerful voice. "Things going okay here?"

"Yeah, it's pretty good here. A little loud but, ya know, kinda fun, I guess."

The answer comforted Gozen more than he showed. He could only guess to how little fun the young man ever experienced growing up. Regardless, other matters required attention. "How are things down at Etecid? Do you feel okay there?"

The question reminded Darou of his father, who always reminded him of how awful work was. "Eh, they talk a lot about how we aren't producing enough there. How they'll shut down if output doesn't increase . . . whatever, it's not like they'd close the company right after they bought it."

"All right, I'll let you go," Gozen said, guiding Darou out of the kitchen.

By now, the smell of smoked coffee filled the kitchen, and the Lady practically cradled the coffee press. It became known throughout the house to be the only time a kid could actually get away with anything: the Lady stood in an aromatic trance.

"That smells ready," Gozen joyfully noticed, the Lady silhouetted by warm vapors. As children vanished, the volume dropped like a tired head on a pillow. Gozen encroached as he and the Lady grinned with anticipation, ready for their five-minute vacation.

Lady Kyoumére pulled the rounded, brass release lever and slid the coffee flask out of the press; a cloud of steam billowed up to the ceiling. Her feminine fingers poured smoked coffee into two small, white porcelain cups that sat neatly on their copper-trimmed saucers. She offered one to her companion, just as Suzu's voice appeared outside the door.

Gozen groaned. "I'll be right back."

He gently set his coffee down and headed for the door saying, "Don't wait up." Needing no further encouragement, the Lady took a quick sip. She happily moaned as the warm liquid slid down her throat.

Suzu had just reached the bottom of the stairs when Gozen stopped her. "Suzu, we should probably get your things upstairs before it gets too late."

His voice had an ability to grab Suzu and lock her in place, no matter how familiar it became. He revealed his keys as they stood at a stalemate.

"Gozen, I think that it might be easier if I just stay in Neko for a while. That way when I go into the city with you, my stuff will already be in there. It's just practical."

Gozen raised his eyebrow. "What are you talking about, Suzu?"

"Well, I don't have that much stuff, so why not keep it with me when we're working, ya know . . . just in case."

Gozen responded with silence.

"I know we said I could stay here, but I don't need watched

after anymore. There's no point to it." She felt confident in her reasoning.

"Suzu, you wanted to leave Kora and come back into the city, and no one suggested you shouldn't feel that way. You stayed in Neko for a while and it was fine, but you can't live in there." Gozen spoke with direct pragmatism.

"Why?"

Gozen leaned in, trying to keep his booming voice as focused as his raising blood pressure would allow. "Suzu, I don't need to give you a reason. We just agreed you would stay here. So can you please get your things and take them upstairs?"

Since leaving Kora, a distant thought clawed at Suzu, who felt compelled to pursue it as directly as possible; the structure of the Tree House would only interfere. Regardless, the current standoff had turned futile. "Okay." She opened her hand for the keys.

"Thank you," Gozen said, watching her walk off full of youthful tension. The smoky smell of coffee then hit his senses, and he headed straight back to the kitchen. When he got into the doorway, Gozen saw what appeared to be Lady Kyoumére already pouring herself a second cup.

"You told me not to wait," she spoke as her voice slipped into a bashful tone. "This is my third cup."

Lucette heard Suzu's travelers thumping up the stairs and then through the hallway. The door slowly swung open, and she saw Suzu entangled in a nightmare of luggage straps. Neglecting etiquette, Lucette let out a laugh. "Do you need some help?"

Suzu took in an exhausted breath. "No, I think I got it from here." She dragged them to the rear bunk, past Lucette, who watched her from a rather comfortable position on a bed. "Back to the old Tree House, huh?"

Suzu dropped the gear and attempted to weave herself out of the traveler-strap-web. "Not for long, so don't get too excited."

"Well, you'll be here longer than me, Miss Adventure. This actually might be my last night." Lucette spoke with tempered expectation.

Finally free, Suzu took the time to fully notice the room Lucette had been living in. Strangely barren, the room lacked any sign of

Lucette's compulsion to decorate everything. "You're leaving me here, alone?"

"I know, I'm sorry. I'm a horrible sister," Lucette lovably confessed. Suzu felt an unusual jab of warmth from hearing someone refer to her as a sister for the first time. She quickly got back to the disconcerting news. "So yeah, explain yourself."

"I know, I know. You just got here." Lucette sat up and got settled. "My cousin Parin went up to Primichi for a job, but he's keeping his apartment here in Chigou. He offered that I could stay there as long as I took care of the place. Pretty hard to pass up, as you can see."

The news felt like a bad aftertaste to her conversation with Gozen. A seeping jealousy then quickly transformed into an alluring new idea. Rapidly, she processed just how much of that idea she needed to share.

"Is it far from here?"

"It's actually west of here in Chacier. The neighborhood feels like a loading dock, but the apartment is a decent size and nicer than you'd think. Plus I sort of have a view of the Chioi river. It's pretty quick if you take the Hotrail," Lucette explained.

A high-speed, underground public train system, the Hotrail became a point of pride for Opaji's shining Chigou. Like the rest of the city's industrial anatomy, it largely hid underground. The Hotrail got its name from the heat one would feel as the giant steam engine in the rear of a train passed by. It ran all evening, carefully monitored by civil Enforcers found on every train in the city.

Stepping over her luggage, Suzu sat down on the empty bed with a developing focus. "So, is it too big for one person?"

"Hah, too big for me?" Lucette burst out. "I grew up in an orphanage; I'd kill a man for a private, full-sized bathroom."

The two young ladies snorted out a laugh. Suzu then swallowed her silliness and spoke directly. "Are you going to get a roommate?"

Lucette quickly deciphered the suggestion that Suzu trickled out. "Well, my cousin said the offer was for me and me alone. He didn't want just anybody running in and out of his place."

"Well, I'm sure once you get comfortable there the place

will eventually start to feel desolate, maybe a little lonesome, and I would graciously like to offer my assistance towards your forthcoming plight," Suzu spoke with excellent enunciation.

Lucette sat inert as if Suzu had just spoken in tongues. She then burst into laughter. "Did you practice that this morning? I think there were at least four words in that sentence I've never heard come out of your mouth before."

Suzu dropped her shoulders and pouted. "I thought I pulled that off pretty naturally."

"Where did that even come from? People up on the farm don't talk like that, do they?"

"No," Suzu confessed. "Well, actually the one guy does, but he's kind of the silver screwdriver in the toolbox up there."

"Fancy pants, huh?" Lucette smirked.

"Yes, he always looks like he's going to the theater."

"Good lookin'?"

Suzu grinned and tried to keep her cheeks from blushing. "He certainly is put together. Nia always felt rather suspicious of him, but enough of that. When do I get to see your new nest?"

Lucette folded her arms. "Actually, I am going over in the morning to move the last of my stuff."

Suzu raised her eyebrow. "Yeah?"

"Yeah. How much can you lift?"

∘ ∘ ∘

Energetic feet echoed through the halls, mixing with youthful voices. Lady Kyoumére floated around, monitoring hyperactive morning-children and prodding late-risers. She typically got up first in the house and never appeared tired. A few children joked that she had a steam engine in her chest.

Lady Kyoumére then heard Gozen enter from outside. "I already put coffee in a travel flask for you, charged and steamy," the Lady smiled.

"Of course you did." Gozen gently bowed, admiring the view. "And now I feel I may actually have a chance of getting through this day."

"New business or old?" The Lady's voice quickly tapered as her eyes shifted towards the sound of scampering feet. A young

man ran around the corner and immediately got intercepted by Kyoumére's voice. "Hilou, no one wants to be knocked to the floor because you decided your impatience is more important."

Hilou stopped on a dime and lowered his gaze, a gesture of respect more than fear. "I'm sorry, Lady Kyoumére."

She stood over him for a breath or two and let the moment sink in before accepting his apology. "Thank you, Hilou. Now go ahead and walk briskly. I'm sure the matter at hand is of dire urgency."

Hilou promptly obeyed. The Lady then turned back to an amused Gozen. "As you were saying."

"Yes, there is business to deal with. I'm going to take Darou to work today. I still have uneasy feelings about that place."

"Do you think he is in any sort of danger there?"

"Not in any explicit way. I just feel that I need to keep paying attention."

"Well, I know he's better off for it."

The suggestion led Gozen to gaze into the Lady's eyes. He had no issue getting lost in them for as long as time would allow; on that day, it wasn't much. The Lady graciously reminded the man as Darou entered the door. "Don't forget your coffee."

Once outside with Darou, Gozen quickly got down to business. "So, you mentioned some doom-talk earlier about not producing enough. Is the output low or are people just blowing steam?"

"I don't know. Our production is barely lower than normal, considering . . . you know . . ." Darou tapered off.

"Considering what?"

Darou hesitated, feeling nervous about blaming the largest man he knew for anything. "Well, it's not your fault really . . . it's just, Tulúki shipments are low."

Gozen stopped as they reached Neko. "Our Tulúki shipments?"

"Well . . ." Darou felt awkward. "Yeah."

The Tulúki crop had been down. Nothing significant, but Gozen didn't want to give Etecid, or whoever ran that company now, any excuse to ruin even one more life. Especially not the young man standing before him. "I'll see if Kora can do anything to help squeeze out a little more for the next delivery."

○ ○ ○

The eyes of an owl set the benchmark for strong vision. Kola had just come from the eastern forest where he and Nia first found each other. Seeing her exit a silo two kilometers away, Kola tucked in his wings and dove down to the farm.

On the ground, Nia had just finished over an hour of Soultai training. She saw Jin working on his precious car, which he seemed to have an endless supply of attention for. She thought of avoiding him by walking around the back but ultimately decided against letting his presence change her course.

"How is she?"

Nia looked towards the muffled voice coming from beneath Jin's car, muffled enough to ignore.

"Suzu, have you heard from her?" Nia glanced out of the corner of her eye and saw Jin slide out from underneath the car. An impulse of etiquette took over, a product of her upbringing, and she reluctantly stopped to look at him. Simultaneously shocking and yet expected, Jin appeared to not have even a spec of grease on his milky face. Nia let out a moan. "Excuse me?"

Walking up, Jin respectfully stopped a few meters away and stood with a formal posture that always felt odd at the farm. "I was simply curious as to whether or not you had heard from Suzu since she left."

Nia immediately felt the tension that she had just worked off in the silo spiral back up her spine. "No, you?"

"Of course not. I can't imagine I would manage correspondence with her before you."

Having taken the absence of Suzu rather hard, Nia knew denying it then would have been pointless, even to an oddity like Jin. Part of her wanted to talk about it, but she could think of a dozen people she would rather have the conversation with. "Well, if that's all I think I better go eat." Nia started to head back towards the house. She could sense Jin's desire to carry on the conversation but ignored it.

He continued. "You seem rather remorseful over her absence. I miss my sister, as well."

The sentiment sounded jarring coming out of Jin's mouth,

making her stop and turn around. She had never heard any words of vulnerability pass through his pretentious, pearly trap before. "I didn't know you had a sister."

Jin remained still as a mental vision of his sibling materialized. "She is five years older than me. We were never that close, but I do think of her from time to time." Nia looked at Jin and felt oddly patient, actually wanting to hear more.

"I know the two of you are not biological relatives, but you are so close it is though you are sisters . . . more than I could claim with my own sister, actually, which is perhaps why I thought to say such a thing."

"It's fine," Nia softly spoke.

A clear image of Suzu then filled Nia's mind as the farm started to fade away. Jin awkwardly stood still, unsure of how to continue, auditioning polite exchanges in his head. A low rumbling noise then materialized as the farm girl clinched her stomach.

"I think I better go eat. I'll tell Clora to leave an extra plate out." Nia started to move towards the house. Jin felt an urge to do likewise as she spoke again. "That way you can still eat while you work." Nia turned her head and went towards the door.

Jin halted his steps. Kola soared in from above and gracefully landed on Nia's shoulder. She calmly began to pet him on the head as he closed one eye, scanning the perimeter with the other. They entered in through the light of the hallway before the door shut them in.

As she passed through the entry way, Gozen entered from the kitchen. Nia's tired eyes popped right open. "I didn't know you were here."

"I haven't been. Just dropping off some paperwork."

"Oh, okay." Nia lowered her head and walked into the dining room, Kola stoically perched up. Gozen watched as Nia sluggishly pulled a chair up to the table.

"I'm heading back into Chigou soon. Do you want to come and hang out with Suzu a bit? I'm sure she'd like seeing you," Gozen intuitively offered.

Nia half looked up with a pitiful groan. "No, I'm sure she probably wants to have some time to herself in the city. It makes sense; she grew up there. I'm surprised she didn't want to go back sooner."

From years of looking after Nia, it took little effort for Gozen to detect when she tried to hide the more vulnerable parts of her heart. Knowing all of what laid beneath; however, he assumed to be an unsolvable mystery. "The city always looks exciting when you're not in it. Over time, a place like Kora looks like a sanctuary," he suggested.

Giving Gozen's comment no reaction, Nia continued her pervious thought. "I wonder what my parents' lives were like. I wish I knew who some of their friends were, what they liked to do every day. I don't feel like I know the place I was born, the place my parents chose to live. I think Suzu wants to remember all of that. I think it matters, keeping the life of someone you loved alive."

The words ripped through Gozen's heart like shards of ice. He knew the place of her birth, the building where her parents raised her. He remembered what it looked like, before and after it burnt to the ground.

"Gozen, I meant it when I asked before. Can you help me find out about my parents?"

The answer had been churning in his chest for so long he couldn't remember what it felt like without it. He hated harboring it, but the thought of releasing it frightened him even more. She looked up to him, the man whom she had learned to be strong and trustworthy, but he lowered his eyes, ashamed of his fear.

Outside, Jin sat perfectly upright, watching the tiny blades of grass casting shadows on one another. He thought of it to be a rather odd waste of time but had no motivation to do anything else. Relaxing his posture, Jin plucked a blade of grass and held it in his hand. For the first time, the small size of a single, broken blade of grass became a conscious and consuming thought. He held it in his palm until the sun disappeared behind the icy rim of the mighty Murde Mountains.

12
HAUNTED

The sound of a civilian-class steam motor faded down the dark street. The Municipal Bairide, a small pay-per-ride transport vehicle, had just dropped off its passenger and rushed away to its next fare. Alone at the bottom of a high-rise apartment complex, Suzu stood with her hair pulled up and the DaiLansu firmly held low in her left hand.

She looked up through the dark fog that covered the upper floors of the building. Tall, strong lines of concrete and steel reached up, seemingly with no end. Deep within the fog, a red light glowed, pulling her upwards from the center of her chest. Hot blood coursed through her body, but her breaths felt cold and steady like an icy river.

A man appeared from around the corner with his hat-covered head hanging down. He walked briskly, tightly holding a paper bag from The Smokehouse Market around the corner. Suzu began to walk forward, their paths converging on a side entrance to the apartment complex.

The man glanced up and noticed Suzu, her identity hidden in shadow. His attention then went to the door as he quickly unlocked it with his communal security key. He took another look at Suzu, who seemed to be headed for the end of the street; he quickly went inside.

Like a spark, Suzu flew to the door and quickly wedged the DaiLansu strap between the door and the frame. The door closed, but the strap pushed back just enough to keep the latch from engaging. She put her ear to the door and calmly waited. Above her a brass address plaque read *2S11 Oraguine Ave*. Fifteen seconds later, she heard the man enter the elevator.

Suzu pulled open the door, passed the elevator, and went straight to the stairwell. Stepping in, she saw a towering spiral staircase, disappearing into scarlet darkness. She quietly headed up the stairs, the deep red light beckoning her from above.

Finally stopping at the forty-second floor, Suzu took a moment to quiet her breathing. Getting up on her toes, she peeked through the safety-glass; all clear. Suzu carefully stepped into the lifeless hallway, her feet silently stepping across the concrete floor. Her ears scanned the environment, eager to pick out even the slightest anomaly from the mechanical hum in the walls. The numbers decreased to 4269, and her feet stopped. The outside world faded away, and she could feel the red glow pulling her in from the other side of the door.

Looking a few meters up, she saw a vent, almost hidden from the light of the hallway. After one final perimeter check, she tightened the large metal buckle on her jacket and then accelerated away from the door. Jumping up, she ran three full strides straight up the wall and then vaulted off to grab the I-beam high above.

Her feet quickly swung up and latched likewise onto the steel bar. High above the floor, she crawled upside down until reaching the vent. Suzu pulled out a small screwdriver and quickly disengaged all four screws in the vent, skillfully catching each with a single hand. She pulled off the vent cover and then smoothly slid inside. The hallway went silent.

° ° °

The rumble of Neko's engine interrupted Lady Kyoumére's sip of smoked coffee. She reached into the cupboard and pulled out another cup and saucer for her friend. Gozen came through the front door, his heavy eyes brightening at the sight of loveliness. Flattered, the Lady handed the tired man his cup of reprieve, and he sipped away in delight.

"No day seems too hard when I get to come home to this."

"Long day in the city, sir?" she thoughtfully asked.

"I had this rather convoluted conversation with an Enforcer friend of mine about . . . well, things I'm probably paying too much attention to." Gozen breathed in the smoky steam.

"I'm surprised that Enforcer talk would wear you out. I'd think you would have developed quite a tolerance for that over the years," the Lady confessed. "Or is there something else?"

Gozen thought through another sip. "Well, I've just been finding Suzu a little . . . I'm not sure how to put this." He searched around between honesty and etiquette. "She's difficult."

A quick snicker escaped the Lady's lips before she could politely hold it back. "I'm sorry, dear."

Gozen followed with his own laugh. "No, I think that is probably the correct response." He cleared his throat. "So how was she doing today?"

The Lady's eyes searched around the space. "You know, I haven't really seen her today except for in the morning with Lucette. I thought perhaps she went into the city with you."

"No, I haven't seen her since I left."

Lady Kyoumére quickly remembered, "Oh, Lucette was finishing moving today to her cousin's apartment. I don't recall Suzu stating that she was going to move out, however. She probably was helping Lucette move?"

Gozen let out a soft groan and pondered the question. "Well, she did mention not wanting to stay . . ."

Lady Kyoumére raised an eyebrow. Gozen's fatigued mind fought to find the correct mixture of words. "Suzu asked to come to the city, specifically. She wanted to stay in Neko, but I told her she couldn't . . . she did want to stay here and was excited to see you, of course, and Lucette, but she wanted to . . ."

Thoughts muddled as the Lady's eyes widened in anticipation. He finally responded. "She is a teenager. At least I think she is."

Lady Kyoumére's delicate fingers reached up and rubbed Gozen's broad back. "And how exhausting they can be, but judging by the evidence here, I think it is safe to assume where our missing girl is." As she rubbed the tension out of Gozen's shoulders, he sighed out a response. "I suppose I should go and check up on her."

"I know you won't sleep a wink unless you do. I'll get Lucette's new address."

Suddenly, the rapid explosion of footsteps carrying thirty-pound bodies entered the hallway: one little boy without a shirt and the later missing his pants. Thankfully, neither had misplaced their undergarments.

"Are you sure you don't want to come with me?" Gozen offered.

"I dare not dream so big. I think you'd better go without me."

o o o

A black Móstique pulled up to the lift garage at *2S11 Oraguine*. The driver put in the key at a switch box and the door opened up. The car pulled in through the security gate and drove to the lift directly ahead. Gears churned as the hiss of steam sounded below, lifting the car up three levels. As it slowed to a stop, the sound of clamping steel echoed from below. The car parked and the driver walked to a tenant elevator, heading straight up to the forty-second floor.

Stopping at 4269, he got out his cylindrical brass key but paused before slipping it in the lock. With the other tenants out to work, the hallway sounded typically quiet, but something seemed off. The hallway had an unfamiliar tone, something he couldn't pinpoint. Finally, the young man unlocked the door, his eyes ready to scan the room within.

From above, he could be seen as he shut the door behind him. His head tilted up, an attempt to focus his ears on the sound of the room. It revealed just enough for Suzu to verify the target of her intentions. Perched up on an I-beam, the young girl silently observed the young man who had killed her parents.

Kits walked forward and casually pulled a Vite pistol out of his jacket. Officially only allowed for target shooting, afficionados knew it for its high velocity, accuracy, and cost. He held it loosely in his hand and headed towards the kitchen. Like a cat, Suzu crawled across the beam without making a sound. With her eyes fixed on the young man's gun, she waited on the two to separate.

Moving towards a stone island in the middle of the kitchen, Kits continued to survey the perimeter. Blocked by a support, Suzu swung underneath and hung from the elevated beam before managing to catch up. A fog of red light swam through the room, fading everything but Kits out of focus. She hung directly above, waiting for him to put the gun down. Impatience grew as her grip began to ache.

Suzu looked past her shoulder to see the retracted DaiLansu

attached to her back. Time slowed down as the strain increased. She longed to grab it and descend down with a strike, knowing it needed to be in a single motion, and soon.

Slowly, Kits placed the gun on the table. Suzu's eyes sharpened while the young man's hand remained on the firearm. She did not want to attack with the gun in reach, but her weakening grip narrowed that decision down to a single option.

Sweat collected on her forehead, and she sensed a drop of it about to fall. A rage swelled in her mind at Kits's indecision. The dark light pulsed. Her fingers began to slip. Then, she saw his hand finally lift off the gun. It remained in reach, but gravity became a force she could no longer overcome.

Suzu reached for the DaiLansu, and her sweat finally fell onto the stone table. Kits's tuned ears led his eyes down to the small splash, and he simultaneously reached back for the gun. Quickly looking up, he raised his pistol, but a second too late.

Already descending and with weapon in hand, Suzu struck Kits square on his firing arm; a shot burst into the side wall.

She got the first strike, but Kits had the deadlier weapon; her action required dominating speed. Now on the ground, Suzu planted her foot and swung for the gun. He turned into her and grunted as the DaiLansu smashed into his shoulder. She tried to step in and keep him from gaining distance to fire.

Still trying to get his bearings, Kits grabbed the DaiLansu with his free hand and they locked up. Getting away from the end of the gun, Suzu sprang up onto the counter and spun onto Kits's back. He awkwardly tried to raise his gun and fired over his shoulder. Suzu ducked, and the shot landed into the cupboards three inches from her head, splinters exploding across her face.

She hung low onto his back to avoid another shot. With her right hand still on the DaiLansu, she reached up with her left and dug her farm-hardened fingers into his throat. Her scream of rage preceded his cry of pain. Now noticing his weight advantage, Kits dug in and rammed backwards. Suzu's spine violently bent over the corner of the cupboards, forcing her to yelp in pain. The steam line coming into the kitchen dislodged and hissed hot vapor up to the ceiling.

Taking advantage of the numbing shock shooting through the girl's body, Kits swung around and managed to fling her down to the floor as her nails tore away from his neck. Suzu bounced off the tile but quickly braced herself and turned right back to Kits, her vision filling with red haze. She knew she needed to be faster than his draw, but before she could even stand, Suzu saw the end of Kits's gun. She dodged low, but his trigger was too fast; the bullet smashed into the heavy buckle on her jacket and knocked her straight to the floor.

A throbbing pain spread through her chest. The impact had forced the air out of her lungs. No time to recover, Suzu looked for the DaiLansu, finding it by her feet. In that instant, however, the red light clouding her mind started to fade, along with her hope. Kits walked up just behind the weapon she so desperately wanted, his gun pointing straight at her. His eyes appeared to her as red as the blood streaking across his neck.

The rage in Suzu's body poured out with the warm tears that started to fall down her face. Her body painfully forced air in and out of her lungs: heavy breaths that purged the resistance out of her, replaced by bitter acceptance. There was no time to do anything. It was over.

○ ○ ○

Putting her last sweater into the drawer, Lucette took in a satisfied breath, checking the time on her colorful Toki. She looked around the newly transformed room, declaring it a vibrant victory over what her rather drab cousin had left behind. Feeling the elation of freedom, she then looked into a box and saw the back of a book wrapped in crimson linen. She reached down to pick it up.

Sitting on the bed, Lucette flipped over the book and read the title, *Tales from the Red Valley*. Children looking to spook one another often resorted to the book's frightening fables taking place in the mysterious, southern end of the Naifin Valley. With her attention completely redirected, she turned to an illustration of a child hiking through the thick forest. Her eyes focused on the center where the trees faded into darkness. Activating the Special with a click, a light shined out of the Toki and onto the shadowed woods, where slowly, a red shape began to appear. It floated above the ground, lurking behind the unaware child at arm's reach. Finally, sloping black eyes appeared within the red figure, as if the ink on the page slowly began to change.

The sound of heavy knocking then echoed through the apartment. Lucette sat up, immediately thinking of how few people she had told of her move. Raising her small hands to her chest, she walked up to the front door attempting to be absolutely silent.

She heard another knock, causing her to jump an inch. Catching the breath she lost, Lucette looked through the peephole. She stood still as darkness filled the view. The shape then turned, and she recognized the double row of dark brass fittings running up the jacket. Not wanting to look like an unkempt girl with no business living on her own, Lucette straightened her colorfully patterned headband as well as her posture.

"Hello, Gozen. What a surprise," she said, opening the door.

"Sorry for coming unannounced. It was a rather recent decision to stop by," Gozen politely stated.

"No complaints. Can't say I don't feel a little safer having you around," Lucette said, leaning in as if telling a secret. "It's my first time having a place all to myself."

Gozen folded his arms. "Is everything okay?"

"Oh yes, yes, of course. Just saying, it always feels safer with the big guy around."

She bounced up on her toes, trying to spring off any worry. Gozen, while typically appreciating her pluck, found the energy suspicious in the moment. "Is Suzu here?"

The discourse paused. Lucette wondered how Gozen could have known that Suzu had moved in with her. It had only been a few hours, and she had kept her chat box quiet.

"No one told me, Lucette. I figured it out myself."

"Right. Hiding anything from you is a rather pointless effort, so I'm starting to realize."

"So?" Gozen asked again.

"Yes, right," Lucette responded, then quickly retracted. "I mean, no, she's not here . . . uhm, would you like to come in?"

"I would, Lucette. However, I'm a little preoccupied with the whereabouts of Suzu at the moment, so why don't you help me with that first?"

"Right." Lucette settled down a bit. "I told Suzu I was moving into my cousin's old place. She thought it would be fun to partner up in the high-tower—be big kids, ya know. I was gonna tell Lady Kyoumére, but I thought Suzu was gonna explode from impatience . . . so . . . ."

"I understand that feeling." Gozen tapped his fingers.

"I know I should have told Lady Kyoumére. I mean, I will tell her, I will." Lucette's apologetic posture quickly burst into defensive excitement. "But it's fun getting to be ladies out on our own, no checking in, not that we want to get into trouble or do stupid things. I don't even like being a troublemaker, but it's . . . ."

Gozen leaned in. "Lucette, I'm not here to scold you. Please tell me where Suzu is."

"Sorry." Lucette started laughing. "She just went into the city to see something. Some place she went with her parents awhile ago."

"It's a bit late. Was she supposed to be back by now?"

"Uhm, yeah. I guess it is getting dark." Lucette had been preoccupied with decoration dreams. "You don't think she's in trouble, do you?"

"No, no," Gozen calmly reassured her. "I'm just an overly protective old man."

"Okay, that's good," Lucette said in relief. "And Gozen, you're not that old."

Gozen grinned, shrugging his shoulders. "So, she didn't say specifically where she was going? No address?"

"No, she just called up a Bairide." Her face skewed. "Which is weird. I'm not sure why she wouldn't just ride the Hotrail." The statement sparked a number of questions into both of their minds. While Gozen explored them in detail, Lucette settled into a ridiculous thought. "It's not like she was carrying a weapon or anything."

○ ○ ○

It was the first time Suzu had ever seen the inside of a gun barrel. The sound of steam still hissed out of the broken pipe. The

DaiLansu lay just past her feet, almost close enough to touch, but it might as well have been across the room. She wiped the tears off her face.

Behind the gun, Kits's face finally came into focus. It looked odd, recognizable, but different than the image that had been warped in her memory over countless nightmares. The shock of seeing it again nearly blocked the pain of a massive chest bruise forming under her jacket.

Kits slowly bent down until his eyes leveled with Suzu's. He then opened the lower cabinet door and reached into the dark. Suzu held her breath, hoping Kits would turn his eyes from her; they stayed put. The steam suddenly stopped its scream and dissipated into the air; he stood back up. In the suddenly quiet space, her own heaving breaths became the only thing Suzu heard.

"Move into the light."

Kits's simple command began to purge the storm of thoughts swirling through Suzu's mind. She began to focus on the moment: pain, breathing, and a gun. Kits waved the weapon past Suzu to where a spotlight hit the floor.

She slid over and Kits followed slowly. Stepping over the DaiLansu, he never moved the gun off of her. As her tired face illuminated, a distant memory crawled from the back of Kits's mind. He spoke slowly. "My curse, my consequence."

Suzu's fingers pressed against the tile floor. The time of clandestine behavior had ended between the assassin and the orphan.

Kits leaned against the counter. "If a person were to tell me that a young lady would drop from my rafters and attack me with some strange mechanical stick, I imagine I'd follow up with a number of skeptical questions; and yet, here you are, and I feel no need to question why."

Suzu struggled to loosen her jaw enough to speak. "You remember who I am?"

"You certainly look older, but perhaps not so different from years ago." Kits spoke with enlightened clarity, the calmness of his voice feeling like poison in Suzu's ears.

"I remember that night like it was just the other day. I wasn't entirely sure what I was doing. I remember being very confused and frightened."

Her throat felt tight. "You felt frightened?"

"I looked into these very same eyes and felt a deep, heavy fear over what I was about to do. So much so that I decided not to carry out the task I was given. And then I was reminded that my decision would possibly bring about a repercussion, a rather severe one at that."

Overhead, the lights only defined the edge of Kits's face, but showed enough for Suzu to see a grin forming. Not of joy, but one of sentimental recollection.

"How could you do that to them?" she said, her voice spilling anger and grief.

Kits whittled down what had been an event of subtle complexities. "Your parents were rather important people."

Her voice raised. "I don't need you to tell me that they were important."

"Of course you don't. I wonder, however, if you understand just how important their lives were becoming to a great many other people. And as we both know, you can't ignore someone that you find intensely significant." Kits lowered the gun a few degrees, his elbow relaxed. "I admired their humility given their skill levels, especially your father's. Although it's probably what left them so open, so vulnerable."

An image formed in the girl's mind, one of a spirited woman's flowing hair and a playful man's charming smile, all around a table covered with fanciful drawings and baked goods. The sweet image stung her soul.

"I admire that you came here." Kits spoke with sincerity. "It shows more conviction than what I was able to muster the first time we met, but I suppose that kind of determination grows over years of survival."

Kits then looked over towards his desk. She waited to see the barrel of the gun drop. Stepping to the side, he kept both eyes and weapon pointed directly at her. Kits then felt against the wall and lifted the cover off a small switch. He triggered it, which initiated a quick buzz.

Suzu watched his every move. "What are you doing?"

Kits slowly walked back to the counter. "Following through with the inevitable."

A sickening chill shot up through her body. She had been suppressing anger for so long that it felt strangely freeing when she finally let it out. That freedom, however, drained out onto the floor as she sat hopelessly alone.

"People know that I'm here." Suzu prayed the statement would project some sincerity that she knew not to exist. Kits just began to laugh.

"I have a confession. I actually knew that you were coming."

Her eyes lit up. "You . . . you couldn't have."

"No, I did," Kits confidently responded. "I am embarrassed to say, however, I did not realize that it was precisely you who was coming."

Suzu sat in confusion, her exhausted mind searching to make sense of the statement.

"I got a message some time back," Kits explained. "Just a simple notification that some young girl from the farm might visit me someday. It was so odd that I almost dismissed it as a mistake, but it was written with such etiquette that I couldn't dismiss its sincerity." As Kits leaned his head to the side, the gun dropped a few more degrees. Suzu watched intently.

"The kind of proper etiquette that I would never expect from someone who worked at a farm."

Awareness struck Suzu as the image of Jin's face flashed into her mind. She wondered what his motivation was for such a strange betrayal. Threatened and angry, Suzu strained for enough strength to hide her desperation. "Like I said, people know I am here."

"No, no one knows you're here." His calmness terrified her. "Any person who had the capacity and heart to come over here and liberate you never would have let you arrive here in the first place, certainly not alone." Kits raised his gun back up.

She thought of her parents, and tears began to form again. She longed for the comfort of their presence but knew it could never come.

"I didn't want to kill you all those years ago," Kits confessed. "Not any more than I do even at this moment." He took a deep breath. "But conviction can grow over time, and I simply can't let some girl loose in the city who wants nothing more than to end my life. Especially one that has shown herself to be rather capable, as you just have."

Kits rubbed his clawed neck as the front door to the apartment opened. Suzu turned her head over to the door. Two men stood in the doorway, silhouetted by the dim light in the hall. She slowly turned back to Kits, desperation in her eyes.

He spoke directly to the men. "Quickly and quietly, and don't let me find out otherwise."

○ ○ ○

Steam billowed across the public street that looked more like an industrial drive. A four-story lift garage squeezed between two buildings, only wide enough to handle a single row of Bairides. The outer lift lowered one of the public transit cars onto the street, the engine echoing between buildings as it left.

The Bairide passed by Neko, which pulled up to the lift garage. Gozen looked across the seat and noticed an illuminated sheet metal sign reading "NorthWest Bairide." He quickly got out and walked to the front door, armed with his stern posture and old Civil Enforcer badge.

Gozen squeezed in through the entryway. The garage had a small maintenance area where two mechanics worked on a pair of Bairides. Near a back wall covered with cabinets, schedules, and shelves, a lackluster man sat at a desk. Hearing the footsteps, he looked up, and then looked up a little more.

"Sorry, guy, but we really don't need any mechanics right now." The garage manager went back to his time sheets.

Gozen took another step forward. "That's quite all right. I'm not here to tinker on taxis."

The manager looked back up. "Well, you certainly wouldn't fit in the front seat of one. So, what, are you lost?"

"I need to know the address that one of your Bairides dropped off a young lady at earlier today."

The manager continued with his papers. "Even if I wanted to

take the time to look that up, which I don't, I can't just hand that information out."

Finished with pleasantries, Gozen dropped his Enforcer badge in the path of the pencil. The manager then lifted his head, pushing his glasses up his nose. "Why didn't you say so?"

"It would have been early to mid afternoon."

"Uhm . . ." The manager shifted a few papers around. "Well, that narrows it down to about three hundred pickups. If you don't have any more specific information I don't think . . ."

"It would have been directly after a pickup at 18W9 Wakune Street."

The manager let out a sigh, "Okay." He then stopped fumbling through the papers and began to actually analyze them. Gozen watched as his finger ran down a list. Three times he wrote on a notepad before looking back up.

"Three pickups at that building today. One of them went to a metalworks, one to another residential building, one to a restaurant," the manager rattled off. "Which one would you like?"

Gozen reached down and took the paper, along with his badge. "Thank you." Without making eye contact, he quickly put it into his jacket.

"Please, help yourself." The manager watched Gozen walk off. "I hope you find her, big guy."

The manager's questionably sincere voice faded away as Gozen stepped out onto the street. Lines of lights ran up towering structures, fading into the stars. The world felt vast, as if anything could get lost in it. Gozen got into Neko and fired up the engine, a roaring hiss announcing his pursuit.

∘ ∘ ∘

His narrow head peeked out the door and looked down the alley. Nothing moved aside from the steam creeping around like a back-alley ghost. Ansel, a lanky man with slick, blonde hair, turned to Guso, who brutishly restrained Suzu. "We're dandy. Bring her out."

Wearing a tattered scarf posing as something more expensive, the blocky Guso followed Ansel into the alley. Suzu, sporting a fresh bruise on her cheek, got dragged out of the doorway. Her heart raced, heating a stomach tinged with nausea.

"Make sure she keeps quiet back there," Ansel said as he surveyed up and down the street.

"Yeah," Guso said as he squeezed Suzu's small arms even harder. "Don't be makin' any sounds."

Ansel stopped along the other side of the alley, stepping out of the light of the street lamps. He pulled out a collapsible spark pipe and lit it, the glow revealing his malevolent face. The sight of it caused Suzu to fight against what was happening to her. She dug in her feet and tried to push back.

Guso pressed down, twisting her arms. "You want me to hurt you real bad?" he said, leaning into Suzu's ear. She could feel the spit fling from between his clenched teeth.

"No," Suzu mustered out of her sore body. Guso lifted her back up and forced her a across the alley until pushing her against the concrete wall. Her feet stumbled and she landed on the ground, letting out a cry of pain.

"Don't make no noise, girl . . ." Guso blurted.

Ansel put a hand out in front of his lackey, reassuring him with a glint in his eye. "Let me know if you see anyone coming."

It took a few spit-laced breaths for Guso to regain control from his primordial rage. He fixed his scarf and then took a few steps back, looking for any trouble coming to disrupt their business. Ansel took a step toward Suzu, who struggled to sit up against the wall.

"Well, well, you're an awfully ambitious young lady, aren't you?" Ansel spoke with irritating confidence. "Went all the way up there by yourself to try and kill someone like that, huh? Or maybe your gears don't match up."

Suzu, who couldn't stomach to look at his face, cast her eyes down. They stopped at a Pocket Claw tucked into his waist band. A favorite tool in street fights, it got its name from a spring-loaded blade hidden within.

"You worried about what I might do with that?" Ansel asked with a predatory sympathy. "Or maybe considering what you tried to do upstairs, I bet you're thinking of going for it and stickin' the both of us."

She kept quiet, but her eyes did not have the strength to lie. Ansel bared his teeth through a crooked smile, and then quickly struck Suzu in the face with the back of his hand. Suzu let out a cry of pain. Guso broke from his guard duty and looked over with a meddling grin. Ansel looked back. "Keep your eyes on the street."

With her crimson cheek swollen, Suzu looked back up to Ansel. He again met her gaze with the back of his hand. The depleted young lady fell to her side, tears of pain mixing with the dirty puddle below.

"You know, I'm real curious what got a little thing like you all the way up there," Ansel said. "Something happen to mommy and daddy? Maybe they crossed Kits, didn't see what would come?"

Ansel then put his hand under her chin and forced her face towards his. His long, dirty fingers squeezed her jaw, forcing her bleeding lips to purse. Suzu felt smothered as Ansel got in close, stealing her air. "Tell me, what is it that he took from you?"

As red light started to fill the edges of Suzu's vision, the world felt distant. Her fingers stiffened and she lunged for his throat but managed just a scratch as he grabbed her wrist. "It's good for you to fight back. It'll make both of us feel better about this."

Ansel then grabbed the Pocket Claw and and pressed it into her swollen cheek before pulling back and striking her again. The metal rod made his fist feel like a rock, smashing out a shriek of pain. The blade popped out of the handle. Suzu frantically grabbed it with both hands, fighting with what little strength remained.

"Very good. All the way to the end," Ansel grinned.

A bright light reflected off of the sharpened metal as Ansel heard the low rumble of an engine. Looking down the alley, he saw three bright lights shining out of the darkness. Ansel quickly looked over to Guso, who had turned his voyeuristic attention back to Suzu.

"Hey!" Ansel barked as he gestured towards the light. Guso snapped to and headed towards the rumbling sound. Ansel put one hand over Suzu's mouth and pressed her head into the wall. Guso formed into a silhouette as he walked into the light.

Gozen's eye surveyed the figure coming towards him, evaluating potential threats. He worked his eyes back past the stocky man and saw something moving against the wall—a crouched figure facing the corner. His eyes focused more, quickly gathering critical information. The figure appeared to be holding something down as a small leg slid out from behind a box.

Feeling an impulse to grab his sidearm, Gozen quickly pushed the idea aside, keeping an old commitment to retire it. All other hesitation then evaporated like sweat hitting a hot stove. The door opened, and he stepped straight out of the cab, his eyes never leaving the small leg struggling in the distance.

Guso faintly saw a figure cut through the headlights, surprisingly large, but his flared rancor pushed him forward. "Hey fella, you took a wrong turn. Why don't you get back in your truck and find another way . . ."

The pushy voice quickly cut off as Gozen reached down, thrusting his imposing hand over Guso's entire face. The startled thug stumbled backwards and reached for the powerful arm holding him up. Gozen's pace never broke as he continued straight down the street, muffling Guso's voice.

A confusing silhouette approached Ansel and he struggled to make sense of it. He looked down to Suzu who kept her weak grip on the Pocket Claw. With no time to hide the squirming girl, Ansel leaned down to her. "If there is any sound out of you, I will hurt you for days."

Slowly, Ansel stood up, exchanging his focus between the girl and the approaching form. Suzu looked rather athletic, but in her broken state he figured he would easily catch her if she ran. He then prepared for the morphing shadow bearing down on him.

Suddenly, the confusing mass then exploded out as Gozen thrust Guso off his feet, slamming him into the bottom of a metal dumpster.

Ansel quickly grabbed his Pocket Claw from Suzu and walked forward, fighting hard to stay in control. Still approaching, Gozen finally saw the hidden body finally come into view. Obscured by blood and bruises, Suzu's eyes tried to turn up towards him. The sight nearly stole his breath.

Taking no chances, Ansel revealed his Pocket Claw and thrust it straight into Gozen's midsection. The veteran combatant's reflexes then exploded. Gozen grabbed the weapon-wielding hand, stopping it from pushing in deep. Before Ansel could react, a crushing force clamped around his neck, followed by overwhelming pain.

Ansel grabbed Gozen's hand right as it lifted him an inch off of the ground. He then felt the bones in his forearm grinding together as Gozen forced the weapon away from his midsection. The Pocket Claw dropped to the ground, its blade reflecting the street light into Gozen's face.

"You shouldn't do this, I'm connected to people," Ansel said, painfully forcing air through his collapsing throat.

"People that have you beat up little girls?" Gozen squeezed harder. "I'm already dying to meet them."

Suzu's swollen eyes widened at the sight before her. She had never heard Gozen so much as yell at anyone. Occasionally he got agitated, typically at her, but a kindness always remained deep in his eyes. Seeing him crush the neck of a man, looking fully intent on killing him, the girl sat in absolute shock.

The blood had completely been squeezed out of Ansel's shaking hand as he felt his body start to go numb. "I'm not gonna tell you nothin'," he said, trying to muster up some grit.

Gozen brought Ansel in closer, his stare drilling through the miscreant's skull. "Then I'm going to tell you what you're going to do. You're going to leave this place, and if I ever see you in this city again, I will put you to an end."

Ansel believed every word the stranger told him, but his groveling ego still managed to crawl out of his mouth. "You think you scare me?" His face puffed out red, speaking through clamped teeth. "I'm not afraid to die."

Gozen then released some pressure around Ansel's throat, allowing blood and oxygen to rush in. The air settled and the alley fell quiet. Gozen spoke with chilling purpose. "No, no, little man, you don't understand. If I ever see you in this city again, I will hide you away, and I will work on you, and work on you until you are begging me to kill you." He got closer, quieter. "But I will not stop until I am absolutely convinced that you mean it."

Ansel's ghostly face shook. Gozen then clenched down again on his throat and let out the roar of a bear. He swiftly swung Ansel's limp body into the lid of the dumpster five meters away. With a thud, Ansel fell on Guso as the lid shut. The two thugs lay silent in the refuse.

The crash of metal echoed down between the buildings and then faded away. Suzu sat motionless, afraid to make a noise, afraid to see Gozen's face. He stood there, towering high above her. Her eyes jumped between his swollen veins and heaving chest, pushing out hot vapor.

Eventually, he looked down to her, his face blank. Unaware of her own action, Suzu leaned away from him. Gozen walked up to her, his face blocking the streetlight high above. Her sore neck strained to see his eyes. The air between them felt cold. Finally, Gozen sat down next to her with an exhausted grunt.

"So are you really injured, or just really, really hurt?" His voice had returned, sounding almost familiar.

Suzu focused on her battered body. "Just really, really hurt, I guess."

As the pressure in the alley settled, Gozen's desire to comfort the girl battled with an urge to question the adolescent madness she had conjured up. He thought of all he had done, all everyone had done to support Suzu, to keep her from getting swallowed up by the city. He wondered why she declined so much encouragement only to run straight into whatever darkness he found her laying in.

While he went on editing his thoughts, Suzu finally spoke up. "I never thanked you for saving me."

Needing a second to pull away from his internal rant, Gozen quietly replied, "It was only a minute ago."

"No." Suzu shook her head. "I never thanked you for taking care of me . . . the day you found me."

Gozen quietly nodded as the impulse to listen took over. Suzu held her knees close to her chest. "I know you didn't have to do that. You didn't need to look after me. You didn't need to put up with me as I made you take me from place to place."

Knots shuffled around in Gozen's stomach as Suzu's voice

started to tremble, coming from a place deep within. "I know I've been difficult. I'm sure there are a lot more worthy things you could be dealing with than me. I'm not sure why you bother with me, but I know my parents are really glad that it was you who showed up at the door that morning. I know they would say thank you if they could."

She felt the words spill from wherever they had long been locked away. Gozen wondered how much he didn't give this young girl credit for, how much more she understood than he realized.

"Suzu, when I first saw you, I had no idea what to do for you. I know that Lady Kyoumére is wonderful and she does amazing things with what she has. Kora is . . . surreal. Sometimes I have trouble believing that with all the problems of this world, such a beautiful place could exist . . . but I still feel like I don't know what to do for you."

The memory of screams started to claw up through his consciousness. Steam, fire, pieces of lives blown into a mangled heap under the echo of sirens. He strained to keep his voice still. "I don't know what it's like to have your parents taken from you, but I feel like you could do well at Kora. I loved watching you with Nia. You two really became sisters."

Suzu thought of everything she had lost, either by force or by choice, and how impossibly far away it all seemed. She thought of Nia's face and her precious DaiLansu in Kits's apartment. She wondered how she could ever face Nia again. She felt like a fool and a thief. She missed Nia, and thinking of her suddenly felt unbearably painful. "I know, but I can't go back."

Gozen had an impulse to refute but instead sat alongside his young pupil on the wet tarmac, a pipe dripping behind them. Despite being three times her size and decorated as a distinguished Enforcer, Gozen looked down at the girl leaning on his arm and felt just as lost as she did. But, they were lost together.

Silence floated around them until a vulnerable voice managed to burrow out into the air. "I can't remember what my parents' voices sound like. I have these memories of them talking; my parents always liked to talk. Especially in our small kitchen. My mom liked to bake. Somehow I still remember the smell. I remember all of the conversations we had there, especially there, but it's just words. I can't remember the sound."

The rest of the city disappeared as she continued. "My mother always took me to see things people made or walk through gardens. She always knew right when everything bloomed. She and my dad would always talk about the city and the land, trying to make it this beautiful place for everyone."

Suzu took a long breath. "I didn't understand why they talked so much about it; it all seemed so beautiful already. It seemed beautiful the way they showed it to me."

She then lifted her head and her voice became more clear. "I liked that they would talk about things in front of me. I didn't always understand all of it, high-tech projects and company policies, but I felt included. I thought it was just something special for our family to do, to take care of the city. It didn't seem like anyone else knew or cared about all the important things we were up to." Her voice dropped again, as if the sound needed to be forced out. "And then someone killed them because of it."

Her words expressed a driving force with no clear direction. "I don't think I can just let everything they cared about end."

Like his little companion, Gozen fought to remember the faces of her parents. "Suzu, I could have killed those two men . . . I almost did. It's a decision I haven't had to face in a very long time. Conviction and duty . . ." Gozen's voice trailed off as thoughts tangled in his mind. "When you opened the door that first time, I looked down and saw this child, lost and alone in her own home. Every day since, I've just been trying to figure out how to look after that little girl. And today I almost completely failed to do it."

Suzu spoke, her eyes sympathetic. "But I'm not a little girl anymore, Gozen. I'm just little."

Gozen looked up into the dim street light that glistened in his eyes. "Then you need to follow where your heart pulls you."

He glanced towards the dumpster housing the silent hoods, long enough for Suzu to notice. Gozen then turned to her with absolute sincerity. "Some mistakes you only get to make once. Don't get impatient with your journey, but don't ever stop."

Meditating on the words, they slowly exhaled a mutual tension.

"So those two guys aren't dead?"

Gozen shrugged his shoulders. "Probably not. Come on, I'll give you a ride back to Lucette's."

Suzu smiled as much as her sore face could muster, and then paused in confusion. "How did you know I was staying there?"

Gozen stood up slowly and then offered Suzu his hand. He gently lifted her up. "You've been on your own for all of one day. It's going to take a lot longer than that before you're able to hide from these eyes."

o o o

On the ride back to Lucette's, Gozen inquired of Suzu how she managed to get into such a situation. She divulged her desire to find those responsible for her parents' death but kept things vague. She wasn't sure just why she didn't want to mention Kits to Gozen just then. Maybe he would keep her from pursuing such a dangerous person and ultimately prevent her from finding the mysterious man whom Kits worked for. Maybe she wanted to finish what she tried to do earlier that night. It was too much to think about, and she just wanted to be in a bed.

Lucette gasped at the sight of Suzu when she arrived with Gozen. The former Enforcer quickly tempered the panic and tended to Suzu's wounds in the refreshingly sanitary bathroom. While Lucette made tea, Suzu asked Gozen about the stab wound she just then remembered him having. He acknowledged it then simply called out to Lucette, inquiring about the status of the tea.

Trying to keep things calm, Gozen stayed until he was confident the girl was stable and able to be alone with her roommate. They finished their tea, a rather comforting blend of local wild flowers that wasn't brewed quite long enough—a fair effort for a young lady new to living on her own.

He said his goodbyes and left the apartment quietly. He walked calmly down the hall and then rounded the corner. Feeling that he was then out of sight and sound, Gozen leaned against the wall as his emotion boiled over. He let it out along a stream of tears and muffled sounds into his sleeve. He felt too tired to hold anything in any more. Equal parts pain and relief, it all escaped until there was no more pressure left.

Gozen then took in a deep breath, wiped his face off with the other sleeve, and proceeded to walk back to Neko. His mind wandered on thoughts of the city he had long ago sworn to protect. There were girls being assaulted in alleys, companies being sold off or traded with no regard for the lives that depended on them. The ideological urban experiment seemed to be fading away from the pristine vision its creator had set up. Gozen didn't understand why Opaji would let his precious Chigou turn towards such a direction. He questioned if the old Lord was either loosing his grip or loosing his mind.

○ ○ ○

Always wanting to monitor the entirety of his grand experiment, Opaji preferred to observe it high above the streets. But as his precious city grew, he realized so did the number of places one could hide from his overseeing eye. For the few close to him, it became obvious that Chigou's usually unruffled creator had grown increasingly suspicious.

Down on the first floor, Daimó had just gotten on to the elevator, quickly heading up for an unexpected meeting with Opaji. Standing behind the operator, he slid an old stone carving out of his pocket. Daimó's eyes bore into the image that he had grimaced at countless times. The carved portrait simply portrayed two downward sloping eyes inside a ghostlike shape, decidedly abstract but painfully familiar. His thumbnail scratched at the stone face, which reminded him of why he chose to follow the course he had been on for so long.

The small relic felt heavy in his hand, a burden that had been there so long he knew no existence without it. His fingers shook with anticipation. He gripped the relic so firmly that he could taste its bitter minerals in his mouth. After decades, the end finally felt within reach. He reminded himself to keep patient. He convinced himself it was not revenge. He swallowed the caustic taste in his mouth and pocketed the graven image.

Daimó entered the office escorted by three armed Sentinels, two more than he felt necessary. He only occasionally met with Opaji and felt the sudden call of a meeting rather curious. Of the many things Daimó orchestrated, only a few of them did he care to officially report to Opaji. Their collaboration was intentionally held at arm's length, and Daimó assumed a mutual satisfaction with it. The big question Daimó always held in his mind, however, was when Opaji would finally discover his absolute plan for the city. Their desires currently overlapped, but he knew at one point their divergence would be fiercely understood by every living being in the valley.

"Do you know what I appreciate about the city, Daimó?" Opaji asked into a glass of Shumé. "It's honest about its ambitions."

Daimó found the question rather sobering, being called into a meeting and immediately reminded of the value of honesty. He looked back to see security exiting the massive office. As the final sentinel shut the door, he made direct eye contact with Daimó before grabbing his gun as if to get it out of the way.

"Chigou, just as Primichi that came before it, was birthed from the womb of progress. Labor pains are a testament to the value of what is born. It is a triumph over complacent fear and the product of steadfast will."

Daimó considered the words, trying to keep ahead of where they were going.

Opaji continued. "Women are the weaker of the two sexes. Some are insecure about it while others accept the physical certainty. The creation of life, however, bears most of its weight upon their shoulders, and a woman feels no need to hide its burden. It is a harrowing responsibility, and they own it."

He finally turned his head to Daimó. "How fatal the error of one who hides from that responsibility. How just the other who rectifies dishonest misuse of such power."

Daimó had never seen such sharp determination in Opaji's eyes before. The old Lord grabbed a folder off of his desk and opened it. "This Dark-spark technology is turning into quite the seductress. Its promise of vast power tempts man to become greedy and betray those who have given it to him. Would you agree with that?"

Daimó had yet to share his true intentions regarding Dark-spark, not even with Kits and certainly not the captain of the city. He felt certain Opaji had not discovered his plans but suddenly began to question if the old Lord had growing suspicions of him. Daimó kept silent, carefully measuring his response.

"How cowardly and vile the man given much opportunity only to deceive the one who gifted him with it." A bitter sadness seemed to flush into Opaji's face. "A disease of constitution that will not be allowed to perpetuate."

For the first time, Daimó compared the physicality of the two men at the window. He felt a strangely primal comfort in assuming he would come out on top of a barbarous conflict between the two of them. He thought again of the holstered guns just outside the door.

Daimó felt his fingers clench behind his back as he finally spoke. "The virtue of progress and the resolution to see it through; woe to the man who impedes its path."

The air between them pulled taut as Opaji continued. "There is a man of increasing value here, developing a technology that could prove quite significant in the growth of industry. His name is Pirou Naizen, nephew to Kasic Vice President Bardin Naizen. Bardin was overly gracious in how much he gave to the young man, who I believe is acting with deceptively selfish intentions. If this Pirou plans on so treacherously repaying the faith given him, as I believe he does, I want to know his intentions in detail, followed by appropriately strong action."

Daimó let out a suffocated breath, now confident that Opaji's concerns were not being directed towards himself. "I will align this misdirection."

"Good," Opaji stated. "Bardin is letting his sentimentality for family cloud his judgment; Pirou has been suspiciously guarded over his new Dark-spark research. However, he has recently relieved himself of his original assistant, Remi Jounaka, and requested for a new one. The opportunity speaks for itself. I will leave you to finding the right man for the job."

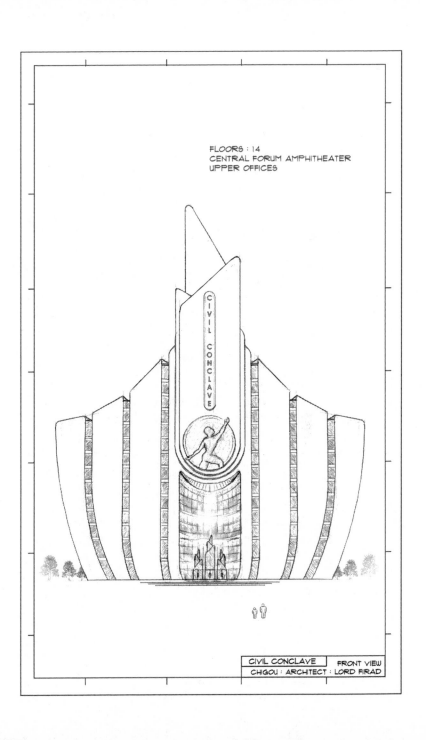

FLOORS : 14
CENTRAL FORUM AMPHITHEATER
UPPER OFFICES

CIVIL CONCLAVE

CIVIL CONCLAVE | FRONT VIEW
CHIGOU : ARCHITECT : LORD FIRAD

13
PERSPECTIVE

She fought hard to see through the forest of human heads waving from the hot wind coming out of them. The steel and wood stage held men in suits just high enough to be seen over the crowd. Surrounding it, massive shafts of metal curved up into the ceiling, forcing all attention down into the belly of the auditorium. Hanging high above the stage, massive steel letters set in oiled brass threatened to crush all below. They unrelentingly spoke two words that described all the monumental pragmatism that happened within: CIVIL CONCLAVE.

Nia tried to hide the fact that she had never been inside the Conclave's main auditorium. She spent as much time trying to decipher the etiquette of its occupants as she did listening to the panel discussion on stage. That day's ballet of policy and proposals centered around an examination of refined Jinouki power versus the emerging Dark-spark fuel technology.

Gozen, who had been making a hobby of resisting Nia's requests to get involved with industrial politics, surprised the young lady by actually suggesting she attend. He had concerns over Jinouki development, as Kora operated as a large supplier of Tulúki, especially to Etecid. Gozen currently headed to the troubled company to deliver a shipment that had been held up for over a week. Unable to split himself in half, the option to solve two problems presented itself; Nia promised to take notes.

The effort to not only comprehend but also quickly write down the rather technical conversations wore Nia out. She tried her best to exude a casual confidence, but the sweat on her forehead, combined with the fact that she was far younger and more female than nearly every other member of the meeting, proved to make such a task rather laborious.

Exhaustion aside, Nia found the room full of bloated men surprisingly intriguing. They discussed one grand concept after another, many of which would impact nearly all of Chigou's citizens. Their seemingly casual demeanor made her wonder how much these men really thought about those lives they so broadly affected. Then, suddenly the pattern of graying hair and puffy suits revealed the blink of a sharp silhouette. Her eyes jumped back and forth from the stage to the obscured figure, until finally able to catch a clear look.

With strong posture and a bit of panache, the young man stood seemingly alone. His appearance didn't beg for attention, but Nia felt he looked downright striking relative to the current crowd of company men. Focusing more intently, she developed a vague recognition about his face. The hall then filled with the echoing sound of the closing mallet, and Nia shuffled to collect her notes. Looking back, she saw the young man already walking towards the exit.

Nia quickly cut through the well-fed crowd, her eyes scanning for the young man. She had wanted to speak to at least one person at the Conclave but had yet to receive a single respectful gesture from anyone.

She made it to the lobby only to find a swarm of graying hair completely void of a single stylish cut. Nia then headed straight out the front doors, trying to calm her frantic pace as she passed between two Civil Enforcers standing at the entrance. Her eyes strained as they refocused, darting around until something grabbed her.

A shining black car had been parked right on the curb, a model she had only seen briefly. With silver lettering spelling *Móstique* on the back, she quickly recalled seeing it once before back at Kora. Her curiosity pulled her straight down the steps, squinting into the window to see if any silhouette emerged.

Converging on the same door, Nia managed to collide directly into the driver. Kits grabbed her shoulder, bracing the mutually staggered young lady. A million options clawed through Nia's frenzied brain until something finally surfaced.

"You were at the farm." Nia spoke the words as if in the middle of a conversation.

With a neutral expression, Kits glanced over the perimeter. "You were waiting for me?"

"No," Nia quickly offered. "I mean . . . well, no." She loudly cleared her throat. "I recognized you in the Civil Conclave. You've been to Kora Farm before; I remember this car. It's kind of unique."

Nia's candid tone pulled Kits away from at least some of his suspicions. "True. Are you here with anyone else?"

"No." Her posture began to loosen up. "I'm waiting for my ride to show up. My name is Nia, by the way."

Kits began to calculate how much info he wanted to exchange with this stranger. "I'm Kits."

As the sounds of the city seeped back into their attention, a specific suspicion materialized in Kits's mind. He began to look around, casually raising his right hand to check the firearm beneath his jacket. Unable to see the particular man whose massive size would stand out in any crowd, Kits reengaged the healthy-looking young lady standing in front of his car.

"So you were waiting for me, and here I am," Kits offered.

"Yes," Nia smiled. "To be honest, this is the first time I've ever been to one of these things, and it's nice to see a familiar face. Even one as vaguely familiar as yours."

"I generally try to keep a low profile, so I'll take that as a compliment."

The statement prodded Nia's curiosity. "So what is it that you do?"

Kits responded quickly, having been conditioned to answer such a question. "Industrial research. Did Jin Aya not tell you?"

"I don't really talk to him a whole lot more than I need to," Nia answered, enjoying any moment she had to take a jab at her rich house guest.

"So you're not too close with the workers up there?"

Nia crossed her arms. "It can be a good idea to be a little selective with how close you get to some people, but we're all generally friendly up there. Occasionally I'd maybe call one a little sister, so . . . yeah, it depends."

A sobering thought materialized, and Kits began scanning for a much smaller individual. "Little sister, huh? Did you bring her along, too?"

Nia felt her energy drop. Kits stood still, internally examining her reaction like a paranoid forensic psychologist. He watched her fidgeting fingers as she finally responded, "No. She moved out a little while ago to live in the city. Girl's gotta grow up one day, right?"

Evaluating Nia's efforts to hide the complexity of her answer, Kits pushed forward. "I thought sisters liked to keep in touch."

"Well, we need our space, too. I'm sure she'll visit soon." She shrugged and smiled.

Kits had forced a reluctant confession from his well-bruised subordinates, who quickly blamed their failure on the brutal giant from the shadows. Having never met him personally, Kits knew enough about Gozen not to trifle with him. He wondered if the resourceful detective was days or hours away from kicking down his door. Alternatively, he suspected the young girl might have kept her revenge preoccupation private. Nia certainly didn't act as though she spoke with a man who had engaged in a life-or-death fight with her little sister.

"So, what made you decide to come to a Corporate Liability Edict gathering?"

"I'm thinking about studying civil development at an academy, so I'm curious about this kind of thing," Nia said. "But you mentioned doing industrial research. What does that involve, besides coming to these things?"

Kits remained thin with details. "A rather wide range of things. Most of them being a bit dull."

"So what about the other, not-dull things?" Nia grinned.

The conversation started to slip into the flirtatious, and Kits felt foolish for pursuing it, but an opportunity began to present itself. Nia seemed a potential source of useful information, but checking the time on his Toki, he knew it had to wait. "Pressing matters that cannot be delayed. Until next time, Lady Nia."

Nia's interest spiked at the abrupt exit. "When will that be?"

"Sooner than you think."

○ ○ ○

Up North at Gris Avenue, impatience pushed Gozen's pulse up. He paced back and forth beside Neko, filled with a week-old Tulúki shipment. A malfunctioning loader at Etecid caused the delay. Darou anxiously looked around the loading bay, trying not to make any sudden moves.

"Is this guy getting paid specifically to waste my time?" Gozen asked in an unusually stressed tone. Darou reminded himself that hypothetical questions should not be answered. Down the alley, a middle-aged man with industrially stained skin and tired eyes came out of a side door.

"There's Cruno," Darou politely stated, stepping back to avoid any potential crossfire. Cruno dragged his feet towards the truck. Gozen took the gesture as permission to start the dialogue and quickly pointed to the trailer.

"So this is getting here a week late. Things sometimes happen, I get that. But last night, I'm told that the tank is fixed, so I spend the entire morning rushing the load back together and drive down here to what appears to be a tank that, in fact, is not fixed."

Cruno took off his hat and scratched the back of his head. "Yeah, it looks like it's actually going to be tomorrow. Sorry to make you wait so long."

Gozen stepped in; Darou stepped back more. "You know, Cruno, after waiting an entire week, one extra day isn't really so different. What I'm more concerned with right now is why I just wasted an entire day's worth of man hours and fuel. Did Darou lie in the wire-type he sent telling me to come down, or did you lie to him when you told him the tank was fixed?"

Darou knew the answer but currently felt strongly the virtues of being a good listener. Cruno conceded a proper explanation. "It looked like we were going to get it fixed today, and I wanted to give you a head start. I should have waited. I take responsibility for that."

Gozen nodded. "Head start, huh? Yeah, you seem all about getting ahead of things around here." Cruno answered with silence. Darou agreed. Finally, pragmatism crept over Gozen, who took in a deep breath. "So you're going to have this fixed by the time I come back tomorrow?"

Cruno put his frumpy hat back on. "If it's not ready by tonight, I'll wire you and let you know."

"Oh, it's going to be ready, Cruno, because if it's not . . ." Gozen took another deep breath. "Just have it done." Gozen quickly got into the cab and slammed the door.

The loud gesture echoed through the alley into a parabolic alloy dish up on the roof. Redirecting the sound waves, the dish had collected the entire conversation into a small microphone connected to an Aunica Pocke amplifier. Kits held the device while peering out over the roof, his ears covered with large headphones.

He took out a field pad and wrote down cryptic notes. Kits made a habit of using his own internal language to keep records that would appear vague at best to anyone trying to gain useful information from them.

As Neko drove out onto Gris Avenue, Kits began to break down the parabolic microphone. He slung it over his shoulder and ratcheted it tight to his torso. Raising his Toki, he checked the time.

Sixteen blocks away, Daimó looked out the window of his unlabeled office. Dots of citizens scrambled below, walking between vehicles and streetlights. His mind pondered the city's potential for chaos and its need for control. He thought of progress; he thought of death.

Daimó then gazed towards a piece of stone on his desk. The shape contained fine details that had been blurred, as if countless years had smoothed them away. On the front, a face extruded out, one that looked similar to his own. The image fostered feelings of sentimental pride, such as with a gift from Father to Son.

He then flipped it over to reveal two long, sloping eyes, simple but ominous. A woman who had seen it many years ago said it looked like a ghost of Goraka. She explained to Daimó about the creature featured in the haunting children's book "Tales from the Red Valley." She divulged the images and stories of all that lurked down in the forbidden forest. She dismissed it as silly fiction, but Daimó needed no such education on what resided in the Red Valley. The carved face linked back to a history that clawed at his spirit. It always led him to think of the people of the valley, but not the ones who thought they had discovered it. He picked at the face with his thumbnail, his teeth grinding in the back of his mouth.

Kits then walked in. His shoes clicked on the cold, tile floor before he set his parabolic microphone kit onto a table.

"And what did we learn today?" Daimó's voice echoed off the floor.

"I think our Etecid man Cruno is starting to reveal his pattern." Kits stayed at the table.

"Has he been thinking too much with his mouth?"

"With his hands, it seems. Gozen, the big man from Kora, is taking a rather aggressive notice of Cruno's inept performance. His tone leads me to think that he is raising suspicions, although I don't believe in anything specific, yet."

The perpetual sound of flowing traffic seeped through the walls. "Kits, do you know how to control the direction of a force more powerful than yourself?"

Kits had become rather accustomed to Daimó's quasi-hypotheticals. Initially quite intimidating, he eventually found a rather enjoyable sense of humor about them. "You become more powerful?"

Daimó noticed a light down below turn green, along with a quick burst from a high-pitched steam whistle signaling the northbound travelers to pass through the intersection. The pedestrians followed, as expected. Daimó's breath fogged the glass. "You know it well enough to predict its behavior, and then simply alter the path in front of it."

Kits mused over the words. At times he would question the larger motivations of his superior but would typically digress to simpler paths. "How would you like me to proceed with Cruno?"

The light over the horizon completely disappeared as Daimó turned around. His vacant eyes were something that Kits never quite got used to. "We converted Karoburn into Etecid as a long-term measure, but I believe its usefulness now parallels that of our mutual acquaintance Cruno. It is time to make way for what is to come."

Despite its seeming vagueness, Kits needed no clearer instruction. He began to walk towards the door and plot his next action. The thought of an imposing man halted his feet. "The large guy Gozen—he seems to be of an investigative mind. Normally I wouldn't be concerned, but if certain situations arise, he may not be so easy to be deal with. He seems like a rather powerful chap."

"Yes, quite a bit more powerful than most." Daimó spoke with calm certainty. "And equally predictable."

o o o

Darou waited alone by the Etecid tank loaders, a garden of pipes and steam. He anxiously waited for Cruno, who had remained unseen since the previous day's hot-blooded forum. Darou checked the time on his scratched Toki just as he heard Neko punctually pull in from Gris Avenue.

Gozen stopped the truck and stepped out, sporting the frustrated face he left with the day before. Darou heard the air sucking in through Gozen's flaring nostrils. Much to the young man's relief, Cruno finally arrived.

"I didn't hear from you, Cruno, so that means this Tulúki is getting offloaded right now," Gozen said with tense certainty.

Cruno's tired saunter came to a stop. "It should be good to load."

"Should be?" Gozen interrogated. "I didn't drive back into the city for *should*."

Cruno strained to lift the weight of his eyelids. "I'm certain it'll . . . it's working. I'll go fire up the loader. Darou . . ." He gestured to the hushed young man and headed back to the door.

Gozen's sharp tongue followed. "That's good. Better to wait until after I get here."

Ignoring the comment, Cruno kept walking. Relieved enough by Cruno's confidence over the fixed loader, Darou finally spoke to Gozen. "You sound a bit dramatic lately. You've been hanging out with teenage girls a little too much?"

"Precisely," Gozen said plainly as he walked back to Neko. "Let's get this over with."

Darou squeaked out a laugh which he prayed Gozen didn't hear. He watched the big man walk around the truck as the sound of doors and valves began to bounce around the loading bay. The young man then snapped his head back, distracted by a silhouette down the alley.

Sitting in shadow, the shape of a sleek sedan contrasted against the light of Gris Avenue. Its sleek, polished exterior looked strange sitting in the dank industrial artery. Darou assumed it to be some high-powered executive who took a wrong turn.

Cruno appeared on the roof and began to open the loader. Vacuum pipes poured seed into a large auger, forcing the Tulúki grain into the holding tanks. The walls rattled from machinery pushing container after container through the alloy circulatory system. Darou looked back down the alley, the car sitting still like a stalking cat. His eyes strained to make out the occupant, instead identifying something oddly sticking out of the roof.

Darou turned to Gozen, assuming the former Enforcer would notice anything suspicious, but the big man kept his frustrated focus on the roaring grain loader. Curiosity spun the young man's head back just as a flash appeared from the end of what looked like a crooked antenna. Darou refocused up towards the roof, but Cruno had already disappeared.

With Gozen still distracted, Darou developed an impulse to investigate the peculiar vehicle. Ignoring the loading process, he slowly walked towards the car, noticing the antenna-type-thing retract into the car. Darou began to make out a figure in the driver's seat, a strong and postured shape looking straight ahead at him. The headlights suddenly flashed straight ahead, and then the car vanished.

o o o

Air whistled over the cab of Neko as trees blurred by in random succession. The silos of Kora appeared as pebbles on the edge of the horizon. Gozen's mind bounced between farm logistics and paranoid thoughts of female teenage ambition.

He looked into his rearview mirror and saw a trail of dust kick up behind a black blur. It took less than a minute before the vehicle reached him. Gozen looked out the passenger window and saw the car shoot past. Rocks pelted Neko's thick metal hood as the hissing engine faded away up ahead. Moaning, Gozen forced himself to think of a steaming coffee served by elegant Lady fingers.

Inside one of the silos, Jin stood under his C22, installing the differential to a prototype all-wheel-drive system. The car was suspended above the ground via a modified lift system produced by Aya Precision; Jin felt a collapsible version served its purposes better.

The silo door opened and Nia walked in, quietly heading for a small lift truck called a Fat Cat. It got its name from the small diamond-shaped headlights and its disproportionately large storage capacity.

Warmed up from a Blashu roll she stole out of the kitchen, Nia prodded. "Have you been in here all day?"

"No, I ate for thirty-five minutes in the house during the afternoon." Jin looked over the finely tuned vehicle that usually emitted an air of speed and power. Recently it began to feel like stuff bolted onto stuff. He simply stared at it.

Surprised that she could in fact care less, Nia decided to keep the conversation going. "You're in here all day and you don't have one word to speak about whatever it is you're working on?"

Jin finally turned around. "Yes, of course. I am demoing a new concept to a potential buyer today. It's the young Lord Kits who was here the other day."

"Kits?" Nia asked with surprising volume and speed.

"Yes." His tone signaled a question as much as an answer.

Her self-consciousness sparked, Nia quickly tried to appear wholly uninterested. "What?"

Again surprised at her punchy volume, Jin spoke slowly. "I'm not sure what. Is there something about my meeting with Kits . . ."

"No." Nia, perhaps too efficiently, denied any significance to the sudden news of Kits and meetings.

The confusion cut short as the sound of their subject shot through the wall. As it got louder, Jin recognized it as a large bore, six-chamber Dark-spark engine with an integrated high-pressure compressor; however, it sounded like it needed a new air filter.

Nia quickly got into the Fat Cat and fired up the steam engine. She pulled up a few meters and then stopped in the path of Jin's blank stare. She threw up her hands, submitting to Jin's persecuting calmness. "What!?"

Jin stood dumbfounded. "I'm not entirely confident I

understand what we are talking about anymore."

Letting out a groan of frustration, Nia charged through the silo's main door on the Fat Cat, escaping Jin's judgmental silence. She pushed it to its top speed, about that of a moderately athletic child. Jin decided to go back to working on his stuff.

Framed in a cloud of dust, Kits pulled up to the house. Nia pulled up to the auxiliary lot and started to look busy, anticipating Gozen's arrival with empty Tulúki crates. Kits got out wearing a dark suit with no tie. Although clad in work clothes, Nia felt rather confident wearing her best-fitting striped pants.

Kits quickly noticed her red hair, which seemed twice as bright in the clear sun. As he started to approach, Nia maintained her attention on the Fat Cat's loader. "Jin's in the silo."

Keeping an eye out for Gozen, Kits found the sight of Nia rather distracting. The memory of Daimó's voice then redirected his thoughts. Nia waited a moment before peeking over at him, noticing his unique walk, like a street kid who grew up sneaking into private schools. In the distance, Neko rumbled over the Long Frost Bridge.

Kits entered the silo to the sight of Jin staring up at the underbelly of his car, still with an unusually lost expression. "You look stumped."

Jin looked over, his blurred thoughts quickly sharpening. "Good day. I apologize that it's not ready to drive yet, but I shall run you through the concept."

Kits walked up to Jin and smirked. "Still running steam, I see. You being sentimental or is Dark-spark a little too complicated for you?"

"This is probably the most efficient engine you've ever seen. I do not believe sentimentality applies," Jin said plainly.

"Emotionally stated as always, Jin."

"Pardon, I said I'm not being sentimental," Jin disputed. Kits smirked in amusement.

Jin continued. "If you are referring to current matters, I don't think the natural efficiency of Dark-spark technology would be appreciated above its rather noxious side effects at this farm. Being here, I've actually developed more interest over Core-thermic energy technologies."

"Why Jin, you're not turning into an industrialist Soran, are you? That's the kind of inner conflict that could drive one a bit mad."

Jin considered his state of being as of late. Conflict and ambiguity had caused a lack of focus that made his mind feel raw. He did not seem to have a swelling love of the natural world, although he clearly noticed those around him who certainly did.

"So that girl out there, does she work here all the time?" Kits asked.

Jin noticed Kits forcing a presentation of indifference. "Are you referring to Lady Nia, the young woman driving the Fat Cat?"

"Yes, the rather fit-looking amber top."

Jin pragmatically questioned the relevance of the observation. "Yes, she is notably athletic and manages quite a bit at this farm. What business are you interested in discussing with her?"

Kits looked away and tried to temper his smile. "Oh, no business really." Hearing Neko finally pull up to the house, Kits then subtly checked the gun holstered in his jacket. A developing certainty had grown regarding Suzu's lack of divulgence over their altercation, but if she had revealed his identity to Gozen, Kits knew that night would prove dramatic. Mentally, he prepared himself for either possible outcome.

Outside, Gozen let out yet another long sigh. Nia heard him while he looked over the black Móstique, speckled with dust.

"You finally get that Tulúki offloaded, big guy?" Nia jovially asked.

Fully distracted, Gozen analyzed its slick surface, juxtaposing everything around it. Nia noticed. "Gozen, I said did you . . ."

"Can't Jin conduct his fancy business deals in the city?"

"I'm still not sure why Jin is here at all," Nia added before heading towards the back of Neko. "But don't worry about Kits, he's all right."

The statement immediately sparked Gozen's keen senses. Realizing what she had just done, Nia kept kept moving, hearing Gozen's heavy feet follow behind.

"You know this guy?"

Nia jumped into the Fat Cat and turned on its engine. She backed up and lowered the rear gate. Gozen patiently walked over to the cab, blocking the driver door.

Nia played it off. "Yes. It is a custom on the farm to introduce oneself to visitors."

Her attempts to temper the inquisition inversely increased Gozen's concern. Nia dropped her shoulders with a grin. "Geesh, all right. I ran into him at the Civil Conclave. We spoke for about five minutes."

Gozen waited for more information.

"What? He's here to see Jin. May I get back to work, Lord Enforcer?"

Gozen finally backed up and the two began offloading the empty Tulúki crates.

○ ○ ○

After the sun had disappeared, Jin finished calibrating the technology Kits's rather esoteric company still only considered investing in; he found the business potential increasingly thin. Jin then decided to deal with the mild aching in his stomach. He packed his tools away and slowly cleaned the workspace to a spotless state.

On his way back to the house, Jin saw two figures silhouetted against the black Móstique. As he approached them, he could see Nia's eyes brightly engaged behind Kits's head. She ignored Jin, and he moved on.

As he neared the house he heard laughter behind him, sounds being pushed out by some kind of youthful excitement. Jin noticed it to be the first time he had heard such exuberance from Nia since Suzu had gone, although not exactly the same. Regardless, Jin recognized that he liked the sound, but less so from Kits. Finally, he made it into the house.

It looked warm like it always did, but everything seemed still. Often Clora would be in the kitchen, or some young worker would be passing through. He forgot why he entered until a rumbling sensation came from his stomach.

Jin entered the dining room but quickly stopped at the sight of Kojo and Gozen sitting silently at the table. They both looked directly at him, their eyes tired. On the table sat a half-empty bottle of Shumé, a distilled liquor made from Blashu and green mountain herbs.

"Good evening, Lords." Jin's spirit spoke with conditioned etiquette. Gozen and Kojo smiled smugly at one another.

Jin spoke again. "My meeting with Kits is over. He's outside with Nia. They're laughing."

With smirks nearly becoming full-blown smiles, Kojo spoke for the pair. "Have a seat, young man."

Neither Lord had ever invited Jin to simply sit and discuss with such jovial timbre. Contemplating the drinking vessel before him, Jin replied, "It's not custom for me to drink during a work day; however, I appreciate the offer."

Kojo slowly filled up the glass and slid it over. Jin's face softened. "I suppose we are finding ourselves in the periphery of twilight. Well then, if I may join two Lords relaxing at the conclusion of an accomplished day," he said, sliding the chair half out.

Kojo let out the closest thing to a laugh that Jin had ever heard from the man. The farmer then took a sip. "You certainly are a first for this farm, Lord Aya. Now please, before this Shumé takes effect and this old man falls asleep in front of his young guest." Jin sat down.

After exchanging implicating glances with Kojo, Gozen leaned forward. "So Jin, tell me what you know about this Kits fellow."

Outside the conversation had carried on long enough for Kits and Nia to end up leaning rather close to one another. Nia had spent most of the time talking about the farm and various elements of her routine. Kits had done little to reciprocate with his own activities. The hour grew late, and neither expressed a rush to leave.

"So what is the name of the company that you work for? Let's start with that," Nia graciously suggested.

Kits hesitated with a smile. "I wouldn't say that I work for a company. At least, not how I'm sure you mean."

His deliberate processing of every question led the young woman to keep thinking of more to ask. "But you certainly must work for someone, right?"

"Yeah, I can say I work for someone," Kits managed to get out.

"All right then, now I almost, sort of, know something about you." Nia caught Kits nearly becoming coy. "So, would I know who this person is?"

"No."

"Not a chance, huh?"

Kits leaned in closer. "Even if you have actually met him somehow, you still wouldn't know who he is."

"Sounds like quite a guy. So were you just lucky to meet him, or are you a boy of privilege like your car-club buddy?" Nia nodded towards the house.

"Not my buddy, really, and I imagine our childhoods could not have been more different."

The answer took Nia by surprise. "You are just full of mystery, aren't you, mister . . ."

Normally for Kits, he avoided wading into such comfortable conversation, allowing for some slipped detail to open a door to Daimó. He took a long, quiet breath. "Bodú. Kits Bodú."

A satisfied smile slowly grew on Nia's face. "Nice to finally meet you, Kits Bodú."

In that moment, a rather odd thought came to the front of Kits's mind; he couldn't recall ever making anyone smile—at least not recently, and not with any kind of sincerity. The jarring sensation led to a desire for more, reminding him of eating food seasoned with salt and vinegar.

Clora then walked up to the pair, causing them to stand up straight. She carried an empty basket covered with a plaid towel. The two young adults leaned away from each other, their perfect timing making the gesture plainly suspicious.

Clora looked at the two with a distinctly motherly grin. "I got those preserved Mimi fruits jarred and ready to be taken to the North Orphanage tomorrow."

"Yeah, I'll take them in with Gozen in the morning," Nia said with forced pragmatism.

Clora glanced over to Kits before speaking again. "Sounds lovely. Good night, you two."

Nia jumped up. "Oh, Mom, this is Kits. He had a meeting with

Jin, but we recognized each other from the last time I went into town."

Clora stepped up to Kits and gently extended her hand. "It's nice to meet you, young man. My name is Clora."

With simple etiquette, Kits gently shook her hand. "It's a pleasure, Lady Clora."

Everyone took in a breath before Clora spoke again. "Well, good night then."

Once she had disappeared into the house, Nia's face illuminated with an idea. "Hey, since you work in the city, why don't you stop by the Tree House tomorrow? I'll be there all day."

Kits hesitated, now being more conscious of how candid he had gotten. "I'm not sure I really have any business in an orphanage."

"Not sure you can handle all those spunky little kids?"

"I've spent plenty of time in them. I'm just not sure why I'd go back to one."

Nia absorbed the sting of the statement. "If you say so."

Standing there, Kits pondered just how attractive he considered that girl. He found pretty faces to be in no short supply in the city, but Nia possessed something altogether different—a combination of qualities he either had never encountered before or at least never noticed. Giving into the feeling, he searched for some practical reason to take Nia up on her offer. "So, how late are you going to be there?"

Two minutes later, the sound of Kits's Dark-spark machine driving off passed through the kitchen walls. Nia's footsteps could be heard approaching the entrance. She ached for a drink from the long talk and headed to the kitchen, her face glowing.

Halfway there, Gozen, Jin, and Kojo greeted her from the comfort of their seats. They sat with nearly empty glasses in their hands and an equally empty bottle of Shumé in the middle. Their half-open eyes hovered over Nia, who felt like she was standing before a jury. Annoyed, she threw up her hands.

"What?"

With the speed of syrup sliding down a spoon, the men all looked at each other with Shumé eyes before bursting into snorts and laughter. Nia accordingly rolled her eyes and went to bed.

14
ORPHANAGE

The cab gently hummed as the pair traveled down to the Tree House, fulfilling a routine delivery. Upon leaving, Nia received a kiss goodbye from Clora along with a short talk about boys from her father. Afterward, Clora delivered another talk to her husband about how much Shumé had been consumed the night before.

Once they arrived at the orphanage, Nia jumped out, immediately confused that Gozen didn't follow. "You're not coming in?"

"No, I need to check on something out west," he succinctly spoke.

Nia squinted. "What's going on over there?"

"Nothing, I hope." Gozen felt fine leaving it at that.

"Gozen, if you're this close to Lady Kyoumére and not coming in, it's most certainly something." Nia crossed her arms.

Gozen lowered his face into the steering wheel. "All interrogators should be teenage girls."

"Aww, you getting picked on at the playground?" Nia quickly inquired.

Gozen rubbed his temples before answering. "I got a wire-type from an Enforcer friend. There might be a mining operation in the West Mountains utilizing child labor. If so, I'm going to help them relocate the kids."

He could see Nia's eyes light up with a vigilante sparkle; he was also in a hurry. "No, you can't go."

"I didn't ask." She wanted to go.

"Because there isn't time for you to do all this here and make it over. Otherwise, I'd ask you to go, maybe." Nia dropped her shoulders. "All right." She then hopped down and got to work. Once Nia finished unloading produce, Gozen caught a glimpse of Lady Kyoumére peeking through the window. They managed to share a single sweet glance before he drove out through the city.

In the back, an onslaught of smiles and high-pitched voices greeted Nia. Although a common occurrence, she reminded herself to always be thankful for it. It humbled her to receive so much love from a group that had already had so much taken from them. She then wrestled with images of the children Gozen mentioned, being used day and night for someone else's profit. A complicated frustration grew inside her as she navigated around swarming children.

○ ○ ○

In the energy capital of Chigou, Kasic employees bustled about as they usually did. A new position had opened up, and the usual line of applicants had arranged a row of chairs outside of an auxiliary office. Inside, a young man, who had yet to give his name to a single applicant, fought the fatigue of tedium.

In charge of a special Dark-spark project, Pirou Naizen had requested a replacement for his current research assistant Remi. Pirou found the young man obnoxiously ambitious towards irrelevant ideologies. Lord Opaji noted the circumstance as an opportunity to investigate Pirou, a man whom he had grown incredibly suspicious of. As one of the top men at Kasic, Bardin Naizen had hired Pirou, who also happened to be his nephew. Opaji found the decision to be foolishly sentimental.

Having been tasked to deal with the problem by the Lord of Chigou himself, Daimó decided to put an agent of subversion by Pirou's side, a crafty person capable of sliding below company ethics. Kits had so far spent the day going through one gleaming poster child after another, very disappointing indeed.

The second to last applicant listed entered, not quite as sharply dressed as his competitors but holding a different kind of confidence. After passing off his resumé, the man stood across the desk and anxiously bounced on his toes. Thin on enthusiasm, Kits asked him to sit down.

"Victou, Victou Despré," the man stated as he bowed before sitting down. Kits groaned while sorting through the stacks of biography. The information seemed applicable, competently presented, and did nothing at first glance to narrow down the decision he needed to make. Something then caught his attention.

Noticing Kits's slight contraction of the eyes, Victou interjected, "I'm sure you'll find that my credentials are easily qualifying. So to assist in your decision-making process, if I may, I offer that any questions you have as to the quality of my person, I am fully prepared to answer."

The words floated past Kits's ears with little notice. He sorted through more papers until landing on a diploma from East Lesai Academy. The applicant noticed how carefully Kits surveyed the meticulously crafted paper.

"I will say, as you look through what is probably looking redundant to you this late in the morning, diplomas and all, that my ability to research beyond the obvious could be of great help. I'm good at seeing through things, you could say."

Kits finally looked up. "So, how did you find your time studying energy development at East Lesai?"

Victou sat upright. "It's a good school, quite small. Helped me get here."

"It's very rare to meet any one from Lesai. What brought you out here?" Kits began to dissect and Victou could feel it.

"Family matters, mostly."

"You have children?"

Victou wanted to divert the question, but he hesitated just long enough to know he couldn't get away with it. "Yes, I have a daughter, actually, but she is away at a camp while I get my new employment situated."

Kits looked at Victou but said nothing.

Victou got back to it. "So, yes, what family man wouldn't want a chance to work in the shining city in the mountains, especially here at Kasic?" Victou pushed the conversation with his enthusiasm, but Kits's smug portrait did not deviate. Victou felt the sweat of his armpits.

"I actually spent quite a lot of time in Lesai," Kits spoke directly.

"Really? That's surprising." Victou shifted in his seat.

"I'm quite familiar with the engineering department at East Lesai Academy. However, I never heard of them having an energy-development program."

The silence returned as Victou held his breath. Kits again looked at the diploma. "This is impressive. I'm not sure how much of this document is genuine, but it's completely convincing. Your hand skills are impressive."

Victou nearly let out an offering of verbal gratitude, which would have doubled as a confession. He kept his stance of silence.

Kits continued on. "Forging such a document to gain employment in a field that holds potential for major industrial disasters could have some very permanent and harsh consequences."

It got harder for Victou to sit still as his mind raced. Kits put the forged diploma down. "And thus, I have arrived at the end of the interviewing process for this job."

Anticipating the threat of punishment, Victou gripped the arms of his chair.

"So you can either choose to be incarcerated, or you can begin work tomorrow."

Victou suddenly experienced perhaps the oddest sense of relief he had ever felt. He played through Kits's offer in his head again, making sure he understood it correctly. "So, what will I be doing exactly?"

Kits kept it dead simple. "Everything I tell you to."

o o o

Rain fell later on in the day, an unusually heavy but otherwise quick storm. People ran for the cover of awnings, avoiding the shifting force they had no control over. A few had prepared for it while others felt its effects crawling down their skin the rest of the day.

Daimó observed the activity from high above, creatures determined to master technology and nature despite their noticeable inability to fully do either. Collectively, however, they had a power that he appreciated, a power he fully intended to exploit. Across the table, Kits had been sitting in a chair for twenty minutes waiting for him to talk.

"Do you question the things I ask you to do?" Daimó finally spoke.

Kits hesitated long enough that Daimó considered the question adequately answered.

"And that is why I selected you, Kits Bodú. You harbor wisdom but you do not take it for granted." Daimó turned around and sat at his desk, his eyes moving towards a small potted Henka plant. "And your meeting with Jin, how is the Aya heir?"

"Rather preoccupied with his little projects. Impressive work, but he seems decreasingly interested with the family company at large."

Daimó noticed the crooked plant skew towards the light of the window. He inserted a metal rod into the middle of the soil and wired the Henka's stem to it. "He is an interesting one. I feel Kora is having an effect on him. I will have to weigh all things in consideration to his usefulness in the future."

It was no surprise to Kits that Daimó would have concerns over Jin, the successor to one of the most powerful industrial companies in the valley. However; the timing and specifics of his concerns often felt enigmatic, and Kits generally avoided asking deeper questions, as they usually just generated more but with even foggier purposes.

Kits then sat back when Daimó did something rather out of character: He looked him in the eye. "And what of you and this transformational Kora Farm? What effect has it had on you?"

Kits answered quickly. "None, really."

Daimó kept his voice calm, a sound that generated quite the opposite in most who heard it. "It's quite all right, my young man. It is perhaps unavoidable to have such a place affect you, especially if you go there with purpose, which you most certainly have done."

Nia immediately came to mind, which lead to thoughts and feelings that he had no intention of divulging. "They are hard-working people there, different kinds of people. Seem to have their place figured out, so they must have respect for each other." Kits knew he still hadn't answered his superior's question yet. "Perhaps, I've learned that just because a place seems like a farm full of Sorans doesn't mean they're all simply misguided idealists."

Daimó put his attention back on his Henka plant. "It is a dynamic institution not to be underestimated. A beautiful piece of land that holds far more than one could fully comprehend in a short time. One could be seduced by such a place."

The statement hovered as if peering down at him in judgment. Kits felt a temptation to defend himself, which itself would have been a confession of some sort. Thankfully, Daimó digressed.

"The Dark-spark initiative has been incubating long enough. It's time to more fully align the direction of industry in this city." Daimó finessed the form of the plant with the wire.

"Steam is going strong still. Jin Aya even mentioned something about Core-thermic energy yesterday," Kits suggested.

Daimó paused—an otherwise plain reaction that, coming from him, stood out like a scream. Kits always felt two sentences behind Daimó in any conversation and had trouble recalling a single time when he actually surprised his superior.

Daimó continued in a shifting tone. "Did he mention that he was developing something? Did you get any sense that his reason for being this far south had to do with investigating Core-thermic technology?"

The question expressed true concern, something Kits rarely sensed from Daimó. The feeling boosted the young man's ego. "He hasn't said anything explicit, but he certainly appeared to have a strong curiosity on the topic."

Kits felt that Daimó was experiencing a very real moment of anxiety. He simply waited as Daimó leaned back in his chair. "Such a curious place. We must keep our eye very close to Kora, Lord Bodú. They may require swift action one day."

A conflicted Kits then moved the conversation onward. "So how do we push Dark-spark forward in the race with steam?"

"It's only a race if there is competition. Otherwise it is simply progress."

Kits thought for a moment. "Getting rid of steam? That seems like a monumental task. It makes up three-fourths of the city's power."

"Not the technology, but that which fuels it," explained Daimó. "Jino?"

"And what is needed to make Jinouki?"

"Tulúki, primarily," Kits answered.

"And who is the largest producer of Tulúki in the region?"

"Kora." Kits felt patronized by such obvious questions.

Daimó explained, "Dwindling Tulúki cultivation is the next step, but I do not see anyone at Kora willingly making that choice. Not that iron-headed farmer Kojo. Not even his ambitious, wandering young daughter Nia." Kits felt his toes clench inside his shoes.

Daimó continued. "But the realization of Kora's full usefulness has yet to come. There is a farmer to the west, Milon is his name. He grows nearly as much Tulú as Kora and uses almost as much for fuel production. I want you to set up a meeting with him on the Unyo airship. He will be dealt with, Kora will respond and provide us with our path for the removal of Jinouki; Dark-spark will ascend to its proper place."

The words rang out like a declaration to a crowd of followers. They reverberated between the walls of the largely empty office. It was the kind of grand remark Daimó ended nearly every conversation with. This time there was an epilogue.

"Oh, and how did the interview go?"

It took Kits a moment to think back to the morning. "Good. I think we found our man."

○ ○ ○

Four feet hung over a bend in the Long Frost River; a pair of athletic runners next to custom short heels swinging in sync. The big Laizóu tree cradled the young ladies as they reminisced. It had been a long time since Nia had seen Lucette, and neither could recall the exact date with any clarity.

"I'm just surprised Parin is having a little torch like you look after his place," Nia offered.

"I know, right!" Lucette responded with exaggerated surprise. "I guess stiff britches trusts this little steam-whistle after all. Although really, I think he was being lazy. I just asked first."

The girls shared a laugh before the sound of the river washed Nia's thoughts elsewhere, towards another young lady who belonged on the branch. "So . . . have you seen Suzu lately?"

Lucette felt discretion and gossip begin to fist-fight inside her head. "Yeah, she just started staying at my place, actually."

"Really?" Nia sat up. The news made the sting of Suzu's exodus relapse. "Oh, fun."

Lucette could see Nia forcing the positivity. "Yeah, she's good. I mean, she's kind of crazy pants now, which is probably why she wanted to stay with me."

Knowing Lucette to be a loving lady, Nia attempted to feel good over the living arrangment. "Yeah . . . that's fun."

Lucette started to feel a little guilty. "Suzu misses you, though. I mean, she just doesn't really say it since she's training for the city's toughest-shortest orphan award or something."

"Yeah?"

"Yeah, it's pretty obvious even though she thinks she's being all sneaky-sneaky Suzu."

Lucette then leaned gently on Nia's shoulder before biting it like an Ice Cat. Nia laughed and pulled back. "Ouch!"

"That did not hurt," Lucette assured her friend.

"Well, it surprised me quite a bit." The sound of Neko's engine then bounced around the house.

"Come on," Nia said before hoping off the tree and running off. Feelings of loss then quickly got replaced with the excitement of investigations. As they got to the front, the girls saw the big man get out along with Darou.

Lucette noticed a grin on Nia's face at the sight of the pensive young man. She suddenly giggled, to which Nia discretely threw up her arms. "What?"

"Nothing," Lucette yielded. "He's not bad looking. It's fine."

"You have a great imagination, Lady Lucette," Nia said firmly.

"I take that as a huge compliment."

Gozen then walked directly up to Nia. "I have someone for you."

The three of them went to the rear of Neko, meeting Darou in the back as the rear door lifted up. As light began to fill the trailer, it revealed the thin body of a young man covered in worn, grimy clothes. Nia began to analyze him, trying to figure out what exactly Gozen expected her to do with him.

Darou called to the young man, who walked out of the trailer followed by three other equally exhausted boys. Nia then looked back into the dark trailer and saw a pair of very small, dirty shoes step into the light, the toe well worn off one of them. She waited a moment, but the hidden figure stayed put.

"Hello," Nia gently spoke. "It's okay, you can come out." Lucette rested her chin on Nia's shoulder as the two saw the small, tattered shoes begin to approach. The warm light then unveiled the sweet eyes of a young girl, covered with layers of dirt and fatigue. Nia bent down to the girl.

"Hey there. My name's Nia."

The girl's silence got interrupted by the grumbling of her stomach.

Nia and Lucette laughed together. "That's my kind of girl."

"I suppose there are things more important than introductions. We have a lot of good food here. Why don't you come tell me what you'd like?" Nia offered her hand. It took a few seconds, but the hungry little lady slowly took it.

Gozen spoke up. "They were part of a mining operation in the western foothills. A lot of kids, but most of them got taken south to other Houses. Chichimou here is going to stay at the Tree House for now."

"Chichimou, how cute is that?" Lucette squeaked before bending down to the girl.

Tired, Gozen seemed fine leaving the meeting, but Nia's curiosity sparked. "How did they get involved? Who was behind it?"

Gozen let out a yawn. "Enforcers busted it up. There were a couple of sentinels there, but they were clearly not in charge of anything beyond yelling at children. We're still not sure who was financing the operation."

"What were they mining? Something illegal?" Nia straightened her posture.

"Not at all. Kurokinojinsper." Gozen said.

"Kikoki-what?"

"Kurokinojinsper. Dark Jinsper."

"The Dark-spark mineral?"

"The very one."

As Nia looked down at Chichi, the thought of the little one working in such a brutal environment pressed on her heart. She developed thoughts, angry and probably futile, which climbed up from her gut. Suddenly, a familiar mechanical sound interrupted them.

Everyone looked up to see Kits's black Móstique park behind Neko. Gozen clinched his jaw while Nia smiled. Kits got out of the car and walked over to them. Gozen carefully watched Kits's eyes while Nia and Lucette noticed his entirety.

"Kits, I'm so glad you came," Nia said, quickly stepping up and giving him an enthusiastic hug. Kits reciprocated awkwardly, as if he had never been hugged before. Nia continued. "So, I'm sure you've met Gozen around Kora. He's hard to miss, obviously."

Gozen remembered no such meeting. Kits thought of the gun well hidden in his jacket.

"And this is Lucette, my very special friend," Nia grinned.

"Extremely special, actually, as you'll undoubtedly find out for yourself," Lucette added.

"Oh, and this is Chichimou. She's new here." Kits and the small girl acknowledged each other with mutual discomfort. Nia continued. "So, Gozen, you were heading back to Kora?"

"I think I'll stick around a bit." Gozen headed off to the kitchen.

"I'll go ahead and get Chichi here some new clothes and then something to eat, so you two kids can go play in the back yard." With a wink, Lucette took Chichimou's hand and headed off. Trying her best to be casual, Nia led Kits around the house towards the big Laizóu tree.

Once Lucette finally got to the kitchen, she saw Gozen and Lady Kyoumére peeking out the back window with smoked coffee in hand. Lucette covered Chichi's soft face with her freckled fingers.

"Don't look, Chichimou. These two have forgotten their manners." The two adults turned around. Lucette released her hand only to see that Chichi had already started eating some Mimi fruit. "So, I guess you know how to eat. That's good."

"Lady Lucette, have you had time to meet this new friend of Nia's?" Lady Kyoumére asked.

"Wouldn't you two shifty characters like to know?" Lucette asked firmly.

"A Lady doesn't ask questions she doesn't want answers to," the Lady replied.

"How are you so classy all the time?" Lucette sincerely asked.

"And shifty is not the same as concerned," Gozen added.

"Well, all I know is that he's a handsome fella, but in that troublemaker kind of way."

"Precisely," Gozen jumped in.

"Now now, let's allow the young man to represent himself." Kyoumére took a sip of coffee.

"Okay, well, I'm going to go spy up close because I'm honest like that. You two keep pretending you're drinking coffee. Chichimou . . ." She looked down to see the little-face look up with orange sticky lips. "You keep working on those Mimiis."

Kits and Nia finished up the more cordial beginning of their conversation by the tree as a pair of kids ran up to the riverbank with a makeshift raft. The two young adults paused to watch what appeared to be an unintentional physical comedy routine. The young boy, not on the flat wood for more than a second, flipped face first into the river.

In the middle of their laughter, Nia ran over to see if the boy had hurt himself. Seeing a small cut on his leg, Nia explained it needed to be washed out due to whatever may be in the water. The smaller boy aided his friend inside, and Nia went back to Kits by the tree.

"Sorry, but that happens a lot here," Nia said.

"You seem rather comfortable with it."

Nia flicked the water off her fingers. "Yeah, it's a little rough, but I do kind of love these kids."

Nia continued. "Lady Kyoumére is great. Lucette helped out a lot, but she's got an apartment now. It can be hard not having your own family, so I like to do what I can." She nudged her shoulder into Kits's. "They would probably appreciate a polished fella like you hanging out every so often."

He pulled back a bit. "No, no, that's not really something for me."

"Oh, come on, they'd love you here. One ride in your fancy car and any boy here would declare you his hero."

His discomfort became obvious. "This just isn't the type of place I like to spend a lot of time at."

Quickly, Nia began to feel bitterness from his words. "What's wrong with this place? Are you afraid you might get some of the poorness on you?"

"No, I just . . ."

Nia interrupted. "These kids have a rough start, some of them really rough, and they can use all the help . . ."

"Exactly, I know how rough it is, and I don't care to relive it."

Nia suddenly recalled Kits once mention being in an orphanage, and felt stupid for not asking about it before. They both took a calming breath.

"Did you grow up in an orphanage?" Nia softly asked.

Kits shrugged off the question.

"You don't have to tell me, but I'd like to hear about it."

Kits felt highly unaccustomed to the heartfelt sincerity in Nia's voice. It made him feel uncomfortable but strangely nurtured. "This place just reminds me of everything I came from, and I have little interest in the past."

He finally looked up to Nia. "Maybe if I had someone like you looking after me I'd have fonder memories."

Nia felt a warmth in her cheeks. "Would you like someone like me being around now?"

Just then a small cargo boat appeared downriver, its presence announced by a roaring engine pouring out a thick tower of smoke. The two watched as it moved forward, its wake pushing elements of the defiled river onto the bank. Behind them, Lucette walked up with Darou and met them at the tree.

Lucette hyperbolically jumped behind Nia and grabbed her shoulders. "Don't look, but I think you're being watched."

Nia looked back to the house. "Seriously?"

"Of course." Lucette nuzzled up next to Nia as Darou swung around and gave himself some space. He made eye contact with Kits, a moment that vanished in a blink.

"So, handsome young man, tell me about yourself," Lucette demanded.

Clearly not accustomed to riffing with peers, Kits deflected to Nia. "Kits does research for an industrialist, I think," she said, smiling. "What is it exactly that you do?"

He quickly chiseled down the facts. "I work for a private company on the development of special industrial projects."

"Fancy." Lucette nodded. "Darou, is that how you describe your job?"

Darou raised his eyes from a typically low profile. "As of today, I apparently save kids from special industrial projects."

Lucette whispered into Nia's ear. "Here we go."

Kits followed. "You work at Etecid, right? On the bottom floor?"

Avoiding direct eye contact, Darou mustered up a "yeah."

Lucette jumped in. "So Kits, give me an example of something you do or have done. Perhaps something special, and maybe even industrial."

Nia began to feel some tension but remained largely amused, as always, by her radiant friend. Kits answered. "Right now we are working with Dark-spark technology quite a bit."

"Ah, I see." Darou added, "Those kids we just saved today were mining for a Dark-spark operation. Pretty corroded stuff."

"That's unfortunate," Kits stated.

"You think so? You sure your boss wasn't paying for it?" Darou kept his eyes to the ground as he developed a smirk.

Nia leaned in. "Darou, I doubt Kits works for someone that runs a labour nursery."

"Someone rich is paying for it, and I would guess it'd be a Dark-spark industrialist."

"Probably true. All the more important to make sure that powerful technologies are controlled by the right people," Kits added, trying his best to stay calm.

"I guess." Darou shrugged.

"Better to fix a problem than to complain about it," Kits slid in.

"And you both try very hard to make the best of what you do," Nia offered with a calming tone.

"Yes, we are in the presence of some very upstanding young men here, Nia." Lucette added.

"Yes, thank you, Lucette." The two girls exchanged a silly look.

"So are you working on how to not make Dark-spark engines vomit toxic clouds every time they're used?" Darou asked as the entire group looked up river at the serpent of smoke crawling out of the ship.

"I have to admit, I get a bit disgusted every time I see something running on Dark-spark. There's no way we'll ever use it up at the farm," Nia said.

All eyes went to Kits, who cleared his throat before answering the rhetorical non-question. "It's a powerful but imperfect new technology. In ten years it'll be more than twice as efficient as steam and the smoke problem will be figured out. Steam is heading towards its deathbed."

"Along with the jobs that go with it."

"Industry advances and jobs die along the way. You just need to make sure you don't die along with them," Kits said rather pragmatically.

"Okay, I think that's enough of the shop talk," Nia suggested.

"Sounds so simple when you just say it," Darou said.

"Push on and live, or give up and die . . ." Kits followed.

"Oh, Kits, please don't," Nia pleaded. "Darou, I'm sorry. He doesn't know about . . ."

Although he appreciated her heart, Darou quickly dismissed her gesture and wished the painfully awkward conversation out of existence. Even Lucette felt an obligation of reverence. Kits however, moved on.

"It's okay. I know about his father." Kits turned to Darou. "I assume you're stronger than him or you wouldn't be here right now. I hear you're a hard worker and good at what you do. When things change, there's no reason you can't take advantage of it."

"That's very inspiring." Darou put his hands in his pockets. "I'm going to check on the exploited children."

With his gaze down, Darou walked up towards the house. Kits watched his hanging posture all the way up until a flash of white dropped from the sky and silently shot right past his head. The young man ducked with a yelp.

"Kola!" Nia exclaimed with excitement.

"Hey, Mister handsome," Lucette added with equal illumination.

"You know that thing?" Kits checked his head for talon marks.

The girls laughed. "This is Kola."

"You're on a first-name basis with an owl?" Kits asked.

"I helped nurse him from an injury many years ago. Now, we just like to spend time together," Nia explained.

"I thought he didn't come into the city?" Lucette asked.

"He has before but it's pretty rare," Nia said.

Kola worked his way onto Nia's shoulder and locked his eyes onto Kits. Their fire-orange color shifted into an icy gray as Lucette pet his head. Kola's fierce focus stayed dead onto Kits, who suddenly longed for the droopy gaze of Darou.

"I don't think your bird likes me very much," Kits nervously suggested.

"No, if he didn't like you he'd be tearing out your eyes," Nia explained. "He's just checking you out."

"Those are comforting words."

"Hah, scared of a cute sack of feathers? You're a funny one, mister Kits, and I am heading in." Lucette gave Nia a kiss on the cheek and then stood up. "Lord, Lady." And with a bow to each of her companions, Lucette walked off. After a few more seconds of judgment, Kola flew up and circled the Tree House.

"All right, well, I better get in and check on the lil boat captain. I'm not so confident in his first mate's ability to dress a wound." Nia slowly slid towards the house before Kits got hit with an impulse. "Wait."

Nia slowly turned around. "Yes?"

Kits walked up to her. "How would you like to take a ride on an airship tomorrow?"

Nia's eyes lit up. "Over the city?"

"Yeah, and maybe farther."

They got closer. "Uhm, yeah, sure. Never really been in an airship before. I didn't realize you had the privilege."

"It's just for work. I'm supposed to tag along and not much else. It'll be nice to have you there."

Feeling strangely shy, Nia felt a bit warm in the face. Kits's voice seemed to have taken on an all new tone of sincerity. Impulsively, she leaned in and kissed him on the cheek. "Thanks for asking."

Feeling rather lovely, Nia walked back to the house. Inside, Gozen still leaned by the window with Lady Kyoumére, the window fogged from their breath.

"Okay, I'm going to get my gun now," Gozen simply offered.

"Oh, I'm sure that won't be necessary." the Lady replied. "I can't imagine any boy trying uncivil behavior with a girl under your care."

Comforted by her poised words, Gozen's mind quickly sobered. "Actually, I would not say with any confidence that I know what that kid is capable of."

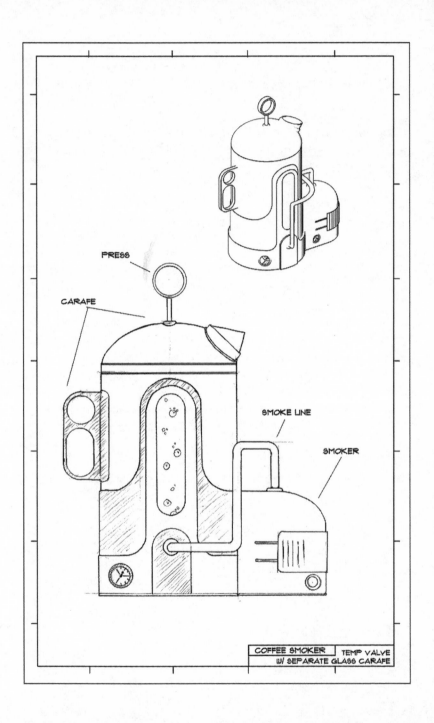

PRESS

CARAFE

SMOKE LINE

SMOKER

COFFEE SMOKER | TEMP VALVE
W/ SEPARATE GLASS CARAFE

15
THRESHOLD

His eyes squinted at the road through vapors rising up from his smoked coffee. Stillness hovered between him and Nia as they drove into Chigou; neither had gotten much sleep the night before.

Despite having an indulgent plate of sweet Blashu rolls that morning, a small storm of cynical thoughts twirled through Nia's head. She wanted to be excited for her adventure in the sky, but driving into the city, knowing her absent friend to be somewhere along the endless streets, her thoughts went backwards.

"So why hasn't Suzu ever come back to the farm?"

The conversation had been thoroughly considered but rarely discussed between them. Suzu's recent goals confused the both of them, accompanied by a subversive tension. Gozen, who had made it a job skill to repress emotions, rarely felt comfortable gushing out from his heart.

Nia had finished holding things in. "I just don't understand why she never visits. I get that she wanted to change it up, move into the city. I mean, I wouldn't mind doing that, but I haven't even heard her voice once since she left."

Gozen looked over to Nia, who seemed to be talking to the road as much as she was talking to him. She continued, louder. "I guess she's staying with Lucette now, and I'm glad she's with her and not roaming around . . . I guess, but I know you've seen her, too. Everyone at the Tree House has seen her. Why does she not want to see me?"

Although he had been checking up on Suzu, Gozen felt lost in his ability to answer Nia's question. As she blinked out a tear, Gozen felt love and guilt wrestling in his chest. He longed to ease her anguish, he feared he didn't know how.

Heavy traffic clogged downtown. Gozen pulled up to Etecid with a plan to check in with the previous Tulúki shipment. As they arrived, however, he didn't much care. The cab muffled the sounds of the city. Nia wiggled in her seat.

"I'm sorry, Gozen. I know you look out for everyone. I shouldn't yell at you." She washed away tension with a big gulp of air. "I just . . ." She sorted through her thoughts.

"Miss your family," Gozen's low voice quietly concluded. They looked at each other with empathetic eyes.

"Yeah." Nia floated down into vulnerable thoughts. Gozen saw a young girl, abandoned but refusing to give up. She had developed so much beauty and strength, but he could never ignore her injured roots. Between them, he always felt the painful memory of a girl who had everything ripped away. So badly he wanted the wounds to heal, but the guilt kept him from ever being able to face them. He had forgotten a life without the toxic mass suffocating his conscience, but he decided it had become unbearable. If something didn't give, he'd either suffocate or explode.

"Are you okay?" Nia saw an unfamiliar Gozen appear shaken.

He drew in air like a man ready to step into a cold lake. "Do you know what I did before I worked at Kora?"

Their voices became gentle. "Yeah, you were an Enforcer, right?"

"I was a Lord Enforcer."

They both took a moment to process the weight of his words. She had never even received direct eye contact from a Lord Enforcer. Thinking of this man, with whom she had sweated and laughed in the fields, holding such an imposing and magnificent role, felt entirely bizarre.

"How was that?"

Gozen's spirit toiled. "It felt significant, as if what I did always carried consequences of much weight. It seemed an honorable responsibility to be charged with. I thought there wasn't a life more noble that I could lead."

"So why did you quit?"

The simple words burned, and he hid his gaze down into the floor. Every utterance moving forward became a struggle. "I was stationed in the south, in Roukot."

"Right, I remember you taking me to the Tree House; one of my earliest memories actually. You must have quit soon after that."

"The Grand Roukot Fire changed a lot of things for a lot of people. I liked working in that district. Hard-working people, honest about who they were. I liked being able to guide the connection between the heights of Chigou's progress and those working down below, making it all happen. That's why I stormed in there that day, a mediator serving two masters."

Nia felt a foreboding force hover above them and Gozen struggled to continue. "Families do not want some Lord Enforcer telling them that they have no right to live in their homes—homes that they've made, but this city demands progress and yields to no one."

Nia sensed the anger and sorrow stuck in his throat. He looked like someone fighting to vomit out what made him ill. Slowly, he managed to look up to Nia with tears welled up in his eyes. "I'm the one who caused that fire, Nia. There were so many families in that building, your family . . . but somehow you survived."

The confession ripped the large man apart. He cried in front of the girl he once cradled across Chigou, saving her from the tragedy of his own doing. He owed her more than he would ever be able to pay back, sentenced to a lifetime of guilt. He bent forward, hiding his desperate humiliation. "I took them away from you, Nia. I took away your family. I'm sorry."

Gozen wanted to hear screams and feel fists pounding on him. He deserved the torment; he deserved to pay for the families he burned away. He wanted Nia to be just and demand retribution.

The words wove through her own pain, one that she had long since understood and faced. She thought of her parents, the memories she had with them and the ones she never would. It was a pain she had endured for so long, but one she vowed to overcome.

Nia leaned over and wrapped her arms around the large, broken man. She put her cheek next to his, feeling pain streaming down. Gently, she spoke, "I forgive you."

Her grace pushed out the burden of pain, leaving his wounds

feeling raw but cleaned. His breaths slowly began to relax. Her arms emitted a powerful warmth and security. Eventually, they let go of each other and leaned back in their seats. The sight of each other's puffy face brought forth an exhausted laugh.

"So what are you doing again?" Gozen asked as clearly as he could.

"Uhm, just going up in an airship ride."

"Yeah?" He refocused. "How did you manage that?"

"Kits invited me. It's some business thing. I think I just get to hang out as his *plus one.*"

"Pretty fancy."

Nia shrugged.

"Well . . ." Gozen considered, "have fun."

He reached over and hugged his young companion again.

"Thank you." And with those words, Nia scurried out of the cab towards the nearest Hotrail station, destined for Chigou's tallest building.

Darou passed her on his way to Neko, and the two exchanged complicated smiles. He finally approached the cab to see Gozen rubbing the tears still running down his face. Darou stopped cold.

"I'll come back." He turned around.

"Hey, come here. It's fine," Gozen assured him. Darou cautiously turned back.

"Yes, men cry."

"Right. I just didn't know you did," Darou confessed.

"Well, when you're done being amazed, you want to tell me that the last Tulúki shipment went okay?"

"I'd love to, but I can't."

Gozen's exhaustion tempered his disappointment. "Okay. What happened?"

"Halfway through the batch, it started reading bad."

"That was a great crop," Gozen insisted.

"That's what I was saying. Oh, and you're really going to enjoy this: Cruno hasn't been back since you dropped that Tulúki off."

Gozen choked the steering wheel. "Ugh. Someone's trying to ruin this plant."

Candidly nodding along, Darou then swapped his thought.

"Wait, you really think so?"

Gozen nodded, "I just might, actually."

Darou considered. "Cruno?"

"He's an idiot, but I'm going to find out who is filling his empty head with ideas."

Gozen fired up the engine and leaned back in his seat. Darou stayed put. "Hey look, with the problems of the last batch, I've heard some talk that we might shut down, for real. There's just so much going wrong."

A matrix of theories mixed in Gozen's skull as he watched Darou sulk. "I'm so tired of this. Can't we just do our job without some mysterious phantom cursing everything we do?"

Darou wanted to offer something. "Maybe I should start looking for a new job. Just in case."

Gozen revved the engine. "They need to be worried, Darou, not you."

○ ○ ○

She had noticed it countless times before, but for the first time she stood at its entrance with the intention of going in. The largest building in all of Chigou, Telakai also housed its most important man. Below the offices of Opaji, industrial leaders regularly met and conspired—a revered tower of influence and mystery.

Looking up, Nia saw the Unyo Mark I Airship docked, being prepared for its voyage. She grinned like a child at the foot of a giant present. Chigouans generally considered the airship to be the most majestic culmination of human ambition. She let out a quiet squeal and walked through the heavy doors.

The lobby looked as if it had been built by ancient gods; everything stood taller and heavier than what seemed reasonable. A surprising lack of occupants accentuated its vastness. She suddenly felt rather insignificant and underdressed, but her excitement pushed her towards the serious gentleman at the desk.

"Name and business please," the Sentinel requested.

"Nia Chiou. I'm here to see Kits Bodú."

She stood on her toes, excited at the idea of her name being on the list. The Sentinel ran his finger down a column of names. "Take the elevator."

Nia nearly asked for the floor when he handed her an alloy tag with the number *137* engraved into it. He sat back down and she headed towards the elevator. Another Sentinel took her tag, opened the massive doors, and sent her up.

Nia barely felt her body ascend until her ears popped. The hum of floors passing by eventually slowed and the doors opened, filling her vision with light. The hallway appeared empty, and not wanting to ride the elevator back down, Nia slowly walked forward. The horizon appeared as her eyes adjusted to the luminescence from the massive window. Suddenly, she saw the city of Chigou as she never had before. It seemed quiet from up above, completely different from the city she knew. Its glimmering intricacies were sprawled out like a map, with everything visible at once. The unfamiliar perspective nearly gave her a second of vertigo.

Looking south, the Murdes cradled a huge forest that sank deep below the horizon. Taking a few steps right up to the glass, it dawned on her that she was actually looking down at Goraka. The legendary Red Valley appeared dark and silent from above, hiding all of its legends. A looming mist wove throughout its lush green hills, churning around like the spirits.

"Believe it or not, you're about to get an even better view than this," Kits said as he walked up the hall. Nia merely smiled, unable to summarize the view before her.

"You ready to go?"

Nia nodded enthusiastically.

They walked up through a narrow stairwell next to a service lift being used to stock the airship. The door up top opened as a gust of wind blew across them. Nia's body became inundated with unfamiliar sensations. Standing on the heaviest structure in the city, she felt nearly weightless, as if a breeze might carry her away.

Up ahead on the loading dock, she saw a familiar man being escorted into the airship. She spoke loudly through the wind and engine noise. "Isn't that Milon, the Tulúki farmer from out west?"

Kits looked over to see the back of the man. Milon had been declared an obstacle by Daimó, who had also suggested bringing Nia for a ride on the airship. The suggestion felt odd, but Kits didn't question it initially; he liked the idea of her traveling with him. However, now on the ship, the combination of passengers seemed downright bizarre to Kits. He knew very well that Daimó never acted sans agenda; some plot had just gotten underway.

"What is he doing here?" Nia asked.

"Just business, whereas you get to play up on the deck the entire time," Kits assured her as he developed a number of his own questions.

They walked up to the edge, and Nia glanced down to an observation deck just a few meters below, extending out from a lounge. It immediately challenged her opinion of how exciting office work could be.

"For the people not special enough for a ride," Kits smirked, pointing to those taking a coffee break just down below.

Nia blushed as a Sentinel opened a brass gate, allowing passage through the railing. Stepping onto the beautifully inlaid wood deck, she felt a tingle crawl up her spine. She couldn't believe she actually stood on an airship. Moments later, the mooring base released the deck anchor, and the Unyo floated backwards. Nia leaned over the rail and saw the streets of Chigou appear directly below her, looking like a living model. Little bumps started to appear all along her forearms.

"I need to go check in, but enjoy the view," Kits said.

Before he walked off, Nia stopped him, her face beaming. "This is pretty amazing, Kits." He agreed and walked off, leaving the girl to her wonderment.

Kits walked down the boardwalk stairs leading to the second floor, just below the middle of the ship. Three exterior doors led to crew areas and a central lobby where he walked in. The wind vanished, and he found himself standing alone with Milon and a Sentinel. The aged farmer sat quietly in the insulated lobby, looking rather sheepish.

Kits passed the Sentinel and headed down the stairwell to the confidential floor. The craftsmanship of the lower level nearly stood up to that of Opaji's Unyo Mark II. He went through a narrow hallway before entering the last door. Inside, Daimó looked out the large bay window that curved from the floor up to the ceiling. Kits again thought of the peculiar mix of passengers and felt his pulse pick up.

"Is your friend the young farmer woman doing well?" Daimó asked.

"I think she'll be rather content with the view up on deck. Do you want me to get Milon?" Kits had a strong suspicion as to the farmer's solicitation, and he wanted to get the matter over with quickly.

"Nia . . . she works at Kora Farm, volunteers with the Northern Orphanage, and has been attending activities at the Civil Conclave. What do you make of those ambitions?" Daimó asked.

Kits suddenly questioned bringing Nia along. "They're strong ambitions as she seems to be a committed individual. She leans towards a compassionate attitude like her parents, but much more open-minded and progressive."

Daimó pondered the words as he turned to Kits. "And what do you make of her opinion on yourself?"

"She seems interested in what I'm doing, *we're doing*, but it's more of a curiosity as she doesn't have any specific information." Kits felt an urge to make her seem as unthreatening as possible.

"Nothing specific?" Daimó asked.

"No, of course I haven't." Kits attempted to hide his growing anxiety.

"If her open mind is as ambitious as you say, perhaps it would be pragmatic to bring her in on our operations. Why not tell her, in detail, what it is that you do?"

Kits hesitated on his answer. He hated the moments when it felt as though Daimó read him like a children's book.

The director continued. "You seem to be graciously accepting of her. Do you feel that would be equally reciprocated? The value of companionship is comprehensible, but what truly is that value if it rests on a foundation of false understanding?"

Kits felt his mind fumbling around in a puzzle. He felt trapped, or maybe desperate. Daimó simplified his thoughts. "Perhaps you should invite her in here for our meeting with the farmer. Her response would answer many questions, don't you think?"

Daimó forced Kits to consider the question he had no immediate urge to address. He wondered if Nia actually would accept him, all of him. It had been a subtle concern that now slammed to the front of his mind. Deep inside he knew that he wanted to know the answer. "I think she has much potential that simply needs time to develop. Another day."

Kits felt his back against an invisible wall but stood his ground. Seconds ticked by and sweat collected on his forehead. Finally, Daimó turned back to the window.

"Very well. As soon as we reach the Mountains you can bring Milon down here. Until then, you should be a good host to your guest."

Kits took what felt like his first breath in three minutes and walked out. He approached a small bar and grabbed two glass bottles of water, drinking the first straight through. He grabbed another, put a CO_2 canister into the valve, and shot the gas into it.

Wind blew onto Kits as he opened the outer door. He walked onto the deck where Nia leaned gently on the railing, looking rather peaceful. Kits calmed his pace and walked up next to her, offering the water.

"Oh, thanks." Nia took the bottle, her face still illuminated.

"Careful with that. You can get arrested if you drop anything off of one of these."

Nia pretended to gasp and then looked back over the brass rail. Down below, the edge of Chigou passed by as they headed towards the mountains. "I can't believe how small everything looks. I feel like I could just reach down and rearrange everything."

"Maybe move Michelou's up by the Orphanage?" Kits pinched his fingers as if moving the cold creamery across town.

"Yes! I haven't had cold cream in so long. Can we go there when we get back?"

"What if I told you we have some onboard?" Kits said.

"No, you do not." Nia held back a squeal.

"No," Kits admitted. "But we should."

Nia punched him in the shoulder, and the two looked back down to the magnificently infinite view. As the airship gained altitude, the Murde Mountains nearly stood at eye level. She imagined them gently guarding the perfectly organized patches of farmland below at their feet. "Hey, so is Milon here to survey his farm or something?"

"Something like that," Kits said plainly, thinking of Daimó and his obscure goals. He again wondered if she knew of anything that had happened between him and Suzu, thoughts that suddenly brought on new anxiety. Looking down at an entire society passing below him, he then wondered if he even truly knew himself.

"So if you could move things around, do anything to the city that you wanted, what would you do?" Kits asked.

Nia glanced over the rail and dreamt. "Oh gee, I'm not sure. I have a lot of ideas but I'm not sure if they're really good ideas yet. I don't want to mess anything up more than it already is. I guess I'd just do whatever I could to make the city a better place," Nia shrugged. "Sorry, that's not much of an answer."

"So what would you do if you messed something up? Really messed it up."

Thinking she generally only slightly messed things up, Nia began to wonder herself. "Just do it better the next time . . . or just never do it again, I guess. There's my big fancy answer."

' Nia still felt a bit overwhelmed by the technological complexity of what they flew on as well as the completely unprecedented view. They stayed on deck for awhile, talking in-between moments of gazing at the infinite.

At one point Nia yelled as she saw Kola fly below them. The white owl circled a few times before landing up on the railing, making an already magical moment slip into the surreal; she explicitly noted that she was flying with her little friend for the first time. Kola sat on the rail and watched Kits before flying back down, leaving the young man again feeling thoroughly assessed.

"I still don't think he likes me," Kits suggested.

"Why are you so worried about my little owl?" Nia leaned her shoulder against Kits's.

"He's really not that little when he's a foot away from your face . . . that and I just don't want my eyes plucked out."

"Don't worry; he approves."

The snowy mountains began to pass below them. Kits felt exposed, like someone stepping out of a pool into the cold air. He leaned his head onto Nia's and felt the warmth of skin mixing with the mountainous atmosphere. He felt like he could stay there forever; they both did. Then the ship began to change course.

"Are we going back?" Nia asked.

Kits jarringly remembered the purpose of the flight and stood up. "I have to go do something." He faintly smiled with uncertain eyes before walking back down the stairs. Feeling the exit to be rather sudden, Nia silently watched him disappear below the deck.

After some time, Nia began to get her fill of massive forms fading into an endless horizon. Deciding that four walls and a ceiling might do her some good for a minute, Nia followed the railing and walked down the steps, getting a good view of the smoothly encased primary turbine engine. Each side mounted one of the impressively large engines, and she imagined jumping up might suck her right into one.

Heading down the outer stairs, she made it to the main walkway and spotted three doors. Peeking inside the round window of the first one, Nia saw what she assumed to be the navigational crew. They all looked rather serious.

The next door opened right up into a well-crafted cabin. The empty space immediately went quiet as soon as she shut the door behind her, smothering the engine's perpetual roar. She relaxed her shoulders and took a walk around the room, admiring the small bar and two large photographs of the airship. A framed painting down the bottom of a stairwell then caught her eye.

Feeling a bit sneaky, she walked down to the lower floor and stood in front of a densely vivid depiction. It illustrated the valley, filled with shining buildings and mechanical towers climbing towards a fiery sun. A line of people ascended along, their backs all towards what she assumed to be the past, or weakness . . . or something. It conjured an uncomfortable mixture of inspiration and oppression.

Then, cutting through the quiet hum of muffled engines, she heard what sounded like a man's scream. Feeling as though she stood in a place she didn't belong, Nia jumped at the noise. It seemed as though it came from down the hall but faded so quickly she couldn't be sure. After playing the cry, *maybe* a cry, again in her head, a curiously protective impulse took over. She walked straight towards the lost sound.

The hallway split around the stairs before converging again into a single brass-trimmed door. She could feel air pressure pulling her towards it. Gently, she put her ear to the polished surface. No sounds came through. Nia wondered if someone was hurt inside. Regardless, she felt compelled enough to slowly push the door open and check.

Kits's back appeared first, along with a surprising gust of air. He suddenly turned towards her, revealing an image that instantly seared into her mind. Behind Kits, a darkly dressed man stood with the iciest expression she had ever seen. Between them, a hatch sat opened to the frozen mountains below. The scream came from Milon, still plummeting to his death.

Kits reached out, panicked with regret. "Nia, wait."

Nia immediately shut the door and sprinted back to the stairs, her heart pounding. She quickly navigated the corners of the hallway, grabbed the railing, and swung up the stairs. She could hear someone ordering a Sentinel, followed by stomping feet.

Nia ran as if her legs gave her no choice. At the top of the stairs a crew member already stood, his arms raised to stop her. Uninterested in anything he had to say, she quickly vaulted off of his chest and launched towards the door, knocking the man down. She ran out onto the walkway and shut the door behind her. Looking at the endless view, realization set in: She was trapped on a floating boat, and the nearest escape laid a thousand meters directly below.

Nia desperately thought of the only door she hadn't tried yet. She ran to the back and grabbed the handle, praying it would open. She ran inside and slammed the door before frantically trying to lock it shut. Her hand slipped off the latch, but after swearing at herself, she quickly managed to bolt it down. Turning around, Nia saw a completely foreign space. Industrial walls filled with engines, turning gears, and axles, weaving between giant gas balloons.

Quickly, she thought to hide amongst the clutter of machinery. As she hastily looked, the overwhelmed girl could hear voices down the walkway. They mixed with the scream of the poor farmer still echoing through her head. She wondered if hiding would even be possible for the entire flight back. She then wondered how she could ever get off undetected. It seemed impossible, and she started to panic.

Then, noticing a small ladder going up towards the top of the airship, she ran through the narrow walkways and up thin metal stairs. She hopped onto the ladder and climbed like a scared cat. She found a hatch at the top and quickly tried to figure out the opening mechanism; below she heard her pursuers reach the door.

Nia grabbed the metal wheel and began to turn it. She could see the hatch bolts slowly disengage. Her forearms ached as they quickly spun the heavy metal wheel. She could hear the door begin to unlock down below as the spring-loaded hatch above her finally flew open.

Bright light and wind assaulted her senses. She stepped up, suddenly looking over the top of the airship. The shining metal surface sloped down to the narrow deck up front, the roaring engines to the sides, and the fins to the rear. Below her, a gang of killers tried to get in. She had perhaps a few seconds to decide where to go. All paths led down.

With a loud clang, the engine door opened, and Kits stepped in with the Sentinel. He looked across the web of machinery and then stopped his search at the open hatch above. "Stay here," Kits commanded.

He ran towards the ladder and climbed up as fast as he could. Kits got to the top and braced himself against the disorienting wind. He imagined Nia standing on the sloping surface or hanging off of some railing. His eyes adjusted, suddenly seeing only metal and sky. He climbed up another rung and desperately looked around the perimeter. Nothing.

Along with the Sentinel, Kits checked every possible pocket Nia could have hidden in, but the engine room proved fruitless. Kits dreaded going back down to Daimó. He made a few more trips around the ship, but the young woman could not be found. Hesitantly, he then headed down below.

Surprisingly, Daimó seemed rather unaffected by the situation. "There are only two ways off of this ship," he said. "She either fell or will need to leave off of the front balcony. Let's hope for the later; you may wait patiently up top."

Kits left and paced from room to room, quietly cursing himself.

o o o

Jin had spent most of the day modifying a Toki that his father had given him years earlier. Tokis generally only had one special function other than telling time, but the young man felt the limitation to be rather sentimental. He worked on it in the dining room of the main house as he found isolation increasingly unpleasant; he could not decide why.

The unmistakable sound of Neko then materialized before Gozen dragged himself into the room and sat across from Jin. The two made eye contact, working through an undeveloped rapport.

"Are you ever not tinkering with something?" Gozen asked.

"I sleep five hours every night," Jin explained. "You look exhausted. Perhaps you should manage your coffee intake. It may be causing an energy imbalance."

"Do you want to brew some for me?"

"I was not recommending it for you, but I was actually planning on having some soon."

Gozen sighed and put his face in his hands. "Jin, I have to hand it to you. You are a very honest young man."

After a quick bow of the head, Jin took a moment to quietly appreciate the comment while working on the Toki. After a minute of work, his mind again shifted. "I have not seen the young lady Suzu in quite some time. I'm curious as to her recent activities."

A deep moan came out of Gozen's throat. Jin continued. "She seemed to be a rather positive source of energy at the farm, and I would be remiss if I did not mention my own appreciation for her presence."

The wire-type machine signaled with its music-box like tone and began to print a message. "Thank you," Gozen's muffled voice addressed the timely communication before getting up.

"You're welcome," Jin naively responded.

Gozen zoned out the young man's continued analysis of Suzu while reading the wire-type. It was from Darou.

Orig: Darou
Attn: Gozen

Source of Túluki contamination found along with Cruno. He was buried in the silo, must have fallen in. They say accident. I say I saw that Kits guy around and I don't trust him. What do you think?

Gozen sobered up fast. His mind aligned into Enforcer formation. He began to sort through a mass of facts until the hum of Jin's voice formed something striking.

"So I was wondering if Suzu had ever visited Kits after all. I found her concern of him rather odd."

"What do you mean? Why would she visit him?" Gozen asked with steel-like hardness.

Jin sat up. "She requested Kits's address right before she left the farm. I found it to be a frivolous request; candidly, I may have even teased her about it. In hindsight, perhaps that was uncouth."

"Did you give it to her?"

"I certainly do not invite the curiosities of young people to interfere with business, but I recall she may have retrieved it from my room on her own."

A chilling realization formed in Gozen's mind. "What was the address?"

"I cannot say with certainty, but I believe . . ."

Gozen cut in. "Was it 2S11 Oraguine Ave.?"

Clarity came quickly. "Yes, actually, that was it. Have you been there?"

It only took a few seconds for the plan of necessity to form. "Jin, I need you to find Clora and Kojo, get them in the house and lock it up. Do not let anyone in until I get back."

"Do you no longer want any smoked coffee?" Jin asked.

"I need you to go right now." Gozen headed to the door.

"What is it?"

Gozen spoke out, declaring his conclusion. "I think Kits is a killer and he has Nia trapped with him."

∘ ∘ ∘

Incessant noise pounded her ears as the vibration had her body going numb. Nia had slid down the side of the airship and wedged herself between the hull and one of the primary engines mounted on the side. Lying on her stomach, she tucked in just high enough to be out of sight from the deck and too low to be seen from the top hatch. Nia feared that even raising her head to look around would reveal her position to anyone standing on the front balcony. The heat of the turbine had her sweating through her clothes as she pressed against the engine housing. Only the wind kept her from passing out.

Her mind raced from thoughts of Kits to how she could possibly escape the ship. She questioned if she misheard, not seeing a murder scene seconds after the act; but she wondered where else the farmer could have gone. Nia just wanted to be back at Kora, seeing the smile of her mother, a simple moment feeling hopelessly far away. She knew getting off the ship unseen would be impossible.

As time went by, she prayed for a miracle. Trapped up in the sky, nothing seemed like it could possibly help. She then saw a strangely familiar sight, the spire atop the Telakai building. It looked odd seeing it from eye level. They were preparing to dock.

Nia quickly thought back to how they boarded: the observation deck, the elevator. A plan formed, and she felt insane for considering it. However, desperation urged her to get off of that hot, noisy turbine. As she slowly peeked up, the loading platform closed in.

Taking in a deep breath, Nia got up and began a sprint along the engine mount. Kits heard her from below on the walkway and called out for her to stop. Her athletic frame ran up along the hull and then slid down right to the top of the stairs. She looked back for an instant and saw Kits running for her.

Nia then launched forward, the loading dock only ten meters away and closing. The path lay clear, and she readied to jump just as she caught sight of a Sentinel around the hull, raising a gun. Kits yelled for the man to stop, but it was just too late.

The Sentinel began to squeeze the trigger and a shot rang out. At the same time the Sentinel felt the gun torn from his hands; a white owl screeched as it flew off with the weapon. Nia heard the bullet whiz past her ear but refused to stop. She jumped over the railing and suddenly saw the city street, 97 floors below her flailing feet. Her body then skillfully swung down off of the long, metal mooring anchor. She slid below to the observation deck four meters down, rolling out as she landed. Kits got to the railing but the ship docked, closing off the view to Nia down below.

Nia recovered and stood up. She quickly wanted to find a door but instead noticed Daimó looking directly at her. His lifeless eyes peered through the curved glass of the airship's lower deck, and in that instant, Nia stared into the face of Suzu's nightmares. The sight felt bitter, and she immediately ran in the opposite direction.

Quickly, Nia shot through the small lobby while hearing gasps from confused visitors. Making it out to the hall, she frantically looked around before spotting the elevator door. Her feet carried her there in a heartbeat, and she slammed the down button. Suddenly, she only heard her own heavy breathing. She heard the chime of the elevator, followed by a gang of angry footsteps, quickly approaching from around the corner.

Nia had no idea what she would do if they got to her before the elevator let her take refuge. She prayed again. She could see shadows come from down a hall, and then the elevator opened behind her and she saw the operator. The most primal impulse she had ever felt took over, and she hit the man square on the chin. He dropped, she ran in and slammed the elevator button nine times.

Kits and a crew of Sentinels rounded the corner just as the doors shut; the air went quiet. The operator moaned on the floor, barely moving. She then thought of what she might encounter at the ground floor. She debated a dead sprint versus acting calm.

Feeling she could probably outrun any man in the building, Nia concluded a sprint would be a safe backup plan. The doors opened with a pleasant chime, and Nia briskly walked out. She kept composure but scanned the environment intensely. Keeping a strong eye on the desk Sentinel, she kept walking.

The chime of a wire-type then rang through the cavernous lobby, and Nia watched like a bird of prey. The Sentinel looked over to her direction, stood up and spoke, "Lady."

Time to run. Nia sprinted full speed and made it past the Sentinel before he had time to grab her. Focused on the front door, she vaulted over a bed of flowers and hit the heavy metal entry barrier with full force; the shock ached through every joint in her body. She growled and pushed the door open. Outside in a world of strangers, she wondered if she should scream for help or keep running. Her head rang fuzzy from the impact.

Her eyes then locked on a vision of relief so strong she nearly came to tears. Neko pulled up to the front of the Telakai building. She ran forward, and the rest of the world disappeared as Gozen came out of the truck. Nia jumped up and squeezed him with what little energy she had left. He helped her get in the truck and they drove off.

○ ○ ○

With temporary workers sent home early, things had gotten quiet at Kora, except for at the entrance of the main house. As Neko pulled up, Gozen saw Legou and Joushi having an intense conversation with the front door. He got out with Nia and they quickly approached the house.

"Hey, would you tell this gold-plated loon to let us in?" Legou excitedly requested.

"I think he's holding the old couple hostage, or something," added Joushi.

Guiding the still-shaken Nia, Gozen walked past the flustered young men to the door. "Jin, open up."

"I hate to tell you, big guy, but fancy face in there snapped. I think that expensive neck scarf has been slowly depriving his head of blood," Legou suggested.

The door opened up; Gozen let Nia walk in first. Legou and Joushi looked at each other bewildered. "We've been out here for an hour." The two young men walked in with their confusion and shut the door behind them.

"Lock it," Gozen commanded.

Jin guided them into the dining room where Clora and Kojo had been anxiously waiting with him. Nia ran up and hugged her mother like she had been a lost child. "I'm so stupid, Mom. I'm so sorry."

"What's going on?" Kojo asked, his arm around his family.

"Nia witnessed Kits murder Milon," Gozen explained.

"Milon? What do you mean?" Kojo anxiously questioned.

Nia finally let go of Clora. "Kits took me up on an airship with his boss. Milon was there; we went out over the mountains. I didn't actually see it happen, but I know they threw him out."

"They killed old Milon?" Clora was at a loss.

"This doesn't make any sense. And why would they want you there?" Kojo asked.

Nia shrugged her shoulders—drained—wishing she had an answer. "I just hid and ran off the ship when we docked. They chased me out of the building."

Gozen stepped in. "There was a Sentinel there that tried to shoot her."

"What?" Kojo was horrified.

"Is this why we just locked ourselves in the house?" Joushi asked.

Gozen collected his explanation. "I think the man that Kits works for is some clandestine industrialist named Daimó. He's very ambitious and very dangerous."

"What has he done?" Legou nervously asked.

"A lot. He essentially orchestrated the Grand Roukot Fire." Gozen felt shame as the words left his mouth, remembering the only time he had ever dealt with Daimó, but he had no time to wallow in guilt. "He very well may be sending people here right now."

Kojo's thoughts rattled. "This is madness."

"We need to notify the Enforcers," Clora suggested.

Gozen quickly tried his best to explain the complexity of trusting the Enforcers when Daimó seemed capable of manipulating their force to some capacity. Although Kojo wanted to protect his daughter, Nia refused to put the farm and family in danger over what she felt was her own foolish mistake. Gozen suggested having Nia hide for a period of time. Their voices raised with their blood pressure, suggesting and tearing down ideas. Panic rose along with the possibility of Daimó's Sentinel's showing up.

"I can take her back to Primichi." The calmness of Jin's voice cut through the frantic storm of conversation. "My family could keep Nia hidden well in the city. We own quite a lot of it."

The volume dropped as everyone looked at one another, waiting for someone to refute the suggestion. In a collective state of surprise, having Nia run off with Jin to a foreign city, one only he knew well, somehow seemed to be the best option.

Gozen offered to stay back, watch after Kora, and deal with any aggression while continuing to investigate Daimó and Kits. He even asked Legou and Joushi if they'd help protect the farm, and in a rare moment, lacking any facade of amusement, they agreed.

A frantic pragmatism motivated everyone. Clora made a basket of bread, dried fruit, and cured meats. Kojo got some camping and survival essentials, just in case. Gozen and Jin took care of fuel and mechanical concerns. Jin ran upstairs and grabbed his Masu. He couldn't imagine actually using the retractable sword on another human, but it seemed relatively logical at the moment. Everyone collected at his car.

"Just take care, no matter what." Clora squeezed her daughter as if trying to merge the two together.

"Keep her safe, I love her more than anything," Kojo demanded of Jin through a trembling voice.

"I will do all I can, Lord Kojo."

Knowing the odd young man to be painfully honest at all times, Kojo believed Jin's words. He then went over to his daughter and whispered, "You're strong and you'll survive this. Just stay safe." Through tears they mustered a nod of trust. Kojo then hugged his family, long enough to feel as though they could never forget it.

With thoughts of protection and fear bouncing around, an image suddenly formed in the mind of Nia. She ran up to Gozen, keeping her distressed voice quiet. "We have to do something about Suzu. What if Kits knows about her staying with Lucette?"

Gozen had been thinking about it since the moment he realized who Suzu went to see on that awful night. "If Kits knew where she was, I think he would have already tried something."

"But what if he finds out and nobody . . ."

Gozen cut her off, trying to keep things focused. "I know some good, trustworthy Enforcers in her district. I'll wire-type them as soon as you leave; you don't need to worry about her."

It took all of Nia's focus for her to keep it together. As her mother cried behind the car, Nia imagined never seeing her little sister again; the world began to feel unbearable. Gozen embraced her and spoke with quiet conviction. "I'll protect your family; you just need to keep yourself safe."

The two nodded their heads, refocusing on the immediacy of the moment. Finally, she and Jin got into his C22. Nia looked back as they drove down the lengthy drive to Long Frost road, onto the path to Primichi.

The family faded in the distance as the elegant mechanical drawbridge came into view. Gozen had raised it when they entered; Jin had never seen it up. Nia told him to stop so she could lower it. She quickly got out but stopped. Her head panned back and forth as the cold river rushed by below her. Jin got out of the car, assuming she might need some mechanical assistance. Unfortunately, something worse stayed her hand.

Looking north and south, they saw two identical black Móstiques idling a hundred meters up either side of the road. "Do you think it's Kits?" Jin asked.

Having been in varying states of panic since she last saw Kits, Nia finally reassessed who he might actually be. She wondered why she had let herself get so close to him; she felt like a fool. An anger then started to grow around an almost overwhelming feeling of betrayal.

"We can go back," Jin offered.

"Whoever it is, I don't want them anywhere near my family," Nia declared.

"We have the faster vehicle. If we can get past I'll get us to Primichi at least an hour ahead of them," Jin calculated. "But we can't outrun the wire. If they have accomplices in Primichi, they'll be waiting for us long before we arrive."

Nia looked at Jin. "I don't want them near your family, either."

In the months that Jin had known her from a distance, only then did he realize what Nia required to care for someone. She risked her own safety for a family she had never met, a privileged family whom no one ever sympathized for, one he offered up for her own advantage; she didn't require anything. Jin stood humbled and amazed.

Nia looked up towards the infinite stretch of the Murdes. Their expanse seemed greater than she could fully comprehend. "We just need to go some place where no one ever goes."

"Like Goraka?" Jin simply considered.

"What?" The suggestion seemed absurd on nearly every level.

"The Red Valley. I believe it to be a place that is essentially forbidden by the entirety of Chigou's citizens. Or am I mistaken?"

Nia thought of legends, a place where mysteries bred enough fear to keep all away. Not a single person who knew its stories entered the valley of death. Not one.

"Nia?" Jin asked as engines idled.

"Lestichi," she replied.

"I haven't heard it called that before," Jin said.

"It's the old path along the eastern base of the Murdes. It's rough, but it goes straight into Goraka, bypassing the city," she explained.

"How do we get there?"

Nia looked across the powerful river to the mountains. "Straight ahead."

They then heard a mechanical roar come from one of the black angels waiting for them down the road. Mad thoughts began to mix with logic. A curious harmony struck between them. Nia hit the lowering mechanism, and the two silently got back into the car. The air felt cool; the field ahead lay clear.

As they sat in the idling car, a moment passed. Finally, Nia squinted at Jin. "You've been working on this shiny contraption every day since you arrived. Aren't you finally going to show me what it can do?"

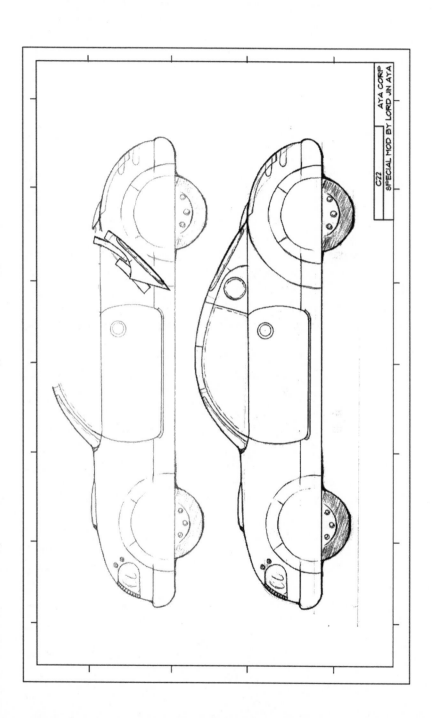

AYA CORP
C22
SPECIAL MOD BY LORD JIN AYA

16
ALONE

A smooth hum from below the car turned into a roaring symphony of steel and steam. Jin grabbed the Bokai wood shifter and threw it into low gear. The sound of pounding metal vibrated through the drawbridge as it touched down. Jin's foot hit the throttle and the car shot off like some wild mechanical animal.

The two black Móstiques kicked up dust as Nia felt her shoulders pushing into the back of the seat. Jin drove his obsessively tuned C22 straight across Long Frost Road and into the field.

Nia pointed to the forest at the base of the mountains straight ahead. "There's an opening for Lestichi just right of that giant Laizóu tree."

Although the opening seemed hidden, Jin easily saw the large tree and accelerated. Nia looked back to see their dark pursuers closer than she had hoped. The C22 proved its quickness, but the uneven ground threw them around. Jin calculated the stresses of every joint in the car.

"I hope the path isn't as forgotten as this field," Jin said.

"Are you worried your Lady can't handle it?" Nia prodded.

"Not especially," Jin stated, then jumped into a higher gear.

After a minute, Nia pointed again as the opening revealed itself. Jin slowed down as they entered the rough path just wide enough for the car to fit. Plants and trees banged onto its metal sides. They tossed around until finally making it up to the intersection. Jin worked the brake, and they spun right onto the path.

Nia looked back through the spray of dirt to see the two heavy Móstiques barging through the forest. Without hesitation, Jin hit the accelerator.

The two black shapes pursued them like demons, but with the

path smoothing out, Jin maintained a distance. Nia had never moved faster in her life. The trees whistled by, one green mass blurring into the next. Exhilaration and fear bounced around in her chest. Bumps and ruts threw them back and forth, but Jin wrangled the C22 back with every obstacle. Nia saw him calmly evaluate every bump and noise as if making evaluations on a test track. She wondered how that infuriating, prim young man, in a dangerous moment of chaos, somehow managed to generate such a sense of peace.

"Jin," Nia said with a smile, maybe the first she ever sincerely offered him, "I am impressed." He looked over as if given dire information. Twenty blurring trees later, the words sank in, and he finally smiled back.

The path seemed to continue for hours. The rush of speed and excitement became almost laborious over time, and stimulation exhaustion set in. Occasionally they saw the metal towers of downtown Chigou through a gap in the trees. The turns got tighter as the slope of the valley began to increase. They felt the temperature begin to rise along with the humidity. Without saying it, they both knew the end of the valley approached.

Nia noticed a cascade of water coming off of a rock cliff above them to the left. Its serenity captured her attention, a moment of calm on a frenzied caravan. A tight turn neared as they drove through the water streaming over the path. Jin braked and immediately felt the car slip sideways. The muddied tires hopelessly clawed for grip but didn't slow down in time; the C22 rammed sideways into a Bokai tree.

The jolt rattled their skulls. Jin painfully turned his neck to check on Nia and the side of the car; both appeared resilient against the impact. Nia rubbed her jaw while trying to recover her bearings. She looked over to check on Jin; instead she saw a flash of light behind his head. In an instant, she felt the Bokai tree explode into her face.

"They're shooting at us," Jin spoke in frantic realization.

Nia tucked down into the seat as the C22 roared up again.

"Are you okay?" Jin asked.

Nia lifted her head and brushed off the bits of wood. "I think so. Am I bleeding? I don't think I'm bleeding."

As they descended, the turns came at them faster as the ground got softer. Jin struggled to keep the intentionally nimble C22 in the middle of the path. The Móstiques roared onward as their heavier mass helped them to grip below the wet topsoil.

"They're getting closer, Jin."

"I would agree," Jin spoke, looking in the mirror.

"Why is that, Jin? I thought this was a first-class machine."

Jin looked at her, feeling protective. "This is an exceptional vehicle, Nia."

Another projectile shot through the windshield, adding bits of glass to the tree shrapnel already on Nia's face. "Well then, stop being an unexceptional driver!"

"I apologize, Nia, but it's not as though I practice driving like this. I haven't even tested out . . ." Jin stopped as an image of gears and axles assembled in his brain. Nia checked on the Sentinel leaning out of the Móstique, pointing his death gadget at them. She turned back to Jin who appeared to be pondering engineering quandaries peacefully at his desk.

"Jin!" Nia exclaimed.

Having concluded that he had in fact finished installing his prototype all-wheel-drive setup, Jin threw a brass lever on the dash to engage the system. Immediately the C22 clawed onto the path with every wheel, and the two felt its force throw them back into their seats.

Although he considered it rather imprudent for a test drive, Jin continued to tear through the winding path. Trees flew by just inches away as Nia checked their pursuers, suddenly having trouble keeping up. The path got steeper as it began to run along a large ditch.

"So where does this path end?" he asked.

"I've never gone to the end. I'm not crazy," Nia said, as they felt the C22 hit a thick root. The speed leapt them out of their seats before slamming back down. "But we have to get away from them somehow and soon."

As the ditch ran along the road, Jin looked down and then back to the heavy vehicles behind them. He started to calculate weights and speeds.

"How far do you estimate this trench goes?"

Nia looked down the winding ravine. "To the bottom, I guess."

"Hang on."

"Why?" Nia asked as the engine howled, thrusting them forward.

Ahead, the path turned sharply to the left to avoid the steep drop, only they weren't slowing down.

"Jin," Nia spoke, questioning his current thought pattern.

Picking up speed, they drove right off the beaten path through a straight clearing between trees. They both gripped whatever they could, and the C22 hit the rising rim of the ditch. The huge trench passed below them as they floated weightlessly. Holding their breath, the pair slammed down hard as it cleared to the other side, debris flying up around them.

With her fingers digging into the seat, Nia immediately looked back to see the front Móstique drive up and attempt the jump. Its large shape vaulted like some hovering tank. Then, an explosion of dirt and metal flew out as the car crashed directly into the side of the trench.

"They didn't make it!" Nia exclaimed with relief.

Jin struggled to reciprocate the feeling. A grinding noise came up through the floor. His muscles ached as he tried to fight through the raw forest, dodging trees like a swarm of insects. He feared further damaging his car but wanted to get far away, fast.

"That sounds weird," Nia said.

"It sounds bad actually, very bad."

Jin kept driving as long as he felt the car could hold out, but it was not long. Getting confirmation from Nia, he stopped the car well out of sight from whoever had been chasing them. He turned off the searing hot engine; they stopped to listen.

"I don't hear anything," Nia said.

She looked around, searching for a sign of what to do next. The area looked exotic compared to the central valley. Everything seemed thick, from the deep green vegetation to the humid air she could feel on her face. Even the sweet and heavy smells of the forest combined into something she had never experienced before. The entire space quietly oozed a sensation of life, but the relief of escape started to mount into a new tension. Nia came to the realization that they sat in a place she had never gone before, where no one ever goes.

"I suspect we have at least thirty minutes before they get here," Jin calculated.

She spoke quietly. "Jin, they're not coming."

Rather curious of her confidence, Jin asked, "How do you know they've stopped their pursuit?"

Nia took a protracted breath as her eyes cautiously looked around. "We're in the Red Valley."

○ ○ ○

Despite standing out like a metal ornament on a holiday tree, the two decided to stay with the C22, which suddenly served only as a large storage trunk. Jin quickly investigated the underside of the car with a custom-built lift. He assessed that repairs might be beyond what he had access to at the time and instead decided to camouflage the car with an assortment of foliage. Nia helped while further explaining to Jin how unlikely it was that anyone, even mad killers, would ever dare to join them where then were.

"Are you quite sure that absolutely no one would be willing to follow us in here? I don't mean to project distrust, but the fear of it all seems a bit hyperbolic."

Nia dug the ground with her toe. "Jin, it's the richest soil in the entire valley and not a single industrialist is down here making money off of it."

"Hmm, that is a rather undeniable bit of evidence. Well explained, Lady Nia," Jin said before getting back to his carefully engineered camouflage pattern.

Nia set down a pop-shelter, built a fire ring out of stones, and then started to collect firewood. She went through the food they had been given and calculated a rationing plan. Kojo also packed some snares and a hunting knife, and she wondered what peculiar animals Goraka offered to hunt.

Camp got set up quickly despite their mutual exhaustion. The two felt cradled by the forest that seemed to hold them in a warm, floating breath. It reminded Jin of his family's two-story greenhouse back in Primichi. Nia got a small fire going, spurring

Jin to be impressed with her ability to keep it from smoking. Ready for a break, Nia sat on a log she had roughly cut, while Jin sat on a collapsible alloy seat with an adjustable back.

Finally still, they listened to the sounds of Goraka. A symphony of biology played all around them as they basked in the rich atmosphere. The air felt tuned to their body temperature. Time went by. They processed what had happened since that morning, eventually landing on their current placement in the legendary land.

"I imagined feeling much more threatened here," Jin stated.

"I know, right? Where are all the flying red devils trying to eat our souls?" Nia wondered. The relief of surviving the day compounded with the exchange of ridiculous words. Despite the assumed danger of their situation, she had never felt more at ease with the rich young man from up north, an heir who had proven to be surprisingly reliable. Sitting in the valley of death, she laughed at the irony. Jin felt farther away from home than he ever had.

"So, what are the stories you hear about this place up in Primichi? If you have any to tell . . ." Nia inquired.

"Well, my mother's grandfather actually knew the first man to come here, a fellow by the name of Martouk, I believe."

"What, are you serious?" Nia asked.

"Yes, not a particularly humorous story, unfortunately. I was told his entire expedition team died, and he turned a bit mad from the whole experience."

Nia chewed on a fingernail. "What did they say killed them?"

"That was perhaps the more fantastical portion of the account. I believe he had trouble explaining the events clearly. Something red killed them; that was it. After that it became a rarely spoken but universally understood doctrine: to enter the southern end of the valley is to enter one's conclusion," Jin stated.

"Okay, so how did your grandfather know this guy?"

Jin thought for a moment. "Well, my great-grandfather's name was Poel Jastoú. He was a . . ."

Nia jumped in. "Wait, *the* Poel Jastoú? One of the founders of the Naifin Valley and the father of modern medicine?"

"Yes, I am charmed that you have heard of him. He is spoken

of quite favorably within the family," Jin tactfully offered.

With her mouth agape, Nia stared for a bit before processing the thought further. "Well, super wealthy people all seem to be related, so I guess I shouldn't be surprised."

Jin found the statement rather curious. "I suppose there is a rather secluded quality to my socio-economic group."

"Is that why you wanted to come down to the farm? Mix it up with us simple folk?" Nia smiled.

With a noticeable hesitation, Jin politely replied. "That might have had something to do with my reasoning."

"And how is that working out for you?"

Jin looked back at his sophisticated vehicle, now sitting crippled in the forest. A scrappy little creature with thick fur called a Rapin sat on the driver's head rest. "Everything seems to be going exactly as I had planned."

Nia squinted. "Why Jin Aya, did humor just manage its way out of your mouth?"

"Despite my relative idiosyncrasies to those at the farm, I do value wit and farce."

They laughed for different reasons. "That is a very normal thing to say."

The words delivered so casually by Nia led Jin to ponder a thought that had been possessing his mind more and more back at Kora. "Yes, I suppose I do not fit so fairly."

"Well, I certainly would not call you a normal person, but I don't think a normal person would have been able to manage what you accomplished today."

Nia sat until Jin decided to reciprocate her smile. She got up and walked over to the car to grab a Lansu. She stood for a moment wondering if Suzu still had her lost DaiLansu, or ever actually took it at all.

"I'm going to check out the perimeter."

"Would you like me to accompany you?" Jin asked.

Nia shrugged. "I won't go very far."

As Nia walked around the camp, their minds wandered, jumping between thoughts of survival and how much their lives seemed to be changing. It became yet another isolating moment for Jin on his curious quest, questioning all of the reasons he traveled so far from home. Nia thought of her family, her feelings bouncing between love, loss, and guilt. Camp remained quiet until the sun started to set.

They prepped camp for the evening and set up the pop-shelter. An endearing moment of awkwardness arrived when they simultaneously compared their combined size to that of the extremely compact tent. Jin gentlemanly suggested he stay awake and take watch for the bulk of the evening. Exhausted, Nia quickly agreed.

Jin got out an electric torch powered by a hand-cranked dynamo with a small battery. It used a red lens that made it easy for one's eyes to adjust from the darkness, a redesign from something his family produced. He then grabbed his Masu and steamed some freeze-dried, smoked coffee, preparing for a long night.

○ ○ ○

The early light woke Nia, who in turn suggested Jin get some sleep. Thirty seconds after he entered the tent, it went quiet for the next six hours. Nia took another trip about the camp looking for small animals and any plants that could be easily eaten. Although a bit out of practice, she soon tracked a flock of plump birds that looked like a type of Chitori but with red beaks.

Jin woke up with his Masu in hand and immediately felt like a fool. He stepped outside to see Nia sharpening the hunting knife Kojo had given her.

"Do you often sleep with that black stick?" she asked.

"Certainly not." Jin rubbed his eyes.

"Hmm, let me take a look at that thing." Nia reached for the retracted Masu. Jin politely raised it and she flipped it around in her hands.

"Be careful not to . . ."

The blade shot out a few inches from Nia's face, which immediately locked in place.

". . . hit those buttons," Jin suggested.

Nia slowly lowered the blade and investigated the curious weapon. "I now understand why you normally do not sleep with this."

"And please, never let me do it again." Jin reached down to slowly turn the Masu in her hand. "You need to hit the thumb and finger triggers together. You figured that out already."

With her face timidly turned, Nia hit the switches, and the blade retracted almost silently. Impressed, she looked it over. Her hand could feel the small squares that protruded from the precision machined handle. "I'm guessing you made this."

"Yes."

"So you were introduced to industrial design as a toddler?" Nia joked.

"Yes."

"Of course you were." Nia handed it back. "Do you know how to use it?"

"I don't understand. I just showed you how."

Nia grinned. "No, I mean *really* know how to use it."

"Oh yes. A caretaker of mine studied Maiishi for most of her life."

"I've heard of that. My instructor explained to me that Soultai was a circle, whereas Maiishi was an angled line."

Jin considered, then smiled. "That is a wonderfully condensed description, actually."

"And I suppose you trained every day of your life."

"Maiishi has four annual days of rest, one for each season."

"Slacker."

"What?"

"Never mind. Let's try something."

Nia recommended Jin take a quick gulp of his leftover smoked coffee that she reheated. A moment later, she led him out into the forest. Nia described the bird that might make for a good meal and wanted him to help catch it. Although they didn't need to hunt yet, Nia wanted to know of some options before they ran out of food.

While in the lead, Nia spotted a single Chitori-like bird eating off of the forest floor. She had Jin position himself behind a tree where he could strike after she flushed the bird out. She then hopped around a Hugou tree and stalked across the forest floor.

Jin peeked around as he saw her quietly creep towards the bird.

Watching her silent footsteps, he kept his fingers on the Masu trigger. Nia then got low, unsheathing her knife in case the bird got within her striking distance first. Four meters away, the bird suddenly saw her and began to fly away just above the ground.

Nia ran after the fat little bird, while Jin popped the sword and gripped it with his sweaty hand. He could see the bird flying right for him. Keeping perfectly still until in striking distance, Jin swung the Masu. The blade whistled as a quick squeal rang out. Jin stood motionless as the the bird writhed on the ground, blood misting around its neck.

In a flash Nia jumped past him and onto the bird. She braced it with her hand and quickly struck it with her knife. The bird stopped moving. Nia put the knife away and stroked the feathers of the still animal, treating it like a sleeping pet. She leaned down and began to slowly whisper what Jin thought to be some sort of prayer or ritual. He found it fascinating, seeing someone have compassion for an animal they had just killed. A small amount of blood dripped from his sword.

○ ○ ○

After another night of taking shifts, the two decided to get scientific with some of the surrounding, potentially edible plants. Being the farmer, Nia became the obvious choice to select specimens. Jin conducted some experiments he had learned in a biology course, rubbing plants on his skin and eating carefully measured amounts. Nia felt confident in her choices but found Jin's tinkering nature to be fairly entertaining. He separated a few samples and explained why he thought they would be safe to eat, smiling as he handed them to her.

She started to see something in Jin that had previously escaped her. A privileged young man bred for confidence, willingly making himself an outsider in a foreign land. She realized how he had never complained about his simple accommodations at the farm or asked for any special treatment. What had once appeared as arrogance now seemed as simple thoughtfulness from an outsider. She smiled, realizing she liked having him there.

They set up another fire and decided to cook some of their findings: a lot of root vegetables and some fruit, which grew larger and higher up than anything found in the central valley. They laughed with mutual surprise over the quality of the meal, both claiming little experience as chefs. Nia reminisced about her mother's cooking. Jin decided which of the family's private chefs he found to be his favorite. At the mention of sweet Blashu rolls, their faces illuminated in unison.

The joy of dinner inevitably juxtaposed into a sobering point. They still sat in a land apparently so dangerous, even the murder squad had not followed them in. Quietly, however, Jin still questioned that theory. He had more concerns over known threats than marauding folklore.

"I imagine living so close, you must have heard quite a few more stories about this place than I," said Jin.

"Hmm, growing up I got a mixture of explanations. From 'It's very dangerous; you can never go in there' to more complicated explanations that were basically scary spirit stories." Nia put another log on the fire.

"I have observed you to be rather adventurous. You never wanted to explore this region?"

"Occasionally you'd hear about someone or some group coming in here for whatever reason. Typically you'd never hear from them again; rarely one person would make it back half alive and crazy. As far as I've heard, no one has ever come out the same way they went in."

Nia's words shot a chill through both of them. Their stay had been peaceful thus far, but it started to feel like luck. Nia tried to shift the subject. "I'm surprised that with how industrially opportunistic Chigou is, no one has tried to come in here and violate the land for all it's worth. Way west of here there's this gate that keeps people out. Long Frost road goes in there, then supposedly it just stops. Kind of creepy."

Ambers floated up in a thin swarm as Jin rubbed his hands together. "Although I haven't told anyone, one of the supplementary reasons I decided to come here was because of Goraka and Suzu's father."

Nia looked at Jin as if his head began to glow red. Her mind processed the sentence she never imagined coming out of his mouth. "I feel like you're about to tell a spooky spirit story, but I don't think this is a good time."

The orange light of the fire lit Jin's face from below. "I had discovered a paper written on Core-thermic technology that had been submitted to my family's company. It proposed harnessing heat from below ground to generate power. Fascinating proposal, but Goraka seemed like the only land where such a technology would work. In reference to our discussions, no one was going to fund that."

Nia spoke directly. "What does Suzu's father have to do with it?"

"The paper was written by Carmin Komou, an engineer at Kasic. I hoped to meet him down here. It wasn't until Suzu told me her last name that I realized he was her father, but since she is an orphan . . . I knew I'd never get to meet him."

His words felt heavy. The thought of Suzu had become almost burdensome to Nia. Her mind wandered to dark and worrisome places. She so badly wanted to talk to Suzu again.

"Have you managed to see the young Lady recently? How is she?" Jin gently asked.

Nia took a long look into the fire. "I don't know."

The conversation quieted down between the tired pair. Darkness crept in behind the setting of the sun.

○ ○ ○

The next morning felt cooler as Jin got up early. Once out of the tent, he quickly moved onto making smoked coffee, realizing how much more he appreciated the comforting drink so far from a proper bed. While staring through the brewing vapors, he noticed Nia curled up in the passenger seat of the C22. She held a Toki in her hand, apparently fidgeting with a Special Jin had yet to know about.

He then heard a mystifying hum through the woods. A minute later he heard it again; Nia seemed unconcerned. He poured his cup of smoked coffee and thought to inquire about the sound with Nia. As he was about to get up, Kola soared just over his head and onto the windshield of the crippled roadster. Jin flicked spilled coffee off his fingers.

Nia's face illuminated at the sight of the bird. Jin realized the sound must have been the Special for her Toki. Although he couldn't recount any Toki having an animal call as its Special, it seemed quite fitting given the scene before him. Jin watched the unlikely friends interact—the animal and the human—intrigued over what he did not understand.

Kola stayed for awhile, always looking stoic, even when Nia would pet his soft head. At one point he even flew off and brought back a small rodent. Nia laughed and thanked him for his gentlemanly gift. Kola reminded her of home, of many other things far away from the forbidden land she was hiding in.

With a proud cry, Kola eventually flew off. Nia got out of the cozy padded seat and walked over to Jin, who asked, "Does your Toki's Special actually call that owl?"

Nia smiled. "Kola? Yes, actually."

Jin thought of the science behind such a thing. "I believe I have heard such a sound before at the farm but have never been able to identify it."

"Well, there ya go. I installed the same Special into my DaiLansu. Maybe you heard that, too, but I don't know where it is. Well . . . maybe I know."

The thought trailed off until Nia's survival instincts pulled her back to the present. "I think we need to figure out when we should go back."

"And how we're getting back," Jin said, noticing the plants leaning against the C22's wheels. "I'm sorry about my question last evening. You obviously miss the young girl, and this probably is not a prudent time to have asked about her."

Slowly, a tear welled up in her eye. Not just because she agreed, but also because of the surprising sweetness of Jin's words. "It's fine. You were just asking."

Jin nodded but felt less and less sure about anything he said anymore. The questions in his mind began to back up, and he had trouble sorting one from another. He took his last sip of coffee but kept the cup in his hand. "Nia, have you ever questioned why I specifically came to Kora? The main reason, that is."

Nia let out a small laugh.

Jin sat up. "I'm sorry, did I say something strange?"

"No, no, it's just . . . yes, I have many times wondered what it was that you were doing at the farm."

Jin fiddled with his cup while the fire crackled. "A long while ago a man came over to our house. I didn't know him personally, but I recognized him. He did something important at the company, but my father typically did not discuss executive matters with me. Commonly he would just leave me to my tinkering."

Nia noticed a long pause after the words which made him sound vulnerable. She waited for him to continue.

"I overheard this man tell my father that he was quitting to pursue some other project he had started, something with helping children, maybe orphans. I remember my father saying things like 'throwing your career away' or 'not necessary'. But the entire time this man kept a peaceful smile on his face. He was listening so carefully to my father, but nothing my father said swayed this man at all; he was completely convinced of his decision.

"When the man left, my father was at a loss. That was very unusual for him. I asked him why the man would leave such a successful career. My father just patted me on the shoulder and walked out of the room."

"He didn't want to explain?" Nia asked.

"No, I don't believe so. I'm quite certain he didn't know the answer. That man was pursuing something that my father didn't understand, and it was greater than what he already had. I think I wanted to know what that was; I wanted to know what all of that was worth leaving for. I supposed, looking at my father in that moment, I wouldn't be able to find out what that was unless I left home."

The thought had never crossed her mind, that Jin came to Kora hoping to find something more meaningful than the industrial empire he left behind. She felt ashamed for what she first assumed of him.

Jin continued. "I didn't know what I was doing when I arrived. I do remember feeling a bit proud, though, and I believe that might have caused some uncomfortable moments. I'm actually quite chagrined over that. I'm sure a formal apology to everyone will be suitable when we get back."

"It's okay," Nia quietly offered.

"But I do remember when Suzu first came and how much time you spent with her. You gave her everything you could, but not out of obligation. Your commitment was very impressive. She went from being scared and pathetic to having an abundance of energy and hope."

Nia noticed his eyes hiding from her. He started to struggle with his words. "Gozen said that her parents were killed. I don't understand how a child could endure such a thing. How brave she must have been. You had your entire family taken from you, as well. You came to that farm with nothing, but you do not act as though you have been robbed of your life. No, somehow you spend all of your time giving. You even gave so much to that hopeless little girl, she was able to live again."

Jin put his hand over his face, covering a shame finally making its way out. "I was born with everything, Nia . . . I was born with everything and all I've ever done is keep it to myself."

Nia watched him cry for the first time, wondering if it was his first time. He looked weak, like a newborn animal, scared and searching in a strange new world. She got up and sat next to him. Gently leaning in, she spoke softly. "Most people don't even go looking for that answer. Maybe you don't feel like it now, but I think you were brave to leave your home and come here. Don't ever stop searching, Jin."

Nia stayed until her friend seemed to find some peace. The fire burned, and Jin sat alone for a while. It became harder to get a sense of time in the Red Valley. Many thoughts went through his mind, questions about the certainties of life. They became lost in the dense sounds living in the forest.

○ ○ ○

In the morning, Nia decided to take a long lap around the camp. She walked for while, her mind wandered and the activity began to feel like a routine. She even seemed to be acclimating to the soft ground and humid air. Still, a deep feeling lurked, constantly whispering that they didn't belong there.

A small and brightly colored bird then flew by her—a whispering bird. Its wings moved so fast they appeared as a blur, keeping its small frame afloat. It zipped around, pointing its long red beak at her. The bird fluttered around and she followed its rather long, thin tail feather.

The bird seemed nearly fantastical as it zipped around, almost too whimsical to be real. Nia stayed quiet, following the soft chirping noise rolling out of its tiny beak. It would approach a tree to investigate and then fly around in long arcs. Suddenly, it held its position, perfectly hovering above a bare patch as if held by invisible hands.

Suddenly suspicious, Nia looked around but saw nothing unusual. She approached quietly, her slim shoes pressing into the soft ground. Then, like a breathing arrow, the bird shot past her. A second later, Nia heard the cry of an owl, and she saw Kola fly after the bird. She smiled, admiring his graceful form. She watched Kola fly away over the canopy of trees and then turn back towards camp. The sound disappeared, and that is when she finally saw it.

Before her in a small clearing stood a featureless, blood-red shape about the size of a man. She quickly hid behind a tree, as years of frightful myths manifested into a scream she desperately fought to keep in with shaking hands.

Praying that it had not noticed her, she slowly turned around, keeping her body against the tree. She rubbed her hands on its rough bark, reminding herself of reality. Cautiously slow, she then peeked around the trunk; the fantastical thing remained. Fear began to crawl all over her skin. The crimson form appeared unbelievably smooth, like some organic capsule, wavering ever so slightly.

It felt as though she stood next to death itself. A desperate urge swelled to get back to camp. She thought of calling out to Jin. She wondered if it had already killed him.

Nia then clenched her jaw as she fought to reign in her thoughts. She took a small step back and silently hopped up to a thick branch. Getting her footing, she swiftly ascended two more branches. Again, she slid back around. The shape had not heard her, or at least it hadn't moved. She became intensely aware of every sound she made.

A hissing sound then echoed in from the direction of camp. Nia recognized it as Jin steaming his coffee, and she fought to keep in a warning cry. She waited for the shape to react. At first it seemed to remain still, but something began to appear. Two round black shapes revealed as it turned. They hung downwards like large, sad eyes from an abstract face. Nia remained absolutely still, wondering if the thing already knew she was there.

Like a phantom, the red shape began to float across the forest floor. It headed towards camp, right towards Jin. The moment felt mad, and Nia thought such a thing could not exist. She then heard more noise from camp and snapped to attention. She looked down at the web of leaves and branches in front of her and picked a route. She began to lightly step across the first thick branch. It started to bend but held her weight. A lower branch stretched just below, and she hopped down before crawling to the next trunk.

She felt her shoes slip on the damp bark with every step. It took almost all of her focus to keep balanced, fighting the need to constantly track the red figure below. Her mind still struggled to reconcile the unreal image floating away, seeing it to be true.

Nia finally began to feel stable traversing the treetops when she noticed camp directly ahead. She saw the back of Jin, the red figure gliding straight towards him. She wondered if it would stop. She wondered how she could warn Jin without making herself a target. Running would make too much noise. She hoped it would simply do nothing, but she thought of the stories, all of them ending so horribly. It got closer to Jin. Nia silently prayed . . . begged it would just stop; it didn't.

"Jin!" Nia yelled, almost as if out of her control. The creature turned its long dark eyes towards the sound of her voice. Jin spun as well, the sight of the bright red mass immediately stole his breath.

The creature began to float towards Nia. Feeling little confidence with any plan, she simply decided to run. With the trees close enough for her to stay above the ground, she moved as fast as she could. Practically stunned, Jin watched the red shape follow Nia. As she started to disappear into the treetops, Jin's mind finally grasped what was happening.

He sprang up and ran to the C22. He reached in, grabbed the retracted Masu, and turned around. Nia scrambled across the branches while the red creature accelerated along the ground, matching her pace. Jin pushed off of the crippled car and launched into a full sprint.

Sensing the creature down below, Nia tried to watch its position, but the unpredictable branches came at her too fast. It took all of her focus and agility to keep from falling six meters to the ground below. Jin followed them, catching glimpses between the trees. In the back of both of their minds, a terrifying certainty resonated that neither had time to ponder: No one had ever looked into the face of Goraka and escaped unharmed.

As Nia focused forward, a new panic revealed itself. Her current path of branches stopped just up ahead. She could see below that the forest floor suddenly sloped down to a cliff, dropping at least thirty meters. Feeling no other choice, she charted a downward course.

Leaping to the lower branches, she precisely landed each step before rolling out as she hit the ground. Panicked, she clawed her way upright as fast as she could, flinging moss into the air.

"Nia!" Jin yelled as he saw her stand. The red shape slanted forward and picked up speed. It slithered around trees as if being pulled on a wire, a wire attached to her. With a huge drop-off behind her, Nia extracted the Lansu and dug her feet into the ground. The shape reached her in an instant. She flung up a cloud of debris with the Lansu and dove around a tree.

Jin watched in fear as his friend disappeared. The red shape then flew across the ground and away from him. He saw Nia quickly get up and brace herself against the tree. She saw the red blur circling around between the trees, its movement gracefully terrifying. Suddenly, it started to circle back towards her even faster. Immediately she knew it couldn't be outrun; she had to face it.

Just in front of the creature, Jin ran urgently fast. As the red blur approached Nia at an opposing angle, she readied herself for the impact. Jin triggered the blade on his Masu and locked his eyes on the target. He lunged forwards hoping to get to Nia first. She raised her Lansu. At once, all three collided.

The force knocked Jin violently into Nia, and they flew onto the slope. Nia screamed for Jin as they quickly slid to the cliff. She clawed at the wet ground but moved too fast to stop. Jin rolled onto his feet and dove as he saw Nia slide off of the edge. On faith, he drove his Masu into the ground and reached down over the drop.

Jin sensed something latch on to his wrist as pain burst out of his shoulder. With half of his body hanging over the edge, he saw Nia clinging on, swinging thirty meters above the ground. Immediately she kicked up with her feet at the cliff wall, but the smooth rock underneath slanted away from her.

"Jin, pull me up!" Nia shouted.

"I can't."

Recovering from paralyzing fear, Nia came to and began to pull herself up Jin's arm. The fatigue barely allowed her to manage one hand over the other. She fought to grip his sweaty forearm when they both noticed it at the same time.

Jin's shoulder had a long, deep cut going across it, either from the creature or his own weapon. Blood started to pour out from below the sleeve folded up just above his elbow.

"Jin, pull me up." Nia's voice struggled.

He could feel the anchoring sword giving ground as he pulled on it, the only thing keeping them from falling. He then pulled on his other, bleeding arm. Nothing.

"I can't even feel my arm. You have to pull yourself up." Jin tried to not panic.

Nia swung her body around and managed to reach higher up his arm, her hand landing on a stream of blood. She flung her weight up but her grip slid down. Panicking, she reached up again. Her frantic hands smeared blood all over his forearm as they desperately tried to pull her up and away from the drop below. She slipped down with every move.

"Jin," she quietly cried. Jin pulled again on the Masu. It slipped, and their bodies jerked towards the ground below. He looked into Nia's eyes and saw desperate fear. She clawed into his blood-covered wrist. As they felt their hands slip apart, the world stopped. Jin saw Nia fall towards the ground below, her screams swallowed up by the world around them.

He lay there, the weight of desperate hope now released. Far away he saw Nia quiet and motionless. He felt numb. Time seemed to stand still except for the plants swaying around her. He could not move. Nothing felt real. The numbness in his arm had spread across his entire body. Kola flew down and landed next to his fallen companion. Jin watched the owl stand over her for awhile, nudging at her cheek. Without a soft touch or even a glance in return, the bird finally stopped.

○ ○ ○

Everything seared with brightness, almost as if the sun had bleached out the colors of the world. With his head buzzing, the ground seemed to float underneath his feet. Jin's lips felt dry and his body begged for water, but his mind had no concern for personal well-being. It had been a few days of traveling slowly, without rest, with every hour fading into the next. His feet scraped across the boards of the drawbridge. Cool, clear water rushed beneath him. He saw a rusted container float along the bank, poison leftovers from his home city up north. Tire marks remained from where they had decided to head down into Goraka.

Jin had trouble focusing his eyes as the horizon seemed to sway. The white owl circled above him in the white sky, casting a shadow around his path. His mind stumbled along with his feet, but he kept walking. A hazy shape in the distance then began to materialize into a home.

Like a slave obeying an unknown master, Jin dragged himself to the farm house. He got to the door and raised his fist. His entire arm looked frail and strange in its coating of dried blood. He meant to knock on the heavy door, but his hand would not follow. The entire journey meant to culminate in a confession, but as the time arrived, he felt entirely incapable. His legs felt weak. A dryness started to form in the back of his throat making it hard to breathe. His fist remained floating in air, unable to move.

Suddenly the door opened to cool darkness. Jin lowered his arm and his eyes began to adjust. He could make out the shape of a small woman standing in front of him. The face of Clora entered the caustic light of the outside. Jin could see her eyes fight to open up until they finally filled with the joy of reunion. A longing smile appeared as she looked around for the one he had promised to keep safe, but Jin stood alone.

The heat in his throat spread out in a wave of utter despair. His dehydrated body struggled to cry as he collapsed to his knees. Utterly exhausted, he began to cry out the pain and guilt he had carried every mile from Goraka. Clora's eyes lowered to the broken young man now simply explaining his story in a wordless confession down at her feet.

In the days since they left, the mother had prepared herself for such news, although the thought made her ill. There were too many feelings to express or make sense of. Her eyes trembled with anguish. A pain began to grown inside her, trying to take over. Instead, she managed to gently put her hand on the young man's head as he continued to weap.

The sound of footsteps then came from the kitchen. She turned to see Kojo standing alone in the hallway. The lifelong partners expressed a thousand thoughts without words. She wanted to hold her husband but could not pull herself away from the shattered child wailing for forgiveness on the ground. Kojo stepped back into the kitchen alone. The world felt unbearable.

17
CHICHIMOU

Rain hit against the window, echoing throughout the empty room. Jin folded the remaining clothes he had into his custom-built traveler; the brass fittings needed polished. He thought of the last thing Nia had ever told him, simply to keep searching. He had never felt more lost.

It had taken Jin a full day to recover enough to utter anything more than a single word. His shoulder required suturing, the rest of his body completely exhausted. Clora took charge of caring for him as it kept her from dwelling on dark thoughts. Kojo couldn't even stomach being in a room with his daughter's failed guardian.

Not until the next day did anyone discover that Jin and Nia hadn't even traveled towards Primichi. He explained the Móstiques and why they chose to travel to Goraka. The end of the story remained unclear and painful like every other story about the Red Valley. Even Jin had trouble making sense of what had happened. Nobody felt compelled to pursue more details; the most important one was already painfully understood.

At one point, Kojo suggested going in to retrieve his daughter, but Clora refused to let anyone go back there. Occasionally, Jin could hear yelling between what otherwise had grown into a silent residence. He had never heard the couple exchange damaged words before.

Gozen stayed around more than usual to help manage the farm as production had started to slide. Kojo couldn't manage things as he normally did, and Gozen tried his best to make it up. The farmhands had trouble filling in the gap left by Nia, who had been involved with so many aspects of Kora. Talk of temporarily shutting down the farm simmered, but moments of wisdom declared such action foolish. Crops at the farm would not simply pause their growth.

After a few more days, Gozen assessed that Jin still couldn't work and Kojo still didn't want to be around him; the necessary change became clear. Through a rather long conversation, Jin decided not to go back to Primichi for a number of reasons. Alternately, Gozen suggested he stay at the Tree House for awhile. While presenting a change of scenery, it also offered a potential opportunity to teach the youth some fine, technical subjects. Inevitably, he assumed Jin would also learn an assortment of things from the orphans.

○ ○ ○

He held a traveler in one hand and a drafting case in the other. Two girls came running down the stairs and passed him on both sides. Jin watched them scamper into the kitchen just as Lady Kyoumére walked out. She looked over his attire and quickly assessed it to be most expensive thing in the house.

"You must be Jin Aya. Welcome to the North Orphanage."

He gently shook her hand with a subtle bow. "It is a pleasure to meet you, Lady of the house. It is very gracious of you to give me accommodations."

"It is not a problem young Lord, as you come with an exceptional recommendation. Please, follow me." With a quick smile to Gozen, the Lady led them through the kitchen. "There is an extra room we just fixed up. Simply head straight through that door. Also, I just made some smoked coffee if you'd like any."

"Thank you very much." Jin bowed again and walked into the isolated room on the edge of the kitchen. It appeared to have been an old pantry, suddenly becoming the smallest room he had ever stayed in. He then set his luggage between some flour and beans.

Back in the kitchen, Gozen took great pleasure in watching the Lady pour him a cup of coffee. "Thank you again for letting him stay. I imagine it won't be long before he is able to head back to Primichi."

"I'm not worried about time. What's one more boy in need of some care." She moved towards Gozen's ear, the old counter creaking as she leaned on it. "Besides, he's certainly the wealthiest person who has ever stayed here. Maybe if he stays long enough we can convince him to buy a new kitchen."

The two shared a refreshing laugh. Kyoumére braced herself gently on his arm, both of them acknowledging that it had been too long since they had seen each other.

"How are Clora and Kojo doing?" asked the Lady, her voice filled with concern.

Gozen let out a long sigh that had been buried deep in his chest. "Clora is managing. She's still fairly active." His voice then paused as his polite decorum floated to the floor. He thought of a mother who would never see her daughter again, who didn't even get to lay her only child's body to rest. He knew Clora practiced generous grace with her pain and tried hard to keep it from burdening others. Gozen wanted to respect her with a more honest response. His voice trembling, he said, "She's . . . she is a very strong woman. She's keeping things together up there, somehow. Kojo has been keeping to himself a lot, more than usual. He couldn't even be in the same room with him." Gozen nodded over to Jin's new diminutive quarters.

The Lady's typically sharp face started to soften. Her mind began to fill with images of Nia, showing up to a crowd of little glowing faces. As a woman in charge of so many children, she had immense appreciation for the time Nia gave to the orphanage. She struggled to think of that healthy, loving girl, now gone. Trying to imagine what Kojo and Clora were going through seemed too much. She wiped a tear out of her eye before turning back to Gozen. "So how are you doing?" She laid her cheek on Gozen's shoulder, feeling the soft rumble of his voice as he struggled to speak.

"It's really hard."

The bittersweet aching of memories fluttered through both of their minds, but far too sweet to make sense of what had happened. The idea of her fate did not seem real but the pain reminded them of its truth.

"Does Suzu know? Nia is . . . was like a big sister to her, and I know how important that was after . . ." Lady Kyoumére put her fingers up to her mouth, trying to manage the words and cries both trying to get out.

Gozen gently brushed her hair back and placed his hand on the side of her face. "I told her while she was alone at Lucette's." The memory stung, and Gozen fought hard to keep his emotions from completely taking over. "She just stood there in shock, like the last piece of her heart had been ripped out. Then she started to cry and yell, screaming questions at me. Why we let her go, why Jin took her into Goraka. She cursed him over and over, wondering why he managed to live while he let her die. It was pretty awful."

The Lady squeezed her dear friend's hand. "Well, I suppose we'll just need to keep watching our kids like we always have. The little one living out in her own apartment. The rich young business owner now living in my kitchen closet." The two cleared out the remaining grief with a much-needed laugh.

After quickly filling up what had only recently been labelled a bedroom, Jin looked outside and noticed the river. He stepped into the kitchen and politely asked the consoling pair if he could walk the grounds. The Lady wiped away a tear while straightening up and offering him some coffee. He gently declined and quickly stepped out of the room, a bit embarrassed at his interruption of what appeared to be some sort of emotional exchange.

Jin walked outside and saw groups of children playing. He walked down the gradual slope and stopped to look at the Laizóu tree. A boy and girl sat up in its branches, laughing and swinging. Behind them he saw the Long Frost river bend sharply, creating a small whirlpool down at the shore. The children looked peaceful and happy. Voices then drew his attention to a group of orphans marching in a circle.

The children hunched over with their arms locked while spinning around and singing. Jin stood still trying to distinguish the lyrics. The cadence reminded him of a chant, a particular kind Jin associated only with children. The sounds of the outside world began to fade as the rhythmic pulsing of the children's words finally became clear.

I heard there was treasure
I heard there was leisure
Beyond all your dreams, beyond any measure

Deep in the woods
the sweet little goods
but monsters can find you, the ones in red hoods
So don't make a sound
and crawl on the ground
for your only hope is to never be found
Turn around, turn around or you'll be dead
all who enter the Valley of Red

Jin felt his neck stiffen as the children's voices raised with the final verse. They rose up out of their circle and all fell on the ground, laughing. A hand then came up from behind Jin and tugged on his vest.

"Hey, why do you dress like that?"

Jin jumped back, turning his pale face down to the source of the tiny voice. A young boy with hair sticking up looked over Jin's white ascot, vest, and pinstriped pants. Needing a moment to catch his breath, Jin finally offered his reply. "It's what I always wear."

"You're really clean for a guy. Don't you work?"

"I do, young Lord. I was working at Kora. Have you heard of that farm?"

The boy's face became crooked, as if Jin revealed himself to be a ghost. The little one quickly ran off and went back to his group of friends. Jin saw him quietly speaking to the others before they suddenly scurried off together. While most of them went back to the house, one went up to another group. The yard then cleared like a chain reaction.

Suddenly alone, he walked down to where the children had been playing along the river. The water looked less clear and had a different smell than in Primichi. Seeing a metal toy car by the shore, he leaned down and picked it up. An odd familiarity then struck as he noticed it modeling the Aya Precision C17, a car his family's company built. An alloy crank came through the top, common of spring-powered gadgets. Jin turned the handle, but when it offered no resistance or noise, he put the broken car down. Jin turned to watch the soiled river swirl in front of him.

As the sun began to set, Jin headed back into the house where he

BEST RIDE IN THE VALLEY

AYA MOTORS

MODEL C17

found a swarm of little creatures scurrying around in complicated paths. Most of them too busy chasing and laughing to notice him.

He could hear Lady Kyoumére shouting orders from the kitchen, instructing the flock to organize in the dining room. Jin walked to the entrance and found the volume quickly drop into silence. The room sparkled with shiny little eyeballs, all staring at him as if ordered to do so.

On the way to the Tree House, Jin had reevaluated why he did not want to go home to Primichi. He felt too feeble to do anything of worth and wanted to exist as inconspicuously as possible. Looking completely unlike every other individual in the house, Jin then calculated his anonymity to be a conclusive impossibility.

Being unanimously observed, Jin slowly walked over to the side of the table. He only then identified the other young man sitting directly across from him. Finally lifting his tired head up after an exhausting day of work, Darou made eye contact with the smug foreigner he had hoped to never see again. Jin lowered his gaze and pulled out the empty seat; the two adjacent children promptly scooted their chairs in opposite directions.

The room quickly came to attention as Lady Kyoumére entered with a large platter of roasted vegetables and pale sausages. Hungry little eyes watched the steam rise over the slices of young cheese and salted blashu bread. Darou kept his seething look onto Jin, who tried his hardest to look anywhere else. The Lady asked young Bris to pray over the meal. As the room politely quieted down, Darou promptly got up out of his chair. Though tempted to call out the breach in etiquette, Lady Kyoumére decided to let Darou leave.

Attempting to observe the protocol of the orphanage, Jin remained quiet as they passed the food around. Conversations and quiet laughter picked up, but the volume always stayed below what Lady Kyoumére found reasonable. After a few minutes, she clearly noticed Jin's still empty plate.

"We have a new guest in the house, but I see our hunger has blinded us from the opportunity to exercise thoughtful hospitality," she said with stern grace. All together, eyes shifted straight down to the table.

"Thank you, Adela." Kyoumére said with unmistakable directness.

Fearing the woman in charge more than any spirit story, Adela leaned forward and offered Jin some bread. Jin thanked the young Adela, who had already retreated back down to her own plate of comfort food. Lady Kyoumére then heard voices from out in the hall and promptly excused herself. Walking to the back of the kitchen, she waited for a moment to see if the conversation was deeply personal or respectfully interruptible.

Darou spoke. "I'm still working a lot, but most of what I do isn't even production."

The voice of Gozen then replied, "What do you mean?"

"Just reorganizing things, like we're packing up. But with Milon gone and Kora not . . . you know, producing so great."

"Well, I think it's going to be okay. Maybe Kojo and Clora can take over Milon's farm for a while. Things will be okay."

Gozen struggled to believe his own words. He had grown tired of giving Darou bad news; the disclosure of Nia's death had been especially unpleasant to share. Reminiscent of his father, Darou tried to keep all of his emotion packaged in.

Gozen then remembered the new addition to the Tree House and felt it wise to warn Darou. "Also, Jin Aya is staying here. He's not doing so good, so he's going to stay for awhile, just to recover a bit."

"Yeah, I don't really feel sorry for him." Darou abruptly walked off as the Lady approached, offering Gozen a warm meal.

∘ ∘ ∘

He pulled the blanket up to his face as the cold air hit his neck. After eventually getting a decent evening of sleep, Jin found himself having trouble getting out of bed. The children had gotten up early for breakfast as they always did, but he stayed in his room, too cold and tired to play the role of resident outsider.

Jin imagined he might spend a lot of time sleeping in the former pantry, but as time passed, he started to feel a bit foolish. He slowly got out of bed and put on his strange clothes.

A little coffee sat in the glass brewer, but Lady Kyoumére was nowhere in sight. He helped himself to the cold remains of the early-morning brew. Jin looked around for a flash steam infuser but noticed the kitchen did not have one; he made a note to install one. Instead, he found a pot and heated it up on the range.

After cleaning up his activities from the kitchen, Jin walked out the back door and found kids gathered by the river. He walked forward a few steps and heard a young voice declare his arrival. The group promptly ran off towards the side of the house with whatever they carried.

Jin stood alone, the steam from his coffee disappearing into the chilly, late morning atmosphere. He questioned the value of his residence at the Tree House and began to consider himself a burden more than a guest. Perhaps that could be said of his entire pilgrimage. He then saw the same broken toy car by the water and picked it up.

As he sat on the edge of the river, Jin saw a cargo ship approach. Its thick black smoke rose up into the sky. He assumed it to be a new model, clearly running a Dark-spark engine. Jin admired its strength and speed but always found the technology to be rather inelegant and, frankly, dirty. He looked back down at the little car in his hand, an old toy running on broken ideas. Alas, it was what those children had.

Jin hurried back to the house, laid a clean sheet over the dining table, then placed the broken toy car on it. Quickly, he ran and grabbed his personal, compact work case that he had put between the beans and flour. He then laid out the impressive array of tools and managed to open up the broken mechanical toy in less than a minute.

He found it to be a rather simple matter analyzing the internal mechanics. Jin quickly noticed that the coiled spring storing the power of the car had broken off. Its interior was relatively roomy and he immediately began to think of ways to improve it, making it faster and travel longer. Jin got to work.

Thoughts of steering mechanisms and available materials danced through his mind. He felt focused and purposeful as he sketched out designs, then gathered pieces and modified them. Jin imagined the faces of the children as he handed them the greatest toy car they had ever seen.

A young girl then managed to sit down right next to Jin, who failed to notice her for a full minute. It wasn't until she moved a custom cut gear, logically placed on the sheet, that Jin jumped to attention.

"Don't touch that!"

The young girl held the small gear in her equally small hands, her big green eyes staring right at him. She slowly put it back, graciously obeying the snippy command. Jin quickly felt a bit imprudent.

"I haven't filed the edges down yet. You could have cut yourself."

The girl sat silent. Jin then concluded he should take advantage of the moment, identifying the child to be the only one at the orphanage not eager to run away from him. "Do you know what that is?"

Her eyes glanced down briefly before speaking calmly. "A part of that broken car."

Jin laughed. "Yes, but it's not going to be broken for long. Actually, I'm going to vastly improve upon its initial design."

The girl smiled. "That's nice."

Priorities shifted in Jin's mind, and he took one last look over his immaculate, makeshift work space. "Would you like to watch?"

The girl shrugged her tiny shoulders.

Jin thought of where to start and estimated the mechanical dexterity of a girl her age. He then realized a pressing piece of information remained missing. "So, what is your name, young lady?"

"Chichimou Despré, but my dad just calls me Chichi."

"Oh, where is your father?" Jin immediately wanted to pull the words back into his mouth, realizing the error in asking such a question at an orphanage.

"He's looking for me." Chichi started to poke at the little metal pieces on the table.

"Did you get lost in the city?"

"No. He sent me to camp, but we went far away and he couldn't find me."

The young girl's words confused Jin. Tempted to ask more, he instead opted for a less complicated route. "So Chichi, may I ask you a question?"

Unaccustomed to having adults ask her for permission, her scrunched face nodded.

"Do you know why the children always run away from me?"

"They said you're the monster."

Such words normally would have seemed rather charming coming from a small child, but they clung onto his neck like cold fingers. "Why do they say that?"

"They don't talk to me much. I haven't been here very long. I just heard them talking about some scary place where a girl died."

Hearing a child he had just met speak those words felt particularly disturbing. It made him feel that there could be no escape from the nightmare. Jin then refocused on the fact that this girl currently chose to spend time with him. "But you don't think I'm a monster?"

The girl gently shook her head before getting back to the array of little gears, sharing in his joy of tinkering. Jin fought back tears. He wanted to reach down, hug the girl, and thank her for something even he couldn't articulate. Instead, he decided to offer something more appropriate.

"So, would you like to help me fix it?"

Chichi's face lit up, framed in messy hair. Jin went through his design plan and explained the process. It all captivated Chichi, regardless of how much technical verbiage she recognized. Once they had gotten the new double spring engine in place, they heard Gozen enter the kitchen.

"There you are," Gozen anxiously said. "Jin, can I talk to you?"

Signaling Chichi to wait a moment, Jin promptly walked over. "What would you like to discuss, Lord Gozen?"

Gozen turned to guard their conversation from Chichimou. "That girl there, we rescued her from a labor camp out west. She was digging up dark Jinsper."

"Kurokinojinsper?" Jin said, glancing at Chichimou. "That's intense physical labor. She's just a small child."

"Yes Jin, that's why we rescued her. Anyway, we found the address of her father and need to take her there, but I have pressing matters to take care of. Could you do that?" Gozen handed him a piece of paper that read '278 B Probisou Alley, Sacoin'.

Jin looked over at the partially completed toy upgrade. "Right now?"

"No, but soonish."

"Yes, I can take Chichimou to her father."

Taking another second to think, Gozen suddenly grew in his concern. "Jin, we don't know much about her father. If he seems to be noticeably unfit, do what you think is best. Also, Sacoin is what you could call a bad neighborhood. You might want to wear something a little less expensive."

"Okay."

Gozen left the kitchen and headed straight for Neko. Jin headed back to the table to finish the car with Chichimou. He decided to hold off on the news of her father as she seemed to be rather joyfully fixated on the task at hand.

An hour later, Chichi tightened the final screw. "We did it!"

"I think we should test it out."

"Yes, we should."

Jin wound up the crank key, and the sound of precision gears purred out. He set the four wheels on the long table, and they watched it launch. Chichimou jumped up and ran towards the end of the table to avoid a horrible, tiny car accident. Filled with excitement, she brought the car back to Jin.

"Can we show the other kids?" she asked.

The young girl's ambition impressed Jin. He thought her enthusiastic proposal might even help to lighten up the tension surrounding his reputation. He then thought of his lost friend Nia and how her relentlessly giving heart shamed him. To her, the children at the House always mattered most.

"I think you should take it out to them."

"You don't want to go with me?" Chichimou asked.

"I'll observe."

With a grin, Chichimou got up with the car and proudly walked towards the door. Jin got up and watched her take it to a crowd of children out by the river. They immediately surrounded her and took to the impressively built toy. Jin stood alone by the house and watched them play for what felt like hours. Chichimou seemed happy.

○ ○ ○

The beast of burden squeezed through the shiny cars of downtown Chigou, getting stares from pedestrians wrapped in suits. As Neko pulled up to the Telakai building, Gozen looked at a wire-type print from Darou which read "Need to speak, meet on roof." He got out of the cab and looked up the towering face; a different man atop a different building needed to come first.

Inside, Gozen walked directly towards the Sentinel at the front desk. "I'm here to see Opaji."

The Sentinel easily understood the words but questioned the large man's choice in speaking them. "Lord Opaji does not take open requests." The man would have looked at the appointment list if a single name existed on it.

"If you ask, I'm sure he'll see me."

"I'm afraid that's not the policy we have here."

Gozen felt in no mood to dance. "Tell Lord Opaji that Lord Z needs to speak with him."

The Sentinel had heard rumors, perhaps legends of the city's most revered Lord Enforcer, who vanished after the Great Roukot Fire. Although a hard proclamation to believe, the massive man in front of him certainly fit the proportions.

"One moment."

Leaning over to the wire-type, the Sentinel quickly hit keys and waited for a reply. A moment later, the machine printed back the answer. The Sentinel respectfully handed Gozen an alloy tag with *138* on it. The former Enforcer walked over to the elevator and handed the tag to the guarding Sentinel, who then took him directly to the top.

After his ears popped twice, the elevator doors finally opened. Gozen looked ahead and saw the space as he remembered it, despite not having seen it for many years. Everything looked expensive and perfectly crafted, surrounding multiple Sentinels who protected the Lord of Chigou.

Gozen approached the guards. The one on the left raised his hand to stop Gozen and then pulled out an electronic baton. The guard activated it, which caused the device to buzz. He then waved it around Gozen. Hearing not a single beep, he allowed

Lord Z to enter.

The next room was nearly silent aside from the typing of Lady Mali Opree. She sat at a single desk, across from a single chair for those waiting to be summoned. The room towered upward into an exceptionally high ceiling, as if to build one's anticipation of ascension.

After a minute of quiet, Lady Opree spoke. "You may go in."

Gozen walked forward as the door automatically opened, releasing a flood of light. Inside, the appearance of implied importance continued, centering around the most costly desk in the city. Behind it, Opaji stood by the massive window, pouring himself a short glass of some amber spirit. He looked over to Gozen and took in the sight.

"Even out of uniform you still strike an impression. I'm not sure any man has yet to match it."

"Thank you for seeing me, Lord Opaji."

"The growth of Chigou would not have been as fast without your work. You accomplished more than perhaps any single Enforcer ever has. Certainly you deserve some of my attention from time to time. Would you like a drink?" Opaji held up the bottle of liquor, one so expensive Gozen didn't even recognize it.

He did want a drink. "No, thank you. I need to ask you for something."

Opaji moaned to himself before lowering the spirit next to a bottle of Shumé. "Lord Z, I do believe this is the first time I have ever heard you ask for anything. Your life after enforcing has changed you, huh?"

"It has, for the better," Gozen confidently said.

"Well, you are a man whose word I can believe. What's on your mind?"

Gozen took a step forward. "The Jinouki producer Etecid, formally Karoburn, has had a string of bad luck lately. So much so I'd say it's not luck. I'm fairly certain a clandestine, Dark-spark corporation is attempting to force Jinouki and steam power into the past."

Opaji took a five-dollar sip. "Astute observation. And how does that concern you?"

"I know you've always supported the growth of the city through advancing technologies, but what's happening to this company is damaging families and has already resulted in some deaths. If it goes on like this, I imagine the consequences will be quite devastating and far reaching."

Turing towards the vast scene outside, Opaji looked down towards the modern industrial quarter, a neighborhood born out of fire. "I know it was hard for you with what happened in Roukot. It was an unfortunate event that accelerated the growth of the region. Progress persevered through tragedy."

"I don't want that to happen again."

Opaji then looked over the entire city. "Do you know what I see from up here? My golden child grown up, and I stand here wondering what role I still have."

He turned to Gozen. "I know you have turned your attention towards the smaller entities of this society, and I appreciate that. I understand the value of work down along the edges."

From up in the clouds, Gozen wondered if Opaji could understand anything below by the dirt. "There are many people down there who just want to do their part, and I believe someone is trying to disrupt that."

Opaji took another sip. "Sabotage and subversion may have their place, but they are not fit to be the foundation of a society. I support perseverance, but it is a disservice to the whole if I perpetuate something proven to be obsolete. If Etecid proves viable, then I will support it. If it gets overtaken by something greater, then progress will illuminate such obsolescence, and I will act accordingly."

Opaji walked up to Gozen and offered him his hand. They shook and nodded goodbye. The meeting gave Gozen what he expected: a vague promise of support. More importantly, it exposed Opaji's concerns of Etilé and the dark figure behind it. Gozen got into Neko and drove straight to Etecid.

∘ ∘ ∘

The thinning work force looked like hopeless machines, overworked and out of date. As he drove into the dock, Gozen wondered if enough energy existed to keep the plant alive. It seemed too much for Darou's father, but Gozen hoped the young man had more life inside of him. He hurried to meet Darou up at the top.

Gozen walked out onto the roof where workers typically monitored production, but currently it appeared empty. He hurried towards the southern edge of the building near the Tuluki loader, hoping to find Darou. With the young man nowhere to be found, Gozen suddenly looked into the dark abyss of the grain loader, and imagined Cruno falling in.

"Gozen."

The big man turned around and spotted Darou pop up from behind an exhaust vent. Carefully watching the perimeter, he walked up to Gozen.

"What's going on? Why did you want to meet up here?"

The typically sullen young man looked especially wretched. "I don't know what this place is."

Gozen never knew the boy to be philosophical. "What do you mean?"

He spoke slowly. "When I was really young my dad worked in a garage, worked on cars. This old man named Heigo owned the space. My dad went to work, did his job, then came home. If there was ever a problem, he talked it over with Heigo and that was it. Simple."

Despite feeling rather anxious lately, Gozen fought to hear the young man out. "So this place isn't quite like Heigo's, huh?"

"They said . . ." The troubled boy questioned his own thought and laughed. "They, who is they? I don't even know who it is that I'm working for every damn day."

Gozen asked, "What did they say?"

"If we don't hit our projected quota of Jino in two days, they're shutting down. That's it." Darou walked over to the edge of the roof by the Tulúki loader.

Gozen kept an eye on the frustrated young man. "How much do they need?"

"Four hundred crates."

Gozen scratched his head. "That's a lot."

"That's impossible. They might as well have said a thousand.

They just want to be done with this place . . . with us."

Gozen took a second to calculate the possibility in his mind. It would be hard, very hard, but not impossible. "We're going to do it."

"Don't bother, Gozen."

"We are, and when we do, we'll get support straight from Telakai."

Darou looked back to Gozen, a man he trusted more than any other. He sincerely wanted to believe him. "Right . . ." He then looked back down to the alley. "You know I used to think my old man was just a quitter. Gave up on life, gave up on me, but I think he figured something out I just didn't see until now. You give your life to a place like this and that's all that happens. They take it."

Gozen took another step toward Darou, who dangled his toes over on the ledge. "You know, this must have been where Cruno got shot. Fell right into the loader." He leaned out a bit, looking straight down the building. "I heard Nia fell off a cliff. I wonder how far she fell."

"You're making me nervous there, big guy. Why don't you cut an old man some slack and let me buy you some coffee." Gozen didn't want to make any sudden moves, but he was prepared to.

"She was great. She was way better than me, so why did that happen to her?"

Gozen could feel the wind blowing from behind them. "Nia was a fighter, and sometimes when you fight you get hurt." He walked up to the ledge by Darou but kept his arms folded. "So do you want to fight along with me or let them have an easy out?"

Darou looked over to his trusted friend. The two stood alone on the roof as the clouds rolled over the setting sun.

○ ○ ○

The Tree House smelled of sweet Blashu Rolls that Lady Kyoumére had surprised the children with earlier that morning. Jin had found himself becoming rather fond of the southern valley treat, which went especially well with smoked coffee. That morning, their sweet taste helped him process a developing thought.

Jin had never spoken to a parent in regard to their child before, nor had he even spent enough time with a child to have such a conversation. Since the oddly brief meeting with Gozen, he had been prudently processing how he would notify Chichimou that her father had been found at a location she inexplicably did not seem to already know.

Downstairs, Jin found Chichimou drawing a picture. He approached her and cleared his throat. "Good afternoon, Chichimou. May I please speak to you about something?"

She looked up to him blankly, having never been asked such a question before.

Jin waited patiently but eventually decided to break etiquette and proceed without permission. "It was brought to my attention rather recently that the staff here has acquired the current address of your father. I am going to accompany you there this very day."

He again waited for her to respond but she remained in stasis. Jin pondered if his presentation was perhaps a bit bloated. "I'm going to take you home to your father today."

Chichimou expressed the subtlest comprehension of the statement by finally nodding. Jin found her delayed reaction rather curious but ultimately satisfactory. "Well, I will give you some time to collect your belongings. If you need any help with travelers, or larger items, I will be happy to assist you."

"I don't have anything."

"Right. Well, I'm going to get a few supplies for the journey across town. I will meet you back down here in just a moment." Jin traveled to his room as Chichi went back to her drawing. Contemplating what one might need traveling the public transit system towards a more challenged neighborhood, he collected a number of small bills, a pocket map, and some dried fruit.

Jin remembered Gozen mentioning something about his attire and took a look in a small mirror. He recalled the lack of ivory neck scarves in the more unpolished areas of Chigou and thusly took his off. He then noticed his Masu sitting on the shelf. He felt an immediate impulse to pack it, although he did not know why. It seemed a rather dramatic item to have while traveling with a child, but the impulse remained extraordinarily strong.

Chichimou turned around as Jin returned and quickly sported a crooked grin. "Where's your scarf?"

"I thought removing it would help me blend into what I was told to be a relatively bad neighborhood," Jin explained, touching his rarely exposed neck.

Chichimou noticed the immaculate shine of his Toki as it poked out of a vest pocket, wondering if it was the most expensive thing she had ever seen. "What is a relatively bad neighborhood?"

"I'm not entirely sure, actually," Jin spoke, immediately realizing the comment could have been somewhat discourteous. "Well, shall we go?"

o o o

More people began to appear as the pair turned onto Long Frost Road. That far north, the main artery had a number of cheap diners and small businesses that created a lot of foot traffic. Occasionally people would smile, but bumping into shoulders proved more common. As they walked south, Chichimou reached up and handed Jin something.

Jin quickly recognized the object to be a rather brilliantly designed Toki. He looked at it more closely, finding it odd that the girl would have such an impressive device. Before he could ask her why she gave it to him, young Chichimou already began to answer. "I found it."

Chichi then grabbed Jin's hand as they continued to walk. At first, he assumed it to be an attempt to get his attention, but she merely looked forward and continued walking. Jin then noticed how other children around them held hands with an accompanying adult and assumed the behavior to be rather appropriate; he put the Toki away.

Jin only needed to check his map twice before finding the Hotrail station, his first time ever entering one. As they moved in, he paused while trying to orientate himself with the array of mechanical gates and pedestrians slinging coins around.

"Why did we stop?" asked Chichi.

Jin deciphered the signs. "I'm unfamiliar with the procedures of the Hotrail."

Chichi pursed her lips. "Do you just walk everywhere?"

"No, I've always had a car."

Chichimou had never spoken to anyone who owned a car

before. "Are you rich?"

Jin thought for a while on how to answer the question before realizing it was not the least bit complicated. "Yes, I am rich."

"That's okay, I'll show you how it works."

Leading him by the hand, Chichimou guided Jin through the gauntlet of mass transit. She allowed Jin to pay for the trip to central Chigou where they would have to transfer trains; Chichimou always loved the sound of coins dropping into machines.

The trip downtown proved more comfortable than Jin had expected, given the surprising deftness of his little companion. He had heard of what was typically referred to as the Hotrail Museum and felt pleased to finally be seeing it. During the construction of the Hotrail system, Opaji found a surplus of artists that far exceeded the space he had allocated for work in his Creator's District. The solution became to allow artists to fill the Hotrail tunnels with art, anything they wanted, as long as they finished in time for the tunnels to be open.

The result became a network of colorful paintings and sculptures, created to be viewed through a window at high speed. Optical illusions, streaks of light, and a bounty of new techniques birthed from the relatively brief time allowed to create such massive works. Over endless days of business commutes, many had grown desensitized to the vast display, but it was truly a sight to behold. Still holding hands, Jin and Chichimou sat in silent, joyful wonderment watching the vibrant cascade pass before their eyes.

Realizing that the Hotrail swap station resided near Michelou's, Jin asked Chichimou if she wanted to get some cold cream; she of course said yes. She took three trips down its famous slide before getting a cone of Spiced Blashu Cake n' Cream with sprinkles. Jin decided on a cup of Shumé and Páts; the green spiced liquor with a dark, sweet, and sticky fruit imported from Primichi. Trying each other's choices, they cordially decided to stick with what they had. It was the first trip to the famous confectionary for both of them.

Eventually the two managed to get back on the lower west Hotrail line, which left them only a few blocks left to walk. Upon getting out of the station, Jin realized it had taken them much longer to get there than he had accounted for. The temperature dropped along with the sun as the buildings turned red.

Jin put his eyes to task as they walked through Sacoin. The neighborhood certainly looked tattered, but nothing announced itself as being particularly dangerous. Chichimou seemed rather unaffected by the scene, or its strange noises that randomly materialized. Busy taking in the broader image, Jin nearly missed the street sign; they had arrived at *Probisou Alley*.

Fairly wide for an alley, it seemed to stretch on quite some distance. About halfway down they found *278 B*, exchanged looks, and then Jin knocked on the door. The quality of the door made Jin question if it was perhaps a temporary entry. He heard shuffling around for nearly a minute before knocking again. Finally, the door opened to reveal a middle-aged man with a rather cautious face. Everyone waited for someone to talk.

Politely, Jin initiated. "Good evening, Lord. I am here as a pseudo representative of the North Orphanage. The young lady here came into our care a short time back, and I believe is your daughter."

Jin moved slightly to let the dim light of the alley better reveal Chichimou's face. He quickly felt odd at the seeming lack of reaction from either of them. The man looked back to Jin as if waiting for more to be said. After continued silence, he finally bent down. "Chichi."

"Hi, Dad."

He lifted his arms and Chichi walked forward to exchange a quick but sweet embrace. A sincere gaze exchanged between them, one Jin found to have some strange ambiguity to it. The man stood up to Jin and led his daughter into the apartment. "Thank you very much for bringing her here. Thank you."

And with that, the man began to shut the door, promptly stopped by Jin's hand. He took half a step into the doorway but tried to appear rather placid. Gozen's instruction had found its way to the front of his consciousness.

"My name is Jin, by the way. Yours?"

Appearing a bit anxious, the man nervously replied, "Uhm, Victou. Again, thank you, Jin." Jin stayed put. "Chichimou came to us from a mining operation that was utilizing children in labor-intensive activities. A rather unsuitable and dangerous situation for such a young individual. I'm curious as to how she ended up there."

He could see Victou's rising anxiety. His eyes shifted around as if worrying about something lurking in the alley. "Yes, thank you very much for taking her out of that place. I was led to believe it was a children's camp, and I intended on having her stay there for a short duration while I found a new job. I had just found out about it myself."

Victou bowed to persuade a goodbye but Jin remained. "Why did you not pursue your daughter when you found out?"

"I knew she was safe with the Enforcers. I was going to head into town tomorrow to track her down. So, again, I really thank you for bringing her."

Having conflicting feelings about Victou's explanation, Jin turned his attention towards Chichi to hopefully gain some clarity towards what to do. She looked as Chichimou always did, calm and unworried. Victou looked at Jin's hand holding the door. The young man felt an urge to stay but felt it might require an uncivil amount of force.

Jin began to slip his hand off the door as Victou began to shut it; Chichi and Jin said goodbye with their eyes. A sound then came from the end of the alley, leading Jin and Victou to both turn their attention towards it. They saw two men walking towards them. The relative darkness made it hard to identify their faces, but looking back to Victou, Jin came to a realization. Victou looked distressed, but not the least bit surprised.

° ° °

His hand traced the drawing of a steam pipe across a large format diagram, mechanically describing a new high-torque engine design. Remi had been tasked to find a more efficient route for the line so that it used less material and kept the steam at an ideal temperature. Although not the most exotic job, the young engineer appreciated the reliability of such work; he then let out a yawn.

Remi's eyes shifted over to a drawing that he had looked over more times than he could remember. Describing an inactive project, it seemed doomed to remain on the wall forever as its designer had long since died. Occasionally, Remi found himself thinking of the young engineer who greatly inspired him, a life cut far too short. The news felt heartbreaking, hearing how Carmin had died with his wife; he couldn't imagine what it must have been like for their daughter. On the verge of being a father himself, he would often wonder how Suzu had managed after the tragedy⎯ that is, until the day he ran into her.

His mind then went back to Carmin's Core-thermic drawing. Remi admired its progressive spirit, a risky proposition with incredible possibilities. He had fantasized about it most while working for Pirou, whom Remi had found to be perhaps the least-giving person he had ever met. It had been awhile since Pirou had removed Remi from his precious Dark-spark development team. It had been an equally long time since the two had spoken more than a few words in passing. With half of the employees having gone home already, it was quite a surprise when Pirou walked up to his desk and actually stopped.

"Hey, Remi. How are you doing?"

In all the years they had worked together, not once had Pirou ever inquired about Remi's state of being. It took a second for Remi to respond. "Fine. And how are you, Pirou?"

"Oh, me? Things are fine. So, it's getting late; you want to go get some coffee?"

Remi became speechless.

"Come on, I'm buying."

"You want to go have coffee with me? Just me?"

"Yeah, we're coworkers." Pirou quickly glanced around the room. "Is that so strange?"

"Yes, actually." Remi thought about it. "But sure, let's go."

A block away from the Kasic Building sat a moderately sized diner called *The Steam Roller*. Typically full, it became a favorite of various professionals looking for good, quick food. It nurtured a noticeably diverse socio-economic array that often generated a loud volume. If one needed to hide a conversation within a bustling public crowd, The Steam Roller easily provided.

A middle-aged waitress with an adorably practical updo

hairstyle poured them their famous *extra-rich* coffee. "You men need anything else?"

"No, thank you very much," Remi replied, enjoying her warm smile at the end of his long day of schematics and meetings. "So, what is it that you would like to talk about, Pirou?"

Pirou had been spending most of the time looking at the crowd in search of familiar faces. Finally, he gave his full attention to Remi. "I can't believe I'm telling you this."

"I'm sure I won't either."

"So this guy that I've been working with for awhile . . ." Pirou looked around again.

"The guy who took my job after you fired me?" Remi raised an eyebrow.

"I didn't fire you. I got you a promotion," Pirou insisted.

"You did not promote me."

"Well, I didn't get you fired. You like your new position, right? Probably more than you liked working for me."

Remi thought about it. "Yeah, probably. So what's this guy's name?"

"Victou."

"Victou what?"

"Uhm, Victou . . . I'm not sure."

"You don't know your assistant's last name?"

"No, he's new."

"Do you know *my* last name?"

"Will you just let me talk?"

Remi grinned, feeling rather content with finally being able to grate Pirou directly. "Sorry, please continue."

Pirou took another quick look around. "So, this guy Victou gets assigned to me; I had nothing to do with his hiring. He starts working for me; he doesn't seem particularly bright, but he does fine. Slowly, though, he starts asking odd questions and making copies of things like he's archiving the work more than doing research."

Remi began to engage more sincerely. "Collecting data is a big part of the job. You sure you're not being a little paranoid?"

"Right, well, I was wondering that, too, so I started asking him questions, checking up on him." Pirou leaned in. "This guy is not qualified to have this job, not at all. I remember when they posted the position, there were a ton of very educated and experienced guys going for it."

Remi's scratched his chin. "So, why hire him?"

"Access to all my work on a booming technology that still has a lot patents yet to be declared . . . maybe he wasn't hired to be an assistant." Pirou tapped the table hard. "I think he's copying all my research and giving it to someone else."

It sounded intriguing, but Remi kept paranoia as an option. "But why would Kasic spy on itself? We did hire him, after all."

"Exactly. So I looked into who hired him, and I can't find anything. It wasn't through human resources, not through the department; this guy just materialized out of nowhere."

The seat squeaked as Remi sat back. "Yeah, that's interesting. So, why are you telling me all of this?"

"Look, we both know I didn't exactly value your particular set of qualities, but you have always shown yourself to be a very honest person, and right now I'm not sure who else I can trust at this company."

"Wow, I think that was a legitimate compliment." Remi took a sip of his extra-rich coffee. "So what, did you just want an ear to talk into?"

Pirou really started to lean in. "I need you to find out who Victou is working for."

"Pirou, I can't risk my career by going around spying on coworkers just to save your project."

"All right, yes, my motivation is predominately self-serving, but whoever this is could threaten the entire company, your career, and who knows what else."

Remi sighed. "Okay, you have my sympathies, but I don't really know what I can do."

"Well, get one of your acquaintances, perhaps."

Remi laughed. "One of my acquaintances? One of my super spy acquaintances? Hmm, it will take quite some time to narrow them all down."

"Laugh if you'd like, Remi, but the entire energy industry could be affected by what this shadow organization . . ."

The young man cut him off. "Actually, I think I do have someone in mind."

18
COMBUSTION

What had been a grieving community frozen in a blue haze, suddenly ignited with activity. Gozen arrived at Kora the day before and immediately gathered all hands to execute the largest and fastest single harvest in their history. Although frantic, it provided a much-needed break from the suffocating vacuum produced from the loss of Nia.

Gozen had been directing young men and women like a crazed band director. The darkening sky reminded him of how little time they had to make the quota. Wanting a quick jolt, he ran inside for some double-coffee and happily found Clora pouring a fresh pot.

"Way ahead of you, big guy," she offered.

Gozen leaned against the counter and cracked his back.

"You are working yourself to death out there," she said. "How young do you think you are?"

"Too young to know better. So how have things been here? Any trouble?" He disliked breaking a peaceful moment with unpleasant pragmatism, but time had become an endangered commodity.

"I keep waiting for some nightmare to show its face, but it's been quiet, nearly lifeless, really."

Kojo then walked into the kitchen with the liveliest face either of them had seen in a long time. "You trying to wear my workers out?"

"I'm trying to keep our biggest buyer from closing shop," Gozen replied.

"Closing for good?"

Gozen had been avoiding the critical question and instead found absurd comfort in trying to achieve the current impossible task. "It's fighting for some chance instead of having none."

Kojo walked up to his wife and gently rubbed her back as she handed Gozen his coffee. "Well, I can't fault you for that."

Gozen graciously took his drink and shoved a sticky braid in his mouth. "I better get back to the circus." With that, he hustled over to the door and opened it to the sight of a young man with a bag slung over his shoulder.

"Oh, excuse me. This is Kora, correct?"

Gozen promptly looked him up and down before taking the pastry out of his mouth. "Who are you?"

"My name is Sheux. I was looking for work downtown at that Etecid plant. This young guy said you'd have work up here."

"You came all the way up here for work? Who did you speak with?"

"Uhm, Darin or Darou. I think it was Darou, but yeah, he said there'd be a lot of work up here for a few days and that the food was really good, and free."

Gozen felt relieved to hear that Darou wasn't giving up. "Come with me."

He took Sheux over to the processing silo where Legou loaded up the first batch of Tulú to be seeded. Legou breathed heavy, overwhelmed doing the job normally handled by Nia. The idea of training anyone in that moment just compounded the stress, but Sheux proved to be a quick learner.

Gozen took a walk around and sized up the progress through the frantic dance of cultivation. He had never seen the farm so busy, and thankfully thus far, void of panic. He started to truly believe they might actually pull it off.

○ ○ ○

Victou stood just inside the doorway, looking like a kid about to get caught stealing. Just outside the door, Jin watched the two shadowy figures approach from down the alley. The lanky man stepped up into the light, quickly followed by a gruff, stockier fellow. Sensing as though he stood in the middle of an impending meeting, Jin readied himself for whatever was about to happen. Victou stayed half hidden behind the door.

"Hey there, Victou, got some company over?" the lanky one asked.

"No, he was just leaving."

"Don't look like it." The stranger suggested noticing Jin's unyielding posture. "So what's your business?"

"I was here dropping off Lord Victou's daughter," Jin said directly.

"Lord Victou?" the stocky one blurted out. "Now that's gotta be a first."

"I didn't realize you had a daughter, Victou. Where was she?"

Victou seemed rather brittle over the question. "Just at the North Orphanage. It was temporary."

Jin looked to Victou, trying to a get a read on the father's face. Victou just looked down.

The stocky man then hit the other on the arm. "Hey, doesn't that big fella work at that Orphanage? The one we ran into over by . . ."

"Yes. That's the one." The lanky one cut off his companion with strange haste but quickly continued. "That Toki looks awfully expensive for someone working at an orphanage."

Jin glanced at his valuable time piece sticking out. "I was asked to help briefly."

"Oh, how giving of you. Did the big guy ask you to help?"

"If you're referring to Gozen, then yes. How do you know him?" Jin asked.

"Not well, actually, but as luck would have it, I have something for him. Would you mind giving it to him? If it's not too much trouble."

Jin's curiosity piled on top of confusion. "What is it?"

"I'm not sure exactly. It's from a young, spunky little dark-haired gal."

A single person stood out in Jin's mind. "You don't mean Suzu?"

The tall one replied, "Yeah, you know her too, huh? Come on, I'll give it to ya."

Looking back, Victou seemed content staying quiet, and keeping Cichi by his side. The short conversation had Jin feeling as if he had jumped onto a moving train to an unknown destination. He followed the young men slowly, feeling good to get them farther away from Chichimou. "Where is it?"

"Just back there by the car." The lanky man began to walk off slowly.

Jin followed behind and began to see their car parked down the alley. The stocky one kept to his side. Jin kept his senses piqued. "And what is your name?"

"Ansel," the tall one replied, "next to you is Guso."

Back at the house, Victou worried over what Kits would think of the entire encounter. That night he had scheduled a routine delivery of information taken from Pirou's Dark-spark project. Victou felt things had been going well thus far as Kits's employer, who still remained anonymous, seemed pleased with what details he had managed to acquire. Having the delivery interrupted by some oddly formal man, unexpectedly bringing his daughter home, made Victou anxious. Watching the men walk away, he anticipated something intense about to happen; he shut the door another inch.

Jin continued to keep each of them in his sight as they moved deeper into the alley. "How do you know Suzu?"

"We have a mutual acquaintance, goes by the name of Kits."

All of Jin's senses focused onto one dense point. In that same moment, Guso released a retracted baton and struck the distracted Jin in the back of both knees. The sting crippled him to the ground, and Ansel turned towards him.

"Jin!" Chichimou's frightened scream rang out from the doorway and down the alley.

Collapsed over his legs, Jin then felt his face collide with the steel toe of Ansel's boot. Jin flew onto his back; he couldn't feel his legs. Chichimou's muffled screams echoed into his ear as Victou tried to console her.

"Shut that kid up, Victou." Ansel commanded towards the screaming girl.

The world hummed; Jin could barely sense which way was up. He struggled to recover just in time to see Guso taking another swing with the baton. Jin had just enough of his faculties to roll his face away and take the blow on his shoulder. Chichi cried out in terror.

Ansel took a few steps toward Victou. "If you can't shut that kid up, Victou, I will."

Jin's blurred vision tried to focus on the girl being held back by her Father. Ansel's barking rattled in his head. Guso shifted somewhere behind Jin who could feel the grimy road on his face. He tried to roll over and felt something poke him in the back.

Almost finished yelling at Victou, Ansel started to walk back. Jin then suddenly realized what pressed into his spine: the retracted Masu. The realization brought forth a swell of clarity. He struggled up onto one knee, bracing himself with a weary hand, his other feeling the triggers of the Masu. Ansel approached Jin with the eyes of a predator.

"Give me that." Ansel pointed and Guso threw him the baton.

Jin took in the deepest breath of his life. Ansel grunted as he struck down. Jin managed to spin out of the way; the sword arcing in a sharp whisper. The momentum pulled Jin up to his shaking feet, and he braced for whatever came next. Guso stood stunned as he faced Ansel, who finally let out a horrifying scream.

Looking down, Jin saw Ansel's hand firmly gripping the baton, about five meters away from the rest of its body. Panicked, Ansel clutched what remained of his arm. Jin looked over and saw the extend blade of his Masu dripping with blood, only then fully realizing what he had done. A breath later, Guso charged towards him.

A second baton came out, and the thug struck down in a frenzy. Jin had just enough time to block it with the Masu, but the force launched it from his hand. The wild animal stumbled past him before coming in for another strike. Jin fought to keep his buzzing head focused.

Guso predictably swung like Jin had encountered a thousand times in his Maiishi training. Jin stepped in to counter, grabbed Guso's arm, and flipped him to the ground in a blink. The flailing brute swung again from his back, but Jin cut off the strike by kicking him in the elbow. Guso yelled in pain and dropped the baton. Likewise, Jin again fell when all of his weight transferred to his more injured knee.

Guso scrambled onto his feet ready to attack. Jin then pulled out his Toki and squeezed it; a six-inch spike popped out. The squatty thug hesitated at the sight, allowing the screams of Ansel to finally break through his consciousness. He ran over to his partner and helped Ansel wrap up his bleeding wound. He grimaced with pain as they stumbled back down the alley, leaving the severed limb behind.

Jin collapsed and sat alone, watching them hobble off with many unanswered questions. He looked over to Victou, who slowly shut the door, his faced drained of color. Inside with his daughter's pulse still stampeding, he gently grabbed her shoulders and tried to calm her down.

"They're gone now, Chichi."

"But we have to help Jin."

Victou thought of what he had just witnessed. "I think Jin can take care of himself."

"No, Dad, he's really hurt!" Chichi's conviction tried to push past her father.

"Okay, Chichi, okay. I'll go look at him and make sure he gets home. You need to calm down though." He gently stroked her short hair. "How does that sound?"

Her breathing slowly settled down and she finally nodded. Victou stood up and took her by the hand. "Now, I'm going to show you where you can lie down for a little bit. Don't get too comfy, though, because tomorrow we're going to get a new place so you can have your very own room."

Victou grabbed the blankets off of his own bed and got a glass of water. He laid the blankets out on a small sofa as Chichi continually reminded him to check on Jin, who still sat alone in the dim alley. Night had fallen onto the valley.

The fire in Jin's blood subsided, allowing a massive flood of aches and pain to fill its place. The once-unfamiliar feeling of being beaten and broken started to become a regular part of his life. He thought of how he got in that alley. He wondered how many people living on that street alone had suffered such pain as a regular part of their life.

Feeling too battered to move, Jin sat there looking at Ansel's limb, laying motionless a few meters away. His Masu still dripped with the crimson aftermath of his choices. The abandoned girl hid behind the rusted door, alone with a father who Jin felt entirely uncertain about. The roar of a Dark-spark engine echoed down the alley as two panicked scoundrels made their escape.

Jin wondered what nefarious things they would scheme, plans for people he had no relation to, people who lived lives drastically different than his own. All logic told him to stop being a fool and head back to Primichi, far away from the pain, far away from the first people he ever thought to call his friends.

o o o

With feet that had not stopped moving the entire night, Gozen looked forward to the drive into Chigou. Exhausted farm hands fought to finish up the monumental shift. Crates of Tulúki finally began loading up, and it looked like the quota was going to get made; only the trip to Etecid remained.

The hired hand Sheux, his face covered with sweat, loaded one of the last crates onto the back of Neko. He jogged up to meet Gozen, who had just finished putting paperwork into the cabin. They met with a mutual, burned-out sigh.

"Crates are pretty much loaded, so I guess that's it?" Sheux asked.

"Yeah, I need to hurry up and get this out of here."

"Great." Sheux let out a laugh. "Looks like we survived."

Gozen nodded. "Glad you came up. Hopefully this goes well and we can get you more work."

With a quick handshake, Sheux disappeared, and Gozen did his final check. Five minutes later, he drove Neko down towards Chigou. His sore feet throbbed with relief as the fields and mountains passed by. He rolled down the window and quietly embraced the moment of peace.

As he entered the city, Gozen's tired mind spun through images of the past. He thought of young faces being beat up by a city, faces he gave promises of hope to. He wondered how much good that shipment of Tulúki would do and for how long. So much felt out of his control, but he knew that day would prove even those at the bottom still had a voice. He refused to let them be discarded.

Neko whipped off of Gris Avenue like a vehicle half its size before screeching to a stop by the loading bay. Gozen hopped out, half expecting Darou to be waiting with a crate loader ready to go. The dock sat nearly empty.

"Darou!" Gozen started to walk towards the building when he saw the young man calmly walking out.

"Hey, was that you screeching in here?" Darou asked a bit confused.

"Yeah, come on."

Darou looked over Neko. "Is this the shipment?"

"Yes," Gozen said hastily.

"There's no way that's all of it."

Gozen leaned in. "You think I'd be here if it wasn't?"

Darou's face faded from fatalism to elation. "I'll get the loader started."

As the young man took off, Gozen's mind got pricked with gratitude. "And thanks for sending help."

"What?" Darou asked, running away.

"Nevermind. Just go."

Having no patience for proper etiquette, Gozen jogged over to the grain loader and fired up the auger himself. He headed to the rear of Neko, grabbed a crate, and hustled it over to the primer tank.

After getting the first three crates loaded, typically a two-man job, Darou appeared from the top and yelled down. "I'm ready. Send it up."

Gozen activated the grain elevator, and the process finally began. Two dock workers then came out and immediately began to help with the crates. Normally, Gozen sat back and watched that step, but he really wanted that Tulúki off his truck. They loaded faster than the elevator could take it up.

Their faces dripped as they sweat out days of built-up tension. The company gave them a quota that it certainly assumed to be impossible. Down below, far away from well-dressed men, callused hands proved them wrong. Gozen knew it may not last long, but they would have to be recognized; at least for today, they had fought and they had won.

The men loaded the final crate, and after a victorious handshake, went back into the building to finish up. Gozen walked back to the cab of Neko and rested his exhausted arms on the seat. He lowered his shoulders and laughed as relief spread through his aching body. He felt ready to leave, go to the Tree House and be taken care of.

Gozen lifted his head and took a step into the cab, but something down the alley caught his attention. A dark shape, simple but refined in its silhouette—a Móstique.

A terrible thought forced Gozen to look up to Darou. The young man still loaded Tulúki up on the roof. Quickly, Gozen stepped down to look for trouble. Right as his foot hit the tarmac, he came face to face with Kits, standing alone. Without hesitation, he grabbed the young man by the throat and pinned him against Neko with a thump.

"What are you doing here?" Gozen demanded in a controlled snarl.

"I'd rather not talk like this." Kits forced sounds out of his crushed airway before emphatically looking down. Gozen noticed a medium-caliber pistol pressed into his side, Kits's finger tensioned onto the trigger.

"Pull that and I'll still have plenty of time to rip out your throat," Gozen squeezed.

"So, how about we talk instead of dying together in a dirty loading dock."

Realizing he easily could have been shot a moment earlier, Gozen slowly released his hand off of Kits's red neck. The young man coughed and likewise lowered his gun.

"Why do you want to talk here?" Gozen asked.

"How are things back at the farm? Must be hard without Nia."

"Don't you ever say her name." Gozen leaned into Kits's face.

"All that guilt, all that pain."

"Why waste an explanation on someone as soulless as you. You wanted this to happen."

"You would think that." Kits clenched his teeth.

"You tried to kill her, you little punk," Gozen exclaimed.

Kits began to heat up. "She was confused and I was looking out for her."

"She died, hiding from you."

"She died because you and all the other fools at the farm sent her off to Goraka."

Embedded guilt flared in Gozen's chest. "We didn't send her there."

"You panicked and let her go, right into the valley of death. What did you think was going to happen down there?" Kits began to tremble.

Through a haze of anger, Gozen caught a glimpse of something he never expected to see in someone he thought to be a borderline sociopath: heartfelt pain.

"So, we hate each other for what happened to Nia. Is that what you wanted to share?" Gozen leaned back as mutual grief hung between them.

Kits cleared his throbbing throat. "You know, even though I can't imagine anyone mistaking one of us for the other, I don't think it's a coincidence that our paths keep crossing. Unlike most people who let this city simply move along, men like you and me push it to where it needs to go. This city was forged and needs to be honed, and where metal hits metal, there we always seem to meet."

"So which crazy old rich man fed you that line of absurdity?"

Kits laughed. It stung his throat. "I think by now you've probably managed to work out who I run for."

Gozen had suspected that lifeless face still pushed buttons, floating around from shadow to shadow like some demon. "Care to set up a meeting? I'd love to spend some time alone with him."

"No, I think your first meeting was so effective he doesn't really feel a need to have another." Kits calmed his voice. "All this time, you've been trying to escape the guilt from incinerating that stagnate, obsolete mass called Roukot, while everyone else has been benefitting from the rapid progress it brought about."

"It doesn't matter where we're at. I'll kill him the next time I see him." Gozen's tone confirmed his sincerity.

"Yeah, I think he knows that. He told me how dangerous you were, and that it would be foolishness to defy you. Lord Z cannot be stopped, and it would be my demise to get in his way. Instead, I need only know what to put in his path."

Gozen felt a truth to Kits's words, and he hated it. "You're not going to get me to do anything for that fiend ever again."

Kits spoke coldly. "Oh, but you see, Gozen, I already have."

The words clenched Gozen's throat as he pressed forward. "What have you done?"

Covered in Gozen's shadow, the smaller young man stood his ground with smug confidence. "I'm a little surprised you gave a stranger so much free range on the farm, especially considering your recent state of paranoia, but I suppose your bleeding heart is occasionally capable of impairing your usually keen senses."

"Shoux . . ." A lingering suspicion suddenly shot to the front of Gozen's mind.

"That young fellow does have such a trusting face, doesn't he?"

Gozen grabbed Kits with one hand and picked him up onto his toes. "What did he do?"

"He simply spread some Akyulose throughout the crates of Tulúki you just loaded into the plant. Pretty harmless until it reacts in the processing furnaces. I'd say you have about a minute before this factory becomes dangerous to within a hundred meters."

His face became petrified with disbelief. The thoughts were too many and too horrible to process at once; Kits began to slip out of his grip.

"My boss would like to thank you for once again being such an effective agent of progress."

Kits's words faded into a hum as Gozen fully imagined what was about to happen. He threw Kits out of the way and ran around the truck, yelling up to Darou. "Stop the loader. Don't let them process that Tulúki. It's going to blow the furnaces!"

The confusing moment of orientation passed when Darou saw Gozen run faster than he had ever seen before. He churned the command through his mind a second time and realized the severity of what he heard. Darou ran for the roof door, and Gozen entered down below. They both headed for the furnace room in the middle of the building.

Kits watched the two disappear before heading over to his car. He knew Diamo would be pleased, but unlike his superior, Kits did not want to personally watch the building burn to the ground.

His Móstique drove out west, following the same path he took with Nia up in the airship. He tried to hurry, knowing the city was about to be in a panic.

Gozen ran through the ground level of the plant, frantically trying to remember the location of the furnace room, simultaneously yelling at people to evacuate. Some assumed he had snapped, but no one seemed interested in getting in his way. A dock loader named Ainou heard the strange cries from the familiar voice and ran into the hallway. He saw the unsettling sight of the massive man running straight at him.

"Where's the processing furnace?" Gozen demanded.

With little thought, Ainou obeyed. "Come on, this way."

He led the frantic Gozen to a perimeter stairwell. The pair ran up three flights of steps, ignoring the quick burning in their lungs and legs. The crash of Gozen's feet echoed up the stairwell followed by Ainou bursting through the door to the *hot level*. Gozen imagined chaos and fire, sirens and screams.

Ainou led them to the furnace room. "What's happening?"

Gozen tried to keep up. "Someone sabotaged the Tulúki with Akyulose."

"What'll that do?"

"Explode the furnace."

"And we're running in there?" Ainou asked, his eyes like saucers.

"I am," Gozen declared. "Go sound an alarm."

Ainou quickly turned around to a side hallway and ran towards the master alarm. Gozen dashed forward and plowed through the furnace room's heavy door. Half-expecting to feel a blast of heat, he found a man not smoldering, not dismembered, but rather sitting with a glass of cold Bollo juice.

Gozen looked up at the furnace and saw Darou appear out of a door high up on a walkway. Their eyes met, and Gozen ran towards the furnace controller. With a dehydrated mouth, he finally made it to the operator, struggling to shout through the mechanical maelstrom.

"Shut it down! You have to shut down the furnace!"

Startled, the operator sat confused. "What?"

"You have to shut down the furnace, now!"

"We can't. Its already got a load of Tulúki in it."

A volley of pistons and sparks echoed through the giant metal coffer. Gozen pointed to the furnace and got right in the conductor's face. "There's Akyulose in that Túluki."

The operator knew the word and what it meant. His eyes shot wide open, and he immediately hit the kill switch on the furnace. Darou walked up closer to the pair down by the controls. A high-pitched whistle sounded out before winding down, cutting the volume around them to half.

Turning towards a panel of valves, the operator quickly gauged the pressure and heat levels; everything seemed normal. "Are you sure?"

"No," Gozen answered, staring at the gauges. "But if the guy who told me is lying, I really need to make sure."

The furnace sat quiet as the three men stood and waited. The operator watched intently as the gauges still held their levels. "I don't know, big guy. I mean, what kind of maniac would put Akyulose in a furnace that big?"

"Shh." Gozen raised his hand. Nothing came at first, but then a low-frequency pulse rattled in from the bottom of the furnace. The men stood still, waiting for the sound to change. They felt a vibration on the floor grate as the sound began to escalate. The operator turned back to the gauges. The pressure and temperature began to move, fast.

"Oh, no."

A second later the fixtures and valves on the furnace started to shake. Gozen turned up to Darou and shouted for him to leave but was drowned out by the blaring siren Ainou finally triggered down the hall. A second later, the top of the furnace erupted into a concussive burst of flame, sending Gozen down the stairs and the operator to the floor.

His head rang with pressure. Gozen struggled to get to his feet, the room feeling like it just jumped up fifty degrees. His shifting vision struggled into focus as he saw the operator holding onto the gauges, straining to pull himself up. Then, in a burst of heat and vapor, they disappeared.

The force blew past Gozen, who tried to focus above the

furnace. The fumes and heat obscured much of the twisted walkway. He did not see Darou; he did not see anything but a smoldering machine about to totally erupt. He needed to get out of there. Everyone did.

He turned around and saw men stumbling through the exit, one of them on fire. With the floor shaking, Gozen fought for balance as he headed to the door. Air sucked into the room as debris pushed out to the edges.

Reaching the burning technician, Gozen grabbed on to the man's flaming jacket and ripped it off. He then picked him up and dragged the man down the hall until was able to stand on this own feet. Terrified cries filled the building from the crowd of frantic workers, pouring out into the hallway like a busted dam.

When he arrived at the end of the hall, Gozen herded the chaos of screams down the stairwell. He looked back to the furnace room and saw the silhouette of a man escaping from the red glow. Gozen thought to run back and help the man, but the inferno burst out and swallowed him. The consuming fire slithered into the cramped hallway as the entire structure started to shake. The building became a nightmare.

As the last worker made it to the stairs, Gozen felt the heat burning his skin. He ran down after the cascade of madness. People tripped over one another. The flow halted as people stumbled into a pile on the second-floor landing. Gozen fought his way down and began picking them up to clear the path.

The madness continued on the ground floor as workers from all over the building formed a sea of hysteria. Gozen tried to direct those too terrified to remember where the exit was. A flaming cluster of machinery fell from the upper floors, falling on a group of panicked workers, swallowing their cries.

Outside, Gozen followed the panic to the back of the loading bay. Some screamed out of their minds while others had become paralyzed with shock, most of them covered with blood and ash. Finally, he looked back.

Etecid was gone. The building vomited flames up to the clouds that morphed into a giant black mass, blotting out the sky. The top of the building hid behind the violent blaze. It melded into a familiar sight Gozen had spent years trying to suppress.

It took only a few minutes for the lives and livelihood of so many to vaporize into flames. He heard sirens screaming in through the alleys. He felt defeated, a fool who thought he could protect the people of the city, again standing in an inferno of his own doing. In the fog of cries, Gozen looked up to the flames and thought he deserved to be in them. He then remembered the young man he left up there alone.

Gozen hurried through the crowd looking for Darou. He desperately wondered how the young man could have escaped from above the flame when so many closer to the ground failed to do so. Gozen's eyes strained to find him, but the young man didn't appear. In an instant, he achingly knew Darou never would.

Bits of smoldering debris then bounced off of Neko's empty trailer. Gozen hurried towards his truck when he saw a cable crash down from the smoke and onto the trailer. A few seconds later, something launched from the smolder and slid down the cable fifteen meters. Gozen ran as it hit the trailer and slid off the side; it looked like a body. He lunged forward and arrived just in time to catch them. Looking into his arms, he saw Darou and the middle-aged woman he carried down the cable. He then set the soot covered pair down.

Letting Gozen take the woman, Darou tried to catch his breath, his white eyes dancing around his ashen face.

"Darou! How did you make it out of there?"

The young man, looking unlike Gozen had ever seen him before, spoke with loud clarity. "I don't know." Darou then looked around and surveyed the troubled scene. "Hey, let's load her and the injured into the truck."

The logical phrase settled in Gozen's mind as he tried to orientate himself to what just happened. Having assumed the young man to be dead, he stood stunned, still holding the woman Darou had just saved by jumping out of a window.

Darou coughed. "Come on, we need to take these people to the clinic."

The young man ran off and began to help people onto the trailer. Other workers tried to limp their way out to Gris Ave.

Through the terror, Gozen then found a moment of victory. He watched Darou, always the victim of a broken world, suddenly being a savior to a desperate crowd. The young man climbed over the remains of his crumbled employer, saving what he could. Gozen then followed as he walked the exhausted woman to the truck. Her eyes suddenly sparked with recognition.

"Hey, you're that man who snuck into the records room."

Gozen thought she was delusional. "You're okay now. We're going to take you to the hospital."

She spoke again, more clearly. "You were supposed to take me out to dinner."

Gozen suddenly remembered her to be the woman who caught him stealing the sales record between Karoburn and Etilé. "You probably shouldn't be talking now."

Darou began to flip crates so people could lie on them. A small amount of order started to emerge, and soon the trailer became full of patients. Gozen got into the cab and drove them off to the hospital, leaving the sirens and smolder behind.

○ ○ ○

Smoke rose up into the clouds; everyone could see the fuel plant display its destruction. From an unmarked office many blocks away, Daimó watched the demolition from high above the street, standing still in the quiet, dry air. The incredibly thick smoke floated down the valley, the southern Murde range being cast in its shadow. He raised a cup of tepid water and took a sip, his eyes remaining fixed on the inferno.

"How effective."

Daimó then looked down at three neatly placed folders on his desk. Anticipating the extinction of Etecid, he already planned on future developments towards an ancient goal that he had yet to fully express to anyone, even Kits. The complexity of his ambition grew, and he knew it would require even more focus to manage properly. The idea had been germinating in him so long it felt extraordinary seeing it finally play out.

His mind stretched between a past known by few and a future known by no one else, at least not in that city. From his pocket, Daimó pulled out a perpetual reminder, the stone carved face that taunted him even in his sleep. He began to grind his teeth, but for the first time he found himself doing so behind an eager grin. Planning had come to an end; only execution remained. He dropped the stone image on the folders and ran his hand across the three labels: one reading *City of Primichi*, one reading *City of Chigou*, and the last brandishing the single word *Goraka*.

o o o

Recovering in his intimately sized room all day, Jin had only heard of the downtown blaze from the children running around. Their language sounded hyperbolic, filled with fright and excitement. The soreness of his body managed to repress most of the curiosity he had of the event. It wasn't until most of the children had gone to bed that he found the motivation to get on his feet. He went back and forth on the idea for a good two minutes, but Jin finally decided to put on proper pants and a vest. While opening his traveler, he internally heard the voice of his mother: *if you're going to take the time to get dressed, then do it right.*

Jin's legs wobbled a bit as he braced himself on the kitchen counter; it felt cold against his bruised hand. A pot of smoked coffee sat warm on the counter along with some Mimi-filled Blashu rolls. He cradled the pot, which felt nice to his chilly fingers, poured a cup, and loaded two rolls onto a porcelain plate.

The cup rattled on the saucer as Jin scooted his double-socked feet across the wood floor. He entered the empty dining room and slowly took a seat at the center of the table. Lady Kyoumére walked by and saw him struggle to get into the chair. She sighed at the sight of the bandaged young man whose fine clothing was hidden under the wool blanket slung over his shoulders.

"Jin dear, is there anything I can get you?"

He turned slowly and struggled to cast a pathetic grin. "Your grace is unmatched, but I am fine."

"I'll be upstairs putting the rest of the children to bed. I'll check again before too long."

Unable to utter his usual etiquette, Jin simply nodded before assessing how much his jaw would hurt eating the rolls. Jin suspended his head over the cup and let the steam cover his face. It flowed slowly and felt warm, better than anything he had experienced since having cold cream with Chichimou. He tried not to think of blood and the sound of flesh getting crushed between bone and metal.

Out of a vest pocket, Jin then pulled out an old piece of carved stone. It had a worn face that looked so ancient one could only estimate its age. His grandfather had given him the relic as a gift, a spontaneous gesture to a curious child. The image resembled the face of a man, but its odd eyes looked eerily lifeless, even for a stone representation. Jin's grandfather had originally received it from Jin's great-grandfather, Poel Jastoú, who mentioned digging it up when Primichi first became a settlement. Little else had been spoken of the object, but Jin felt it hid a deep matrix of secrets. Ever since he had made it back from the unthinkable events of Goraka, he had become obsessed with the graven image.

He then pulled something from another vest pocket and set it down on the table. Its glistening, perfectly machined surface of brass and alloy seemed to repel the stone relic it sat next to. Behind Jin, the front door opened. He could barely make out the sound of heavy footsteps through the pressure of his swollen head; he didn't bother to turn. Slowly the steps approached, revealing themselves to be from an unusually slow-moving Gozen. The big man sat down across from him, the two making a rather ragged-looking pair.

Having seen blood and bandages all night, Gozen made little notice of Jin's broken state. Instead, his eyes fixed on the two objects neatly resting on the table. Jin hung his head over them, looking like a frail, anemic old man. The round shape reflected the light from a small lamp, suddenly sparking something in Gozen's mind.

"Why do you have Suzu's Toki?"

Jin slowly looked up, his face wincing from his injuries. He put his hands on the table, pushed the stone relic aside, and slowly picked up the Toki. "Chichimou found it before I escorted her to Sacoin. I was puzzled over how someone could neglect such an immaculate device. I suppose it makes sense now, as you say it is Suzu's."

Gozen stared at the forsaken little treasure. "It was a gift from her father; he never got to give it to her. I hoped she would be able to figure out its Special, but as you have it now . . ."

Just then, Jin slid his fingers across the device and into an odd position. The Toki face opened up beneath the glass as a perfectly clear *click* emitted, followed by an unworldly glow. Although Jin gave it no reaction, Gozen swiftly sat up.

"How did you do that?"

"I've had a rather long day to myself," Jin stated with tired, focused eyes.

"What is that light coming from? Certainly any battery would have died by now."

"It seems to be from some chemical compound that is well beyond my proficiencies. Carmin Komou most certainly is . . . was a master engineer."

The two sat there quietly as the small device softly illuminated their battered faces. In the warm glow, Gozen finally acknowledged Jin's assortment of bandages, shifting the concerns of his conscience. "Where is Chichimou?"

"With her father, as you requested."

Gozen's tolerance of bad news had worn thin. "Things don't appear to have gone so well. But I take it you didn't leave her in danger, did you?"

Jin raised his eyes but a few degrees as his mind struggled to make sense of what did in fact happen. "I'm not sure . . ."

Gozen groaned, but before he could reply, Jin continued.

"I . . . we, actually, located her father. Quite a savvy traveler, young Lady Chichimou. I could not quite make out the reaction they had to seeing one another. Strangely placid, really . . . then those others arrived."

Watching Jin's mind trail off towards incertitude, Gozen felt impatience heating up his face. "Jin, what happened. Who arrived?"

For the first time that evening, Jin looked squarely at Gozen, his pale eyes looking especially ghostly. "They asked about you."

Gozen furrowed his brow. "What?"

"They mentioned Suzu as well."

The big man quickly leaned into Jin, who became further confused by his own words. "You ran into people at Chichimou's house, and they mentioned me and Suzu?"

He struggled for an answer as he sat under the old blanket. Gozen's impatience peaked. "Jin!"

"Quite a curious thing, is it not? The stocky fellow knocked me down and then . . ." Jin's hands gripped the blanket in tighter around his shoulders. "I do believe I severed that tall man's arm. It accompanied me in the alley as the two men hastened off without it. He very well may have bled to death . . . that is quite a thing to say."

Right then, Gozen thought of the first time he had killed a man as an Enforcer. He had trained for it, prepared himself for the possibility, and yet none of that seemed to matter. Months passed before Gozen stopped having nightmares, seeing the man's lifeless face looking back at him in a pool of blood.

Jin lowered his eyes again. His hands were almost completely drained of color. "I left Lady Chichimou with her father. I think she is fine . . . I'm not quite sure." His trembling voice then let out a laugh, as if to release the compression building up inside him. "Oh, they mentioned Kits as well. I do believe they work for him."

Gozen's probing mind then locked onto a memory of two men whom he wanted . . . threatened to never see again. "Jin, look at me. What were they doing there?"

Jin shook his head, as if trying to jar a memory loose. "I always felt it was a bit strange how Kits conducted his business. It was always a rather guarded affair, never quite revealing who charged him with his inquiries. Perhaps his interest in my work blinded me to the obvious. I was too self-absorbed to see how little trust should have been offered him."

Gozen moaned as the weight of shared blame pushed down on his shoulders. "We all made that mistake, Jin."

Jin retreated further back into his blanket. "I remember so many times hearing Nia talk of things she so passionately wanted to do, people whom she valiantly fought for. I remember you and her parents worrying about her, being excited over her potential. It seemed like there were so many things she was going to do, wonderful changes she was going to be a part of." Jin lowered his head more, fighting to keep his composure, bowing for forgiveness.

"I'm sorry none of you will be able to see what she would have done."

Jin struggled to get every word out. "I never formally apologized for failing to bring Nia home as I swore to do. I don't believe her father wishes to hear from me, but if you're willing to hear it, I deeply regret my failure in protecting someone you all greatly cherished."

The young man's guilt pushed out tears that his pride tried to hold back. Gozen clenched his fist as he heard yet another life cry in anguish, poisoned from an inescapable grasp lurking out of the darkness. He had spent years enduring the pain of working families, poor children, and then even this privileged young Lord from across the valley. The pain became ignited by a nameless man, scarring all who fell within his grasp, exempting no one.

"I know the man who charges Kits with his actions. It is a man I have met but once. I cannot really say who he is except that he is no one. I can't really say where he is except for anywhere he wishes. He is a fog of death that I have tolerated for far too long."

Jin then remembered the horrible things that the children in the orphanage discussed before he got up. "Did he instigate the fire at Etecid yesterday?"

Gozen wondered just how many lives this man had destroyed, how many aside from even the ones Gozen had allowed himself to execute. "Even when I quit the Enforcers, I embraced my oath to fight within the law of the society I was part of. I tried to oppose this man within that law, but he has no regard for such institutions. He works around or through whatever he must to achieve his end. Since this man chooses only to operate from the shadows, that is where I will go."

The chair creaked as the former Lord Enforcer stood up. He gazed down at the young man who had never looked more broken, but Gozen knew that junior Lord held a potential that should not be wasted.

Gozen spoke out. "Nia wanted to fight for this farm and for the children of the city. She had little fear, so I tried to protect her from the darkness she had yet to find. In the end, it found her anyway." He then leaned forward. "Jin, if you really wish to see

Nia's fight continue, you should join me."

With that, Gozen began to walk out, hoping to find a face less battered than his present company. As he reached the doorway, Jin finally responded, "Just the two of us?"

Gozen turned around. "Well, if you think of anyone else . . ."

INQUISITION

Night had long since fallen as sounds of the city spilled into the quiet alley. Pirou stood nervous and cold, rubbing his arms in an effort to deal with both. Remi checked the time on his Toki, patiently anticipating the arrival of who they planned to meet. Suddenly, a distinct, sharp sound echoed down the alley.

"Are you sure about this person?" Pirou asked as he nervously tried to identify whoever—or whatever—had made that sound from the shadows.

"If you need someone who knows the industry and can sneak around like a cat, I think this is the person you want."

"Well, he certainly isn't punctual," Pirou noted.

" Maybe she's already here."

"Wait, what?"

"Well, maybe. I don't know. Like I said, she's sneaky."

Pirou got struck by a thought. "What do you mean, she?"

"Yeah. And don't let her age fool you, she knows the business. Very athletic, too."

Pirou scrunched his face. "You didn't bring me here to hire some teenage girl for espionage, did you?"

"I would like to point out right now, Pirou, that the prejudices you just clearly stated are part of the reason why no one will suspect her. Trust me, she's a ghost," Remi said confidently.

Pirou questioned his sanity. "I can't believe I asked you to help with this. I am not hiring a little girl to singlehandedly conduct a clandestine investigation on the largest corporation in the city."

He started to walk off; Remi watched. Suddenly, a white owl silently swooped down the alley nearly clipping Pirou's head. Letting out a squeal, Pirou quickly ducked as the bird soared down into the shadow of the alley.

"What insanity was that?" Pirou exclaimed. "Since when do owls fly in the city?"

As he and Remi looked into the shadow, they could see two glowing eyes peer directly at them. Then, the owl appeared to hover towards them. Its white body stood upright, floating in the darkness. "What's going on here, Remi?"

The young man calmly stood, watching the floating bird. A silhouette then appeared under the owl, both moving into the street light. Before them stood a young, fairly short lady who indeed looked rather athletic. The white owl remained firmly on her shoulder. In the opposite hand she held a long, rather menacing-looking staff.

Quite the opposite of what Pirou expected. "Who are you?"

"You contacted me." The girl replied with mettle, her dark hair pulled back revealing sharp eyes.

"This is her?"

Remi nodded.

"I hope we didn't come out here just to exchange awkward glances in the cold," the young woman said.

Pirou grumbled and then finally took a few steps closer to her, trying to keep a sensible distance from the carnivorous bird. "All right. I'm in need of someone who can collect some information."

"Anything specific?"

Pirou looked back to Remi and rolled his eyes. "How do I know I can trust her?"

"You're asking a stranger in a dark alley to spy for you," she interrupted. "Trust is clearly something you already lack."

Pirou folded his arms. "Okay. I need to find out who my incompetent assistant Victou is feeding information to regarding my Dark-spark project. My guess is that it's either some crazy, anti-Dark-spark Sorans trying to sabotage my project, or some jealous schlep trying to steal my research . . . possibly even someone from Kasic. Maybe it's whoever is busting up the Jinou production all over town. Maybe it's that vigilante engineer and his loony, Soran wife who died a couple years ago, haunting me from beyond the grave. I don't know."

The young lady glanced over at her father's former coworker and then back to Pirou. "It is a bit unusual for a man to design a dam and then protest against its existence along with his wife. Perhaps it's more interesting still who then killed them because of it."

Pirou snapped up. "Wait, you know who killed them?"

Remi leaned in. "I told you, she's good."

The irritated expression on Pirou's face quickly dropped. "You don't think . . . but what if it's the same people who . . . oh no. You can figure that out, right?" He nervously rubbed his throat.

The confident young woman scratched the owl's neck. "It'd be a bit silly of you to come out here and ask me if you didn't think I could."

Pirou groaned. "Okay . . . will you?"

"So just to be clear, you want me to investigate who killed a former Kasic employee, discover their interest in you, find out who is behind destroying all the Tulúki producers, and see if they are using your assistant to steal information on your Dark-spark development?"

"Yes," Pirou stated. "Please, yes."

Suzu grinned, Kola sitting stoically on her shoulder. "Looks like I'm your Lady."

SWEET BLASHU ROLLS

INGREDIENTS

For The Dough
1 lb. 2 oz. (4 cups) blashu flour
⅓ cup crystal sugar
½ oz. (4½ tsp.) dry yeast
½ oz. (2 tsp.) salt
4 eggs
4 oz. (½ cup) tepid milk
8 oz. (1 cup) unsalted butter

For The Filling
⅓ cup orange mimi-jam
(warmed)
4 oz. (½ cup) melted butter
¾ cup dark-sugar
2 T. monnican spice

Combine all of the dry ingredients in a bowl and mix well. Then, add the eggs and milk to the dry mix until combined. Take the combined dough and place onto a floured surface. Knead the dough and begin to incorporate the butter, one chunk at a time. Continue kneading for a few minutes making sure the butter is all combined and the dough has become shiny and smooth (no need to be delicate).

Allow to rise, covered, until it has doubled in size.

Take the risen dough and knead again for a quick bit. Roll it out onto a floured surface making a large rectangle. Spread out the orange-mimi jam in a thin surface across the dough. Follow with the melted butter, dark-sugar and monnican spice.

Cut into long triangles and roll into balls, going from the flat end to the pointy end (see figure, above right). Place into a buttered dish, allowing room for them to bloom. Once they have gained in volume, bake in an oven at 350°F for approximately 30 minutes or until lightly brown.

Cory Sheldon grew up between the Cuyahoga Valley National Park and Akron, Ohio (an industrial curiosity, formerly the nation's fastest growing city). After graduating with an industrial design degree, he spent several years designing tires, directing films, and creating a movie theater. While teaching film and design at a local college, he decided to write his first novel, which turned into his first series: Valley of Progress.

Learn more about Valley of Progress online

MORE BOOKS ∘ BLUEPRINTS ∘ ADVERTISEMENTS
READING MUSIC ∘ ARTWORK ∘ MAPS & MORE

valleyofprogress.com